BLANK SPACES

Cass Lennox

RIPTIDE
PUBLISHING

Riptide Publishing
PO Box 1537
Burnsville, NC 28714
www.riptidepublishing.com

Blank Spaces
Copyright © 2016 by Cass Lennox

Cover art: L.C. Chase, lcchase.com/design.htm
Editor: Chris Muldoon
Layout: L.C. Chase, lcchase.com/design.htm

ISBN: 978-1-62649-484-8

First edition
November, 2016

Also available in ebook:
ISBN: 978-1-62649-483-1

BLANK SPACES

Cass Lennox

RIPTIDE
PUBLISHING

For anyone who thought they were unlovable.

TABLE OF CONTENTS

CHAPTER ONE

Vaughn stood in front of the wall, the sinking feeling in his stomach rapidly turning into plunging freefall. Around him, the silence of the gallery made ample space for him to take in a deep breath. And another one. Just to make sure he was awake and seeing this right.

Because a very obvious blank space sat on the wall in front of him instead of a showcase work of art. A delicate arrangement of threads sewn from a canvas onto clear plastic piping to resemble a dark, fragmented wormhole reaching towards the viewer, to be precise. It was visually arresting in a kind of nightmarish way, and it was also one of the main pieces of this exhibit.

Despite all his deep breathing, it remained missing.

"Shit." He looked around, but every other piece still rested safely on plinths or on the wall or *in* the wall, in some cases. "*Shit.*"

He dug his phone out of his pocket and dialled his manager, Maurice. While he waited for Maurice to pick up, Vaughn walked swiftly around the gallery, keeping a desperate eye out for black threads attached to canvas. Maybe the cleaner had lost his mind and moved it. Maybe one of the owners or the artist, Jai Yoon, had sold it but hadn't logged the sale. Maybe, just maybe, there was a *nice* explanation for the disappearance.

But no, everything else was in its place, except for an empty bag of chips some cretin of a visitor had left in one corner. He dumped it in a nearby bin.

Maurice wasn't picking up.

Vaughn tried again. And again. But by the time he'd checked the front desk, the stationery closet at the front desk, the manager's office, and the storage closet at the back of the gallery, Maurice still hadn't answered. He gave up. "*Shiiit.*"

This was the third piece this year. Not good.

He went back upstairs to the office, tapping in the entry code on the way. He was the only person there, because Vaughn Hargrave was the lowly gallery assistant (read: office grunt) responsible for opening the gallery on time. This being the art world and today being a normal working day, no one else would show up until just before lunchtime.

Not today. He *had* to get his manager here. Failing Maurice, the owners. The police. Somebody. He turned on his laptop and ran to the filing cabinet that contained the physical copies of sales made through their gallery. While he thumbed through last month's receipts, he dialled Maurice again. He'd found nothing for the piece by the time the voice mail kicked in.

"Maurice," he said thickly, "another piece is missing. The Yoon. Get here *now*." He hung up, then navigated to the contact info of the owner, Angeline. He took a deep breath and pressed her name.

She picked up on the first ring. "What is it, Vaughn?"

"The Yoon's not here."

"Excuse me?"

"Jai Yoon's piece, *Entrance*. It's not here; I've looked everywhere. It wasn't sold. It wasn't misplaced. It's *gone*."

She sucked in a breath. "What did Maurice say?"

"I can't reach him."

"I'll handle him. Take down the plaque and put some folding chairs in that space. Open the gallery on time. I'll be there in half an hour."

"But what about—" she hung up and Vaughn exhaled heavily "—the police," he said to his phone. It promptly vibrated in his hand and he saw Angeline's name on his screen. He picked up.

"Vaughn." Her voice was extra crisp. "On second thought, don't do anything I just said. Also, *do not* call the police until I get there."

"Yes, An—" She hung up. Normally her distinct lack of manners grated on him, but today he was grateful for the brevity.

Vaughn put his phone away and returned to his laptop station. As he opened his inbox, his mind raced. This was bad. This was really bad. If this turned out to be another theft, no one would want to exhibit at their gallery, and if no one wanted to exhibit at their gallery, they'd go out of business, and if they went out of business, he'd have to get another position, and he really, *really* didn't want to do that. This assistant position, awful as it could be, had him working with art and exhibitions and meeting people in Toronto's art scene; it was worth the ego management and terrible pay. Finding another job like this one? Soon? He didn't even want to think about how difficult that would be.

And who would want to employ someone who'd had multiple pieces stolen while in their care? Not that he personally was responsible for the artworks; no, the owners Angeline and Cressida were, and perhaps the expensive security team supposedly available 24-7 to respond to breaches in the very high-tech security system they'd installed earlier this year. Only, they hadn't responded to this because there hadn't *been* a breach. Vaughn would know, because he'd turned the damn thing off half an hour ago when he'd arrived.

The security upgrade. The 24-7 monitoring team. There was an idea. He called them and asked for a system report of the last week.

Then he sat down and breathed deeply for a moment. There wasn't any reason to panic. Not yet. Perhaps not at all. Angeline would arrive and they'd call the police and the police would pretend to do something about the gallery space—though how pictures of a blank wall would help them figure out what happened, Vaughn had *no* idea—and then he'd open the gallery and direct visitors and answer calls and fetch sushi for Cressida like normal. Nope, no need to panic.

So. While he waited for Angeline, he could review emails and answer inquiries like he always did. Yeah, he could totally do that. He was gonna do that right now.

The very first email he looked at was from Jai Yoon, wondering if she could bring her family for free that day, to show them the piece. They'd flown in from South Korea to visit her and wanted to see her work on display.

A strange garbled noise left his mouth, and he clapped one hand over it. *Keep it together, Hargrave.*

Maurice chose that moment to call him. *Thank you.*

"Maurice," he answered in relief.

"Vaughn, why the hell did I just have Angeline scream at me on the phone?"

Because you didn't answer your phone when I called, you prick. "The Yoon is missing. I looked everywhere, but it definitely is. Angeline is on her way." He paused. "Jai Yoon wants to visit with her parents today."

Maurice swore. "That is the last fucking thing we need. I don't care what you tell her as long as she doesn't come in today. Have you called the police yet?"

"No. Angeline said she wanted to be here for that particular honour."

"Of course she did. God. Okay, I'm on my way. Don't touch anything." He hung up.

Vaughn looked at the email from Yoon, wondering how the hell any of them were going to tell her that her piece had been stolen. She was an up-and-coming talent, a few years out of Emily Carr University, and had been nothing but polite and friendly and accommodating; the idea of telling her *Entrance* was gone was physically sickening.

Nope. No way was he doing that.

He took a deep breath and typed, *Due to a family emergency, we unfortunately have to close the gallery today. I'm terribly sorry about this, Jai, and about the short notice.*

There, that would do. A few more platitudes, and the email was sent. Great.

How were they in this position again? *Again?* It was ridiculous. Perhaps it was just as well that they'd renewed their insurance and lowered the deductible. The thefts earlier this year had stung. Combined with the security upgrade, Vaughn had to wonder just how well the finances of the Delphi Gallery were doing right now.

Despite the constant worry tugging at his mind, he managed to process a few emails before he heard the click and slam of the downstairs door. He sprang up and ran down the stairs into the gallery's ground floor.

He found Angeline standing before the blank wall, legs wide and hands on her hips. It was telling that she still had her snow boots on; normally she paused to take them off and slip into heels once out of the snow. She glared at the wall as though it had personally offended her. "This is a fucking disaster."

"Maurice is on his way."

"That is the least that man could do." She glanced around the room. "Nothing else touched. Jesus. We have a carved rock estimated at $600,000, a triptych at half a mil, and this asshole takes the cross-stitch project worth a couple grand. I don't pay myself enough to deal with this shit." She rubbed the bridge of her nose. "Did you check the closets?"

"Yes."

"The office?"

"Yes."

"The receipts?"

"No sale recorded."

Angeline scowled, her fine dark features narrowing. "Damn it."

"I called the security company for a log of the last week."

She looked at him for the first time, squarely in his eyes. "Good."

Praise. From *Angeline*. Vaughn would have swooned had he not been so stiff with nerves.

She turned back to the wall. "This piece isn't necessary for the December exhibit," she muttered to herself.

No, it wasn't. Their December exhibitions were famous for their seasonal themes. Their annual shows were one reason Vaughn had been so happy to get the position: he'd be involved in curating the exhibition every year and organizing the Christmas party that accompanied it. Last year they'd done pagan roots, with works related to First Nation winter celebrations and druidism and even some Celtic imagery. The year before that, holiday pop art. This year it was interpretations of Christian symbolism, and some of it was very dark. Yoon's piece certainly fit the tone of the exhibition, but not the religious theme.

"No, but we still have to do something about it," Vaughn said.

"Is the coffee machine on?"

"Yes."

She turned abruptly and marched towards the office stairs. "I'll call the police." The gallery phone rang at the front desk. "Answer that." She disappeared through the door.

Vaughn rolled his eyes and jogged over to the desk. He picked up the phone. "Delphi Gallery, how can I help?"

"Hi," said a throaty voice down the line. "Could I speak to the gallery owners?"

"Who's calling?"

"I'm Jules Mitchell from the *Globe and Mail*. I understand you have an exhibition featuring Jai Yoon at the moment, and I was hoping to interview her there with her work. Are you the right person to talk to about that?"

Fuck. Me. Vaughn wanted to slam his face into the desk. "Unfortunately we're closed today for a family emergency."

"Not what I asked, but okay. I wanted to arrange it for next week."

Next week. Would that be enough time to straighten this out? Who knew. But he couldn't turn down publicity outright. "I'll make a note for my manager to call you back." He took down the journalist's details and pencilled a date into the appointment book. If Jai Yoon still wanted to be associated with them next week, they'd need the good press coverage.

Maurice arrived as Vaughn finished up with the reporter. He stomped snow off his boots in the front entrance, his habitual scowl present as Vaughn put down the phone.

"How are you so calm?" Maurice demanded. "We've been robbed, you know."

Vaughn's jaw dropped. "I'm not calm."

"Could've fooled me. Look at you." He gestured at Vaughn. "Not even a goddamn wrinkle in your jacket. Let me guess—the maid ironed that for you this morning?" He came around and scanned Vaughn from head to toe, shaking his head. "And the always-present inappropriate footwear. It's winter, in case you hadn't noticed." He shook his head again. "Is the coffee machine on?"

"Yes."

"My God, you did something useful."

Maurice went up the stairs to the office as Vaughn looked down at himself. He was wearing his usual workwear: a decent shirt, quality blazer, trousers, and loafers. What was wrong with dressing respectably? To give Maurice credit, it was November, so the loafers *were* kind of out of season. But it wasn't like he'd actually walked here in them, he just preferred to feel the floor under his feet.

And knowing how to use an iron didn't mean he had a *maid*. Jeez. Maurice could be unnecessarily grumpy without coffee.

The front of the gallery had wide glass windows that extended from the first floor up to the second floor. The desk where he currently stood faced the front door and a small reception area and coat hooks. Melting slush from Maurice's and Angeline's boots streaked around the door and doormat. Outside, the sun shone in a cold blue sky, making the snow glisten. People moved past on the sidewalk in bulky coats and big scarves, and the deli café opposite them had Christmas decorations up already.

Of course it had to be a beautiful day when they found out they'd been robbed. *Again.*

Vaughn dug into the drawer of the desk and pulled out the Closed Due to Unforeseen Circumstances sign and put it up on the front door, then locked it. That done, he reluctantly went up into the office.

Angeline was on the phone to the police, pacing the carpet near her desk in stockinged feet, and Maurice was frothing milk for his morning cappuccino. Vaughn returned to his laptop and saw a reply from Yoon: *So sorry to hear that. Will the gallery be open next week? My family will still be here and I have a paper interested in interviewing me there.*

"Maurice," he began.

"Not now," Maurice snapped. The milk spat at him.

Angeline hung up and turned to Maurice. "The police are on their way." She gave a deep sigh, then jabbed at her phone to call another number. "Hi. I hold gallery insurance with you, and I need to report a theft."

Vaughn's phone buzzed and he glanced at it. His friend Devon wanted to go out tonight. That meant drinks and a club. Not really Vaughn's idea of a good time these days, but after today? He texted back, *God yes please*, and put the phone down as Maurice sat next to him, cappuccino firmly in hand.

"What?" Maurice asked.

Vaughn explained the Yoon interview situation, and by the time he'd finished, Maurice looked ready to throw something. "Perfect. Just fucking perfect. Fuck you too, universe."

"It might be really useful. I have the reporter's details downstairs if you want them."

"What do you *mean* your colleagues flagged it?" Angeline snapped into the phone. "No. That's unacceptable. What's your name? Jonah?"

Maurice rubbed his eyes. "Look, don't answer Yoon yet. Wait until Angeline's free to talk it over. We'll have a powwow on how to handle her and the reporter."

That seemed sensible.

"Put me through to your manager, Jonah."

Vaughn raised one hand to run it through his hair, remembered he'd spent an embarrassing amount of time styling it full of gel, and lowered it again. "Maurice, she's not going to be happy."

"Who?"

"Yoon."

"No shit." Maurice sipped his cappuccino, eyebrows drawn. "We'll tell her what we told Berkley and Katzenjammer."

Vaughn grimaced at the memory. Both of those artists had been upset when their work had been stolen, but Berkley had been extra irate, threatening to sue and have them closed down. Delphi insured for theft, unlike most galleries, so in the end it had worked out, but the bad news had made the social media rounds anyway. Artists inquiring for exhibition space had dwindled a bit. Thankfully the Katzenjammer theft had been relatively low-key in comparison, mostly because Vaughn had managed to soothe the artist enough that he hadn't ranted much online.

This? This could threaten the gallery's existence. Yoon was new and exciting enough for this to be of real interest to people.

"Sorry and we'll refund her the sale value of the piece from our insurance claim?" Vaughn said.

"What the hell else can we do?"

He had a point.

"Are you kidding me?" Angeline demanded. "Are you actually kidding me? Fine." Her tone indicated things were immensely not fine. "I'll expect you here exactly at eleven o'clock, *Garrett*, and if the police aren't finished by then, you'll have to wait. Good-*bye*."

She punched the End Call button and raised her face to the ceiling. "Fuck insurance lemmings. Fuck them all."

Maurice raised his eyebrows at her. "Yeah, fuck them. What happened?"

"They don't believe it's been stolen."

"*What?*"

Watching this was better than reality TV. Vaughn didn't think he'd ever seen Angeline this furious.

Wait, the insurance lemmings thought *what*?

"This guy said it sounds suspicious. He has to come down here to see the damage, view the police and security reports, and establish for himself that we have a valid claim." She shook her head. "Un-fucking-believable."

"They don't think we have a valid claim?" Maurice was turning purple. Vaughn backed away from the cappuccino. "Our claims were plenty valid earlier this year. What makes this one different?"

"Like I know?" She turned sharply and picked up her shoes. "Vaughn, go downstairs and open the door for the police. Maurice, finish your fucking coffee and get the paperwork ready for the lemmings." She wedged her feet into the heels. "I'll make sure nothing else was taken and call Cress."

Both Vaughn and Maurice winced. Cressida, Angeline's partner in life and in the gallery, wasn't going to be happy about this. And when Cressida wasn't happy, no one was.

Jonah looked out of the taxi window and wanted to scowl at the gallery.

He'd had this insurance investigator gig for two months, and so far things had been pretty smooth going. He got outside the office, got to meet lots of people, and got to visit plenty of swanky places—like this one. Sure he hadn't been doing it long, but he could spot real whiplash a mile away by now and was developing a gut instinct for the big problem claims.

Like this one. Jeez, when Customer Services had bounced him this doozy of a claim, he could've killed them. An art gallery—loaded if the premiums were anything to judge by—two claims already that year, and now a third one discovered literally that morning. He'd scanned their claims history when he got the phone call (of course he did, because he took his job seriously, unlike some of the hosers in the Home and Contents Department), and three in one year struck him as very, very weird, considering they'd only included theft on the insurance eighteen months ago. When Garrett had taken over the call, he'd thought the same thing.

So now he and Garrett were doing an on-site evaluation. An immediate one, which meant their other appointments were pushed back thanks to these guys being whiny and rich. Doing insurance for companies like this pissed him off.

Hell, the mere sight of Delphi Gallery pissed him off. All concrete and glass, pretentious fancy eggshell-blue tiles on the path to the door, and a stripe of matching blue paint down one side of the façade. He supposed it was artistic or something. Along with the Yorkville address, the place looked exactly like the kind of ridiculous, trivial überwealth he detested. Not even the police car in front of the building ruined the impression.

He and Garrett left the taxi and walked towards the door.

"It's good the police are here," Garrett said. "We can hear their summary directly."

"Yeah, but the official report won't be ready for a few days. Is it even worth being here right now?" Not that Jonah would openly admit to it, but his thoughts on that were something like *No freaking way.*

Garrett shrugged. "Scoping things out before they have a chance to get their story together is worth doing. Take notes about the staff, the piece that's missing, the estimated value of it, any security measures, all the usual stuff."

"We know about their security measures. They installed a high-grade system after the second theft in order to reduce their premiums."

"We still need to corroborate the situation for our side of things."

Yeah, okay, true, but did that mean they had to drop everything and rush over here like the gallery was burning down?

They paused in front of the door, which had a big sign saying *Closed Due to Unforeseen Circumstances* in nice lettering. Through the door and the glass windows beside it, they could see a young man sitting at a desk with a laptop. Garrett rapped on the door, and the man looked up.

Jonah's breath caught. Holy shit. The guy was *hot*. Tall and lean, in a form-fitting blazer over a patterned, collarless dark-blue shirt, cheekbones you could slice cheese with, and curly dark hair around his face. Grey eyes. Clear pale skin. *Mmm.* Jonah would bet money he looked even better without the expensive clothes. He could just picture it: a hairless chest; thin, hard torso; long cock—

The guy moved out from behind the desk, and Jonah saw he was wearing deck shoes and green pants. The shirt's pattern was light-blue *tulips*. Lust careened to an abrupt halt. Who the fuck wore green pants? Willingly? And deck shoes in winter? *Rich boys who don't have to worry about wet feet or walking in snow, that's who.* This guy probably took taxis everywhere.

He shook his head to clear it. This was work, not a bar. *Focus.*

Gorgeous opened the door. "Can I help you?"

"We're from Laigh and Sanders," Garrett said.

"Please come in." He opened the door wide for them. Jonah followed Garrett in, making sure to stamp the excess slush off his boots on the way. A place like this, dirt stains would show up like mud on snow. In fact, he and Garrett probably stood out like sore thumbs in their cheap suits and bright snow jackets.

"You may hang your coats up there," Gorgeous (but badly dressed) said, indicating coat hooks on one wall. "I'll inform my colleagues that you're here."

"And you are?" Garrett asked.

Gorgeous paused on his way into the gallery. "I'm Vaughn Hargrave, the gallery assistant. Please excuse me for a moment."

If the shoes, clothes, and job weren't enough, the name sealed it. Hargrave was the name on a shiny plaque on a very shiny building near Jonah's office, one that he walked past every day. Gorgeous was Money. Jonah almost bristled at the way he sauntered off, not least because those pants showed off a mouth-watering ass. It was better than his, which wasn't fair, as he had to spend two hours a day at the gym for his and Hargrave looked like his idea of heavy lifting was a latte instead of a cappuccino.

"You okay?" Garrett asked, shrugging off his jacket. "You look like you drank cold coffee."

"I hate places like this."

"Art galleries?" Garrett glanced around. "Not my favourite kind of place, but good for a date. Girls seem to like staring at random shit on walls."

Jonah wasn't about to tell him that he wasn't into girls, or dates to galleries, or dating at all. His ideal date was a drink before being fucked against a wall. Definitely couldn't tell his boss that. "I don't get art."

"Me either, bud." Garrett picked up a pamphlet on the front desk. "Oh hey, a Christmas exhibition. That's fun." He frowned as he thumbed through the pamphlet. "Oh. None of this looks very Christmassy."

Jonah glanced over his shoulder in time to see a picture of a naked woman on a cross, bleeding from places he'd rather not think about. That *was art?* He'd rather stick with insurance.

Hargrave returned. "My manager says he'll meet you upstairs. Please follow me."

They were being shunted out of the way already. Jonah glanced at Garrett, then decided to push back. "Do you mind if we see where the piece was?"

Vaughn smiled apologetically, smooth and practiced. "Unfortunately, the police are still surveying it."

Garrett stepped forward. "I'll meet with your manager while my colleague looks at the scene."

Jonah shot him a grateful glance. He definitely wanted that spot scoped out for their own peace of mind.

Vaughn glanced between the two of them, his rich-boy good looks tugging at Jonah's dick. Ugh, he was cute from *all* the angles. "If that's how you'd prefer to do things, Mr. . . . ?"

"Garrett Barlow. This is Jonah Sondern."

Vaughn nodded. "The space where the piece was is through there, Mr. Sondern. Please follow me, Mr. Barlow." He led Garrett to a door in the next room, punched a key code in, then ushered Garett through it.

Jonah moved in the direction Vaughn had indicated, behind the desk into the next room, which was a large clear space with paintings and random shit on the walls. Columns with stuff on top of them or pinned to them were dotted around the room, and there were two police officers talking to a fierce-looking woman in heels and a long skirt. She had to be Angeline, the owner, who he'd "spoken" to on the phone earlier.

They stood in front of an empty section of wall. There was a plaque on it, presumably for the stolen piece, and the police officers were taking pictures and notes. Jonah stepped forward, hoping to see for himself if there were any cracks or obvious smudges or scrapes in the paint on the wall.

There wasn't anything.

Huh.

So he, the police, and the gallery owner were all staring at a wall featuring a grand sum of nothing on it. What kind of information could be had from *that*?

Talk about feeling like a chump.

Angeline caught sight of him. "Who are you?"

"Jonah Sondern, claims investigator from Laigh and Sanders." He had the full intro *down* by now.

Her lip curled. "Ah. You. Vaughn should have taken you to see Maurice."

"My colleague's with him. I'm here to survey the site." He nodded at the police officers, who were giving him that steady, expectant look law enforcement seemed to do so well. "Officers, we're here from the insurance company to investigate the legitimacy of the claim. I wanted to ensure we're all seeing the same thing."

The officers glanced at each other, then at Angeline. She looked ready to throw something.

"We've searched the building and the piece is not here," one of the officers said. "How it happened is the real question."

Yeah, the million-dollar question for his company.

Jonah scanned the room. There was some crazy shit in here. One piece looked like someone had scrawled black pen on a canvas, but the pen marks were actually black threads. One painting was of mangled shapes in shades of yellow and orange. Another painting was literally a huge wall's worth of white paint and one smear of red. And one of the columns had a gigantic *Q* hanging from it. *What is that even supposed to be?* Hopefully the stolen piece wasn't as nutty as the rest of the art here. He had no way of judging how valuable any of this stuff was, not beyond *I wouldn't pay a dime for it.*

"No break-in?" he asked.

"We'll provide details in our report," the officer said smoothly.

Great.

Vaughn appeared beside Jonah, startling him. Shit, he was tall—Jonah's eyes were level with Vaughn's chin. Damn it, not only was the guy loaded and a clothes freak, Jonah also had to look up at him? Nope, seriously not fair.

"I have the security log here." Vaughn held up papers in one hand, then gave them to the police officers.

"We'll need that," Jonah said to him.

"I left a copy with my manager to give to your colleague."

Jonah tried not to glare (up) at him. For someone who willingly wore tulips on his shirt, Money was organized.

And *really* handsome up close, which meant he was leaving unfair and travelling into downright *unjust* territory.

"We're done here," the officers said to Angeline. "You're free to open the gallery to visitors; we're not going to get any more information."

Angeline walked the officers to the door, which meant Jonah found himself in front of an empty wall with Vaughn. He took his phone out and snapped a few pictures, then put it away, feeling silly. This wasn't exactly a straightforward burglary; there wasn't a sign of breaking in and none of the other pieces seemed to have been touched.

Also, standing next to what had to be the son of the guy who ran that expensive-looking company near Laigh and Sanders was awkward. Jonah eyed him and wondered what he was thinking. He didn't look at ease; his arms were crossed and he had the slightest frown on his face as he gazed at the wall. Jonah half wanted to sigh; he even looked hot *frowning*. Just how beautiful was a guy allowed to be?

"What did it look like?" Jonah asked.

Vaughn jumped, then collected himself. "The piece? It was a three-dimensional construction of plastic and thread on canvas." He uncrossed his arms and made a roughly tubular shape in the air in front of him. "It looked like the tunnel to a warren or another place on the other side of the canvas. It represented the experience of reality shifting, of travelling from one place to another despite physically staying put."

What the...? "So... like a portal?" Portals he roughly understood. He'd enjoyed what little he'd played of the *Portal* games, though the physics of them had made his head hurt.

Vaughn smiled. Jonah's breath caught *again*. Whoa. A smile like that could blind a guy. "That's exactly right," Vaughn said warmly.

"But what did it *look* like?"

Vaughn frowned, then pointed at the artwork with the thread on the canvas. "That's a similar piece from a different artist. Similar black thread, only sewn through clear plastic tubing attached at a right angle to the canvas. It looks like the threads are hanging in the air. Quite remarkable."

It kinda sounded creepy as fuck, actually.

Heels clicked behind him and Jonah turned to see Angeline. She came up to him with her hand outstretched, a piece of paper in it. "The case number," she said icily.

He took it. "Thank you, ma'am."

"I suggest we join Maurice and your colleague upstairs." She turned and walked away.

Clearly not a suggestion. Jonah followed, noticing how Vaughn fell into step behind him. He automatically gave a small hip wiggle, then reminded himself he was working *and* that he didn't like moneyed brats who didn't understand the concept of warm shoes in the winter, no matter how beautiful or smiley they were.

He did glance back as they climbed the stairs, just to see if the guy was checking him out. How could Vaughn not, when Jonah's ass was in his face? But no, the guy was looking down. Jonah turned to the front, a little confused. He had a great ass, as qualified by a vilifying number of men who'd know. And Vaughn *was* gay, right? Dressed like that and working in an art gallery, he had to be. Jonah's gaydar was pitch-perfect, and it had twanged the moment he saw the guy.

Or maybe that had been his dick.

Anyway, it didn't seem to matter what Jonah's gaydar had picked up—Vaughn hadn't noticed any of Jonah's more prominent attributes by the time they reached a small office on the next floor of the gallery. He barely looked up from the ground, let alone at Jonah.

Angeline led them to a small meeting room where Garrett was sitting opposite a weaselly-looking guy with a bad haircut and a permanent scowl. Jonah figured this was the famed Maurice.

"Angeline. You're finally done with the police?" Maurice said as they entered.

Garrett stood, extending a hand. "Good morning. I'm Garrett Barlow."

Angeline briskly shook his hand. Jonah stepped forward and introduced himself to Maurice.

The guy had a handshake like a wet noodle. "Maurice Palomer."

Jonah resisted the urge to wipe his hand on his pants after Maurice let go, then sat next to Garrett, who shot him a grim look.

"Anyone want coffee? Water?" Vaughn asked.

"We're fine," Angeline said, sitting down. Maurice just waved his hand at him.

Vaughn nodded and left the room. Jonah settled fully into the meeting, taking in Garrett facing off against Maurice and Angeline, and the stack of documents in the middle of the table.

Maurice sat forward with an insincere grin. "We were almost done here, weren't we, Garrett?"

"Not really," Garrett said.

"As done as we could be without the police report."

"I'm not certain we have full details of the—"

"The police have confirmed the theft, right?" Maurice said.

"Yes." Angeline's tone was hard. "They're doing the report right now."

Garrett picked up the documents in front of him. "I still have to verify the documentation you've provided us."

Maurice smiled. "We can leave you here to look through it if necessary."

Garrett returned the smile, but his was as false as Maurice's. "Could you also provide the reference numbers for the claims earlier this year?"

Maurice and Angeline glanced at each other. Angeline narrowed her eyes at Maurice, who stood. "I'll get them for you now." He walked out the door. "Vaughn, why didn't you—" The door shut behind him, cutting off the rest of his sentence.

The three of them sat in tense silence. Angeline glanced at them. "You're not the people we met last time."

Jonah put on his most winning smile. "We're in the Investigations Department. This is the first time our company's flagged your claims as worth investigating."

Angeline raised an eyebrow. "You don't say. Jonah, right?" She didn't sound impressed with him. Then again, she hadn't been impressed on the phone either.

Jonah tried not to visibly bristle.

Garrett passed the papers to him. "We're just following procedure, ma'am."

"Really? Isn't procedure us sending in scans of all that documentation in front of you? And maybe a few calls to ensure you have everything you need to process our claim?"

"After you upgraded your security system," Garrett said, "we didn't expect another claim."

Angeline shot him a hot glare, then abruptly sat back against the chair. "Honestly? We didn't expect to be filing another one."

Unlike Maurice, who reeked of insincerity, she seemed genuine in her anger, so Jonah believed her. She was moving from anger to frustration and disbelief, which was a typical emotional trip people took during visits like this. It wasn't like he didn't get it: theft was nasty. Made you feel dirty and exposed. Evidently even rich people felt that.

Jonah flipped through the papers. He found a paper-clipped log from the security company and put it on top of the stack. Hopefully there was a nice entry of someone tripping the system, and they could settle this quickly.

"I'm glad to hear you say that," Garrett said.

"It's weird." Angeline was frowning. "Our security system is top-of-the-line. It should've caught a fucking mouse moving around, let alone a person and a painting with a goddamn tube sticking out of it. Vaughn says the system was turned on when he arrived this morning." She leaned back, took a deep breath, then forcibly relaxed into her chair. "So why the need for a personal visit?"

Garrett shifted in his chair. "We—personally—feel this needs a personal touch."

Angeline raised an eyebrow. "You *personally* do, eh?"

Jonah did a mental head slap. *Nice one, Garrett.*

Garrett glanced at Jonah. "We like to look after our clients, Ms. Dufort, even though this doesn't seem straightforward to us. It helps to meet the people actually affected." He gave a warm smile, no indication whatsoever that Dufort's wealth said *jump* and they were jumping. "However, I feel I should warn you that if we're not convinced by this—" he tapped the papers in front of Jonah "—and the police report, then we'll have to refuse to pay out for this claim. I hope, of course, that it won't come to that. We'll be sure to investigate this thoroughly." He stood, which was cue for Jonah to stand. "Thank you very much for your time, Ms. Dufort."

Maurice opened the door, a piece of notepaper in hand. "I have the references . . . here," he said slowly, obviously realizing they were about to leave.

Jonah took the paper and added it to the stack with an overbright smile. "Thanks!"

Maurice's eye twitched.

They all went through the office to the stairs. Vaughn was nowhere in sight. Jonah was a little disappointed; he'd kind of wanted to cruise that ass again. Then they came in view of the front desk and saw Vaughn there, standing and tapping at the laptop, ass nicely showcased in those dumb green pants. Another breath escaped him.

Vaughn looked up and watched them as they retrieved their coats. "I hope you got everything you needed."

Ever *so* polite. Was this guy even real?

Garrett nodded absently. "Yes."

"When can we expect to hear from you?" Angeline asked as she and Maurice stopped next to Vaughn. Jonah pulled on his coat, surveying the scene: the three art gallery staff in one line beside the desk, watching him and Garrett pulling on coats with papers firmly in hand.

"The normal timeframe is six to eight weeks," Garrett said. Angeline's brows drew closer together warningly. "But, uh, given the, ah, delicate nature of this claim—"

"And the amount we pay each month," Angeline added.

Jump, monkeys, jump.

"—we'll fast-track it," Garrett finished.

Angeline's smile could have frozen meat in seconds. "I would greatly appreciate it."

"Thank you," Vaughn added.

Jonah zipped up his coat. "Yeah, thanks. Bye."

And with that they left the art gallery and its badly shod, gorgeous-assed assistant.

Garrett breathed a heavy sigh of relief as soon as the door closed behind them. "Oh my *God*. She's more intense in real life than on the phone."

Jonah couldn't agree more, but unresolved frustration niggled at him. Not that it took much to get him horny, but shit, that guy really got to him. He couldn't say why—normally he stayed clear of the moneyed guys, because he hated the little differences that reminded him of just how dirt-poor he was in comparison—but this one had slipped past. *Then again, hot is hot.* Money and terrible clothes didn't make him any less objectively good-looking.

Once they got back to the office, he was going to jerk a quick one out in the washroom, then make plans for the evening. And those plans were going to involve his favourite pastimes: friends, dancing, drinks, and sex. He grinned to himself as Garrett hailed a taxi. Yup, he'd process the paperwork, make a few more claims visits, head home, pretty up, and work this out of his system tonight.

Perfect.

CHAPTER TWO

Vaughn stood in the club entrance, surveying and judging. It was so new it still smelled faintly of varnish and paint, and it was filled with the kind of people who watched Toronto's nightlife like hawks, swooping in on anything fresh and exciting. People like his friend Devon, who currently led him and their friends into the place as though he'd been here dozens of times before. Retro neon lights illuminated booths and seats and the bars, while men—and some women—ground to decent trance music on the dance floor.

Yes. After today, Vaughn wanted nothing more than to let go and dance.

But first they had to do the drinks and shouting-over-the-music stuff. His friends were largely people from LGBT groups at his university and accompanying partners or friends; despite working in the art industry, Vaughn hadn't picked up any new queer friends to bring to one of these nights. Possibly because he seemed to fly under the radar in the industry. Artists and the people who worked with them tended towards eccentric and open-minded anyway, so it was difficult to put labels on people from the get-go. Identifying them and inviting them to these kinds of nights wasn't worth the effort or embarrassment if he gauged wrongly.

Really, if he had to be honest, he'd found it increasingly difficult to label *himself* these days. Standing here, gazing at the dance floor and aching for a drink to help him chill out, Vaughn was very aware that his friends were here for other things, things that didn't occur to him until he caught sight of people on the dance floor touching each other in ways that were decidedly not dance-related.

But now wasn't the time to nitpick or get deep about the nature of nightlife venues. He was with friends, there was booze to drink, music to dance to, and a rough day to forget. He could certainly be here for those reasons alone.

Devon flirted with one of the bartenders and got them a free round of shots on top of their order. Vaughn knocked his back, then washed the cheap, sugary taste out of his mouth with a vodka mixer. The guys moved to a table near the dance floor and immediately lined up to survey the offerings.

"Interesting crowd," James judged.

Devon scoffed. "Please. It's full of twinks."

"You like twinks," Vaughn said.

Devon winked at him. "Yes, but I wouldn't call them *interesting*."

"It's full of twinks with good taste," André said, a grin lighting up his face. "And good stylists."

Vaughn scanned the dance floor. Young, lithe men threw themselves into the rhythm of the music and into each other. Bodies undulated, hands sneaked past collars and under hems, lips grinned or kissed, and chests were slowly bared. And yes, the majority of them were unusually good-looking, typical of the kind of people who chased the new and undiscovered. Shiny shoes, form-fitting shirts and pants, the odd vest top despite the winter snow outside, and artfully mussed hairstyles. Dotted among them were a few older men looking for action and women giving themselves up to the music, free from any undue attention.

He envied them slightly.

Banish the thought, Vaughn. Being touched by complete strangers was part of the gay-bar experience. And while he wasn't here to pick anyone up, being admired wasn't a bad thing.

"Anyone promising?" Devon asked him.

"I should ask you," Vaughn replied.

Devon was fastidious in two things: his choice of clothes and his choice of hookup. If Vaughn had a dollar for every time Devon had pointed out an exceptionally beautiful young man to him, he wouldn't need to worry about paying his bills. Devon had been like that for as long as Vaughn had known him, which was since Vaughn's first year of university. Devon had been the student union president, president of the LGBT group, and head of his business class; now he was circulating the departments in his father's pharmaceutical company in preparation for running it. If he dedicated as much time and energy to that as he did to circulating the Toronto gay club scene, Vaughn had yet to see proof of it.

"You said you needed to blow off steam." Devon waved at the crowd below. "Go blow." His grin was sharply illuminated by pink neon, and Vaughn rolled his eyes.

"I'd like to have a civilized drink first." He held up his vodka.

Devon barked out a laugh and clapped his shoulder.

Energy thrummed under his skin, and he suddenly needed to get out there. Work had turned almost farcical by the end of the day—Angeline in a terrible mood, Cressida in a worse one when she eventually showed up, and Maurice griping about every little thing, while Vaughn tried to welcome visitors, make sense of the log from the security company, and manage more media requests to see Jai Yoon's exhibition. God forbid any interest happen *before* one of the major pieces was stolen.

At least he hadn't had to tell Yoon about the theft; he'd been at the front desk when Angeline had made that call. He'd still received a furious email cancelling the interview, with a promise to never exhibit at Delphi again, but that did mean he hadn't had to speak to her.

Of course, after that, the same reporter had wanted to come in anyway to do a piece on theft and insurance. Maurice had said no, Angeline had said no, but Cressida had said yes, and somehow that meant the rest of them were outvoted. Vaughn didn't want to imagine the inbox the next day, once the news hit the arts and culture circuit.

Stop. None of that now. Time to forget all the bullshit of working life.

He knocked back his drink and set the glass down, the buzz from the alcohol adding to the buzz in his skin. No one else seemed ready to dance, though. He turned to Devon. "Another?"

Devon grinned and raised his glass. "Absolutely, compadre."

Vaughn returned to the bar, bought a round for everybody, and carried it back to their section. In that short time, Devon had attracted the attentions of a young man with earrings, blue hair, and the impossibly toned body of a dancer. Another of their crew was leading someone else into the fray of the dance floor. People were acting quickly tonight. Vaughn set the drinks down and handed one to Devon.

"Thanks, babe," he said.

"No drink for me?" Toned pouted, brushing a finger down Devon's T-shirt.

Devon took a hefty gulp, then pressed his mouth to Toned's. Vaughn saw liquid dribble from one corner as the gulp passed from mouth to mouth. His stomach rolled. That couldn't be hygienic.

Judging by the stars in Toned's eyes as he swallowed, he didn't give a shit. "Oh *honey*," he breathed, gripping Devon's shirt and kissing him fiercely.

"It's so fucking unfair," James shouted to Vaughn as he accepted a glass from him. James raised his drink in thanks, then sipped it. "Ten minutes and he's pulled the hottest queen in here. How does he do it?"

Vaughn shrugged. "Maybe you should have done it in five."

James shook his head. "Yeah right. If I tried that trick, I'd have spit rum all over myself *and* him."

They regarded Devon and Toned as they made out, then James shook himself and downed the drink. "Come on, let's dance."

Finally. Vaughn finished his too and followed James into the heaving mass of the dancers. Alcohol and sugar lit up his nerves and heightened his senses.

Being part of a hot, almost claustrophobic press of people was perfect—he was lost in the collective sway of humanity, movements orchestrated by rhythm and beats, bouncing and dancing. *So good.* He ground against James, who wouldn't get the wrong idea, working himself into a sweaty, pulsating state of thoughtlessness.

The odd hand wormed over his ass or stomach or pec, but Vaughn gently pushed them away and they stayed away. This place was great, he decided. Not as handsy as some of the other bars in town. The music was decent too.

James backed away, prompting Vaughn to check on him. A guy behind James was rubbing his stubbly jaw against James's neck, and James practically swooned into his arms. Vaughn grinned and turned to give him some privacy.

Only to be confronted by the sight of a blond man sandwiched between two taller, dark-haired men. Blondie kissed one of them fiercely, hand digging into the guy's jeans, while the guy behind him pressed closely up to him, groin rubbing against his ass, one hand stroking Blondie's dick through his obscenely tight pants. *Jesus.*

Vaughn began to move away, because watching sex on the dance floor wasn't ever his idea of fun, when he realized he recognized the sandwich filling. It was the insurance guy from earlier that day, the short one who'd aggressively worked his way into the gallery.

He stole another look. Yes, it was him. The straw-like hair, the compact, lean body—now on display in very tight clothing—and the strong jaw and nose. Muscular arms reached down towards cock and up into hair. The guy was just as consumed and lost to the world as Vaughn had been moments ago.

What was the guy's name again? Barlow? No, Sondern. Jonah Sondern.

Vaughn felt the beginnings of an evil grin. So, Jonah the intense insurance lemming was into men. Plural. At once. Who'd have thought?

The guy at Jonah's back tapped Jonah and the other man on the shoulder and leaned forward to speak. Vaughn turned quickly, not wanting to be seen by Jonah.

Ugh. He couldn't linger on the floor now that Jonah was there. Given James was otherwise occupied and Vaughn was suddenly very aware of how thirsty he was, it seemed a good time for a break.

Weaving his way off the dance floor, he found his friends still talking over drinks, and he sat down. A few waters later, they headed back onto the dance floor, where he got one glimpse of Jonah and his partners before the crowd obscured them.

After the third song, the drinks caught up with him and he beelined for the washroom. Inside, the stall at the end of the row was locked, moans issuing from within. Vaughn spotted a few rolled eyes from guys leaving the place as he took a spot at a urinal.

"Shit, I'm coming," someone in the stall groaned.

Vaughn was abruptly very tired and ready to call it a night. This had been good, but peeing into a grimy urinal while men fucked in the stall behind him suddenly seemed a complete waste of time.

Did he really want to keep doing this? Coming to places like this, watching his friends pair off for a few hours or the night, listening to other people have sex *in a washroom*, for God's sake. How could anyone be aroused in a place that stank perpetually of piss and pubes, let alone consummate that arousal with other men peeing around them? It was beyond him. Maybe there were other ways to burn off a crap day. He should take up a sport. Running. Rock climbing. Or he could try a straight club with some of his school friends; sex in straight places just didn't happen with the regularity of sex in gay clubs. He could dance and pee in peace.

Better yet, he could try to actually focus on painting. Be more consistent about it. Work it into a schedule and get pieces done. It wouldn't burn off energy like dancing would, but it would definitely leave him feeling better and not being exposed to other men's bodily fluids.

He shook himself and zipped up. He was washing his hands when the end stall unlocked and two men left with a spring in their step; Jonah the insurance lemming followed with a victorious grin lighting up his face. He looked like a tomcat fresh off a successful hunt. Every line of his body radiated languid ease and satisfaction—until his eyes met Vaughn's in the washroom mirror and the victory dropped from his face.

Vaughn felt his blood freeze. The guy's mouth was swollen, there were burgeoning love bites on his neck, and his hair was mussed beyond redemption—there was no doubt about what he'd been doing. The satisfied expression was gone; now he looked like he'd seen a ghost.

Or rather, *his client*.

This had to be embarrassing for him. Vaughn would've been embarrassed for sure, so the best thing to do was probably ignore him. Jonah'd appreciate that, right? Tactful silence could cover a lot of sins. He washed his hands and walked out without a backwards glance.

Outside the door, he managed about two steps towards his friends, but found his arm gripped from behind.

Evidently Jonah had other ideas.

Vaughn was yanked to the left and pulled through a door to the smoking area outside the club, the hand painfully tight around his arm, and he didn't resist as Jonah marched him into a shadowy corner. The smoking area had two die-hard smokers shivering in the cold air, and Vaughn could taste smoke in each icy breath, the harsh chemicals adding to his unease. His heart beat quicker—what was Jonah doing? What was happening here?

Jonah pushed him against the back wall and caged him, no mean feat considering he was four inches shorter than Vaughn. "You," he snarled, warm breath escaping in a white burst.

Vaughn crossed his arms. "A pleasure to meet you again, Jonah."

"What the hell are you doing here?"

No sign of the lemming now. "None of your business." Vaughn let his gaze rest on the guy's neck. Wow, those men had gone to town there. "And whatever—or whoever—you're doing is none of mine."

Jonah visibly bristled. "Damn right it's not. This won't leave this club. It doesn't mean you can just ignore it like it didn't happen."

Okay, maybe Vaughn had made the wrong decision. "I didn't think you'd want to talk about it. I'm practically a stranger." When Jonah's expression didn't change, Vaughn added, "A stranger who doesn't care what you do in your free time."

Jonah leaned in. "You're not a stranger. You know who I am. Don't pretend like you don't."

"Right." What did Jonah want from him? "Sorry . . .?" Their breaths came in cloudy gusts against each other's face now.

Jonah's head cocked to one side. "So you ignored me on purpose. That's not how I roll and how the people I know roll. What were you gonna do? You gonna bring this up at work? Get me into trouble?"

Vaughn's head spun. What on earth was he talking about?

"Because it's not going to work. I don't respond to blackmail, pretty boy." Jonah poked a finger into Vaughn's chest. Somehow, when he said it, *pretty boy* wasn't a compliment. "My work won't give a shit about me being here, so don't even try it."

"I don't know what you think I'm trying to do," Vaughn said slowly, "but blackmail isn't it."

"Oh, so you just happened to be here? In the newest gay club in Toronto? The same day your company files a very, *very* suspicious claim?"

Vaughn frowned. "My friends like to go to places like this. And what do you mean, suspicious?"

Jonah's eyes narrowed. "If your friends are the ones who like it, what are *you* doing here?"

"Dancing." It sounded stupid the moment he said it.

"*Dancing.*" It sounded even stupider the way Jonah echoed it.

"And drinking. And talking." Vaughn gestured towards the club. "Plus, hot guys. What's not to love?"

A vindicated expression briefly crossed Jonah's face. He leaned back slightly. "So . . . this is a coincidence."

"Yes." Vaughn was shivering. *Fuck*, it was cold. He couldn't feel his face anymore. "I promise. Just a coincidence."

Jonah's arms dropped to his sides and he hugged them to himself. It was hard to tell in the shadows, but Vaughn thought he was blushing. "Okay. You, uh, you heard a lot of what happened in there . . .?"

"I think everyone who used the washroom in the last ten minutes heard you."

Jonah scowled. "Hey, *twenty* minutes at least." The scowl receded. "And you're not going to say anything? To your workmates?"

"Or to yours." Great, now Vaughn's face, arms, *and* legs were numb. "That's not how I operate. Look, can we go inside? I'm freezing."

Jonah nodded once, stepping away. They hurried back into the club, the sweaty, alcohol-infused humidity wrapping around them like a welcome blanket. *Much better.* Vaughn rubbed his arms, trying to encourage feeling in his hands and limbs, and noticed Jonah eyeing him up and down, a strange conflicted expression on his face.

Vaughn glanced down at his clothes. Had he spilled a drink on himself? "What?" he asked.

"You clean up nice."

Of course he did. Clothes made the man. "Thank you." He couldn't really say much about Jonah's clothes, except that they were so tight they rendered themselves unnecessary. But he did look good. "Likewise."

Jonah gave a small half smile. "So you're into hot guys?"

The answer to that was loaded. "I like them." Which was true.

"Got your eye on anyone here?"

Was he being chatty or was he flirting? That seemed like a flirty question. But Vaughn wasn't sure why Jonah would flirt with him, given what had just happened. Probably making conversation. "No. You?"

The smile dropped from Jonah's face. "No." He shook his head as if to clear it, shifted weight to his other foot. "Anyway. You sure . . . You genuinely don't care about . . . ?"

Vaughn could definitely see a blush now. "About hearing you being fucked sideways for *twenty* minutes by two guys in a washroom?"

Jonah crossed his arms, giving a curt nod. Back to business.

"No. I don't." Vaughn cleared his throat. "I mean, it would be nice to pee without listening to coitus, of course, but it tends to come with the territory." As if to illustrate his point, two guys with their hands down each other's pants slammed into the wall next to them and proceeded to breathe all over each other.

Jonah smiled. "Right. Fine. Okay. So we're cool?"

An arm slung itself around Vaughn's shoulders. He looked over to see its owner, Devon, grinning tightly. "Vaughn! Darling! Who's this?"

Jonah reared back, raising one eyebrow. His back straightened, arms uncrossed, and suddenly the languid tomcat was back. He openly scanned Devon, the eyebrow remaining high.

Was he interested in someone else that quickly? Maybe washroom threesomes weren't all they were cracked up to be.

Vaughn gestured between the two of them. "Devon, this is an acquaintance, Jonah. Jonah, Devon."

"Nice love bites," Devon said.

"Yours aren't too bad either," Jonah replied.

Vaughn craned his head back. Sure enough, there were bruises on Devon's neck and collarbone. Toned seemed to have quite a big mouth, judging by the size of some of those hickeys.

"Dancers." Devon's eyes glittered with delight, then his focus snapped back to Vaughn. "Listen, I'm done for the night. Can I give you a ride home?"

Vaughn nodded. "That would be kind, yes."

Devon planted a kiss on Vaughn's cheek. "Glad to hear it. Come on. Nice to meet you, Jonah."

"See you." Vaughn waved at him. Jonah raised one hand uncertainly, and Vaughn turned away.

Devon pulled him closer as they walked through the club. "*Him?* Seriously?"

"What?"

Devon shook his finger. "He's got a reputation. Total slut. Don't bother, Hargy."

"Don't *bother*?" That seemed harsh.

"No. You'll catch something." Devon glanced at him. If Vaughn didn't know better, he'd think Devon was *worried*. "Listen to me. I get out more than you do, so I see the guys who do the rounds. He's one of them. Fun for five minutes, but not because of the conversation, you understand?"

Vaughn rolled his eyes. "I can handle myself, Dev."

"Yeah, yeah, buddy. You handle yourself so well you bat away every guy who tries to dance with you but go after the one who just finished a threesome." Devon guided him back to their friends and jackets, and took his arm off Vaughn's shoulders to yank on his winter blazer. "And don't think we're not gossiping about it."

André perked up. "You met the threesome guy? I heard he took it up the ass for *both* of them."

Devon shot a look at Vaughn as if to say, *See?*

"I didn't realize talking to him was going after him," Vaughn replied dryly.

"You are the pickiest gay man I know." Devon helped Vaughn into his own coat. "So, yeah, for you? Talking is the equivalent of attempting a pickup. Believe me, darling, you can do so much better. In conversation partners as well as hookups," he added. "Maybe try for guys who trick one at a time at least."

Vaughn didn't agree. Talking with Jonah had been intense and kind of fun.

And despite being *picky*, though that wasn't the word he'd use, and not generally inclined towards hookups, he didn't think sex was bad. As long as it was consensual and adult—and that threesome had certainly sounded like both of those—he didn't really care what sex other people had, or how much.

It just wasn't interesting.

So he didn't care for Devon judging the guy purely because he'd gotten laid. Knowing Dev, it was nothing more than sheer jealousy. Wasn't an anonymous, no-strings threesome one of the ultimate gay fantasies?

"Leaving so soon?" André asked.

"Tell me which one the threesome guy is!" James called.

Vaughn shook his head. "Have a good night, guys."

A chorus of good-byes faded into the music as he and Devon made for the entrance. They waited only a few minutes in the freezing cold and relative quiet of the street before a car drew up to meet them and Devon urged him in.

"I thought you weren't supposed to use Bogard for something like this," he said to Devon as they settled in the car.

"Bogard doesn't mind, do you Bogard?" Dev asked loudly.

"No sir," the driver answered. Vaughn gave his address, Bogard put the car into gear, and it lurched forward.

"Still by yourself in the apartment?" Devon asked.

"Yes. And no, you can't crash."

Devon rolled his eyes. "I wish. I have a departmental presentation tomorrow morning, and my father wants to have breakfast with me." He pulled down a mirror from the roof and examined his neck. "Shit. Extra-high collar tomorrow." He sighed and leaned back. "Speaking of annoying parental units, how are yours?"

Vaughn shrugged. "Same old." His mother organized events for people and charged them plenty of money for the privilege, while his father managed a company that ran mutual funds for the people who propped up Toronto's financial district. They'd been doing the same things with the same people for as long as he could remember.

"How's your brother?"

Vaughn knew that searching tone. He eyed Devon. "He doesn't discuss his trades with me. Stop trying to dig for inside information. Apart from being illegal, it's really very tacky."

Devon's eyes went innocently wide. "Honey, what on earth do you think of me? I was *genuinely* inquiring after your brother's health."

Sure. But there *was* something Vaughn could share. "He's engaged."

"Seriously? Already?"

"Yes." It *had* been a quick engagement. Vaughn didn't like to think about the implications that had for him.

"So when's the wedding?"

"Next autumn sometime." Vaughn was too tired to remember the date.

"Who's your plus-one?"

"Haven't thought about it."

"Gosh, don't overwhelm me with your excitement."

"His fiancée is the daughter of one of Dad's partners. It's all very medieval." Perhaps the truth was that Vaughn didn't want to think about it. Now that Merril was engaged, his parents would turn their attention to him. He could foresee months of weekend brunches listening to stories of young men his mother knew. Being the younger brother had its benefits, like distinct differences in expectations regarding career aspirations, but not dating someone suitable wasn't one of them. "Suitable" meaning anyone who was responsible and kind and wouldn't snort the family money up their nose or sink it into vanity projects—a surprisingly difficult prospect in the circles his parents moved in.

He was twenty-six. Still young enough to push back on unsubtle inquiries about his social life without any arguments. Merril had never had that luxury.

"Do you think one of your father's partners has a gay son?" Dev laughed at the idea.

Vaughn glared at him. "Don't even joke."

"Well, darling, you know *I'm* always here."

"I'd rather marry a girl."

Dev scoffed and punched his shoulder.

Vaughn smiled at him. For all Devon's crassness, they'd been friends a long time. When Vaughn had started uni, he'd just figured out he liked men, but hadn't slept with anyone, and Devon had been only too eager to help him out. Their relationship, such as it was, barely lasted two months before Devon slept with someone else. Vaughn hadn't particularly minded; without the sex to distract Dev, they could actually have a conversation and develop a friendship.

It wasn't a friendship Vaughn's parents liked, but he suspected they wouldn't mind as much if Devon ever attempted civility.

His parents knew he was gay, and while that wasn't ideal or what they'd have wanted, he knew they vaguely expected him to find someone and marry him. Devon at least kept Vaughn out on the scene.

The problem was, Vaughn wasn't sure he'd find a boyfriend at all, let alone one who'd marry him. It had been four years since Vaughn had touched anyone intimately. Or kissed anyone. Or slept with anyone. It wasn't for a lack of offers—gay clubs seemed to attract the kind of men who enjoyed hookup culture—it was that he found the whole experience of sleeping around kind of tawdry and underwhelming. He knew he wasn't supposed to. He was supposed to be like Devon and his friends and Jonah the insurance lemming: excited to be on the prowl and happy when he got laid. But he wasn't.

It was a shame, because he also didn't like the prospect of justifying his bachelorhood into his old age.

"Well, if you ever change your mind, it would help me out a lot." Devon flopped over and put his head in Vaughn's lap. Vaughn looked down, ready to push him off if he got handsy. It sometimes happened still, particularly when Dev'd had too much to drink. "My parents actually like you."

"My parents despise you."

"And you know I'd cheat on you discreetly."

Vaughn rolled his eyes. "Let it never be said you're not romantic."

Devon yawned, then blinked sleepily up at him. "I can't believe you talked to the threesome guy," he muttered before closing his eyes and dozing.

What was so unbelievable about that?

CHAPTER THREE

Jonah asked for a red eye in the coffee shop. The barista blinked back at him. "It's a black filter coffee with an espresso shot in it," he explained. The barista's eyebrows rose. Another memory from last night swam in front of Jonah's eyes and he grimaced internally. "Better make it two shots."

"Sure thing." The barista turned to make his order.

It was his own fault he'd barely slept last night. The realization that he'd been heard having a loud threesome in a washroom by the hot gallery assistant had been like a smack of snow in the face. It was a shame things had ended like that, because hand to God, the threesome had been amazing. Blowjobs all around, then one guy in his ass, the other on his cock, safe in the understanding that they were only here to get off. He'd sunk into it, riding the sensations of hands and mouth and cock, the stress and anxiety of the day just draining away. Perfection. One of his top three hookup experiences. He could have been carried home in a bucket, he'd been so relaxed afterwards.

Until he'd seen that gorgeous face in the washroom mirror. *Fuck*. He would never forget the way his spine had crawled when he'd recognized Vaughn and realized that he in turn recognized Jonah.

Or the moment when Vaughn decided to ignore him and walk out.

Jonah had been stunned—and *furious*. He came out of a stall with two other guys, was spotted by some rich guy he'd met that day, and *nothing*? Who ignored something like that? Rang a few alarm bells. Money like Vaughn used stuff like this for bad ends; Jonah had seen it before in the petty, fucked-up circumstances around certain insurance claims. He wasn't going to let anything bad happen to him. No way was Jonah letting him just walk away. Nope.

Plus he'd called it: Vaughn was gay. Which made it worse in a way, because Vaughn was gay and had ignored him earlier that day too, and Jonah didn't understand why. They knew each other. They were attractive. At the very least, Vaughn could have *acknowledged* him as a member of the same team.

So of course he'd rounded the asshole up and let him know there was no way Jonah would let him hold this over his head.

But instead of a bout of catty insults or vague threats of blackmail, Vaughn had seemed genuinely at a loss. Totally surprised and maybe even a little offended at the blackmail idea. And he'd promised not to tell anyone they worked with about that evening. Pretty much the best-case scenario.

Jonah hadn't expected that. *Whoops.*

The espresso machine began brewing the shots and the smell alone helped perk him up.

He also hadn't expected Vaughn's boyfriend. He had been a blond, heavier version of Vaughn, with a horse sewn on his shirt and perfect teeth and the judgmental snarl that had been missing from Vaughn's face. They looked good together, a matching set of coiffed hair and high thread counts. Rich guys in their rich clothes in a rich relationship. Only, the boyfriend had hickeys that Jonah didn't think Vaughn had put there, judging by the surprised way Vaughn had noticed them.

Not that Jonah cared.

Just . . . it seemed a little wrong that Vaughn was so into Blondie that he hadn't cruised Jonah's fine ass, yet Blondie could get his rocks off with someone else and not get called out for it. Were they open? If so, that was a shame. Open relationships seemed like a complicated case of denial, but what the hell did he know? He'd never been in a relationship long enough to experience monogamy, let alone variations of it.

Not that any of it was his business.

But the whole thing had left a sour taste in his mouth. He'd gone home earlier than he normally would have, the nice effects of the mind-blowing sex completely gone, and tossed and turned all night.

He'd never been . . . not *caught* exactly, but seen like that before. Not right after. Not by someone who knew him professionally. It was a weird, unsettling feeling.

Now he was totally underslept. Sated, but tired. And he didn't want to go to work, for the first time since starting the job.

Jonah paid for the coffee and took a big mouthful, enjoying the way the hot liquid ran down his throat and warmed him up. Outside, the November sky was overcast and full of snowy promises. He strode as quickly as he could through the slushy streets to the insurance company.

It was on Bay Street, in one of the glass skyscrapers, and stood shoulder to shoulder with financial consultancies and banks. The day of the interview, Jonah had squared his shoulders and eyed the building, saying to himself, *You are mine and now is my time.* Of course he'd aced the interview; he'd dreamed of working somewhere like this since he'd been twelve and his third foster dad had told him he would never amount to anything.

He almost wished he'd kept that guy's details just so he could call him up and tell him he'd amounted to freaking Bay Street in Toronto, and he currently earned more per month than that guy had made in three, so he'd be debt-free way before he turned thirty. So maybe twelve-year-old gay foster kids were more than a tax write-off, *ya jerk.*

Shoving that in the guy's face would be sweet. But Jonah had cut the cord with every set of foster parents he'd had, had even changed his last name before going into university to emphasize just how much he'd moved on, and he felt damn good about it. Living the dream was better than throwing it back in people's faces.

He grinned to himself as he walked with other suited, coffee-carrying employees through the wide streets and into the skyscrapers. Christmas decorations were already going up on the lampposts and outside the buildings. Snowy streets, tinsel, glossy intimidating buildings, coffee he hadn't even had to think about being able to afford. Yup, he'd made it.

Once he'd settled at his desk, however, he reconsidered whether making it was all it was cracked up to be. On his desk was the Delphi file with a Post-it saying *WE NEED TO DISCUSS – G.*

Awesome. Jonah resisted the urge to slam his face into his desk. *Shit.*

He logged into his workstation and started loading the programs he needed for the day, then picked up the file and went to Garrett's office. Garrett ushered him in, and Jonah closed the door, wrapping them in superficial privacy.

"What"—*breathe, Jonah, it's fine*—"do we need to discuss?"

"Good morning to you too." Garrett's voice was dry. "Look through the security log."

The security log? Oh yeah, the security log they'd requested.

Huh. Seemed that Pretty Boy had made good on his promise to keep his mouth shut.

Jonah flipped the folder open and spent a silent five minutes perusing the log. It detailed each entrance covered by the Delphi security system. There were three: front door, back door, office door. Every single entry was logged. The legend key included an abbreviation for forced entries; it didn't show up at all on the report.

He looked up. "This supposed burglary didn't trip the alarm."

"Yeah." Garrett wore the most serious expression Jonah had ever seen. "Don't you think that's weird?"

"You think it would have?"

Garrett sat back. "Here's a test, Sondern: you tell me."

Jonah thought through the situation. The police had searched the building and verified the piece stolen. The security log, from a reputable company and provided by the claimant, said the security of the building had not been compromised at any point. There were a few logical conclusions he could draw from that.

"Okay, option one," he began, "the piece was taken by someone who works there, hence the lack of break-in. Option two, the piece was stolen by a professional who somehow got the details and bypassed the system. Option three, the report has been tampered with."

Garrett smiled. "That's what I thought too. As well as various unlikely iterations of all of those."

Jonah studied the report. It was a printout of a PDF document. Easy enough to edit. "I think we should request the security log ourselves and cross-check."

"Agreed."

"But it wouldn't make sense for them to fudge it like this, not if it already helped their claim," he thought aloud. "I'd expect to see a breach of security, rather than a lack of one."

"Exactly. Which means . . ."

"This is legitimate."

Garrett's hands gestured *Go on*. "And if it's legitimate . . .?"

"Then we're assuming the thief knew the codes, which brings us to two scenarios. One: the thief works in the gallery. Two: it's an outside job."

"Exactly." Garrett stood and rounded the desk so that he could glance over the report too. "I'd say the first, but there *is* a slim chance that someone got pass codes for their security system and/or hacked them. It's rare, but it happens."

Jonah frowned. "So we're thinking it's an inside job. They're covered for theft. Are they covered even if the thief is an employee?"

Garrett nodded. "The insurance is in the name of the company, and the company is owned by Angeline and Cressida Dufort. Unless it's proven that one of those two stole the painting, it wouldn't be fraud, it would be legitimate theft." He tapped the paper. "Get the official log from the security company. And maybe it would be good to talk to the employees, see what these log-in patterns mean. Confirm if this is accurate."

Jonah glared at him. "Is that really my job?"

"We," Garrett stated grandly, "are insurance investigators. We decide if what we have received is the full truth and if that truth falls within the guidelines and areas articulated and covered by the policy."

"Yeah, but that 'truth' thing? Not us who actually decides that. The police do. The report is due today or tomorrow. If they say it's stolen, we have to treat it as stolen and wait for their conclusions on who did it. We should at least wait until we get the initial report before making any kind of decision on this. We can't definitively refuse or pay anything until the police have caught someone."

Garrett sighed, then shot him a proud smile. "We'd have to pay even if they don't catch the guy, but you're right. You know upper management likes us to refuse claims, but I'll help you push back on a final verdict until we get some proof one way or another. Go do what you can for now." He went back to his seat.

Jonah gazed at the file. "This is going to be a complicated one, isn't it?"

"Oh yeah. And considering how minted they are, we need to tread carefully."

Jonah quirked an eyebrow. "How d'you figure that?"

"This is . . ." Garrett rubbed a hand over his face. "You know, you met them. They're not happy about this, and they want a payout yesterday. Unhappy rich people always pull the lawyer card at some point." Garrett pointed at the folder. "These people can afford a good lawyer. Hell, one of them's probably married to one or has a family member who's one. We want to avoid litigation. Make it happen."

Jonah stood and saluted with the case file. "Got it."

Garrett smiled. "Good. Any questions, give me a shout."

Jonah left Garrett's office, a troubled feeling in his gut. Finding out the truth behind a claim was what he did, and he liked to think he had a good sense for when someone was bullshitting him. Sometimes things turned out to be really simple, but sometimes not. This had the potential to get fuzzy around the distinction between fraud and theft, especially if the police couldn't establish who did it. If they were right about this, this would leak into a grey area, one in which they were at odds with entitled rich people. Grey areas and entitled rich people led to contention, and contention cost the company money. Garrett was right; they'd have to tread carefully.

He could totally do that.

For the rest of the morning, he pored over the documentation already provided for the Yoon theft. Everything seemed to be in order: the description matched Vaughn's, the valuation was depressingly high, the picture attached was creepier than he'd imagined, the artist details were all correct. He chased up the police report and official version of the security log, received and checked the log, established both provided versions as correspondingly exact and therefore truthful, then chased the police report again. Then he spent the afternoon pretending to go over another claim's documentation, but googling the gallery and its staff members instead. Most of them had online CVs available for general perusal. Vaughn, however, didn't. Shame. Headshots could be hot.

It was odd that he didn't, not when that kind of job seemed pretty dependent on who you knew and where you'd worked and being visible. But maybe it wasn't completely unheard of—Jonah knew jack about the art world. So what if Vaughn wasn't on LinkedIn? Or didn't have his own website (unlike his managers, Maurice, Angeline, and Cressida)? If he was as lackadaisical about self-marketing as he was about hearing acquaintances orgasming several feet away, then Jonah was betting he just didn't give a shit.

Oh well. It wasn't like Jonah didn't remember what he looked like. Especially last night—*wow*. The stupid gallery outfit had been replaced in the club by a simple blue T-shirt and tight black jeans. He'd practically looked normal. And his clothes had emphasized his lean figure, the planes of his body, the angle of his jaw, and the way his eyes went all dark under the club lights. When Jonah had dragged him outside, he'd definitely noticed how the cold had perked up the guy's nipples. Sitting there in his crappy little cubicle, Jonah realized he had a semi from the memory.

No. Absolutely not. Rich, boyfriended, and not interested. *This one is off-limits.*

But still hot. Jonah was only human.

And Jonah was also at work. He resolutely closed down all Delphi-related tabs and returned to the claim already in front of him. There. Done. No more Delphi Gallery or hot assistant thoughts for now.

The next few days ticked by in Jonah's usual routine: coffee, work, gym, sleep. Notably, he wasn't called into Garrett's office and given a lecture on unsavoury rumours, so it seemed Vaughn had kept his promise. *Good job, Vaughn.*

On Friday, he woke up with the usual itch in his bones. Horniness, desire, need, whatever people wanted to call it, he had it, and bad. By the time he left the house, he'd decided to go out that night and see who he could find. He didn't want to be topped again, not after earlier this week. As he bought his morning coffee, he debated what he was in the mood for: a barely legal, sweet twink? Someone older? A bear? It wasn't often that he wanted someone big and hairy on him. He wasn't sure he was quite there this time. So perhaps just some average gay bar with a mix of guys, a smorgasbord of types. He'd find someone cute and willing and hung and enjoy himself.

Today was looking up already, and he'd only bought coffee.

Of course, waiting for him on his desk was a police report for the Delphi Gallery. Reading through it, it appeared the police had realized what he and Garrett had guessed—namely that there was no forced entry and thus the theft was highly suspicious—and were investigating further. Also, to Jonah's surprise, there were details that didn't match the gallery documentation.

Garrett wasn't surprised when Jonah brought in the report. He glanced over it, then picked up his phone, grinning at Jonah as he dialled.

"Hello, Ms. Dufort? We received the police report." Pause. "I'd like to come down and discuss it with you." He frowned. "Mr. Palomer, then. Yes, today." He glanced at Jonah. "I was thinking before lunch, actually." Jonah nodded. "Great! We'll be by shortly." He hung up and fixed Jonah with a pointed look. "Ready for more 'discussions' with Delphi?"

Nope. Jonah didn't want to go back there. "All we can say is that we can't approve the claim just yet. Can't we do that over the phone?"

Garrett grinned. "Personal touch, remember?" His grin dropped. "Plus, I want a word with Mr. Palomer. Some of the details don't match up between the police report and the gallery documentation. The description of the piece and the valuation seem a little off."

"You don't say." *What a surprise. Not.*

"Do you have anything else you need to do this morning?" Garrett asked.

Jonah fixed a smile on his face. "Nope."

"Great. We'll leave in thirty minutes."

And that was how Jonah found himself walking into the Delphi Gallery for the second time this week. What a freaking joy.

Vaughn sat at the front desk, laptop at his fingertips, as polished as the first time Jonah had seen him. *Okay, this could be someone's version of joy.* No blazer today; instead he wore a cable-knit sweater, beige chinos, a different pair of deck shoes, and a green scarf with daisies. He looked up and stared, obviously surprised to see them.

"Mr. Barlow! Mr.—" the hesitation was only slight "—Sondern. Welcome."

"We're here to see Mr. Palomer," Garrett said.

Vaughn stood. "Of course! Please follow me." He closed the laptop and tucked it under his arm, then led them up the stairway to the office.

Maurice didn't look happy to see them. "Nice to see you again." His voice was about as flat as his handshake. "Can I get you coffee? Water?"

"Coffee would be great," Garrett said.

"Vaughn. Now."

Jonah almost gaped at him. What the fuck was *that* tone? Then Vaughn swished past them to the kitchenette at the other end of the office, and Jonah's jaw did drop. How could Vaughn let this punk talk to him like that?

Maurice led them to the same meeting room, and the moment they sat down, Vaughn came in with two cappuccinos and placed them in front of Garrett and Jonah without looking at either of them.

Jonah watched him leave out the corner of his eye. Vaughn's face was serene, but Jonah would have been mad enough to spit in the milk. He eyed it suspiciously.

The door shut, and Garrett leaned forward. "Thanks for meeting us on short notice, Mr. Palomer. We received the police report today, and we wanted to check in with you on how that report affects the claim for the Yoon piece."

Maurice pulled his greasy smile. "We went over the report this morning, and we're glad that the police are actively investigating how the theft occurred. I'm not sure how that would affect the claim, though." That smile stayed wide. "The piece is confirmed stolen."

"Yes," Jonah said, "but by whom?"

Maurice shot him a withering look. "Does it matter?"

"It does," Garrett said. "The insurance policy covers theft by a third party."

"And?"

"The theft has been established, but not the third party."

Maurice's smile dropped completely. "Are you suggesting that one of *us* stole this piece of art?"

"No, not at all," Garrett said soothingly.

"Because we at Delphi *love* art," Maurice began. Jonah wanted to roll his eyes. *Here we go.* "We seek out the best up-and-coming artists and showcase them before many others do. We *want* people to see the best that Canada and the world have to offer. We love what we do so much that we took out that policy on theft when no other gallery of our calibre and size does." Maurice tapped one finger on the table to emphasize his points. "We want our artists to trust that we will take care of their work to the full extent of our abilities."

"We appreciate that," Garrett said. "We're very impressed with your dedication and sense of responsibility. We adore supporting companies like yours."

Jonah *had* to learn to lie like that. *Amazing.*

"Then why are you waiting for the police to investigate this crime before paying out a substantiated claim?" Maurice demanded. "Your company paid out in a matter of days for our prior claims."

Yikes.

"We haven't outright declined," Jonah jumped in. "These circumstances aren't as, uh, straightforward as prior claims." *Because we smell a rat.* "We just want to make sure we have all the information we need to make the right decision for all parties concerned."

Maurice turned red.

"It can be a slow process when circumstances aren't clear-cut," Garrett added. "We want to reassure you that we're just as invested in getting a definitive result from this investigation as you are."

"You just want the piece recovered so you don't have to pay out," Maurice snapped.

"Wouldn't that be the ideal situation for everyone? Especially the *artist*?" Jonah asked.

Maurice visibly collected himself. "You're right, but given how the other pieces weren't recovered, how likely is it that this one will be? Surely you're just wasting time and delaying the inevitable."

Jonah wanted to sigh. This guy was like a pit bull with a toy in its mouth, only he wasn't playing around or letting go. He absently sipped his cappuccino and almost choked. The milk was scalded.

Now there wasn't even the help of coffee to get him through this.

The insurance guys and Maurice emerged from their meeting forty-five minutes later. Vaughn heard them coming down the stairs while he was welcoming a visitor. After the visitor paid the fee and went in, he turned around.

Maurice seemed pissed off, but that wasn't exactly new. Jonah and Garrett were tired and drawn. Having had meetings where Maurice was on a rampage, Vaughn knew exactly how they felt. He checked the time—just after noon. Pity. A little early in the day to look that drained.

Well, at least Maurice's policy of excluding him from "important" meetings had worked out well this time.

Jonah caught his eye and headed towards him. Vaughn stilled, wondering what the guy wanted. He hadn't expected to see the insurance lemmings back so soon—it had only been a few days. There had to be some new development; Maurice had been sulking over something earlier that day, but Vaughn knew better than to ask. If the insurance guys were here now, perhaps that development was the police report. He didn't know what it said, but it had to be something major for the insurance guys to physically come here to talk about it. Judging by the wary expression on Jonah's face, he definitely wasn't pleased to be here.

Given events earlier this week, Vaughn couldn't blame him.

"Hey. Hargrave." Jonah stopped just in front of him, his gaze fixated on Vaughn's neck for some reason. He shook his head, then looked Vaughn in the eye. "Gotta ask you something. You free for lunch today?"

Lunch? What on earth for? "Unfortunately not," Vaughn said.

"Busy with someone else?"

"I usually catch up on emails during lunch."

Jonah eyed him. "Seriously? No time off?"

Vaughn shifted his weight. "Well, officially I get an hour, but why do you even—"

"Awesome." Jonah pointed a finger at the window. "Meet me at that deli across the road. The one that's all decorated for Christmas already. See you there in . . ." he glanced at his cell phone ". . . ten minutes." He went back to his manager and Maurice.

Vaughn gazed after him, felt himself staring, and whipped back to his laptop screen before Maurice caught on. Lunch with the promiscuous insurance lemming? Why? What could he want? If this lunch thing was related to the claim—and Vaughn was fairly certain it was, because why on earth would anyone want to bring the other night back up—he would need to tread carefully.

He watched the insurance guys leave. Jonah went across to the deli almost straightaway, while the other one, Barlow, used his cell to make a call. Maurice turned from the door, his face dour.

"I'm having lunch out today," Vaughn told him.

"Whatever."

Vaughn snapped his laptop shut, locked it away, and retrieved his coat. He swapped his shoes for his snow boots and put up a Ring for Attention sign on the desk, because Maurice couldn't be relied on to staff the front desk constantly or to care about a detail like an explanatory sign. Jonah's manager got into a taxi and drove away as Vaughn crossed the road and entered the deli.

Jonah was ordering at the counter. He glanced at Vaughn, then did an idle sweep of his body that seemed practically instinctual to him. "Hey," he said. "I ordered food."

The server turned to Vaughn. "You two ordering together?"

"Separately." Vaughn stepped up to the counter. "The lasagna, please."

Jonah stood by quietly as Vaughn paid. Jonah took their table numbers, Vaughn picked up their drinks, and they found a table and sat down in silence.

The silence continued.

What was his deal? Jonah seemed uncertain and tongue-tied, his eyes darting from Vaughn's face to the deli surroundings.

Now that Vaughn had a moment to study him, he realized Jonah was younger than him. Not by much, perhaps only a few years, but something about him said he was still growing. Under bright café lights, his blond hair turned sandy, and his hazel eyes stood out in a long, serious face. In his suit, he appeared every inch the dedicated young graduate in a new job that Vaughn was starting to suspect he was.

The graduate who was apparently having second thoughts about ordering him over here for lunch.

"I like this deli," Vaughn said, hoping to break the ice. "Their wraps and salads are excellent."

Jonah looked relieved. "Oh. Good."

"You picked a good place for us to have lunch during this very mysterious conversation."

Jonah went red. "Yeah. Okay. Got it." He pulled out his phone. "It's just . . . I have some questions I want to ask you about the piece that was taken."

Vaughn frowned. "We've already submitted the documentation—"

Jonah waved dismissively. "Yeah, yeah, but I just want to be triple sure about the details. Do you mind? What was the name of the piece?"

He hesitated, but it seemed entirely aboveboard. "*Entrance*. Artist is Jai Yoon."

"And the dimensions?"

Vaughn went through the description of the piece in great detail. By the time he was done, their food had arrived. Jonah glanced longingly at Vaughn's lasagna, but dug into his salmon salad without mentioning the food.

"And the sale value?" Jonah asked after the first mouthful.

"Ten thousand dollars."

Jonah's fork paused. He tapped the number into the phone. "Seriously?" His voice sounded strained for some reason.

"Yeah."

"It's thread and plastic. How the hell does something like that sell for \$10K?"

Vaughn sliced his lasagna. "The value of art doesn't lie in its physical materials, or not *just* in its materials. It lies in its message, its mode of expression, its creativity, the hours put into it, the marketplace value of the artist, and so on."

Jonah had a confused expression on his face. "I don't get it."

Figured. Most people unaffiliated with the arts industry didn't "get it" either. Vaughn privately thought it should be something Jonah should have a rough idea of, if only for his job. Then again, artwork valuation for insurance purposes *was* a murky, fuzzy area. Interesting, but not straightforward. Jonah seemed like the kind of man who preferred straightforward.

Vaughn elected not to elaborate, as it would easily take the rest of the hour, so he chewed his lasagna carefully, appreciating the flavours of tomato and basil and meat. He licked his lips to catch a spill and cut another piece, ignoring the way Jonah stared at him.

"While we're asking questions," Vaughn said, "you mentioned something interesting the other night, in the club. Something about our claim being suspicious. And now you're here, asking me questions for which you should already have answers. What's going on?"

Jonah took a few moments to slice his salmon into smaller pieces.

Vaughn suspected he was buying time. "You'll lose the texture if you cut it up that small, by the way."

Jonah shot him a hot glare. "I do *not* need your advice on how to eat my food."

Touchy. Was that fair? Probably. "Our claim isn't straightforward?" he prodded.

Jonah stabbed at his plate, skewering leaf and herb and salmon. "In a nutshell."

"Why isn't it straightforward?"

"We can't process it until the police finish their investigation. They need to at least establish that a third party stole the piece."

Ah yes, the police. They were proving tremendous fun. They'd returned and pored over the office and keypads for the security system, then had insisted on checking everyone's homes for the missing piece. Not that Vaughn had minded too much, though he was infinitely grateful that the Yoon was nothing like his own work in his studio, but Angeline and Cressida had been furious. Of course, the police hadn't discovered anything in any of their homes, so now there was a detective popping in and out, asking questions and examining the gallery spaces and getting in the way of work.

Like Vaughn really needed someone else getting in his way. Maurice and Angeline were worried to the point of distraction and hadn't done a thing besides drink coffee and bitch at each other and try to smooth over the media. Cressida had refused to leave home, claiming the stress was too much. The last few days had felt like Vaughn was running the place on his own, what with greeting visitors and doing cash counts and answering emails and providing the odd tour *and* booking musicians for the gallery's Christmas party *and* talking to the detective whenever she had questions.

Wait a second: *establish that a third party stole the piece?*

"You mean that it wasn't one of us who stole it," he realized.

"Basically." Jonah shovelled another forkful of vegetable matter into his mouth, his eyes on Vaughn's plate.

Oh, for God's sake. Vaughn cut a piece off. "Would you like to try some?"

Jonah's gaze flicked up to his and turned hostile. Vaughn wanted to sigh. What was with him and *glaring* every time Vaughn asked him a question?

"No," Jonah practically spat. "Do you have any idea how many calories are in lasagna?"

Calories. *Give me strength.* Vaughn lifted the piece he'd cut off and chewed it deliberately, eyes locked on Jonah's. He swallowed. "I can't say I do, no."

Jonah also swallowed, even though he hadn't actually been eating. "Cheese. Pasta. Beef. The unholy trifecta of dairy, wheat, and red meat; it's the worst thing you could possibly eat." Jonah's fork stabbed into his salad again. "I don't eat that kind of stuff."

"You're missing out." Vaughn forked an especially cheesy piece into his mouth. Mmm. Bliss. He closed his eyes briefly, it was that good. Swallowed. "Was that all you wanted to ask me?"

"Huh?" Jonah was staring at him again.

"About the piece. Was that it?"

"Oh, yeah." Jonah's face turned thoughtful. He really was very expressive. "I'm not accusing any of you of stealing the piece."

"No. You're just assuming one of us has until the police say otherwise. They searched our houses and found nothing, you know."

Jonah rolled his eyes. "Oh, like it couldn't be somewhere else? And we'd get the money back if it turns out that this *was* fraud? I don't think so."

True. They'd get the money, but Angeline would take them to court first. Maurice had been muttering about doing that anyway. "I concede your point."

Jonah grunted through another mouthful of food. He startled abruptly, then dug into his pocket and pulled out his phone. His face went white.

"What's wrong?" Vaughn asked.

Jonah swallowed, choked, grabbed his water and chugged it, then took a deep breath, and put his phone back in his pocket. "Nothing."

Damien Hirst's latest attempt at art was nothing—*this* was something. "If you need to call someone, I won't mind."

Jonah scowled at him. "I'm *fine*. Drop it."

Okay then. He looked down at his plate, unsure of how to keep the conversation going now that Jonah had very effectively shut it down. For someone who'd invited him to lunch, Jonah didn't seem to actually want to talk to him that much. And now he was scarfing down his food like it would jump off his plate if he didn't. Why on earth was he eating salad when he clearly wanted something more filling?

Vaughn had about half the lasagna left, and he picked at the sauce as an awkward silence filled the table between them. This sauce was a proper ragù: rich, tomatoey, filled with basil and oregano and minced beef and mushrooms. Maybe his lunch companion would be more amenable to just this part of the meal?

He scraped out a sizeable amount of the sauce into a spoon and held it out to Jonah. The guy eyed it in surprise, then glared at Vaughn *again*. "I said I didn't want any."

"I know. But this has no cheese or pasta in it." He kept the spoon up. "It really is very good. I think you'd like it."

Jonah put his cutlery down. "Okay. That's it. I wasn't going to say anything, but now I totally am. What are you doing? What would your boyfriend say?"

Boyfriend? "Excuse me?"

"You heard me."

"I don't have a boyfriend."

A faint pink limned his cheeks. "The other night. The guy who took you home."

"*Devon*?" Vaughn chuckled. The very idea. "No. Definitely not. We're friends."

"He practically pissed a circle around you." Jonah did go fully red now, and ducked his head slightly. "Sorry. That was inappropriate."

And snapping at him for offering a bite of lasagna wasn't? Honestly, what were this guy's priorities? Vaughn shook his head. "He's protective. It's nothing personal." No way was he telling Jonah what Devon had said about him.

That eyebrow rose again. "Uh-huh. Still not sure he'd approve of you flirting."

Flirting? Good God. Calorie-conscious *and* delusional. Vaughn knew how to pick them. He set the spoon down. "I'm not flirting with you."

"Really." Jonah's voice dripped with disbelief. "You don't call putting food in my mouth flirting?"

"No, actually. I share food with my eating companions regularly." Vaughn mentally replayed their conversation. "What part of the last twenty minutes was flirtatious?"

Jonah's jaw dropped. "Are you kidding me? Just how oblivious are you?"

Jesus. Okay. Clearly they were having separate conversations here. Whatever Jonah was experiencing, though, Vaughn didn't want to be involved. Since when had simple conversation been so badly misconstrued? Vaughn decided he'd had enough, both of the lasagna and of this touchy, surly man.

"I mean," Jonah added just before Vaughn could push his plate aside, "do you have any idea what your face does when you're eating?" He gestured at Vaughn. "Seriously, you have this expression like you're eating the most delicious thing on the planet. You look like you're about to have a Meg Ryan moment."

Vaughn frowned. "And my enjoyment of food means I'm flirting with you?"

"When it's like *that*? Where I'm from, yeah."

"And where's that?" Vaughn genuinely wanted to know, so he could make sure he never visited.

"Toronto, pretty boy."

Huh. "I'm from Toronto too," Vaughn said, "and I've had many meals with people who somehow managed to not worry that I'm flirting with them."

Jonah's mouth turned into a grim line. "You're angry."

"I don't know what kind of people you spend time with," Vaughn was careful not to be curt or loud, "but I don't flirt with someone I barely know, who's handling a delicate work-related matter, and who clearly doesn't like me."

Jonah blinked in surprise.

Vaughn pulled his napkin off his lap and set it next to his plate. "I think we're done here." He made to stand.

Jonah's hand shot out and pressed on his. "I'm sorry." He'd gone very red. "Please stay and finish your food."

"I *am* finished."

"Look, I . . . Wow, seriously? You've only eaten like half of it. Hey," he added, pressing down harder on Vaughn's hand, keeping him pinned there. "I totally misjudged this. That doesn't usually happen." He seemed to be scrabbling for words. "I mean, we're both gay, we're both attractive . . . you know how it goes."

Like he'd give him that. "Not really."

"I misread the situation. I didn't mean to offend you. I'm sorry."

Vaughn hesitated. Jonah's hand was warm on his. Weighty. Was he *squirming*? He looked contrite, but he had backtracked the moment Vaughn had reminded him of their work, not before. "If you're saying that just to stay on my good side for work, there's no need."

Jonah frowned. "The work aspect freaking sucks, not gonna lie, but after this claim is filed, I'll be out of your hair. I investigate lots of claims, you know? We're a big team. So we might not see each other again, even if your gallery makes another claim. Except"—he tentatively took his hand off Vaughn's—"in clubs." He fidgeted with his cutlery, his fork scraping through the film of dressing coating his plate. "And I've been meaning to say thanks for that, by the way. For not saying anything to your people."

This was a different person than the one who'd cockily told him to meet in this deli, and the one who'd told him off for flirting. This one seemed almost *shy*. Well, maybe *shy* was the wrong word, but certainly uncomfortable. It reminded Vaughn of that small moment between them in the club before Devon had interrupted them, the one where their focus had been entirely on each other. No posturing, no anger.

It was a nice change. He liked this person.

Vaughn sat down again. "Like I said," he responded slowly, "I don't care about that. Outing you about something so personal isn't the decent thing to do."

Jonah shrugged. "'S beside the point." *Scrape*. He snagged the last tomato and rolled it in the dressing. "Not everyone would see it that way. If my manager caught me in that situation . . ." He shuddered. "Oh God. No. I can't even think about it."

Vaughn couldn't help smiling at the idea of Mr. Barlow in a gay club washroom. He was fairly certain the man was straight, what with his choice of suits and the wedding ring on his finger. "I'd say his wife would have bigger problems than him hearing you."

Jonah's face jerked into a smile. "Oh my *God*, could you imagine? Ugh." A moment later, his expression clouded and he shifted in his chair. "You know, you're wrong. You said I don't like you. And, I mean . . ." *Scrapescrapescrape.* "It's not that I don't like you. It's more like I don't know you."

"You've glared at me for most of lunch. That's what I meant."

"Oh." He went red again. "I thought you were being all pretentious and coming on to me or something, so I was trying to put you off."

Vaughn studied him, genuinely trying to understand this guy's perspective. "Right."

"You're not though." Ah, it seemed the idea had finally sunk through. He dropped his fork. "You're genuinely, *genuinely* not hitting on me." His eyes went wide. "Oh my God." He sat back, face clearing from embarrassment to disbelief.

Vaughn shifted uncomfortably. "Is that, er, strange?"

Jonah shrugged. "Yeah. But that's okay. I get it now." He leaned forward with a mischievous grin. "So what are you into?" His voice was barely a whisper.

"What am I—"

"Yeah. Queens? No, wait, bears? Because I've been there. We should swap notes."

Oh no. "I, uh, I don't really have a type."

"Seriously?" Jonah held up a finger. "Ah, I get it. The boyfriend. I know, I know," he said quickly. "You said he wasn't actually a boyfriend, but you *want* him to be, right?"

"No!" Vaughn forced himself to lower his voice. "We dated for a few months in university, but that didn't work out, for good reasons." Reasons like insanely mismatched libidos and the multiple other people Devon had fucked without telling Vaughn.

"Like?"

"Like it's none of your business."

Jonah waggled his eyebrows. "It totally seemed like you two were together. Maybe he wants you back. You should think about it."

Him and Devon. God. Vaughn really *would* rather marry a girl. "I'm not really a relationship guy."

Jonah's eyes lit up, and he grabbed Vaughn's hands. "*Me too.*" God, he sounded absolutely delighted. "I just can't, you know? Free and easy. No strings. It's the best way."

Vaughn blinked in the face of so much cheerfulness. "Actually, I just find it simpler—"

Jonah nodded. "Yeah, yeah, I hear that, I *hear* that. No one hassling you to cook food and deal with bad moods and sleep with only one person. Totally get that."

Vaughn gently tried to extricate his hands. "That's not what I—"

"Hey, I'm cruising tonight. You wanna come with?" Then his eyes narrowed and he let go of Vaughn's hands. "Actually, maybe you shouldn't. You're too hot to be a wingman."

"I'm less than ideal at being a wingman." Vaughn sometimes missed signals. It was why he stuck to dancing and drinking. "I don't do cruising."

"What were you doing earlier this week, then?"

"Dancing."

Jonah rolled his eyes. "Oh yeah, I remember. Anyway, come with if you want to."

"I have plans, sorry." He did. Now. If earlier that week was any indication of Jonah's typical night out, Vaughn knew better than to even attempt that.

"You sure?" Jonah's expression was teasing. Vaughn thought perhaps Jonah knew he didn't really have plans, but he didn't seem to mind. Evidence suggested his clubbing strategy was just fine without a wingman.

He smiled anyway. "Yes. Have fun."

Jonah's eyes danced. "Oh baby, you *know* I will." He glanced at Vaughn's plate, then reached for the spoon and put the sauce in his mouth. Vaughn watched the emotions play over his face as he tasted it. Desire. Appreciation. Enjoyment. A small expression of guilt as he put the spoon back down.

Ah. Now Vaughn understood Jonah's earlier assumptions. *Whoops.* If Vaughn's face was even half as expressive as Jonah's, then perhaps he should watch it when he ate something delicious.

"That *is* good," Jonah declared. "Are you seriously going to leave half of it there? That's a total waste."

When Vaughn asked if he wanted it, Jonah pulled the disgusted face again and told him where he could put it, making Vaughn laugh at how ridiculous Jonah was.

By the time Vaughn had the remainder of his food wrapped to go, his lunch hour was almost up. They left the deli, and Jonah called for a taxi. Vaughn waved good-bye to him and loped back across the road to the gallery, foil container in hand. Remarkable. He'd never brought leftovers home before. Funny how slight censure from certain people made one want to do things to please them. Plus, this would be great for dinner tonight.

Upon entering the gallery, he saw Maurice at the front desk, a thoughtful expression on his face and a packet of pickle chips in his hand.

"Did you just have lunch with the insurance guy?" he asked through a mouthful of snack.

Vaughn bent down to take off his boots. "He happened to be there."

"Yeah, and you both just happened to leave at the same time. Had a nice long chat with him, eh?"

That certainly didn't seem leading in any way. "I suppose."

"So what's he like? Nice guy?"

Vaughn thought about Jonah dropping the lemming act to tell him off for cheating on an imaginary boyfriend. The apology afterward had been nice, but he had been up-front and honest when many wouldn't have been. "On the whole, yes."

"Making friends with the enemy." Maurice sounded approving. "I like the way you think. Keep it up, Vaughn."

Vaughn went still, then studied Maurice's face. He was happy. He was *happy*? Maurice was never happy with him. What did he mean? Keep what up, exactly? *Friends with the enemy*?

Vaughn frowned as he slipped his feet into today's loafers. Maurice seemed to have drawn some weird conclusions there. "Friends," he echoed. "I'm not sure I'd go that far."

"Well no, not *yet*." Maurice winked. "But you could just, you know, slip in a good word for us, ask him how his work's going, how claims are processed, what would help them process faster. That kind of thing."

Ah. Vaughn straightened, feet firmly in light, cotton-lined comfort. "Maurice"—he leaned his head to one side—"I'm not sure it's going to be that kind of friendship."

Maurice grinned and tapped the side of his nose. Then he glanced at his watch. "You took the full hour, eh? I thought time was getting on. Back to the grindstone, Hargrave." He grasped his chips, turned, and made for the office. Vaughn frowned after him in confusion. Maurice sounded *chipper*. It was a little disconcerting.

He stashed his boots in the nearby closet, sat down behind the front desk, put the sign away, and set up his laptop. Almost right away, the detective, a fortysomething woman called Meyer, strolled past from within the gallery, startling him.

"Lunch out?" She nodded at the foil container next to him.

"The deli across the road." Had she been in the gallery long?

She glanced through the window at the deli. "Hmm. I might try it one of these days. Mr. Palomer sounded happy just now."

Oh yeah, she'd been here long enough, for sure. "He misunderstood something."

"That right? You *did* have lunch with Mr. Sondern from Laigh and Sanders?"

Vaughn stared at her. She studied him back, face innocent and open. She *had* heard what had Maurice said. "Yes. We had lunch."

"Is that something you often do together?"

"No. First time."

She nodded. "And how was it?"

Vaughn shrugged. "Delicious. They source local."

She crossed her arms, and her expression turned intent. "Did he ask you any unusual questions?"

Plenty, but nothing that had made Vaughn uneasy. Except... "He asked me about the Yoon piece." That was weird, right? Or wasn't it? "It's odd because everything I told him was in the documentation we gave them earlier this week."

She raised an eyebrow. "Uh-huh."

"That's all. We talked about that, ate food, then talked about ..." He couldn't mention meeting in the club. Or the gay thing. Or the calorie-counting thing. God, did detectives learn that hard stare in detective school? "... growing up in Toronto."

She nodded. "Sure. Thanks. Have a good day, Mr. Hargrave." She retrieved her coat and left the gallery.

Bizarre.

Not that he had time to think about it, as he was now back to front-desk duty. He turned to the screen and saw the twenty unread emails that had pinged into the gallery inbox during lunch. His eyes glazed over.

That lunch had been one of the weirdest experiences he'd ever had. Jonah was something of a puzzle: he was so young and yet so direct and confident. *Meet me at the deli. I don't eat that stuff. Are you kidding me?* Blunt too. But quick to apologize and be contrite. All in less than an hour. Being him had to be exhausting.

But that *face.* A literal canvas for his emotions, each one clear and vivid. He'd be an artist's dream to sketch or photograph.

Insurance probably wasn't a good fit for a face like that.

Then the way he'd utterly transformed in those last ten minutes or so. His excitement had lit him up and his whole body had become animated. Just because . . . what? They'd established they weren't interested in each other? Jonah'd thought they shared a no-relationship preference? Something like that.

Well, whatever worked. Talking with a happy Jonah was far nicer than talking to a surly Jonah.

A notification blinked at him on the laptop screen, catching his eye. *Menu confirmation, call caterers.*

Right. The Christmas party for their December exhibition. He brought up the menu choices and began considering canapé options. Once he'd decided those, he sent back his choices and called the catering company to confirm rough numbers.

What else needed to be done?

He pulled out the checklist. Pieces: to be set up next week. Date: confirmed. Musicians: confirmed. Catering: contacted and double-confirmed. Guest list: invites sent out to patrons, friends, artists, reporters, and investors. He sent a few chaser emails for those who hadn't RSVP'd.

"Vaughn."

He looked up sharply. Cressida stood in front of him, coffee cup in hand and sunglasses on. Her sunset-red hair curled wildly about her head, and her nail polish matched her hair colour. She wore heeled black leather boots, purely to spite the slushy streets. She lowered her sunglasses to reveal bloodshot eyes. Perhaps *bed* meant *in a bottle of gin* these days. "Are those leftovers, honey?"

Vaughn pulled the lasagna closer to himself instinctively. Hungover Cressida had fierce food cravings. "It's from the deli across the road. Very affordable."

Cressida laughed. "I've never seen you with a doggie bag before. How are things today?"

He shrugged. "Yoon is still angry. Detective Meyer just left. We've had thirty visitors. The insurance company is waiting for the results of a police investigation before deciding on a payout. I'm chasing guests for the party."

She grinned. "Yes, the party! I had an idea for it last night." She stepped closer. Vaughn shoved the lasagna into a desk drawer, just to be safe. Cressida leaned forward. "We should have a choir."

Vaughn blinked. A choir? For a party they'd planned two months ago? Which was now exactly three weeks away? And for which he'd already booked the music?

"A quartet is so *traditional*. We need something with presence, grandeur, *gravitas*." She gestured at the large, open space of the entrance foyer. "Something that will really wow while emphasizing the whole religious theme, you know?"

Not possible. "It's a *great* idea," he said carefully, "but I think it's too late to book something like that. Uh, Angeline would know. She's upstairs." Here was hoping Cressida would take the hint.

"Thank you, honey!" She flipped her hair back and swanned past him to the upstairs office.

Thank fuck.

Vaughn sighed. She might be hungover, but at least she was still in a good mood. He, though, was suddenly very tired.

CHAPTER FOUR

J onah squinted into the foggy club. His friends had moved spots while he'd been buying a drink. He walked around tentatively, sipping his whiskey and Coke. Why did everyone look the same in the dim light?

He hadn't planned to meet friends tonight, but they'd bumped into each other, and the more the merrier. Not like they were going to stop him from pursuing fun. He'd been itching to get here since this morning, but lunch had boosted the desire tenfold. The way Vaughn ate food should be outlawed—his expressions, how his long fingers handled a knife and fork, his tongue darting to catch drops of flavour, and that cool gaze locked on Jonah throughout it all. Shit, he was getting hard just thinking about it now. The guy seemed oblivious, which was hilarious when it wasn't kind of ridiculous. What handsome guy like Vaughn didn't realize he was being even unintentionally sexy? In spite of the weird clothing? If Jonah had Vaughn's height and wealth, he'd be working it like crazy.

At least they were on the same page about relationships—*such* a relief. For all his sexiness, Vaughn totally read as someone who'd want something serious, but luckily Jonah had misread that, so it was fine now. They understood each other. Jonah could handle any level of flirting, intentional or not, as long as it wasn't aimed at anything longer than a quickie. Like Vaughn had said: it was just simpler.

And that revelation he'd dropped—that the sale value of the piece was apparently ten thousand dollars. That was *not* the two hundred thousand dollars listed on the claim documentation. When Maurice had confirmed over the phone that the documentation was "absolutely fucking correct," Jonah'd had fun emailing that contradictory info to the police that afternoon.

He'd also managed to get over the other big lunchtime surprise. When he'd seen that text from Claire, his last foster mother, he'd almost had a heart attack. What were the odds that *she* still had his number? And why was she contacting him? It had been years. Of course, he hadn't read the message. No way. He'd just deleted it. He was done with anyone from his past.

Tonight, he was going to go hard and long with the hottest guy he could find.

His friends turned out to be next to the dance floor, finishing their drinks and eyeing the availability. Men after his own heart, truly. A few were university buddies from Ryerson, the rest were guys they'd met in the year since graduating, through work or hookups. A good crew to hit the bars and dance with. Looking at them now, Jonah thought Vaughn might fit in well. *If* he didn't wear dumbass shirts and scarves and shit. Maybe next time Jonah ran into him, he'd get his number and convince him to come out with them.

Jonah reached his friends and was pulled into a hug by Adrian, a Ryerson buddy.

"Bitch, where'd you go?" Adrian shouted.

"Bitch, the bar." Jonah held up his drink.

"And we thought it was some twink's pants."

"All in good time."

Adrian grinned and clapped his shoulder. "Spotted anyone yet?"

Plenty, but it was a case of which were willing. Jonah took a hefty gulp of his drink. "Some potentials. You?"

Adrian's eyes danced. "Oh yeah." He leaned against the table, both relaxing and showing off his chest in its tight T-shirt. "Babe, were you at Derelikt earlier this week?"

"Yup."

"Ah."

"You hear shit?"

Adrian smiled. "Nothing I haven't heard before." He reached over and pinched Jonah's cheek. "I will never get over the filth that lies behind this baby face."

Jonah batted him off. His phone buzzed in his back pocket, and he pulled it out. Another text from Claire. Seriously? Annoyance washed over him, and he put it away.

"Pest?" Adrian's eyebrow lifted.

"Something like that."

"Uh-huh." Adrian wisely dropped it. "*So*, how's the job going?"

"Good." He didn't want to think about work. "Yours?"

"Eh. It goes." Adrian leaned in. "I saw Zay recently. She's not looking so great—do you know anything about what's going on with her?"

Zay was a mutual friend from Jonah's business course. She was as smart and ambitious as he liked to think he was, but they'd lost touch in their final year—too focused on graduating, she'd found a girlfriend, he was job-hunting. The typical stuff.

So this was news to Jonah. "No. Haven't spoken to her in, like, a year. She's not looking so great? What does that mean?"

Adrian shrugged. "She's all tense and snappish. Not like she used to be. And she's working retail. It's not right. I don't know, dude, it's a gut feeling." He patted his stomach.

"I'll text her." Jonah pulled out his phone, scowled at Claire's text, deleted it, then texted Zay.

"Cool." Adrian nudged him. "You know, we could do something together with her. I haven't hung out with you in months. What gives?"

Jonah eyed him. What was this? "We go out all the time."

"Yeah, but we can do things other than help each other hook up." His gaze caught on someone and he inclined his head. "Eleven o'clock, in the mesh vest."

Jonah sized the guy up, then shrugged. "Kinda short."

"Since when has that ever stopped you?"

"Just not feeling it." He sipped his drink again. Another man's shape among the dancers stood out. He zoomed in on him: fairly tall, toned, slim body, stubble, dark hair long enough to clutch. That itch flared into a fire, one that spread all over his body, incited directly by the stranger. He set his drink down.

"Jonah's on the hunt," Adrian crowed as Jonah started stalking towards the guy. He was spotted after a few steps, and he slowed to let

Tall, Dark, and Stubbly look him over. Shuttered eyes scanned him up and down, then his target smiled. Jonah's heartbeat increased and he tried not to smirk. As if anyone would refuse to play when he knew the game so well. Smugness wasn't attractive though, so he kept back his smile until he'd sauntered up to the man and administered his opening gambit: his hands ran over the guy's pecs and traps, pressing in gently until they cleared the shoulders and he could grab one wrist on the other side. In short, sliding right into the guy's arms. Tall, Dark, and Stubbly's smile grew larger and his hands gripped Jonah's hips securely.

"Hi." Jonah gazed into his face. God he was hot. Those hands felt *amazing*.

"Hey there," Tall, Dark, and Stubbly replied. "You wanna dance?"

"Only if you suck my dick later."

Tall, Dark, and Stubbly laughed, hands moving lower to grip Jonah's ass. *Oh yeah.* "You're on."

And: hooked. The familiar thrill ran through Jonah, and he began dancing under the guy's hands. The next move would happen within this song: one of them would let his hands explore. Someone would try for a kiss somewhere. Bodies would get closer. Shirts would be teased open. Groins would rub together. Eventually they'd leave the dance floor for a dark corner or the washroom. Jonah would feel the heat of being pressed against another body, fucking or being fucked by a man he didn't know, letting his desires carry him hot and aching until he came.

It didn't matter by whom or how or how many saw; whether it was sucking, thrusting, licking, rubbing or jerking; as long as he got that heady, satisfying rush, throbbing aches, and a hint of danger, he was happy. Free. Orgasms and hard hands releasing him from the everyday shit he didn't want to think about or remember. He could float on a wave of sensation, safe in the knowledge that he was needed, that he was desired, even if just for a few intense minutes.

It took a week, but eventually Jonah arranged to meet Zay after work for quick drinks. To his surprise, he was looking forward to seeing her. Meeting girls for drinks—well, meeting *anyone* for just drinks—wasn't something he seemed to do these days. Why was that? And how had he let so much time go by since talking to her? Sure, okay, towards the ends of their degrees she and her girlfriend Parry had gone grunge (and not in a retro way), and started mixing with other people, and he'd lost track of her. But that didn't excuse it. How many university friends did he keep in contact with? Not many. Maybe he could change that, starting with Zay. It would be good to see her.

Then he actually did see her, and he reared back in surprise. Zay was a shadow of her former self: she had dark circles under her eyes, she'd lost weight, and the long, black, unfairly beautiful hair that was her heritage from her Lebanese mother was entirely shaved off. Jonah watched her slip into the booth, martini in hand, and tried not to show his shock.

"Hey, Jonah." When he didn't respond right away, she raised an eyebrow at him. "Go on, sweetness, say it."

Oh, hell no. "You look more like a lesbian than the last time I saw you."

A smile glimmered on her mouth. "I'm not sure whether to smack you or thank you for that. I know I look like shit." The smile disappeared. "The last year has been tough."

Jonah might need a martini too. Something stronger than his microbrew, because he wasn't sure he wanted to hear what *tough* meant to Zay without a decent amount of alcohol on hand. "Let's hear it."

She started with graduating school and moving in with Parry, then finding work and Parry getting and dropping work and spending all their money on what turned out to be drugs. And not okay drugs like marijuana—the bad ones. The addictive, claw-your-mind-out ones. By the time she had reached their breakup, her moving places and jobs, and shaving her head, Jonah had decided *tough* was an understatement. That shit was on the level of stuff he'd seen in foster care.

"Babe," he said breathlessly, reaching out a hand.

She took it. "I'm okay."

"Like hell."

She squeezed his hand, her face turning fierce. She looked briefly like the woman he remembered. "I promise, I am, sweetness. Really, I am. I'm not good, I'm not great, but I'm okay. I've got work, and I have savings, and I'm thinking about going back to school, you know? So my life isn't in a shithole, got it?"

He nodded, and she gave his hand another squeeze, then let it go.

"Tell me some good stuff. You still fucking your way through Toronto?"

He rolled his eyes, then launched into his new job and the kind of injuries and damage he'd been asked to verify so far. Before he knew it, he was on a roll about the Delphi Gallery and the stolen piece. "You should see the picture of it," he said in feigned horror. "It looks like the opening to a gigantic funnel-web spider lair."

She shivered. "Ugh."

"How is that art?" He sipped his beer. "And the *people*! They're insane, Zay. All artsy and crazy. The gallery assistant wears the dumbest shit."

"Oh yeah?"

He gestured. "Patterned shirts and this scarf thing and *deck shoes*. In winter. He's a freak. And you should see the way he eats food. He *shares* it."

"What's weird about that? I share food."

"He looks like he's about to come from eating it, *then* he shares it. That's what's weird. Plus he's rich. You can tell by how his clothes cost more than my degree and by how the hedge fund around the corner from my job is run by his *dad*." Jonah knew he was ranting now, but he couldn't seem to help it. "His only redeeming feature is his ass. For real."

She lifted an eyebrow. "His ass?"

He nodded. "Oh yeah." He cupped his hands.

"Is he straight?"

Jonah shook his head.

An evil glint took residence in her eyes. "How many times have you sucked him off?"

Jonah's jaw dropped. "He is my *client*. I don't suck off clients."

"That's where you draw a line?"

"Not that he'd be interested anyway." Jonah's fingers worried at the label of his overrated microbrew. "He ignored me when I cruised him. I don't think I'm his type." The memory of that still stung. Only a little bit. Not much.

Zay pulled out her phone and began tapping at it.

Jonah frowned, a little miffed. "Hey, I thought you'd be all over what I just said. I can think of like three jokes off the bat."

She grinned at the screen. "How about we try cruising him again?"

"Huh? *We?*"

She held up her phone to show the gallery's hours. "They're open late tonight. Let's go. I want to see this fine ass."

Jonah sputtered as she drained the rest of her martini, stood, then wound her scarf around her neck. She grinned at him. "Coming?"

"No. *No.* It'll be weird."

She leered. "You promised hot ass."

He was aghast. "You're a *lesbian.*"

"Lesbians appreciate fine asses. I certainly do. Frankly, I think I deserve to see one after this past year." She had her coat on now. "Move yours or I'll go by myself and tell him about *aaalllll* the fun times you had at university."

She'd definitely do it. Jonah downed his beer, then ran after her, struggling with his coat.

Fifteen minutes later, they were there. Zay marched them in, so lit up with purpose she almost outshone the soft gallery lighting. Jonah felt his stomach sink as Vaughn looked up from his laptop and went wide-eyed. "Mr. Sondern."

He was wearing a grey shirt, lighter grey cardigan—an actual *cardigan,* all thick-knit like something grandmas wore in movies—and dark-red pants. And the daisy scarf again. *Oy.*

At least his hair looked good. All thick and tousled around his face, like he'd been running his hands through it.

"Hey," Jonah replied.

"We're closing in twenty minutes."

"Is that so? Okay, no prob— Ow!" Zay had dug her elbow into his side, and he glared at her. *Who needs friends?* Clearly reconnecting with old friends was a terrible idea. Next time, he'd stick with the gym and a quick frot on the way home.

She elbowed him again.

"Do you mind," he gritted his teeth, "if I show my friend around the gallery?"

Vaughn frowned, which was good, because that meant the answer was no, and Jonah could march Zay out of here and never talk to her or Vaughn again.

Vaughn opened his mouth—obviously to order them out right away—and Zay sailed forward.

"Hi." She extended her hand. "I'm Zay. Jonah told me all about this place and I just *had* to hustle us over tonight."

Vaughn visibly switched tracks, smiled warmly at her, and shook her hand. "Pleased to meet you, Zay. I'm Vaughn Hargrave."

"Zay, we should get out of his hair," Jonah said. *His nice, thick, dark hair. How does he get it all shiny, yet tousled like that?*

Wait, what the hell was he noticing that for? *Focus, damn it.*

She made puppy eyes at Jonah. "But I *adore* art. It's been *so* long since I visited a gallery, and this one is *so* hard to get to because I work *all* week." She turned to Vaughn. "You don't mind, do you, Vaughn, honey?"

Vaughn went a little pink. "No . . . No, of course not." He pulled out two pamphlets. "I have to ask you to be quick, but I won't charge you entry."

"You are a *doll*," Zay said. She winked over her shoulder at Jonah, and he rolled his eyes. The infamous Zay Fayed-Smith charm. Poor bastard hadn't had a chance.

Neither had Jonah, come to think of it.

They were handed a pamphlet each and ushered into the first room beyond the foyer. Jonah lingered behind, watching her work. She batted her eyes, then grasped Vaughn's arm and asked him about the closest piece on the wall, a weird thing that looked like a square Venn diagram but with two colours and some illusion effect that made it look 3-D. After Vaughn had explained it to her, dropping words like "two-toned" and "optical effects" and "bas relief," she dragged him over to the column with a *Q* hanging off it, more questions flying out of her.

To Jonah's surprise, Vaughn didn't fall for it a second time. "I really do need to be at the front desk." He gently unhooked her arm from his. "Art is more satisfying when you draw your own conclusions from it." He smiled, polished and genteel. "I'll come find you when I close up." He moved away.

Zay and Jonah swivelled around to watch. Zay gave a low whistle, and Jonah tugged her away before Vaughn could hear and turn back.

"*Nice*," Zay whispered as he steered her to the other side of the room. "I can see why you like him."

Oh no, he knew that expression on her face. "I don't like him," Jonah replied.

"Okay, why you're attracted to him."

"I'm not attracted to him." Not *much*. And not in that cardigan.

She scoffed. "Honey, you're attracted to everybody."

"Everybody my side of the gender spectrum that's hot." They stopped in front of a canvas filled with splashes of paint. Boring. He turned and leaned toward her. "We came, we saw, let's go."

She glanced around. "No. This place has some cool stuff. We should look around now that we're here." Then she walked away, apparently caught by a painting on the next wall.

Jonah gaped at her, groaned internally, then scanned the room for something that made any kind of sense to him. A piece near him seemed promisingly simple: it was all lines and colours over the top third of the canvas, a soft cream colour across the remaining two-thirds. He stared at it, wondering why the artist had added so much stuff at the top, but left the rest of it bare. Weird. Art was so weird.

"I like that one too," Vaughn murmured.

Jonah jumped. "Fuck!" It echoed in the room, causing Zay to turn and hush him from the other side. He flipped her the bird, then quickly jabbed his hands into his pockets at the amusement on Vaughn's face.

"It's just you and her tonight," Vaughn said. "I decided I might as well lock the door a little early. Don't worry about making noise."

Please. Art galleries were like museums and churches and shit. No loud noises allowed. Not that Jonah really knew *why* that was the case, but it was.

"I meant it when I said I'm sorry we came in late like this," Jonah said hurriedly. "Not my idea. All hers."

"Really?" Vaughn looked at the painting. "I'd never have guessed."

He'd never have . . . Wait, was he being *sarcastic*? Damn that relaxed tone of his. Did he think Jonah didn't like art?

Okay, he didn't, but that didn't necessarily mean he wouldn't willingly come to a place like this. Like, he knew art. He'd been to art galleries before. Okay, *an* art gallery. Okay, he'd been to the AGO. Once. For a school field trip. It had been fine. Lots of depressed-looking people and angels and soapstone carvings and pictures of snow. Nothing he couldn't have seen in a book, but getting out of school was fun, so the AGO was better.

But the art in the AGO was nothing like the stuff in here. "What kind of art is this?"

Vaughn eyed him. "Contemporary and abstract."

"Yeah, but how come this is all lines and colours and—" he waved "—*emptiness* and stuff? Why wouldn't someone paint a thing people can actually understand right away, like a person or a chair or some shit?"

Vaughn seemed to mull it over. "Art is all about perception." He pointed at the piece. "This artist could have painted a chair. But she didn't. Why would she paint something abstract instead? What are you seeing here?"

Was that a trick question? "Lines," he replied warily.

"And?"

"Colours."

"And?"

He glanced at him. Vaughn gazed back patiently. "And nothing else."

Vaughn pointed at the mess at the top of the painting. "What kind of colours are they?"

Big punches of blue and green and pink and orange. Lines slashed through them in slivers of gold and red. "Bright." *Duh.*

"How have they been applied?"

Jonah crossed his arms, feeling like a kid. "It looks like the painter freaking stabbed the paper."

"Canvas. And yes, exactly." Vaughn made a gesture to carry on. "How would you describe that?"

The colours *mocked* him, swear to God. "It's a mess."

Vaughn's face lit up. "*Yes.*"

What the . . . Was he getting this right? "How would *you* describe it?"

"Chaotic. Cloudy." Vaughn frowned thoughtfully. "Loud and eye-catching. Opaque."

Jonah could tell he was holding a few words back. Probably some fancy art terms or artists that Jonah wouldn't understand. Well, screw him. Even if Jonah knew jack shit about art, he could play whatever game this was.

"And what about the rest of it?" Jonah gestured to the creamy expanse below the mess. "There's nothing."

"Absence is as important as presence, in art." He paused. "In most things, actually."

What the shit did that mean? "In English?"

"The artist *could* have painted this in. But she didn't. She left it bare for a reason." He pointed up. "Why is it busy up there, but not down here? The lack of something here is meaningful. It contrasts the mess up there, and the mess contrasts how bare it is down here. The two define each other, and the absence therefore takes on its own significance. It could be colourful, but it isn't, and we have to think about it."

Jonah stared at him. Vaughn was like lobster—dressed up and on a roll. He was giddiness and joy, words spilling out of him like he couldn't hold them in. *This guy really loves this stuff. Wow.* Jonah almost felt bad he didn't get what the hell Vaughn was saying.

Vaughn grinned at him. "What does that expanse look like?"

"Like a freaking unfinished painting."

"Does it? Why off-white as a colour? It's a thin layer—you can see the canvas through it. She didn't have to paint over the canvas, but she did, barely. To finish it. It's intentional."

So it was intentional. So *what.* "Then let's ask *her* what she meant by the stupid painting," Jonah grumbled.

Vaughn shook his head. "No, no, it's out of her hands now. *You're* the one looking at it. You're bringing yourself to it, all your experiences and feelings."

"Right now I feel stupid."

Vaughn shook his shoulder. "Don't get frustrated. There's no wrong way to look at a piece of art." His voice was warm. Almost as warm as his hand on Jonah's shoulder. Vaughn stood super close, like Jonah-could-*smell*-him close, which was doing strange things to his gut and dick. It was confusing to feel horny *and* intellectually inadequate.

Jonah had to not focus on that. "*I* think there is. Look at this. What the fuck even is this? It's like this one line of interesting shit and a whole lot of uninteresting shit. And the interesting stuff is right at the top. It's *distracting*. If I was going to make something people wanted to look at, I'd fill the whole canvas up with that part."

"Imagine what that would look like."

Jonah could. The whole canvas would be covered with the bright colours and slashes and it would look— "Crazy," he realized. "Even more of a mess. Like too much to look at." He frowned. "Wait, is that a thing? Limit the crazy so it's a pretty mess instead of a huge one?"

"That is indeed a thing."

"So, mess is nice but in small doses?" Jonah gazed at the cream colour. It was so . . . so . . . "It's bearable when everything else is quiet," he said slowly. "It's easier to enjoy when the rest of it is calm."

Ugh, no way he got that right. He sounded stupid. *Way to go, Jonah, make a joke of yourself and piss off this hot guy in his workplace by being a clueless dumbass.* He should've stuck with insurance. Also, mental note: never let Zay take him anywhere cultural again.

Vaughn still hadn't said anything. When Jonah looked over at him, Vaughn had a big, proud smile on his face. Jonah's insides jolted as though he'd been struck by lightning.

"Did I get it *right*?"

"There's no wrong or right in interpretation," Vaughn said. "Within reason."

Argh, what kind of answer was that? "Look, did I say something stupid or what?"

Vaughn shook his head. "No. Not at all." He gazed at the painting. "You said something quite profound. Perfectly valid." He turned back to Jonah. "Would you have thought that if you were looking at a picture of a chair?"

Vaughn was enjoying this. Jonah was squirming, his face turning red. It would've been cute if he didn't seem so frustrated and uncomfortable. And it was definitely entertaining to watch him puzzle through a piece of art, to actually make some sense of it.

Vaughn was glad he'd stuck a sign on the door and closed the place fifteen minutes early. Like anyone else would be crazy enough to visit an art gallery on a Canadian winter night fifteen minutes before closing. Not that Jonah and his friend were *crazy*, but last-minute visitors weren't always this pleasant.

"A chair could mean something like that." Jonah crossed his arms.

Ha. Stubborn. Vaughn had seen that expression before—on kids refusing to admit someone else was right. Jonah had seemed pleased at figuring out this piece for himself, just briefly—not that he'd said as much. A small, proud glow lit inside Vaughn.

"That's not to say a chair isn't worth depicting," Vaughn said. "It is. Or that chairs are simple. They're not." The obvious ones came to mind—Van Gogh, Matisse, Kosuth. "But that's not what *this* piece is about."

"Nice work, sweetness," Zay said, startling them both. Jonah cursed in surprise, then followed it with an apology.

Vaughn had completely forgotten she was there.

Zay wasn't someone he'd immediately pick out as a friend of Jonah's. She had recently shaved hair, a piercing in her nose, and tendrils of tattoos curling over the edges of her shirt, which was a hockey shirt with its sleeves torn off. The look was completed with a long-sleeved striped undershirt, skinny jeans, and stocky purple boots that would make any butch girl fist-bump with pride. Where Jonah was clean-cut masculinity, she was punk through and through.

She peered at the painting. "I see this as excitement on top of the crap of everyday life. Something glaring and sharp and beautiful over the boringness of that beige colour."

"It's *cream*," Jonah said.

"You *would* call it that."

"Oh my *God*—"

Jeez. If Zay's features weren't Middle Eastern, Vaughn might've mistaken them for siblings, not friends. "You're both right," Vaughn said. "I can see both of those interpretations in this."

"You know," she mused aloud, her eyes on Jonah. "I've never ever seen Jonah interpret art before."

Jonah went red. "He basically led me through it!"

"Yeah, but you're Jonah Sondern. You fuck, sleep, and make money." Her grin was pure troll. Vaughn could practically see each turn of the crank as Jonah became more and more incensed.

"This is someone I have to *work* with," Jonah hissed at her, gesturing at Vaughn.

She glanced at him. "Betcha knew that about him already."

He was never going to forget that club encounter. "Yes," he admitted.

Jonah threw his hands up over his head. "Unbelievable."

"I'm *just saying*," she said, "that it's good to try new stuff. You totally need a hobby. Maybe art appreciation."

Jonah gaped at her. "Are you for real? The fuck I need to appreciate art for?" He glanced at Vaughn and went even redder. "Uh, no offence, man."

No offence? Man? He *did* realize he'd just insulted Vaughn's career choice, right? And that he was so absolutely wrong it was laughable? Art was basic. Art was fundamental. Art predated *writing*.

Vaughn opened his mouth to start on his favourite rant, Why Everyone Should Love Art, when Zay stepped in. "Say, Vaughn, you're into art and fancy clothes. You like other stuff too?"

"Yes," he replied in surprise, his brain still caught on the primacy of visual representation and communication in ancient and prehistoric human society.

"Like what?"

Vaughn shrugged. "Theatre. Movies. Spending time with family, friends. Food. Video games. Rea—"

"*Video games.*" Zay poked Jonah, who'd crossed his arms and was sulking. "Dude. You're the only person I know who doesn't game."

What? Nearly *everyone* played a game of some kind these days. Vaughn stared at Jonah, who looked like the kind of man who'd make time regularly for some first-person shooter raids. He was still in his coat, but had opened it, revealing business wear—perfectly clean shirt, slacks, boots, suit jacket with a rather nice lining, a thick and elegant wool scarf. Nothing big brand that Vaughn could recognize, but it all fit well. Sharp, modern, sleek. Emphasis on the *modern*.

"You don't game?" he asked.

Jonah rolled his eyes. "I *have* played games. It's just not something I *do*." He poked Zay back. "And it's not that strange."

Zay grinned. "Vaughn, don't you think he's missing out?"

Vaughn couldn't help it. *Turn the crank.* "Yes, I do."

Doesn't need to appreciate art, indeed.

"Could you recommend something for him?"

"Yes."

Jonah groaned. "Oh my God, you guys."

"And you have your own console, right?" she asked Vaughn.

"Of course."

"You could totally walk him through a game."

Vaughn nodded. "Yes, I could." His brain tripped over what she had said. "Wait, excuse me?"

Jonah's jaw dropped as she clapped her hands excitedly. "There. Jonah, you're going to his place and joining the rest of our technology-addicted generation in playing controversially violent games."

Vaughn suddenly saw *exactly* why they were friends. That had been masterful.

Apparently Jonah realized it too, because he looked overcranked. He grabbed her arm. "One sec, Vaughn." Then he dragged her towards the entrance.

Masterful, but deluded. What on earth had she been thinking? It had been years since Vaughn had dated, but he still recognized a setup. Perhaps she was well-intentioned, but good *Lord*, it was ridiculous. Him? With Jonah on his sofa? Playing, what, *Halo* or *GTA*? He couldn't even imagine it.

Actually. Maybe he could. He could see Jonah getting frustrated with the Xbox controller and ranting about it while Vaughn cowered at the other end of the sofa.

Jonah and Zay hissed at each other near the foyer. Vaughn checked his phone: five past. More than time to kick everyone out. He started towards them.

"—n't hurt, you know," Zay was saying.

"That's so beyond the point I don't even know what to tell you," Jonah snapped.

Zay glared at him. "What, you too good for games?"

Jonah glared right back. "Bite me."

"You can't handle one afternoon of shooting zombies or strippers or some shit?"

"You *know* I can, but this isn't just me we're talking about." He gestured towards Vaughn, then both of them jumped as though they'd just seen him. Jonah swore. "Why do you keep *doing* that?"

"Doing what?"

Zay glanced between them, then turned to Vaughn. "You don't mind him crashing your place for an afternoon and shooting zombies, do you?"

"He does if you volunteer his place for him," Jonah seethed.

Vaughn quirked an eyebrow. "You seem quite invested in this. Don't *you* have a console, Zay?"

"I did, but my ex hocked it for drug money."

Ah. Wow. Okay. That would make things . . . difficult. "*You* can come over, if you feel so strongly about it," he offered.

She shook her head. "This isn't for me, this is for Jonah." She cast severe side-eye at him. "Who needs to do something beyond think about his calorie intake or his next blowjob."

Vaughn couldn't really comment on that last one, but he was with her on the calorie thing. "You're welcome to come over, if you want to."

Zay turned a wide grin on Jonah, who shook his head and sighed deeply. "If I agree to this, Zay, you will buy me dinner tonight, lunch the next time we meet, and let us leave *right the fuck now*."

Zay punched the air. "Yes! Deal!"

Jonah turned and beelined for the door. Zay grinned at Vaughn. "You don't mind, do you, honey?"

Vaughn wasn't sure he had a choice.

But it was true that sometimes his apartment was a little too quiet. And he enjoyed playing games with people. Jonah's expressions alone would probably be worth it. And if Jonah relaxed and got into it, the way he got into talking about art tonight and gay culture over lunch last week, then it might even be fun.

Maybe—and this was an exciting thought—Vaughn could sketch him.

"No, it's okay," he said. "I like gaming with friends."

Zay winked at him. "Thanks." She paused then, said in a loud stage whisper, "He needs friends."

"*Zay*!" burst from the door.

"Bye, honey." She walked away.

Amazing.

Vaughn locked the door behind them, then closed down his laptop, secured it in the office, and turned off the lights. He changed his shoes, keyed in the security code to turn the system on, then ducked out quickly and triple-locked the door.

It was snowing, and the flakes were soft against his face as he went home, feet crunching in the new layer on the street. Blackness pressed down overhead, but the orange light from streetlamps and the occasional festive twinkle of fairy lights kept the night at bay. The odd person moved past, bundled up against the snow and cold. After the chaos of the day, he enjoyed this walk, the peace of it.

Once home, he said good evening to the concierge staff, then took the elevator up to his apartment. Inside, he kicked off his shoes and flexed his feet against his floor. *Ahhh.* Nothing could beat the feeling of freed toes. Nothing except freed toes *and* food in his belly— he rooted around his kitchen for something to eat.

His apartment was a typical two-bedroom place, fairly small and compact, but the kitchen was a reasonable size, and he'd turned the second bedroom into his studio. His parents had bought the apartment for him as a graduation present, and the living area had a nice view southeast, across the city and Lake Ontario. He'd managed to paint the view a few times when he'd first moved in.

Tonight, however, he took in the Toronto cityscape, plate of spaghetti bolognese in hand. The city was distorted through a veil of snowfall, lit up by streetlights and the sporadic moving cars. He liked doing this, looking at it from above. He enjoyed seeing cars and streetcars and buses move along the streets, imagining the varieties of lives and scenes playing out below. Children going to school, people bustling to and from work, the cinema, hockey, museums, shopping.

Tourists. Couples on dates. Dog-walkers. People hustling and people meandering. Lives happening.

Zay and Jonah were out there somewhere, probably bickering over food. Their visit had been hilarious but also mystifying. Why *had* Zay pulled Jonah over to the gallery and set them up like that? Had she done it because she'd meant that stuff about Jonah needing a hobby, or had Jonah expressed some kind of interest in him?

The implication of that nearly made him drop his spaghetti.

He turned away from the window and forked it into his mouth.

No, Jonah couldn't be *interested*. Not in a relationship kind of way, and not with Vaughn. He'd said as much last week. She had to have been doing that interfering friend thing that friends liked to do.

As the savoury, spicy flavours of meat and tomato exploded on his tongue, Vaughn was reminded sharply of the ragù he and Jonah had shared, of Jonah's expression as he'd tasted the sauce. The mix of delight and slight guilt unique to Jonah.

His fingers itched to set it down on paper.

He took the food into his studio and put his sketch pad on his drawing board. A few swipes of his pencil later, and he stared at the lines he'd sketched. The briefest hints at the curve of a cheek, eyes, mouth, and nose. The expression wasn't quite right. He ate more spaghetti as he analyzed his outline. Cautiously, he added a few more soft lines, then, frustrated, started over in a new corner of the page.

Before he knew it, a few hours had passed, his pencil needed sharpening, and his dinner was gone. He had several sheets of sketches in front of him, all of a long, full face in varying stages of delight, disgust, or guilt. The faces didn't look exactly like Jonah, as Vaughn needed the original in front of him in order to get the planes of his face just right, but he thought he'd captured Jonah's features and expressiveness. The exactness of that expression eluded him, but he'd managed something like the guilty desire he'd seen. He was happy.

He stood up and stretched, flexed his bare feet to warm them up, then padded swiftly back to the kitchen. Dirty plate deposited, he returned to the living room and the view, which remained bright and busy. When he checked the time on his phone, it was close to midnight.

The quiet, the peace, the dark, the soft solitude of creation and his own think-space—all of this was pure bliss. Some might—and had—said his time would be better spent doing laundry or cooking a proper meal, perhaps catching up on a popular TV show or going out with friends or family or reading a book or, you know, spending time with a boyfriend.

Vaughn was the first to agree with people who thought like that—doing laundry regularly would be logical and adult and actually really helpful, because he didn't like shopping for clean clothes when he ran out—and he *did* do those things when he wanted or needed to (except the boyfriend part).

It was just that the art, the musing, the slow movements between spaces, and the sheer mental freedom that came from having no one else there, that was all-important. More valuable than laundry, or even dating.

Those of his friends inclined to artistic pursuits understood it completely. Hell, those of his friends trying to run a side-business were envious of him. "You're lucky," they told him, "so lucky you don't have—" and then listed one or more of the following: roommates, a demanding job, intrusive parents, a child, a pet, a spouse, a boyfriend.

He wasn't sure he was *lucky* he didn't have those things. They came with their own benefits, like company and structure and conversation and entertainment and hugs. And love. But it had been a conscious decision to live alone and to devote most of his spare time to artwork, and it had been a very easy one to make. Perhaps that was why he didn't consider it luck; such an easy decision didn't seem worth associating with the whims of fortune.

Sometimes the solitude shifted into loneliness, and when friends weren't free to do something, he was a bit stuck. But he was used to that, and he could deal with it. He didn't *need* conversation or someone waiting for him at home all the time. Just . . . once in a while.

Perhaps he was lucky in that he could live without those good things around him 24-7. Some people couldn't.

Tonight was a night where the peace settled pleasantly in him. Vaughn sighed happily, retrieved a glass of water, then padded back to his studio. Done with attempting the expression of someone who wasn't there, he put the sketches aside and pulled an easel with sturdy paper on it towards him. He squeezed a decent blob of red acrylic paint onto a palette, then took a clean brush and added tiny dabs of blue, green, and yellow to make it a rich, deep carmine—the kind of red that screamed tart, savoury, tasty, bloody life. Then he began painting.

CHAPTER FIVE

Jonah scanned yet another piece of documentation and wanted to scream. Why couldn't some people fill out a form? How hard was it to put a date of birth in the right field? God, matching this stuff up across all submitted documents was a nightmare. No wonder so many of his colleagues were trigger-happy with rejections *due to incomplete paperwork.*

It didn't help that he was still annoyed about the previous night. After that shambles of a gallery visit, he'd made Zay buy him food at some local late-night eatery and had promptly reamed her for trying to set him up with Vaughn. Not that she'd given a shit or backed down.

"I wasn't trying to set you up," she had said. He'd scoffed in disbelief and she'd held up a hand to keep him quiet. "Seriously, I wasn't! I think he's a nice guy, despite the whole preppy thing. You need more friends."

More friends? "Who says?"

"I do." She'd leaned forward. "Here's the thing about you—all you do is sleep, work, and have sex. You did that at university and you're doing it now. Did you know there are LGBT running clubs? And volunteer groups? And book clubs? There are other ways to interact with gay guys than sleeping with them."

He'd bristled. "There's nothing wrong with what I do in my spare time."

"No, but sweetness, it's okay to do other things with people than rub genitalia." She sipped her drink. "When was the last time you met Adrian outside of a club?"

Jonah fixed her with a Look, because he had this particular question down. "House party."

She groaned. "Doesn't count. Betcha got with people at that party."

"No, I didn't." He had, but she didn't need to know that.

"I'm not trying to attack you," she'd said, turning serious. "Or judge you. It's just that . . . this is us seeing each other for the first time in like a year, and all you've talked about are hookups and your job. And this assistant guy. When we were at Ryerson, all you talked about were hookups and the course load. There's more to life, you know?" She gestured at herself. "I got caught up in Parry and our group and all that shit, and when everything fell apart, I got out and realized I hadn't spoken to any of my old friends in months. Didn't know where to find them or where to meet new people or what to do in my spare time outside of my apartment." She smiled at him. "That Vaughn guy is a total nerd, but he's nice. And you two seem to get along. What's the harm in spending time with him?"

When she put it like that, Jonah couldn't argue with her. He tried though. "He's money."

"So? He's still a nice guy." She pointed at him. "And weren't you always talking about making bank? One day you'll be money too. Maybe you can pick up some tips."

He *supposed*.

Zay went all smug, knowing she'd won. Considering the recent crap she'd been through with Parry, he'd decided he could stop arguing and just roll with this.

And now, at work, he realized he had no idea where Vaughn lived or the best way to contact him to arrange this stupid gaming session.

On top of this craziness with Vaughn and Zay, Claire kept calling him. Who knew why she seemed so anxious to get in touch now, as none of his other foster parents had done that. He'd left her home as soon as he'd turned eighteen, determined to strike out on his own and forget his crappy childhood.

In retrospect, Claire had been the best parent of all the homes he'd been through, but after thirteen years of foster care, he hadn't been focused on enjoying the scenery. No, he'd wanted out of high school and into university as quickly as possible. Five years and lots of part-time work and grants later, he'd done it—a degree, minimal loans, and a well-paying job that would help him blast the rest of those loans away. The most important thing was independence, though. His own money, his own clothes, his own place that he shared equally with other people. It had been damned hard at times, but he'd done it on his own, with no help from the federal government or any of the people who'd so-called "parented" him.

So he ignored her latest call and text.

His desk phone rang, and he picked up.

"Mr. Sondern?" said a female voice.

"Speaking."

"This is Detective Meyer. I'm investigating the Delphi theft and wanted to speak with you about that email you sent regarding the valuation of the Yoon piece. Could you please go over how you established this 'true' sale value?"

He explained about the conversation over lunch with Vaughn. "Said it straight off the top of his head. No thinking about it."

"Right. Is he the one who filled out that paperwork from the Delphi Gallery?"

"I have no idea."

"And why did you meet him like that? Why dig for information you already had?"

Jonah shifted in his chair. Somehow he didn't think *the Delphi staff are a nest of overcaffeinated shitheads and I don't trust them to aim in the bowl, let alone courtesy flush* would make a good excuse. Vaughn being the clear exception. He cleared his throat. "After reading the police report about the theft, we felt there were suspicious elements to the incident and thought we should clarify things with more than one member of gallery staff."

A significant pause on the line. "I'm going to need better evidence than your gut instinct and hearsay, Mr. Sondern. Get Mr. Hargrave to state this second price in writing."

His heart sank. "The email's not enough?"

"Not if it's from you." The sound of typing came down the line. "Do you need his email address?"

"No." It was on the documentation from the gallery. "I'll get a confirmation from him and send it to you."

"That would be great. Thank you, Mr. Sondern." She hung up.

No time like the present. He pulled out the contact info and sent an email asking Vaughn to confirm the quoted valuation. Twenty minutes later, the reply appeared in his inbox. He opened it.

The Yoon piece is valued at CAD 10,000.

Your memory is terrible.

-V

Ha. Jonah found himself smiling. He forwarded it to Meyer, then started typing a response. Another email from Vaughn dropped into his inbox before he finished it.

By the way, your friend was quite the tour de force yesterday evening. I will understand if you would prefer to bow out of her suggestion of a game night.

-V

Jonah rolled his eyes.

She made me promise picture evidence before she'll buy me lunch. Let's just do it. I'm free tomorrow evening or the weekend.

Jonah

Vaughn wrote back confirming tomorrow and gave his address and phone number.

Which was how Jonah found himself in Yorkville after work the following evening, staring at a big, shiny building. All concrete and metal and glass, it was typical of the Yorkville area, and it left a bad taste in his mouth. He'd passed a ridiculous number of yoga studios, juice bars, Starbucks, and boutiques displaying clothes without price tags on his way here. Every building was white, grey, black, or beige, with odd flashes of blue, red, or orange *tastefully* applied. Even the Christmas lights and decorations seemed elegant rather than garish.

Trust Vaughn to live in Yorkville. Trust him to live a fifteen-minute walk away from the art gallery. Jonah, like most commoners, had to commute thirty minutes to work because, while he earned reasonable money now, he didn't like spending half his paycheck on rent. How the hell could Vaughn afford to live here?

His free lunch from Zay was going to be worth all of this, he'd make damn sure of it.

His phone buzzed in his pocket. He glanced at it. Claire again. He ignored it and took a deep breath. Despite the fanciness of the area and this building, all he was going to do was play some fucking computer games. *No big deal.*

He went into the building and was stopped short by a concierge. An honest-to-God *freaking concierge.* The guy held Jonah in the lobby and called ahead, actually called Vaughn to make sure Jonah was expected. What, did he think Jonah was some random person trying to get into their building? He was wearing a *suit.* Then the guy waved Jonah through, like he was suddenly worthy of entering this shiny, rich building full of shiny, rich people.

Jonah seethed until he stepped out of the elevator and found Vaughn waiting in the hallway. He'd come from work too, judging by his clothes—blue-and-black patterned slacks, a sea-green shirt with the grey cardigan, and bare feet.

Bare feet. In *winter.*

"Good evening," Vaughn said.

"Hey," Jonah replied.

"You find the place all right?"

It was literally the biggest building on the street. "Yeah."

"You came straight from work?"

"No, I wear suits for fun."

Vaughn laughed. "I have spare sweatpants if you'd prefer to change. Come in, please." Vaughn gestured towards an open door behind him in the hallway. "*Mi casa.*"

Jonah went through the door and found himself in a space larger than the house he shared with six other people. A small entryway with a closet and coat hooks led to a living room with a huge L-shaped cream sofa, a coffee table, and the biggest TV Jonah had ever seen. A bookshelf beside it contained DVDs and games. Large windows gazed out on a magnificent night view of Toronto. The far wall was a dark, woody maroon that appeared to run the length of the apartment, forming the hallway to the rest of the apartment; the other walls were off-white except for the wall opposite the maroon wall. *That* wall was taken up in its entirety by an intricate mural of a snarling lion, full of whorls and patterns and vibrant colours. Jonah could only imagine the amount of work and money that had gone into it.

On his right was an open-plan kitchen with a breakfast bar and stools, steel fittings, and what looked like a marble countertop. A bowl of brown bananas sat on the counter, as well as plastic bags of groceries, papers, and pens. The floors were wood, broken only by a few bright-blue plush rugs in the living area.

This was what money could get you. God*damn*.

Vaughn closed the door behind him, making him jump. "I'll take your coat."

Jonah let him take it, then toed off his shoes and moved to the windows, drawn like a moth. "You *live* here?" His voice came out all strangled for some reason.

"Yes."

It was hard to tell at night, but he thought the view looked out over Cabbagetown and the Distillery District, with Lake Ontario an abrupt inky black beyond all the lights and buildings and roads. "Holy shit."

"It's a nice view."

"*Nice*, he says. It's incredible." He spun around. "You know, I've seen your last name on a fund company in the city. Just how wealthy are you?"

Vaughn grimaced, but Jonah refused to feel bad about asking the question. "It's not my wealth. My parents bought me this place as a graduation present."

A *what*? Jonah had to hold on to the windowsill to stop himself from falling over in shock. "They must *love* you."

"I'm not sure what your point is." There was an annoyed edge to his voice.

Jonah wasn't sure either, and the large dose of envy wasn't helping. "My point is that *my* graduation present was a degree and LCBO's cheapest bottle of bubbly, and I gave them to myself. Why do you work if you have this kind of money in the family?"

Vaughn crossed his arms. "I work because if I didn't, I'd go nuts. What would *you* do if you didn't work?"

Visions passed before Jonah's eyes of watching movies and going out and partying all the time. Then, because he couldn't do those things all day, they faded to him reading books and going on walks around the city. Maybe booking tickets to other parts of Canada, like

Montreal or Vancouver. Or to the States. Or whole other continents, like Europe or South America.

But without money, he couldn't do those things. Without the money from work, he'd end up homeless and scrounging from the government.

Again.

"I'd learn how to play video games," he said sweetly.

Vaughn rolled his eyes. "Of course." He walked around the bar into his kitchen. "Something to drink?"

"Anything nonalcoholic."

Vaughn opened the fridge and frowned. "Uh . . ."

Jonah looked around the rest of the place while Vaughn searched. The hallway beyond the kitchen led to four doors. So, a bedroom, a bathroom, and judging by the distance between one door and the next, one of them was a closet. The last door—

"I'll give you a tour." Vaughn had noticed him gawking.

Now he *did* feel rude. "Uh, it's okay—"

"Here." Vaughn waved him forward. Door one: "Closet." Door two: "Bedroom." Jonah got a glimpse of a blue room with a king-size bed and bedside table with a lamp. Door three: "Bathroom." Door four: "Studio." Vaughn held this one open, allowing Jonah to get a good peek. He saw bottles of paint on a table, a stack of pictures against one wall, a roll of material leaning against another wall, an easel with faces on it, and another easel with a canvas containing vibrant red streaks—then the door was shut in his face.

His own freaking studio. *Of course.* "You aren't messing around with this art thing," Jonah remarked. He glanced at the mural in the living room. Was that . . .?

Vaughn followed his gaze. "That's mine. I paint something new on that wall once or twice a year."

Jonah gaped at him. "Get *out*. You did that?"

Vaughn blushed, which was a nice look on him. Jonah turned back to the mural. No freaking way. It was so realistic.

That right there was one major perk of owning a place. Painting it the way you wanted. Changing things because they were yours. If it were up to Jonah, he'd settle for hanging up a picture and calling it a day. Not that Jonah knew Vaughn well or anything, but the fact that he'd painted a massive picture on one of his walls and redid it whenever he felt like it seemed a very Vaughn thing to do. "Man, that is serious talent."

Vaughn was red now. "No. It's practice."

Jonah smirked. "You're all flustered."

He waved at Jonah dismissively. "Hush, you. Go sit. I'll set up in a second and we can get started."

Jonah kind of wanted to keep Vaughn all bothered like this. With his face pink and his hair floppy, he was *so* different from the polished assistant shtick. Jonah couldn't help wondering just how far down that blush went.

Hold it. Wait, don't *hold it. Not yet. At least wait and see how this goes.* Sure, he wasn't officially here for sex, but that didn't mean platonic fun couldn't turn into other fun. Happened all the time in porn. Why not when playing comput—video games? Yeah.

Jonah sat down on the huge sofa, twisting to study the mural, because he really couldn't get over it. It looked professional, as far as he could judge things like that. All bright and vibrant, a total opposite to the plain maroon on the other wall. He could see brushstrokes where Vaughn had really gone at it, frenzied and messy and thick, and there were delicate details outlined in brushstrokes so thin he half wondered if they were pen. The lion's teeth and face were fierce and perfect, the mane a blur of gold and brown brushwork. He pulled out his phone and took a picture.

If Vaughn could paint something like this, he could definitely sell his work somewhere. "Why are you working in a gallery if you can paint like that?" he asked, putting his phone away.

Vaughn came over and placed a glass near him. "I'm not exhibition good."

He poured something amber and sparkly into the glass, then set the bottle aside and crouched by the TV. An Xbox and controllers emerged from the cabinet underneath.

Not exhibition good? Not likely. "Uh, for real, dude? You are." He sipped the drink. Ginger ale. The guy couldn't have soda that normal people drank? This was all he had? Maybe he should just be grateful it wasn't tonic water. He put it down on the floor near the sofa.

"Like, I know I'm not some massive art critic," he continued, "but if you can paint *that*, you can totally sell your art."

Vaughn smiled at him over his shoulder. "You haven't seen the rest of my work. That's an easy figurative piece. Nothing to brag about."

"Dude, I can't think of anyone who could paint a freaking lion like that." He meant it. He really couldn't. And Vaughn didn't think it was enough? Why was that?

The TV was on now, Xbox logo on the screen, and Vaughn was pushing buttons on a remote. This platonic fun thing was . . . great.

"I can think of many." Vaughn picked up a controller and handed it to Jonah. "Thank you," he added, his hair flopping down across his eyes. "But believe me, it's not a big deal. I did art history at university, and I know what the greats are capable of. I'm almost entirely self-taught, and I barely know what I'm doing. You're being very kind, but I'm just an amateur."

Jonah stared at him. *Wow.* So humble. Almost awkward. It was . . . well, it was unexpected. With the blush, maybe even cute.

Too bad he was in total fucking denial of reality.

Jonah scowled. "Oh, so my opinion doesn't count because I didn't learn all about the grand history of art?"

Vaughn quickly shook his head, but Jonah was just getting started.

"Weak, man. *Weak.* Are you listening to yourself? If I had your talent, I'd be painting all the things and getting my name out there. I'd be shoving my pictures at people and telling them they're crazy for not buying them. I can't be the first person to say this to you. Do you at least have Tumblr or Instagram or something?"

Vaughn frowned. "What's a Tumblr?"

"Jesus." Jonah pointed at him. "You. Open a goddamn Tumblr account. Put pictures of your shit up on the internet, see the reception you get, *then* tell me I'm 'being kind.'"

Vaughn's mouth was open. "Uh . . ."

"You won't regret it." Jonah noticed the game logo on the TV screen. "Whoa, we're playing *Halo*?"

Vaughn blinked, visibly processing the change in conversation, then nodded. "Yes. If that's all right with you."

Jonah looked at the controller, properly taking it in for the first time. Oh God. The back of his neck prickled with sweat, and his hands felt all clammy. "You know, I'm really, *really* not so great with these," he blurted.

Vaughn had turned back to the screen and was doing *more* setup stuff. "I'll put the game on a nice setting for you."

A nice setting. Jeez. He was being babied already. "Don't do that. Isn't there a normal setting?"

"Sure." Vaughn settled himself on the floor, legs crossed, his thumb flickering over the controller. On the screen, the title *Halo: Reach* loomed large. "Sorry for not having anything better than ginger ale," he said abruptly. "When I picked up groceries after work, I forgot about drinks." He pressed buttons that bypassed the credits and went to the menu.

Oh God. This was happening. Like Jonah gave a shit about the drink options anymore. "It's cool." He felt like he was at school. Specifically, like he was about to take a test for which he hadn't studied.

Getting in this guy's pants sounded better. That was a test he knew how to pass. And it was *guaranteed* to be fun.

Vaughn finished adjusting the settings of the game. "Are you signed in? Press Start." He stood fluidly, sat down on the sofa near Jonah, then crossed his legs.

It was official: the guy was way nicer to focus on than the stupid game. Jonah totally ogled. Vaughn's body was all lean and long, neatly framed by those otherwise stupid hipster clothes. His hair was long enough to have a slight wave around his ears and down the back of his neck. His toes wiggled as he got comfy, and Jonah eyed up to the bend of his knees and along his thighs, the way the material of his pants stretched over his legs and crotch—

"It's on your controller," Vaughn said.

Jonah's gaze jolted to his face. Vaughn waited, calm, as though he hadn't just caught Jonah ogling his crotch. *Oops.* Jonah blinked at him, then studied his controller. Start button. Right. He pressed it.

After a few more screens of setup—during which Jonah didn't look at Vaughn again because being caught crotch-staring once was enough—the co-op version of the game finally went into its intro. Jonah watched in silence, knee jigging up and down. Something about supersoldiers and aliens and investigating a communications relay.

Or something. What the hell ever. He waited through forever of cutscene until they were dropped off a chopper into the game.

"How come you're so nervous?" Vaughn asked as they moved their characters down a hillside with their team. Jonah could at least manage that. He accidentally pressed X and his gun tried to reload. That seemed an important thing to know.

"Who says I'm nervous?" He was just glad he was part of a team doing the story and not in the multiplayer shootouts that his friends had preferred at university. Here he maybe had a chance of actually shooting something at some point. Maybe.

Their characters reached a building, and he hung back, letting Vaughn's character go into it ahead of him.

Then Vaughn's hand landed on his jittery knee, stilling it. "Don't be so jumpy. We haven't even seen any Elites yet. This is just scouting right now."

The hand was nice, but— "*Elites*?" What were those? Aliens? Scary elite aliens?

Vaughn flashed him a grin, his hand returning to his controller. The guy was winding him up.

"I'm totally going to die," Jonah groaned.

"So what?" Vaughn settled back, apparently completely at ease.

"*So* it's lame to die."

Vaughn shrugged. "But you respawn instantly. Don't be nervous. You're playing for the first time. Just have fun."

Have fun. *Yeah*. Have fun trying not to shoot himself. Which one was the shoot button again?

An hour later, he zoomed in on a hidden Elite and fired until it grunted and fell over, then raced into the room as their team drew fire away from him. He managed to sneak up behind another Elite crouching behind a shield and pummel it to the ground, just for fun, then reloaded.

Moments later, the area lit up like Canada Day. He ducked for cover from the explosions. "What the fuck?" he gasped.

Vaughn's thumbs and fingers gripped his controller as he tried to manoeuvre closer to the main fight without catching enemy fire. "Ship nearby," he grunted. "Mission's almost done. Equipping the rocket launcher."

A few more minutes of desperate firing, several well-aimed rockets, and one cloaked Elite later, the mission was done. The cutscene started playing, and Jonah whooped. "Fuck yeah! Teamwork!" He held his hand up for a high-five, and Vaughn slapped it with a grin.

They settled back, pleased with themselves. Jonah couldn't believe he'd lived this long without playing *Halo* properly.

Well, he could, really, considering the homes he'd grown up in, but he'd been *missing out*. "I have *got* to get one of these." Without a crew of yawping nineteen-year-olds giving him shit for every move—and him giving it back—he felt a lot more comfortable with the controls. Like he could actually play. And this game *was* basically a series of adrenaline rushes.

Vaughn was surprisingly cool too. Like this, immersed in the game, bitching and yelling, he seemed like any other guy. Totally different from the polished assistant Jonah had first met in the gallery and from the blushing guy who insisted he couldn't make art.

"I think Zay would approve."

Right. Zay. *Time for proof.* Jonah pulled out his phone. "She'd wet herself, she'd be so happy. She'd come over and play it so often, it would practically be hers." He held the phone up and snapped a picture of him and Vaughn on the sofa.

"Hey!"

In the picture, Vaughn had a caught-in-the-headlights look on his face, and Jonah had pulled a quick pout. Perfect. Jonah sent the picture to Zay. "There. Evidence."

"She was quite, uh, adamant you do this." Vaughn fidgeted with the controller. "Any idea why?"

Because she's a nutcase who thinks I need help. "She thinks I need a hobby."

"I take it she doesn't consider clubbing a hobby."

"Nope." Jonah took the opportunity to leer. "Not the way *I* do it."

"Was she . . . serious? About you needing friends?"

Way to make me look pathetic, Zay. Hey. "Hey. *Hey*." Jonah waggled his finger at him. "I have friends, okay? I'm not some loser who doesn't know how to have fun." He paused, then conceded, "She maybe had a point about platonic fun though."

Vaughn's fidgeting eased. "Good. I thought so. I got the impression she was trying to set us up, but I was sure I was mistaken."

Oh, man, that was in an envelope on a *plate*. Jonah leaned forward, pulling the sly grin he knew guys loved. "You don't have to be mistaken about that."

Vaughn's eyes widened. He cleared his throat. "Didn't we have this conversation already?"

Lunch. Right. "That wasn't about some friendly blowing in between alien kills."

Vaughn exhaled sharply. "Wow. That . . . Uh, thanks, but no." He went red, eyes down on his controller. "Zay didn't invite you over here for that. You, uh, might need to practise the platonic part."

What the— *Damn.* He couldn't remember the last time he'd been shut down that quickly. How the hell was he going to rescue this? *Ugh.*

"You know, I was having a good time." Vaughn's voice was quiet. "Just with the game and you. I thought you were as well. Are you bored?"

Guilt thudded into him like so many bullets. "No, dude. I'm not bored." He really wasn't. He'd just . . . Why *had* he hit on him? It was like some kind of reflex for him. Cute guy: fuck him. Jeez, maybe Zay had a point.

Okay, time to move on. "It's just some fun to add to this. A suggestion, is all. No big deal."

Vaughn went red again. "Ah. Right. Of course."

"Get the next mission started already, pretty boy."

"Okay." Vaughn pushed buttons, then shifted and recrossed his legs. Jonah very clearly did *not* look anywhere near his crotch. In not looking at Vaughn's crotch, he noticed Vaughn very much not looking at *him*.

Had he messed this up? They'd had a chill vibe going, all teamwork and swearing and giving each other shit as they played. It *had* been fun. But Jonah couldn't help how aware he was of the guy, with his lean frame and wavy hair and bare feet. Vaughn nagged at the edges of his attention, always there.

But that didn't mean Vaughn felt the same attraction. After that shutdown, it was pretty damn obvious he *didn't. Oh man.*

Jonah sat back, determined to move them both past that little awkwardness.

The next mission was more difficult. Both of them swore their way through it, at the game and at each other. At one point Jonah shoved Vaughn for messing up a shot and Vaughn immediately shoved him back, the tension from before evaporating completely. Good.

"You know," Jonah remarked, during another cutscene, "you don't strike me as someone who'd be into these kinds of games."

"No?"

"You're all . . ." He gestured to the apartment and to Vaughn himself.

Vaughn glanced down at himself. "What? Alternative? Artistic?"

Ha. No. Jonah would have said *Rich and intellectual and on a whole other level above the yahoos who normally play this.*

He must've pulled a face, because Vaughn snorted. "Hey, even artists like to blow stuff up. Need to, even." He recrossed his legs, his lean body flexing in a way that made Jonah ache. "Besides, *Halo* is a fantastic franchise. It'll be a classic. Everyone should play it at least once." He reclined against the sofa, gaze flicking between the game and Jonah's face. "It does surprise me that you're not already an aficionado. Did your parents forbid video games?"

"I grew up in foster homes."

Whoops. He hadn't meant to tell him that. Jonah eyed him, waiting for a reaction.

Vaughn's eyebrows raised, but his gaze was on the screen. "And does foster care disallow gaming?"

Damn it, his voice was as dry as the goddamn Sahara. Jonah decided he could dish up some reality for this smartass. "Depends. Some parents thought we were violent enough already. Some of us would have stolen the console or games. And some of the families decided only their *real* kids were good enough to have gaming consoles." He made sure to really stare at Vaughn, emphasize his point. "Let's just say it wasn't a priority for me to develop an interest."

"By 'we,' you mean other foster children?"

"Yeah."

Vaughn frowned. "If you were living with people who would judge children like that and withhold entertainment on that kind of basis, I'd be—"

"Nah, nah, dude. Some of the teenagers *would* have stolen it." Jonah paused. Most of the faces had blurred together, but there were always the standout few who'd been particularly fucked up. The ones with anger issues and stolen knives, the ones who used a wall instead of toilet paper, the kleptos and the ex-gang members, and the ones who gravitated towards people's junk at weird moments. Looking back now, they'd all needed help and boundaries, but a couple of them had been downright dangerous. "Most of us wouldn't," he added. "But there was usually one asshole who couldn't be trusted."

Vaughn was quiet, watching him with steady grey eyes. Silence filled the space between them, and Jonah tried to gauge it. Was it pity silence? Or was it awkward silence? When he'd told Zay about his foster background, she'd been awkward, then overcompensated by asking him too many questions.

Gunfire distracted both of them, and they returned to the game.

"Were there some nice places where people didn't assume you were a thief?" Vaughn asked a few minutes later as their characters sneaked through the landscape between checkpoints.

"Sure. Didn't stay anywhere long, though." Claire's place came to mind. He'd been there the longest—two years, which actually made it the exception. By then, he'd been past caring, but it had definitely been one of the better ones.

"That sounds difficult."

Difficult. *Difficult.* Understatement of the year. Jonah was done with this topic. "It was what it was. I'm over it."

Vaughn paused the game and stood up. Jonah blinked. What was this? Was he mad? Or upset? What were they stopping for? He gestured at the screen. "Hey!" He tried to keep his voice light. "We playing or what?"

"One moment."

Vaughn went into the kitchen, then came back with a goddamned *spread*. Jonah sat up. Hummus, raw vegetables, flatbreads, stuffed vine leaves, olives, falafel, cured meat, roasted peppers, and taramasalata were arrayed out before him on a massive tray. A feast. An actual feast of expensive delights.

"Oh my God," he breathed.

"I wasn't sure if you were hungry." Vaughn settled back on the couch casually, as though he hadn't just blown Jonah's mind. "Dig in."

"This is for me?"

Vaughn looked at him weirdly. "You're my guest. Of course it's for you."

With crappy memories of foster care still lingering from their earlier conversation—food had been part of the bad times, like the uncertainty about what foods were okay to eat in each new placement, or the occasional meal withheld as punishment, and other kids stealing his snacks—this gesture just about made Vaughn Jonah's new best friend. He'd expected to eat once he got home, not for Vaughn to serve up freaking gourmet Middle Eastern food.

Fortified, they continued playing, Vaughn reaching over for the odd bite of something as Jonah dug in.

"This is really good," he said around a mouthful of falafel as they ran through another area.

"Thanks. Nearby deli." Vaughn made a noise in the back of his throat. "Enemy up ahead."

Jonah focused on the game as they sneaked up on a camp of aliens. They dispatched the site, then moved on. "You do this a lot?"

"What?"

"Play games with people and buy them deli goodies?"

He could hear Vaughn's smile in his voice. "Usually I order something in, but I remembered your unholy trifecta and decided I'd make some effort for you."

Unholy trifecta? Right: dairy, red meat, and wheat. He'd remembered that?

"Oh my." Jonah kept his voice dry. "I'm so honoured. You're eating healthy stuff just because of little old me."

Vaughn scoffed and fired a few shots at him in the game.

The rest of the evening went like that, shooting the shit while they shot at aliens. Jonah didn't mention the mural behind them, and Vaughn didn't bring up the foster stuff. By the time Jonah decided he had to go, he actually felt sad to call it a night. He'd kept up. He'd had fun. Without a glimpse of dick. He hadn't even been distracted by Vaughn's ass.

Well, not much.

He put down the controller at the end of the current mission. "This was awesome, but I gotta call it a night."

Vaughn pulled his phone out of his pocket to check the time and winced. "Me too, actually. Shame, I was having fun too." He paused. "Would you want to do this again? Finish the game?"

"Yeah, man." Maybe he could try not embarrassing himself with the offer of an unwanted BJ next time.

They left the huge, comfy couch and stood before the front door, Vaughn leaning against the wall as Jonah wrapped himself up against the cold.

"Let me know when you're free next," Vaughn said.

"Gotcha." He patted himself down, checking he had everything, then turned to the door.

The guy had actually *opened the door* for him. Jonah couldn't believe it. *Dork.* Artistic, rich, kind of ridiculously nice dork. He stepped through, waved good-bye, then took the elevator down.

Jonah hummed to himself on the way back to the TTC. Yeah, that had been a great way to spend an evening. Free food, fun gaming, cute company. Had he been at home, he'd have been trawling Grindr or watching porn. Given he did those things almost every day anyway, even he could admit that this was a good change. Maybe Zay was onto something with this making friends thing.

Okay, Jonah. Face facts. He outright *knew* she was onto something. Foster care, with all the shuffling around, hadn't really lent itself to keeping friends, not when he was a kid. He'd make a few at whatever school he was at, then have to move on. University had changed that, but if Jonah was honest, he'd found friendships kind of strange to navigate once they got going. Sometimes he'd pissed people off over things he hadn't even known to do, like invites to hang at his place occasionally, or to sit and just listen to rants rather than tell people to get over themselves.

Friendship groups were weirder still: all these people hanging out with each other and bitching about each other at the same time, then getting mad when they found out about it but still remaining friends somehow. Or just hanging out because it was convenient, even if you didn't like other people in the group. How the hell did that work?

Hooking up was so much easier—you came, you saw, you got a yes, you came again, you left.

He thought he'd managed to get the hang of friendships by the end of university, but then everyone scattered and only seemed able to meet up for the odd housewarming party or catch-up over drinks. At least people still talked to each other on Facebook. That was cool and easy to handle.

Really, he could probably do worse than hang out with someone new. Vaughn was a decent guy, despite the clothes and money. Totally chill. He'd handled the foster thing better than most people did; he got the hint to shut up and move on. Fed him. Didn't linger on Jonah's stupid attempt to proposition him in his own home.

Ugh, *why* had Jonah done that? The guy was hot, yeah, and all he'd said was no, which wasn't the end of the freaking world, but looking back now, Jonah cringed. Vaughn hadn't given any signs of being interested—he'd just been *nice*. Hindsight was a clear-sighted bitch. So yeah, Vaughn was all right, and Jonah reckoned he deserved another playdate without being put on the spot.

That said . . . what *did* it take to make the guy say yes?

CHAPTER SIX

Strictly speaking, Vaughn's work laptop wasn't meant to be used for personal stuff, but he figured if Maurice could lurk on Reddit, and Angeline on pottery blogs, Vaughn could do some social media research.

He glanced around the foyer, then scrolled through the Tumblr search feature, absolutely astounded at the artwork popping up. Some of it was just famous pictures, and there were plenty of beginners and people still honing their skills, but a lot of the sketches and photorealistic images were nigh on amazing. Even if he didn't know half the people or characters being drawn, the skill and deftness on display were awe-inspiring. There were seriously talented people out there.

And Jonah thought Vaughn should put his work up on this site?

He had his doubts. Obviously there was a mix of talents, and a *mass* of content, so it wasn't as though he'd stand out. In fact, there was *so much* good stuff that he wasn't sure he could even compete. What would be the point of even trying?

Plus a lot of the really popular stuff had to do with something called *Supernatural,* and he had no idea what that was. He'd only figured the title out after reading the hashtags.

He googled it.

Ah. Okay.

But . . . why were the users of this site so hung up on a horror show about demon hunters?

In fact, the more he clicked through and explored, the more he realized that the popular artwork was nearly all fanart of TV shows he'd never heard of. He didn't do fanart. Maybe this wasn't the right site for him.

On an impulse, he typed *Halo* into the search bar.

Two minutes later he was setting up an account.

"Vaughn!"

He looked up and smiled at Cressida, quickly flicking his inbox up over his internet browser. "Hi."

She held her usual coffee cup in one gloved hand, hair tucked back under a toque. "You were so focused," she trilled. "Keep it up!" She shrugged off her jacket, water from melted snowflakes flashing under the gallery lights. "Has that reporter come in yet?"

Reporter? The call from last week came to mind. The reporter from the *Mail*, the one who'd had Yoon cancel on him after the theft had gone public. He wanted to write another article instead and was due to arrive any minute. "Not yet," Vaughn said.

"Good. Tell me or Angeline when he does." She clipped past him sharply.

He returned to setting up the Tumblr account. He reached the option to input a username and paused. Oh. *Oh.* The possibilities.

His phone vibrated in his pocket. He absently pulled it out, then cursed as it slipped from his fingers onto the ceramic floor. The back cover popped off and there was an audible crack; when he picked it up, he found a spiderweb of splintered glass radiating from one corner. Shoot. It still seemed to work, so he put the back cover on and unlocked his phone to see who'd texted him.

Jonah: *Yd was fun. Thx again. Btw I took a pic of ur mural and posted it on fb and it got lk 50 likes.*

Vaughn's heart stopped. He'd done *what*? His fingers scrabbled across the broken screen.

Vaughn: *What? Why?!*

Jonah: *Bc its good, thats why.*

Vaughn: *I didn't give you permission to do that!*

Jonah: *Hey its all good I sed u were the artist and stuff.*

Vaughn was tempted to smash the phone completely. "That's not the point," he muttered. The phone on the front desk rang, because of course it did, and he picked it up. "Delphi Gallery."

"Hi, honey, it's Mom."

Perfect. Freaking perfect. Sybil Hargrave, with the inner demonic knowledge granted to people upon becoming a parent, had phoned at exactly the wrong time. "Mom," he hissed, "you shouldn't call me at work."

"What if it was an emergency?"

"*Is* it an emergency?"

"Are you free for brunch this Saturday?"

Oh, for God's sake. "No, Mom."

A knowing note crept into her voice. "Are you painting? Still? Because if that's all you're doing with your free time, you can keep the morning aside to see me."

"It's important, Mom—you know that."

"I know it makes you happy, sweetie, but there are other things in life."

He took a deep breath. "I'm otherwise engaged."

"Oh?"

"With a friend." He'd have to call Devon and tell him to cover for him.

"It's not Devon, is it?"

Another text popped up from Jonah: *I no all abt plagiarism dont worry. Ur credited. Important thing is ppl who dont no u liked it. Thats lk OBJECTIVE proof that ur art is gud nuf to share.*

"No, it's not," Vaughn muttered. That was so *not* the point.

"Then who is it?" his mother said.

Whoops. "Uh." Damn it. His mind raced, thinking of university friends, work people, clubbing friends . . . "Just someone else."

His eyes fell on the text from Jonah, and the idea of saying the name *Jonah* to his mother, of implying there *was* a special someone else, was strangely tempting. Stupid and more trouble than it was worth, but still tempting.

Time to put the phone down before it distracted him again.

She gave a small, excited gasp. "Honey, is this someone a *date*?"

Laughable idea. "No—"

"Because you know I'd love to meet anyone you're seeing. *Anyone.*"

He winced. He hadn't dated since university, as his mother was very aware. Even at university, he hadn't really gotten the hang of it.

Even the nicer guys had seemed to expect sex straightaway, and he was . . . Well, he wasn't into that.

"It's not a date. It's a friend thing."

"Well, date or not, as long as he's not Devon, then he's very welcome to come along. Merril will be there with his fiancée, and my friend Justine is bringing Katie with her, so it won't be just us old people." Great. His brother too?

"Mom, fifty-two isn't old."

"Please say you'll come. I think Katie wants to ask you a favour for a film project."

Katie. Justine. It took a few seconds, but he remembered them. Justine ran a very successful dance studio and Katie, her daughter, was studying film at university. She'd been a few years below him at school. Red hair. Chewed gum incessantly. Hardly surprising, with a mother like Justine. She seemed the kind of person who expected minty freshness every time someone opened their mouth.

A man walked through the front door, and Vaughn could have kissed him. "I'll get back to you about brunch," he said into the phone. "I have to go. Bye, Mom." He hung up quickly, cutting her off, and smiled at the visitor. "Hi."

The guy was slightly overweight and had a beaky nose. Vaughn took in the fake North Face jacket and leather messenger bag and air of presumed authority. *Media.*

He smiled widely at Vaughn. "I'm Jules Mitchell from the *Globe and Mail.*"

Not just any media rep, a *journalist.* "Welcome to the Delphi Gallery," Vaughn said with a cheerfulness he didn't really feel. "We're expecting you." He typed an IM to Angeline informing her the reporter was here.

"Awesome." The reporter shrugged off his coat and hung it on one of the hooks near the front desk. "Have you worked here long?"

"Three years."

"Nice." The reporter looked around. "Not too shabby."

Vaughn wanted to roll his eyes. *How good of you to approve.* "The owner will be with you shortly."

"Yeah." The reporter ambled over to the desk. "So, how's it going?"

Vaughn gazed back at him. ". . . Fine?"

"The claim for the Yoon piece, I mean. I heard that the insurance company isn't playing ball."

A reminder of the reporter's visit popped up on his screen. Vaughn's quick glance at it jogged his memory—*Mail reporter article on insurance and theft.* "Is that pertinent to your research on art insurance?"

"Maybe." Mitchell had picked up a pamphlet on the December exhibition. He opened it and winced.

The stairway door opened behind Vaughn. "Hi," Cressida called. She and Maurice strode up to Mitchell and shook his hand firmly. Introductions over, they steered Mitchell into the gallery, Maurice shooting Vaughn a glare for some reason. *Nice.*

Vaughn exhaled once they'd gone. His phone blinked at him, and he realized he'd missed a few messages from Jonah.

Was that a bad thing to do?

Im sorry if that was the wrong thing to do.

Vaughn had to reread the conversation to remember what "that" referred to. Right, the frankly offensive act of taking a picture of his lion mural and putting it online *without asking him.* And at least fifty people had seen it. Probably more. Oh God, what if people had shared it?

Wait. Wasn't that a good thing? Vaughn gazed at his phone, then at the laptop screen, where the Tumblr setup still waited. Then he looked around at the gallery, at visitors examining pieces and Maurice talking in a low voice to Mitchell, and at the front desk where he'd stood for almost three years now.

Then he thought of the time and evenings he'd spent creating pictures and murals, only to place them in portfolios or storage for "later." There were canvases stacked against the walls of his studio room and in his bedroom. His sketchbooks took up their own shelf in the living room.

Maybe later was now.

He could imagine Jonah's expression as he'd written those last two texts: defensive but direct and sincere, much the way he'd apologized in the deli café over lunch. He wrote back: *The mural was on private property, so you should have obtained my permission before taking a picture of it and distributing it. Yes, that's a bad thing to do. I know you meant well, so I'm not angry at you.*

He turned to his laptop and typed in the username *fresh-delusions* and a password. Seconds later, he was a bona fide Tumblr user. He passed the news onto Jonah, and instantly received: *YESSS!!!!!* Then a moment later: *srry again.*

A Tumblr account and—he ran one finger over the cracks in his phone screen—a damaged phone. And someone who thought he had talent.

If Vaughn were being completely truthful, Jonah's vehemence about that mural last night had been a surprise. He'd had plenty of friends who'd seen multiple murals he'd done, and while they'd all been very complimentary, they hadn't exactly ordered him to push himself online. No one had literally pointed at him and declared the mural good enough to share. Jonah doing that had been surprising, but also gratifying. Unbelievably so.

Not that it hadn't occurred to him to go online—nearly every artist had a website these days—but Jonah had been so absolutely convinced. And Vaughn, like anyone who'd taught themselves a skill, *knew* he wasn't brilliant. He absolutely knew it. He was okay, and he did do some things well—like the mural, which had been a lot of fun—but the mural was a clear-cut thing. It either looked like a lion or it didn't. It was the more abstract work he'd done that caused him doubt.

After all, if he had any talent, surely someone would have told him so? His parents or his brother or his friends, the ones he'd shown pieces to. Devon had always looked over a picture and declared it "absolutely fucking excellent, darling," but when he said that about every piece, the praise fell a bit flat.

Whatever it was, whether it was the sheer blunt conviction of someone he barely knew or a cumulating desire to do something about his art, this did feel like a positive step. He could feed work online anonymously, gauge a reaction, then perhaps take things further based on that.

This all felt kind of good.

The phone rang again, and he picked up. "Delphi Gallery."

"You can't be that busy if you can answer the phone ten minutes later."

He closed his eyes. "Mom, come on. I'm at work."

"I'll keep it quick, honey, I promise. So am I putting you and your date down for brunch next Saturday?"

"No. It's not a date, and I'm not free."

There was a frigid pause. He readied himself. "It's been a month since I last saw you," she started.

"I know—"

"You're my son. I get it, you have your job and your independence and your friends, but I need to see you too."

"Mom—"

"I just worry about you. You know that, right?"

"Yes, I—"

"And now that Merril is finally engaged, it's just made me realize that I never hear any stories from you about the boys you date."

He closed his eyes, mortified. "Mother, *please*."

"You *are* dating, aren't you? I mean, I know you never seem to go for anyone I introduce you to at my charity functions, but surely you meet nice boys through work? Maybe an artist?"

He wasn't having this conversation. He *refused* to have this conversation. Especially here at work. "*Mom*—"

"You don't have casual sex in bars like so many gay men seem to do, do you? Or in baths? That's not the way to meet a nice boy."

His jaw dropped. "Mom, what on earth are you talking about?"

"Honey, when you told your father and me you were gay, we did lots of research. I read articles on LGBT rights every week. I'm completely up to speed on how gay culture operates."

Really? *Really?* This was news to him. "I don't know if Toronto even *has* baths. No one I know does that these days. Not that I would even if we did." What was he saying? "Look, I know you mean well, but . . . God, Mom, no, okay? Don't worry about that stuff."

Her voice turned concerned. "Sweetie, it's my job to worry about you. Your sex life is your own business, I know that. But you're using protection, right?"

He wanted to slam his head into the desk. Jesus *Christ*. "Mom, I'm twenty-six. We covered the Talk already. I don't need this."

"Okay, honey, okay. Your dad and I just want to know that you're meeting people and having fun."

"No, you just want to know when you can announce another wedding."

She laughed. "I do love parties. But"—and the laughter left her voice—"it's not about that, sweetie. It's about you being happy."

He rolled his eyes. "The same way Merril is happy?"

"He *is* happy. Dana is a lovely girl."

"Dad practically pushed them together."

"They're so cute."

He took a deep breath. "Mom. I'm fine. Singledom is great. Work is great. I'll see you when I next have a free weekend." He glanced around to make sure no one could hear him. "And for the love of God, *please* stop researching gay nightlife."

"Don't be embarrassed. I realized it's not *that* much different to straight nightlife nowadays. It's pretty reassuring."

"Mom, I need to go."

"Call me, honey! I want to hear about your dates! Love you!"

He hung up, then stared at the receiver. The gallery phone didn't have caller ID. Maybe he could convince Angeline to get that so he could avoid talking to his mother *ever again.*

What was more pathetic: the fact that his mother was asking about his sex life or that he didn't have one to talk about? He picked up his cell and tapped out a message to Merril: *Mom just called me. Please tell me she asked you insanely intrusive questions about your love life when you were single.*

It was almost worth being engaged to never hear questions like that again. *Baths?* He shuddered. He couldn't handle sex one-on-one, let alone in a public space with others looking on. How the hell did his *mother* know about them?

And what was with worrying about him meeting people? He was fine without dating and sex. More than fine. The last time he'd had sex, it had been entirely typical of all the sex he'd had up to that point: not good, but not *terrible* either.

He'd gone to bed with the guy, happily kissing and touching him until the underwear had come off and things had become serious. Vaughn remembered how routine it had felt—more kissing, then going down on the guy, him going down on Vaughn, then Vaughn lubing them up and frotting the guy into orgasm. Vaughn's had followed, but like every other orgasm in his life, it had been pleasant but nothing to literally scream about. If he were to paint his feelings about sex, the colours would be a bland, muddy neutral somewhere between grey and darker grey.

The feelings *after* sex were worse, when he lay back next to his partner and wondered if this was it, if this was all there was to sex. Mechanical and formulaic. *Boring.* Not that he would ever say that to whomever he'd just slept with; that would have been terribly inconsiderate, especially when *they'd* always seemed to have a great time.

Which somehow made it worse. There had to be something wrong with him, because other people didn't react like this. Other people wanted sex. They *needed* it. Especially in relationships.

That last not-so-sexy time, he'd lain next to the guy and felt a kind of choking despair, hollow and lonely. Because the guy had been all smiles and cheerfulness, but Vaughn *hadn't.* Doing this sucked. It really, really sucked. He hadn't known what he was doing wrong, and he'd been—and he remained—*tired.* Tired that sex was the normal thing to do. Tired of pretending this was something he really wanted.

He'd realized that he wouldn't ever get away from doing it, not if he wanted a relationship. Sex would be expected at some point, even if not right away. Would be practically demanded, considering how some men behaved.

More hollowness and detachment. More nights like that one, of meaningless touches and pretending he was enjoying himself and letting the physical stuff take care of itself, then lying next to someone who was in a completely different headspace, with no way of sharing it with them. That was what had waited for him if he'd kept agreeing to hookups and dates. Years of it, if he fell in love with someone.

He couldn't do it. Not when it made him feel that lonely and upset, and when he rationally and objectively didn't like it. It wasn't soul-suckingly awful, but it also wasn't fun.

So he'd stopped.

Admitting and articulating it to himself had been difficult, but the logical conclusion was that if he didn't like or want to have sex, then he didn't have to. At all. Ever again, if he so chose. After all, no one was holding a gun to his head about it.

Realizing that had been the best part of his dating experience at university. Such a *relief*.

And so he had taken sex off the list of things he did.

For the most part, it had been great. He went clubbing without expecting to get laid, just looking to spend time with friends, dance, drink, banter, then go home and sleep undisturbed. He focused on the people he knew and liked. He met new people and tried new things completely unshadowed by the prospect that something sexual might happen. His art flowed freer, in brighter colours. People said he seemed happier. He didn't seek out men, he just admired them, and it was so much easier. Better. Lighter.

There was no way he could tell his mother all of that.

Or anyone else. Who could possibly understand that? He barely understood it himself. His experience went against the narrative that he understood about sex: namely that all men wanted sex all the time, and there was something wrong with them if they didn't. That was definitely alive and well in gay spaces. Hell, in hetero and public spaces too. He practically swam through it if he wanted to dance in a club.

But well-meaning questions like that, from his *mother*, were difficult to listen to. If dating wasn't such a minefield of expectations, and if he thought there was any sort of chance of having a relationship without sex, he'd maybe be more open about what he wanted. He might even go through the motions of dating. But that didn't seem likely or realistic. Not when today's dating culture included apps to facilitate quick hookups.

His phone lit up with a text from Merril. *Oh yeah she did. Your turn now, asshole :p*

Heartening. Vaughn sent back a few choice emoticons to his brother, then slumped over the front desk. His parents were gunning for his love life now. Great. Just *such* a pity he didn't have one.

Last night with Jonah was probably the closest thing to a date he'd had in recent months. Video games and some compliments about his mural and a diverted attempt to take things to the next level. In retrospect, Vaughn wasn't surprised at Jonah trying for more, not when Jonah so obviously had sex on the brain. No, the crazy part was that Jonah had wanted to do more *with him*. It was kind of nice to feel that he was an option for someone, but it was even better to say no and for that to be okay too. Okay enough, in fact, that Jonah had stayed and hung out.

Kind of ideal, in Vaughn's opinion.

It wasn't like he couldn't imagine making out with the guy, because that would probably be awesome. It was just that things wouldn't stop with kissing. They never did. And sure, he knew how to give a blowjob, so while he could picture doing that too, it wouldn't be as fun as kissing—hence the no.

Not a great loss, but he did regret losing the chance to kiss Jonah. That probably wouldn't happen again.

No to sex and thus to the love life.

At least he had art.

Jonah stared at the tarp fluttering over the hole in the side of the house. He glanced down at the paperwork. Huh. *Drunk driver drove into living room* was not, in fact, a mistake or a joke.

The homeowner stood by, a sour expression on his face. "You believe me now?"

"Oh yeah," Jonah said.

"I sent a picture with the claim. And a police report. Makes me wonder what you're doing out here."

Neither of which had been in the paperwork he'd received, because if they had been, he *wouldn't* be out here. Jonah bit back a sigh. Someone had lost them, either accidentally or deliberately. Either way, he was now freezing his ass off in front of a sorry-looking house in eastern Toronto. Someone's head was going to roll back at the office.

Jonah scribbled a big *CLAIM IS VERIFIED* note on the top sheet and turned to the homeowner. "I'll make sure this gets through to the right department. You can expect a payout in the next few weeks."

Once he was done with the homeowner, he called a taxi. On his company's account, of course. After that, he found a text from Zay waiting for him: *Sooo how did gaming go?*

He fired back a quick, *Fine.*

To his surprise, she called him within seconds.

"Just 'fine'?" she asked incredulously.

"Hi to you too. Aren't you at work?"

"Yeah, but I'm bored. What do you mean, 'fine'? Did he turn weird?"

"No. He's a nice guy." The taxi pulled up and he got into it. The driver confirmed the office address and they were off. Jonah sat back, grinning. Nice to have paid-for transport like this.

"Hmm." She sounded suspicious and a little disappointed.

"Why do you want to hear about game night anyway?"

"Did you two seriously *just* play games?"

"Yeah."

There was a pause. "Is he actually gay? I just assumed . . ."

Jonah turned to look out the window. Snow-covered suburbia passed by, familiar and repetitive. "I've seen him out in gay clubs."

"*I've* been to gay clubs."

"*You* are actually gay."

"And female. My point is . . . he seriously didn't hit on you? Not even a little bit? I expected him to."

Jonah scoffed. "Zay, what the hell? You were the one who said I should hang out with guys instead of sleeping with them."

"I meant it, too. But . . . you're you. I expected *some* level of flirting. Like, successful flirting. He was so into helping you figure out that artwork, I thought he might have a crush."

"He doesn't." They'd definitely covered that. "But I think we could be friends." Which was true. Vaughn was a fun guy, when he wasn't being awkward or dorking out over art. And even the awkwardness and dorking out was kind of cute. Plus, Vaughn had taken his advice and joined Tumblr, or so he'd said. That was good, because the guy definitely needed to get his work out there. That humble, modest, *I'm not good enough* bullshit wasn't flying with Jonah, so he was glad to see Vaughn listening to him.

The line had been silent a little too long. "Zay?"

"Sorry," she said, "I thought I heard you say, 'I think we could be friends.'"

"I did."

"Jonah Sondern, infamous sex machine and master of threesomes—"

"Hey, how do you know—"

"—has just told me he could *be friends* with another gay man. Excuse me while I faint."

He had to laugh. "Stranger things have happened."

"My baby's growing up," she fake-sniffed down the line.

"Oh my *God*, Zay. I'm hanging up."

"I consider this excellent personal growth, you know."

"Bye." He hung up and rested the phone on his lap, grinning stupidly. She was a good friend. He should have kept in better contact with her.

His phone vibrated in his hand. He rolled his eyes, swiped to answer, and put it to his ear. "Zay, I think you need more friends too."

"Jonah? Is that you?"

He froze. That warm, firm voice was for fucking sure not Zay.

Claire.

Shit. *Shit.* Her voice hadn't changed a bit. Just hearing her speak brought back memories of lectures and food. Mostly lectures. God, she'd enjoyed lecturing him. And laying down the law: *Wash your hands before dinner. That's not how you cook an omelette. Did you do your homework? Where were you today? Clean your room. Iron your clothes. Be nice to the little kids.*

"Hi, Claire," he managed.

"I'm so glad you picked up!" No mention whatsoever of the fact that he hadn't picked up for the last week; that was typical of her. "I'm calling because a lawyer contacted me on behalf of your birth mother."

Everything went silent. The hum of the taxi, the chatter of the radio, the sounds of other cars outside—everything faded. All he could hear was the blood rushing through his head.

"Jonah?" she said, when he didn't answer. "She contacted me because social services couldn't trace you. You changed your name and moved, and you didn't give them this number." She paused. "I'm surprised it still works. I wasn't sure it did, but I was going to keep trying for another week before giving up."

He'd bought his first cell phone just before leaving the foster system. He'd written down a false number on the documentation, but he'd given the real one to Claire when she'd asked for it. The phone had changed since then, but he'd kept the number. And he'd kept transferring hers, for some reason he couldn't articulate to himself.

His chest hurt. He forced in a breath. "What do you mean, a lawyer?"

"I wasn't given any details, but I have a number here for the lawyer. All she told me was that she needs to contact you regarding your birth mother." She hesitated. "Is that something you want?"

He didn't know. He couldn't know. "I need to think about it."

"Okay. Do you want me to give you the number now?"

"I'll think about it."

"Fine. I'll hold on to it until you tell me what you want to do." Her voice turned hesitant. "It's good to speak to you again. I'm glad you picked up. How are you doing?"

How was he doing? He was numb, and it had nothing to do with the winter outside or the barely adequate taxi heating. He garbled out, "I'll speak to you later," and hung up, then stared at his cell as if it were about to bite him.

His mother wanted to get in contact. The person who'd singularly condemned him to home after home of stressed-out, overburdened, sometimes terrible people; and caseworkers who barely cared; and foster kids who stole his things or beat him up; and schoolkids who thought he looked funny because his clothes were always too small or too old or too weird; and a life with no money, no home, no parents, no siblings, no *family*. The woman who'd left him outside a Metro store almost twenty years ago, with an ice cream and the clothes he wore, suddenly wanted to talk to him again.

Unbelievable.

And through a lawyer, no less.

The bright screen of his phone blurred before him. He was tempted to throw it out the window, to smash it into pieces too damaged to put back together. What a mistake, answering without checking the caller ID. Always a mistake to invite the past back in.

Even though he'd kept Claire's number.

This was too much to handle. He didn't want to think about this. He also didn't want to go back to work and sit in a cubicle like nothing had happened.

The Grindr app icon popped out at him from the cell in his hand, orange and familiar and beckoning. *Oh.* That was the answer. Sex. Someone to push him against a wall, scrape his skin so hard it almost hurt, make him come, help him remember who he was now. He was an adult. He had a job. Money. Looks. Youth. He pressed the icon.

"We're here," the driver said.

Jonah looked up, blinking. They were parked in the drop zone outside his office, in downtown. He glanced back at the phone, photos and text spilling across his screen. A new message appeared while he gazed at it.

What was he doing? He was still on the clock.

He closed the app and nodded at the driver. "Thanks. You got the account number, right?"

"Yeah. Have a nice day."

Jonah left the taxi and walked swiftly into the office building. Shit. Tonight was officially a club night. He would return the drunk driver paperwork and advise someone's manager that documents were being lost, finish out the day, have a quick workout, then hit the clubs or the bathhouses or bars and get laid.

That was exactly what he did. Rough, furious fucking that drove all thoughts—lawyers and mothers included—out of his head. The only way he knew how to get to that safe, floating place where he felt achy and good and nothing else mattered.

CHAPTER SEVEN

November moved into December, and Jonah didn't call Claire back.

It was fine. He just needed to think about it. That whole . . . mother thing.

Not that he could in any real depth, because work had ramped up with lots of weather-related claims all of a sudden, like winter had surprised people or something. Jonah'd received a bunch of texts from Adrian, Zay, and Vaughn, but had ignored them to focus on his work. After all, people were losing paperwork.

No updates from anyone about the stupid Delphi Gallery theft.

He'd been eating a bit more because colleagues had started bringing in Christmas cookies and candy. So he'd had to push it in the gym, as abs didn't stay abs unless he worked off the excess. Honestly, he needed to cut back on the cookies, but they were *homemade*. It was criminal to ignore them. At least the Grindr and bathhouse guys appreciated the extra gym effort, and *wow*, had they appreciated it.

He shifted in his chair at work, feeling a definite ache in his ass. *Oh yeah.* Being stressed-out meant he was practically entitled to some hands-on relaxation. Get him out of his head. When was the last time he'd been laid this much? University finals, maybe. It was a good feeling, knowing he could reel them in with a message and tasteful (but honest) dick pic. The prospect of a hookup at the end of the day was sometimes the only thing that got him through the grind of work and gym.

Today was looking extra promising: Garrett had brought in his own special lemon-and-pepper cookies, chest and arms day loomed, and Claire had stopped texting him, although Vaughn, Adrian, and Zay still bugged him.

His desk phone rang while he was staring at his cell phone and trying not to hit the Grindr app, and he gratefully picked up.

"Hi, Jonah," one of the receptionists' crisp voice said, "there is a Mr. Maurice Palomer and a Mr. Vaughn Hargrave to see you."

Oh hell. What were they doing here?

"They said you're expecting them?" she added. *I bet they did.*

"I'll be right down." He hung up, then ran over to Garrett's office.

Garrett looked up in surprise as Jonah almost skidded into his glass door. Jonah opened it and gabbled, "Thdelpepldensters."

He frowned. "Excuse me?"

Jonah took a deep breath. "The Delphi people are downstairs. They said we have a meeting with them. Do we have a meeting with them? I wasn't told about a meeting. *What meeting?*"

Garrett sighed in annoyance. "No. We don't have a damned meeting." He stood and dug through the paperwork on his desk. "But if they're here, then I guess we do now." He pulled out their file, and they walked to the elevators.

Jonah had the ride downstairs to think through why the Delphi people could be here. Detective Meyer had received his forwarded email from Vaughn confirming the sales valuation, thanked him, then gone silent. The police didn't have any updates on the investigation. He and Garrett were waiting on the final report before making a decision.

They had nothing to say to these guys.

The elevator doors opened, and they went into the foyer, where Vaughn and Maurice lingered on uncomfortable chairs. Maurice spotted them and gave them a fake smile. Vaughn stood as they approached, his smile as warm as Maurice's wasn't. Guilty heat spread through Jonah—it had been two weeks since lunch with Vaughn, one week since game night. He'd meant to finish the game with him, but he'd ignored Vaughn's texts trying to arrange it. Looking at him now, in his stupid rich-guy clothes (at least he wasn't wearing another flowery scarf), with his stupid handsome face wearing that stupid happy smile, Jonah thought he didn't deserve a smile like that.

They all shook hands, then Garrett signed them in and led them to the elevator.

"This is a pleasant surprise," Garrett said cheerfully in the elevator.

"We wanted to return the personal visit," Maurice replied.

"Oh *hey*, you didn't need to do that!" Garrett turned to Jonah. "They didn't need to do that, did they, Jonah?"

"Not at all," Jonah said. He noticed Vaughn turning aside to hide a smirk.

"It's not a problem," Maurice said magnanimously.

Vaughn straightened his face with visible effort. "How is work?"

"Same old," Garrett replied. "You know how it goes."

"Oh sure." Vaughn's tone indicated he knew nothing at all about how it went.

The elevator doors opened.

"This way." Garrett walked forward.

Jonah hung back, his eyes going straight to Vaughn's ass. Again. This time it was showcased in cigarette trousers that would have looked stupid on Jonah, but for some reason looked like sin on Vaughn. Slim legs and a tight ass, shown off to perfection. He was ridiculously thin for a man who could scarf lasagna for lunch on a standard workday. Jonah sighed and lifted his eyes to Vaughn's back. Not good for him to be spotted cruising a client.

In Garrett's office, Jonah closed the door behind everyone and they all sat down.

"We're here because it's now December and we've swapped out the pieces on exhibition in our gallery," Maurice started. He went on to talk about how Yoon's creepy thread artwork still hadn't been recovered and the police investigation was ongoing but hadn't found any evidence of fraud, and surely there was a set amount of time that their insurance had to pay out within and blah blah blah. Jonah had heard this all before. He could've called it the Entitled Angry Customer Act, Manager Version.

Vaughn sat with his arms crossed, a slightly bored expression on his face, as Maurice talked. Jonah had no idea why he was here, given Maurice was doing all the posturing. Occasionally, Vaughn sent a veiled look at Jonah; he was probably thinking the same thing.

Jonah exchanged glances with Garrett, who also appeared to have realized Maurice was just here to rant to an audience. Hopefully Garrett could hustle the guy out with minimal manoeuvring, because Jonah's temper wasn't up to coaxing this guy down. Perhaps he was in the wrong area of the business. *Or perhaps the guy is just an asshole.*

Half an hour later, Maurice wasn't any closer to being mollified. However, he did glance at his watch and turn to Vaughn abruptly. "It looks like this might drag on for a while. Angeline will be done with the press soon, so she'll need you back right after lunch. Say your thing and go."

Vaughn visibly returned to the scene in front of him. "Oh. Oh! Okay." He sat upright. "We're very disappointed by the way you're treating us."

Uh-huh. That sounded real convincing from the guy who'd spent the last half hour asleep with his eyes open. Jonah barely managed not to scoff.

Maurice was watching the pair of them for some reason. He nodded at Jonah. "Yeah. Exactly." Maurice turned back to Vaughn. "I need a while longer. I'm not sure I'm getting through to these guys."

Garrett looked ready to punch something. "I assure you, your message is very clear, Mr. Palomer. Unfortunately, our position remains the same. We're waiting for the police investigation's conclusions, and until then we cannot in good conscience make a decision one way or the other. Just like your assistant, my colleague and I have other work we need to attend to, including chasing the police on the status of your claim." He stood. "If you'll please excuse us, I think it's time we ended this meeting."

Smooth. Jonah wanted to applaud Garrett. He stood up and opened the door, ushering the Delphi Gallery people through with a grand gesture. Vaughn rolled his eyes at him as he went past, which made Jonah grin.

"You'll make sure they sign out okay, Jonah?" Garrett said, not moving from his desk.

Oh, you bastard. Jonah shot him a hot glare before grinding out, "Sure, no problem."

Garrett winked. "I'll save you some cookies."

Sure, like cookies would make up for managerial betrayal.

Then he was on his own with the two of them in the elevator. Maurice bristled with unexpended frustration while Vaughn seemed calm, but whenever he met Jonah's eyes, obviously fought a smile. *Ha.*

Downstairs, Maurice signed out with a flourish, then scowled at the two of them. "God. I need a walk. I'll meet you back at the gallery, Vaughn." His expression cleared and turned crafty. "Take the full hour again." He stomped off, leaving Vaughn and Jonah stunned at the reception desk.

"What the hell was the last half hour about?" Jonah demanded.

Vaughn wrote his sign-out time. "I believe," he said quietly, "the term is a 'dick-measuring contest.'"

Jonah snorted with laughter, then clapped a hand over his mouth in an attempt to cover the fact he'd *snorted* in public. "Holy shit."

"I'm fairly certain Maurice lost." Vaughn offered Jonah a shy smile. "I think he thinks that we're close friends and that I have an in with you. If you can forgive how ridiculous this was, it would be great to have lunch again."

He didn't have to think about it. "Yeah. Let me grab my wallet."

A few minutes, one wallet, and a coat later, the two of them were out in the freezing street. Vaughn turned to him. "Anywhere in particular?"

"Somewhere cheap and quick."

They frowned at each other a moment, thinking, then Jonah had it. "TD Centre? Or is that too lowbrow?" he added, only half-teasing.

Vaughn's eyebrows raised. "Lowbrow? I'm not that fussy." They started walking towards the TD Centre, moving quickly to keep warm. Christmas decorations flapped in the wind and Jonah's cheeks stung with the cold.

"How have you been?" Vaughn asked.

Jonah shrugged. "Busy."

"I understand completely. Turning over exhibitions is surprisingly difficult." He started going on about moving paintings and sculptures out and moving other ones in and the stresses of not damaging them. "At least it's done now," he said by the time they entered the TD Centre food court. "I can focus on wrapping up the Christmas party planning."

"Christmas party?"

"Yes. The gallery has one every year." Vaughn went a bit pink. "It's invitation-only, but I'm in the charge of the guest list. If you want to come, I could add you."

Jonah could just imagine the type of party it would be. "Let me guess: swanky clothes, fancy drinks, little nibble-y party food things on trays."

"That's about the gist of it, yes."

Him, at a party like that? No way. "Nah. Not my scene."

Vaughn cast a surprised glance at him. "Really? You're very sociable. I think you'd have fun."

Jonah studied him. Vaughn looked like he was being honest. *Hmmm.* "You sure? I think your manager would follow me around to make sure I don't wipe my hands on the curtains."

Vaughn rolled his eyes. "We don't have curtains in the gallery." He paused. "Though there is a black veil hanging from the ceiling in one room. Barinski's latest piece. Very dramatic. I'd be surprised if no one touched it, even accidentally. In any case, the caterers will provide napkins."

Was it just Jonah or was conversation with this guy sometimes like banging his head against a brick wall?

They paused in the food court to see what was on offer, then made a beeline for iQ in silent agreement.

"I got enough going on," Jonah said as they stood in line. "But thanks for the invite."

Vaughn nodded.

They waited in silence for a few minutes. Jonah shifted from foot to foot, resisting the urge to look at his phone.

"So, what else has been happening?" Vaughn asked. "Have you seen Zay lately?"

Zing. Another stab of guilt. "No."

"Really? I thought she owed you lunch."

She did. "Look, I've had some stuff come up, work's been crazy, and I just had this asshole client yell at me and my manager for half an hour. That's pretty much been my week."

Vaughn laughed. It was a nice sound, and it let Jonah relax. "Maurice has been like that for days." Vaughn shook his head.

"I'm sorry about him. If it's any consolation, he's been bitching at me as well."

Yeah, Jonah got the impression he did that. "You know, it's not okay for a manager to give you shit all the time." Definitely not in the way Maurice doled it out. "You should hand it back to him."

Vaughn rolled his eyes. "Please. He'd have a meltdown and take the gallery with him. I find it best to get on with my work and let him have his tantrums."

"Nah, dude, I've seen that shit before." Jonah had met bullies over and over again at the schools he'd been to. He'd learned damn quickly how to fight back. It had come in useful in new foster homes too, the ones where other people sometimes thought the idea of personal property was just that—an idea. Once he'd realized that people didn't give a shit what ideas they had when faced with the threat of a fist, life got a bit easier. When he'd learned how to give attitude and back it up when necessary, he'd found less of his stuff went missing and people left him alone.

Vaughn didn't seem to have learned that lesson.

"You *have* to give it back to him," Jonah pressed. "Stand up to the guy. He'll back off."

Vaughn shot him a look he didn't understand. "I ignore him most of the time. Don't worry, he's nothing I can't handle."

Jonah privately disagreed, but hey, what did *he* know, right?

"Thanks for the concern." Vaughn hesitated. "You okay? You seem kind of . . . tense."

"That's a lie." Jonah leered at him. "I'm super relaxed. I haven't been laid so much in forever."

Vaughn stifled a laugh. "Oh my God."

Jonah grinned; he really *was* cute, laughing like that. He should laugh more. Inspired, Jonah launched into stories of the hookups he'd had in the past week: the guys he'd met (and screwed) on the way to his gym, a crazy grunter in a club, the odd person in the city after work. "All dressed up in this suit, right, like I think I saw Armani cuff links or some shit," he said as they inched closer to the counter. "It's freezing, and we were in a doorway somewhere. He was like ten years older than me, but he wanted me to talk dirty to him—like, dom kind of dirty, go all hard on his ass, practically do him raw and no lube. In Armani cuff links." He shook his head. "Probably a stockbroker."

Vaughn was watching him with a mixture of fascination and disbelief. "And you did it?"

"Yeah. With a condom." Jonah shrugged. "Not really my deal, kink, but I can manage dirty talk for fifteen minutes."

"It's not really your deal? Why would you do it, then?"

Why would he . . .? Jonah stared at him. "What do you mean? It's *sex*."

"Yeah, but I thought a fundamental part of sex is having the kind of sex you want."

"Just because it's not something I *like* doesn't mean it's not worth having." Jonah reran those words over and grimaced, because *ugh*, he could have phrased that better. "It's just, like, an experience," he tried again. "An overall good experience, but not the best. Like . . . like chocolate."

Vaughn raised an eyebrow. "Chocolate."

"My favourite chocolate is dark chocolate." Well, that was the only chocolate he allowed himself to eat these days. "And that guy was milk chocolate. Not my favourite, but still chocolate."

"Sex is so intimate, though." Vaughn frowned now. "I'd assume you'd want it to be as good as possible each time."

Jonah clapped his hand over his mouth. Oh good *Lord*. That was . . . That was so *sweet*. He thought sex was intimate? Wow. *Wow*. And that said a lot about Vaughn. Clearly he was the guy who wanted and had dark chocolate. Just dark chocolate. Jonah wondered what it said about him that he was willing to have milk chocolate. Sometimes a lot of it. Did Vaughn judge him for that?

Maybe not, because he was going red and waving his hand. "Don't say it. Your face is an open book. I know sex is whatever you make of it. Don't say anything. My point was, life is short. You should have the sex you want, not just settle for what you can get."

Oh, for fuck's sake. It was only sex. Jonah glared at him. "I *am* having the sex I want."

Vaughn's hands flew up. "All right! I just thought . . . Never mind."

"No. You thought *what*?"

Vaughn turned away, blushing fiercely. Jonah realized that perhaps a food court near his work wasn't the best setting for this, but if anyone had a problem, they could just not listen. Oh hey, Vaughn's ears had gone all red too.

"It's not really any of my business," Vaughn said, "but if you're having all this great, relaxing sex, even if it's not 'your deal' but it somehow still is, then why do you look like you're ready to break something?"

Jonah's phone suddenly weighed heavy in his pocket with the unanswered texts and the phone call he had yet to make to Claire.

"I also don't see how that stops you from answering a text," Vaughn added. There was an edge to his voice Jonah hadn't heard before—anger? Annoyance?

He rubbed the back of his neck. No, he wasn't proud of that. "Sorry."

"Sure."

"If it helps"—and maybe it would—"I ignored everyone else's texts this week."

Vaughn raised an eyebrow, but didn't respond to that because they'd reached the head of the line. After ordering, Jonah ran for seats while Vaughn collected, and soon they were settled with food. Jonah forked through his box of delicious health. Protein, greens, seeds, nuts—all the good things were there. *Take that, cookies.*

"I think you should respond to your texts," Vaughn said, turning the food in his box over with his fork.

"What?" When Vaughn just gazed at him, Jonah swallowed his mouthful of spinach and amaranth. "Like, now?"

"Yes."

Jonah crunched another mouthful, studying Vaughn. He didn't like being the person on the phone when talking with someone else— but then again, he *did* need to respond. And Vaughn looked serious.

Hell with it. He first answered Zay with an apology and a date for dinner next week, then glanced over Adrian's text messages. Two invites, one to a club a couple of nights ago and another to a toga party that Friday. A toga party at *Carson's.* Oh man, Carson was a queen and a half—that was going to be *crazy.* But Jonah had missed out on a night with Adrian and the guys. That sucked.

Why had he done that? Ignored his friends like this? He needed to get a grip.

"That looks like a good message," Vaughn remarked.

"Oh yeah." He glanced at Vaughn, mentally stripped off the jacket and added a toga, then decided to linger over that image because it was a nice one.

"I hope whatever's in there is better than whatever has you so tense."

"I'm *not* tense."

Vaughn's fork pointed at his shoulders. "You're all hunched over, shoulders are up, chin is down, and you have your cell in a very tight grip."

Jonah straightened, forced his shoulders down, chin up, and put his cell on the table. "Better?"

"Much."

"It's just . . ." His thoughts churned over the past week. He could share the overall shape of the problem without going into the stupid details, right? "There's this . . . thing. It came up suddenly, and I don't know what to do about it. Kind of freaked me out. So I ignored everyone." He opened Vaughn's texts and wrote: *Hows Sat?*

"Is it anything I can help with?"

Him? With this messed-up mother-lawyer thing? Jonah didn't think so. "Nah."

Vaughn's phone dinged, and he pulled it out.

Jonah gaped at the screen. "What the hell happened to your cell?"

Vaughn's fingers swiped across it. "Dropped it."

"But that's like a five-hundred-dollar phone!"

Vaughn smiled at him. "All the more reason not to replace it just yet." He unlocked the screen and Jonah saw his backdrop was a picture of daffodils. Not a stock image; it was a painting—one that Jonah even vaguely recognized. A Canadian artist he'd researched in grade school. Helen somebody. Trust Vaughn to have that as a background picture.

And ha, I know some art.

It was quickly hidden by his text. Vaughn read through it, then looked back up at Jonah, eyes crinkling. "Saturday is perfect."

The way he said it sent Jonah's stomach spiralling away and heat flooding through his veins. Something about those grey eyes and that happy expression. Jonah swallowed.

"Good," he croaked out. He looked down and stabbed at some sweet potato and egg, wondering why he suddenly felt so spacey. "So," he added hurriedly, "you got any hookup stories you wanna share too?"

Vaughn shook his head. "I didn't go out this week."

Jonah gestured impatiently. "Look, some of those guys were on Grindr. I didn't exactly go far to find them. You're on it too, right?"

Vaughn raised one eyebrow. "I'm not on Grindr."

Oh good *God*. Jonah stared at him in shock. "You must be *dying* for some."

"I'm really, really not."

"How? It's been over a week—that I know of," he added, not wanting to presume too much. "I'd be climbing the walls, dude."

A strange expression crossed Vaughn's face. "I'm fine. Don't worry about me." He glanced around. "I'm amazed you're comfortable discussing this stuff in public."

In public? *Wait a second.* "What's the matter? Am I too loud for you?"

"No. Not at all." Vaughn shifted his weight though.

Suspicions rose thick and fast. "You *are* out, right?"

"Yes." Vaughn shot him a reassuring smile. "It's just that I tend to talk about these things with friends while clubbing or at home with glasses of wine."

Wine. Jesus effing Christ. Of course he did.

"It's not a criticism of you," Vaughn added.

"It's only sex." Because it was, and everyone had it. "I can talk about it in public if I want." Jonah narrowed his eyes at Vaughn. "Anyone who's uncomfortable because it's gay sex doesn't have to listen."

Vaughn sighed heavily. "I *agree* with you."

And he'd somehow changed the subject. Goddamn it. Jonah swung it back around. "Nice try, but I can't stand by and let a brother dry up. So what's your deal? No relationships, I know, but no Grindr either?" Now that he was thinking about it, Grindr had some really skeezy guys on there. He could see someone like Vaughn wanting a different kind of casual meet-up. Really dark chocolate. No milk at all. "You prefer meeting people in person? Seeing what they're like before sleeping with them?"

"Can we just drop this?" Vaughn had gone red again.

"Because"—oh, and this was genius—"I'm going to a toga party later this week with a friend, and you should definitely come along." The more Jonah thought about it, the more he liked the idea. Carson always had hot guys at his parties. Vaughn would be a hit. "Guy like you would have no problems getting some there." He pulled out his phone. "I'm going to text you the details."

"Thank you but no," Vaughn said stiffly.

Jonah looked up at him. Had he offended him again? He hadn't wanted to do that.

"I don't do casual sex or hookups or sex parties." Vaughn's voice was stilted and low. "I used to do that, but it's not all that... interesting to me."

Interesting? *Interesting?* Jonah could remember one of his foster sisters telling him he should never use that word in an essay because it was essentially meaningless. "What do you mean?"

Vaughn became very intrigued by the contents of his box. "It's complicated, is what I mean." He glanced around. "I don't really want to explain it here."

Jonah took a mental step back. Okay. *Okay.* Not every gay guy was into the scene the way he and his buddies were. He knew that. Hell, he'd even met (and blown) a few shy guys back at university. Geeky, serious guys so eager for a boyfriend that they had their hearts broken several times in a row before finding someone. Serious Boyfriend Material. Vaughn totally read that way too, but he'd said he didn't do relationships, *sooo* that sounded like his tastes were *very* selective...

Understanding hit him like a punch of cocoa to the tongue. "Oh, you're into BDSM!"

Vaughn hid his face in his hands and groaned. "*No.* I'm not. Really not. At all."

Not BDSM? "Another kind of kink?"

"No."

"Furries?"

"Absolutely not."

He grinned, liking this game. "Cars?"

Vaughn emerged from behind his hands in surprise. "*Cars?*"

"That's a thing."

"Really?" He shook his head. "No, nothing like that."

He looked embarrassed, maybe even slightly upset. That wasn't a good sign. Jonah's stomach twisted. What if . . . What if it was a bad experience? He'd seen some messed-up kids in foster care, ones who'd been abused by their parents or guardians or even by foster parents. Was it something like that?

The idea of Vaughn being one of those kids sank an icy hook into his chest. "Is it bad?" he asked before he could stop himself.

Vaughn rolled his eyes. "Will you just," he started, then stopped when he focused on Jonah. His face softened, and he reached out to touch Jonah's wrist. "No." His voice was gentle. "It's nothing bad. Just complicated."

Thank fuck. Jonah's sheer relief burned almost as much as Vaughn's fingers on his skin. "Good." Jonah wasn't a total asshole, and he could take a hint. "Consider the topic dropped. But you're still coming to the party."

"Why?"

"Because I want you there." Jonah realized it was true as he said it. He really did want him there. He wanted to see what Adrian and Carson thought of him.

Vaughn had gone bright pink. "Oh. Well. But I should . . . You should know—"

"Do your interesting, complicated sexy thoughts not allow toga parties?"

Vaughn's mouth twitched. "Not necessarily."

Jonah couldn't look away from his lips. There was a shine of salad dressing on them. As he watched, Vaughn licked the dressing away in one smooth flick of his tongue.

Jonah's mouth went dry, then, "I want to see you in a toga," spilled out.

Vaughn's eyebrows rose.

He'd actually said that. *Whoops.*

"There's not much to see," Vaughn said.

"I think I'll be the judge of that." Jonah waggled his eyebrows, raising a smile from Vaughn. "And *I'll* be in a toga too."

The pink deepened. "I, uh, well . . ."

And: hooked.

Vaughn wasn't sure when he'd agreed to this party, but standing on the steps of said party was too late to be arguing with himself about it. When had he made the decision to go? Had it been that afternoon, as he'd helped a stressed-out Angeline and Maurice inventory and photograph every single art piece in the December exhibition because "just in case"? Or had it been during that lunch in the TD Centre food court a few days ago? When Jonah had said *"I want you there,"* with that serious expression on his face, and Vaughn's stomach had exploded into flurries of butterflies? Or had it been during the stream of texts in the two days afterwards, alternately begging him to come and threatening him if he didn't? Was he really the kind of person who was charmed into coming to a party by a threat like *If you don't come I'll fill your apartment with bees*?

Evidently so.

That promise of Jonah in a toga had seared images into his brain. He *did* want to see that. For sure. He maybe wanted a picture to use as a drawing reference later. He maybe just wanted to look at Jonah. That was definitely something he liked doing: looking at him and listening to him and watching him react and joke. And thinking about kissing the hell out of him.

That was partly the problem. Because that's all he wanted to do with Jonah, and Vaughn had an inkling that Jonah had maybe, *maybe* been hitting on him when asking him to this. Or he might do something tonight.

He shouldn't be here. He shouldn't encourage Jonah, even indirectly, in thinking they were on the same level where parties and sex were concerned. That Vaughn was like any other normal guy.

Only, Jonah's expression when he'd said *"I want you there"* had little claws that had hooked into Vaughn. The stricken concern he'd shown when he'd asked *"Is it bad?"* to Vaughn's vague excuse for not elaborating on his sexual habits. Simply *him*, in all his fierce, furious energy. Tiny claws sinking deep into Vaughn's skin and mind.

He pressed the doorbell.

After all, he was already there, and he could always attempt to *explain* his thing about sex. Or keep putting Jonah off, *if* he was interested. And who said this would turn sexual anyway, right? It wasn't like Vaughn had never been to a toga party before; Devon had been fond of them at university, and once the novelty had worn off, it was in essence like every other house party.

Someone stumbled to the door and opened it. A burst of heat and light hit him in the face, and Vaughn blinked to see a lithe young man wearing a toga and a smile. He scanned Vaughn, then leaned enticingly against the doorframe. "Well, *hello.*"

Vaughn was wearing a coat and jeans. Quite what there was to lust over was beyond him. "Hi. I'm a friend of Jonah's."

"You could be a friend of my grandmother's, and you'd be welcome here." He extended a hand. "Carson. *Enchanté.*"

He shook it. "Vaughn. I brought my own—" He was yanked inside.

Carson held his hand firmly, his free hand grabbing the zip on Vaughn's coat. "Let's get the bad winter clothes off you, sweetie." He pulled the zip down. "In here, it's July."

It certainly felt like it. The heat was blasting. Vaughn's coat was lifted off him as he looked around. He stood with Carson in a hallway, which led to several open doors and a staircase. A few men lounged at the foot of the stairs, and two ran into the hallway from the living room, one chasing the other up the stairs. Music played from somewhere else in the house. Not everyone, he was glad to see, was wearing a toga. Perhaps he'd get away with his T-shirt and jeans.

Carson flung his coat carelessly into a nearby closet and started tugging at Vaughn's sweater. "Come on, arms up."

Vaughn kept his arms firmly down. "I don't normally let strangers strip me."

"Honey, I already *told* you my name."

"Carson!"

Thank you, party gods. Vaughn looked over to see Jonah walking out of the living room, a sheet wrapped badly around him and a beer in hand. A laurel crown rested on his blond hair. His legs and feet were bare, as were his abs and half of his chest. It was a hairless and very toned chest. Physically stunning and everything Vaughn had imagined, only better. Real. After all, Vaughn appreciated the male form as much as anyone.

But by God, he'd made a travesty of his toga. It wasn't even close to authentic. Togas were meant to cover the body, not show it off. Vaughn's was practically a monk's cowl in comparison.

"Carson, he's barely through the door." Jonah gave an evil grin. "Why isn't he undressed already?"

Carson flipped his hair. "I'm *trying*."

Jonah pointed one finger at Vaughn. "Pretty boy. Behave."

Unbelievable. Vaughn sighed. "Could one of you at least get me a drink?"

Carson lit up, then took off, leaving Jonah smirking at Vaughn. "Hey." He spun in a slow circle. "What do you think?"

Vanity, thy name is man. He had to know he looked good, despite the haphazard toga. "Bacchus himself would approve."

"Who?"

Vaughn picked up his bag and pulled his toga out. "Where can I change?"

"What's wrong with here?" Jonah's eyes danced merrily.

Vaughn should've known.

"Yeah, buddy, what's wrong with here?" asked one of the men on the stairs.

It was too public, for one, but he could tell it would be easier to play along. They all grinned, waiting. Vaughn peeled off his sweater, then his T-shirt. Jonah's smile grew wide and filthy as he watched, sending Vaughn's stomach into somersaults. Vaughn jerked the toga into place over his bare chest, making sure it reached to his knees, then took off his jeans, shoes, and socks, to the obvious disappointment of his audience. He tucked the clothes into his bag.

"You forgot something," Jonah said.

Vaughn raised his head. "Oh?"

Jonah stepped forward and traced one finger down Vaughn's chest, from clavicle to navel to groin, scraping against the fabric and igniting a slow line down his body, until he reached the edge of Vaughn's boxers through the sheet. Then his finger pushed under the band, pulled it away, and let it snap back against his skin. Inches from his dick. Someone on the stairs exhaled slowly.

Okay. Yes, that *was flirting.* That was expert flirting. This was Jonah, after all. Vaughn should've seen it coming—well, not *that* specifically. Were Vaughn anyone other than Vaughn, he'd probably be half-hard and ready to go after a move like that—but that wasn't who he was. He just thought it was amusing.

But honestly? Sometimes it was a real fucking shame. Right now he'd give almost anything to be able to flirt back, to answer the challenge in Jonah's face. Or, to be precise, to *want* to touch back and to meet that kind of sexiness with his own. To be sincere about it.

"They stay on," he said.

Jonah raised an eyebrow. "Got something that needs help staying in place?" He sipped his beer.

God. So edgy. So *funny.* So completely out of Vaughn's league. Why the hell had he decided to come tonight?

Because my apparently latent masochistic tendencies have decided to test the light of day.

"My gigantic dick," Vaughn replied, to guffaws from the peanut gallery. Jonah folded his arms, hopefully mollified for now. Vaughn knelt and retrieved the wine he'd brought, then tossed his bag into the closet on top of his coat.

Jonah stared at the bottle in his hand, aghast. "You brought wine."

What was the problem? Wine was requisite for a toga party. "Yes." He held it up. "It's Greek."

Jonah blinked, then laughed. "Unreal."

Carson returned, almost skidding to present Vaughn with a can of beer. "Here, honey— Oh!" He gazed Vaughn up and down, then turned on Jonah. "You bitch. You *knew* he was going to change while I was gone."

Jonah blithely sipped his beer. "You were the one who jumped to get him a drink."

Carson *tsk*ed and turned back to Vaughn. "And he brought wine!" He fanned himself. "Oh my God, Jonah, where did you *find* him?"

Vaughn handed him the bottle. Carson took Vaughn's arm and marched him into the living room, Jonah following.

People lounged on the sofas in the living room or stood around chatting with drinks in hand. Vaughn spotted two figures in one corner grinding against each other before he was steered into the kitchen. Carson deposited the wine next to a pile of assorted bottles, and positioned Vaughn against a cabinet. Jonah stood next to Carson and together the two of them studied Vaughn intently, eyes scanning his body.

He was too sober for this. "What is it?"

"Your toga covers too much," Jonah replied.

"But," Carson said, "it *is* authentic." He smiled at Vaughn. "You've done this before, haven't you?"

"It's not my first toga party."

"But it's your first toga party at *my* house." Carson reached forward and brushed his hands over the panels of material covering Vaughn's chest. "And as host, I have full veto over toga design. Authenticity sucks." He began pulling at the panels to try to rearrange them to display Vaughn's nipples.

Vaughn was casting about for a distraction while trying not to laugh—Carson's hands were ticklish—when the doorbell rang. Carson threw his hands up with an, "Oh my *God*, we're so *popularrr*!" and ran out.

Vaughn set the laughter free.

Jonah grinned. "Carson's right, you know. Show some skin."

"He's delightful."

Jonah held up his beer. "Welcome to the party."

Vaughn touched their cans together. "Thank you for the invite."

"Don't thank me yet." Jonah leaned in. "I have the bees on standby."

Vaughn could smell him. Fresh yet salty, like sea spray. "Your threats are no longer valid. I'm here."

"Yes, but you have to have a good time too."

"That won't be a problem."

"No, it won't." Was that a promise?

"Jonah!" Another man joined them, beer in hand and a sheet around his waist. Dark curls flopped around his face. "Is this the guy?"

Jonah nodded. "Adrian, this is Vaughn."

Vaughn held out his hand. Adrian took a firm grip and pulled him forward into a fierce kiss. When he let him go, Vaughn let out a surprised breath. Whoa. *Completely* unexpected. Adrian grinned cheekily at him. "Hi, Vaughn."

"Hello, Adrian," he said stupidly.

Jonah's face was an interesting mix of disapproval and envy. Adrian's grin turned sly, and he wrapped one arm around Jonah's shoulders. "Tastes good," he leered.

"You're worse than Carson," Jonah muttered.

"I bet you *feel* good too," Adrian added, eyeing Vaughn's toga. "Not that you're giving away much."

Vaughn gestured to his toga. "This is how a toga should be worn."

"Very nice and grand and shit, but—" Adrian gestured to his own "—allow me to disagree."

"*That* is a bath towel."

Adrian fluttered his eyes. "Exactly. Easy access."

Oh, good *God*. This was like first year of university queer society all over again.

"Noted." Was it him, or was his voice sounding strained already? He sipped his beer.

"Some of us don't need to show off all our assets, Adrian," Jonah said.

Adrian reached down and grabbed one of Jonah's assets—and firmly, judging by Jonah's jump. "Some of us need to chill out." He planted a kiss on Jonah's cheek, then let go and took a few steps over to Vaughn, who readied his own assets for a grope. Instead, Adrian reached up and kissed him again. A warm, brief kiss. No tongue, thankfully. "Nice to meet you," he said, that cheeky grin in place again. "The rooms upstairs lock. I hope I'll be seeing you up there later."

Jonah let out a frustrated huff and grabbed Vaughn's hand. "Come on, I'll introduce you to some *nice* people."

Adrian winked, then waved in farewell.

Vaughn was pulled into the next room, another living space. Here the music thumped and people danced—and it was a mix of men and women. The men vastly outnumbered the women, though. It reminded him of the Village's gay clubs, which was reassuring, though the average age here was significantly lower, perhaps around twenty at a guess. It meant there were at least a few people here intending to socialize rather than screw. And a fair number of them had proper togas too.

Jonah led him to a cluster of men at the edge of the room. "Guys!" He gestured between them. "Vaughn! Vaughn, the guys!"

They introduced themselves. Vaughn caught a Tom and a Jeremy and maybe a James, but that was it. They all waved and seemed friendly. Three of them were watching something on a phone while the other two and Jonah immediately started scanning the crowd. Vaughn moved to see what was on the screen.

It was a recording of the hockey game from earlier in the week: Leafs against the Bruins. Vaughn hadn't had a chance to watch it yet and immediately latched on. "How're they doing?"

"First period, ten minutes left," one of the guys said, "and nothing's happening— Oh!" The Leafs scored on-screen, and Vaughn drank his beer, rapt.

Someone prodded his arm. He looked over to see an unimpressed Jonah. "Watching the game doesn't count as having fun."

"I respectfully disagree."

"It's cheating. Plus, where were you on Wednesday when the game was actually on?"

Vaughn smiled. "You said to come here and to have fun. And lo, I am."

"Lo this." Jonah flipped the finger at him. "Finish your drink and dance."

Vaughn glanced at the game. "After this period."

"*Now.*"

Jeez, *pushy*. Vaughn finished his beer, put it down, and followed Jonah out into the dancers. Unlike in a club, people here seemed to prioritize dancing rather than scoping potential partners. Jonah received a few hugs and shoulder pats, while Vaughn received smiles and surreptitious glances. He began dancing, the beer kicking in and relaxing him, and as he slowly surveyed the crowd, it hit him that he was the oldest person there by several years.

He bent to Jonah's ear. "How old are you?"

Jonah shot him a surprised look. "Old enough."

He shook his head with a laugh. "Not like that. I feel old."

"What?"

He had to shout over the music. "I feel old here!"

Jonah shook his head. "Nah, nah, we're all, like, just out of university. You're good."

"Like, just out of university." Jesus. No wonder they were all so fresh-faced. Jonah seemed perhaps a year older than that, so twenty-three? Twenty-four? The way he scanned the crowd made him seem a lot older.

And the way he stopped scanning and focused on Vaughn was very adult indeed.

Jonah stepped forward, arms wrapping over Vaughn's shoulders, bringing their bodies together. Vaughn's mouth went dry as Jonah's face came within inches of his.

"I've been wondering about those mysterious, complicated sex thoughts of yours," Jonah said, his body moving with the music against Vaughn's.

Mysterious—? Oh, lunch. Right. Wasn't that *some truth.* How could something as simple as *I don't like sex* be so complicated? Vaughn regretted even hinting at it.

"They're really not worth thinking about." Vaughn's throat was tight. His hands had attached themselves to Jonah without him realizing it, slowly pressing against his waist and rubbing over the fabric of the sheet.

Jonah smiled, sly but happy, setting off a series of shocks in Vaughn's head and gut.

Look at him, at them; Jonah was *there*, literally there in front of him. In his arms. Vaughn could feel his breath on his lips. He'd never have another chance like this again.

He kissed him. The softness of his mouth gave way to the fierceness of Jonah's response. His arms tightened around Vaughn's neck, keeping them close. Vaughn luxuriated in the sensations of holding Jonah, of kissing him like this, the rush of blood in his head and thrill in his chest. Rare. Precious.

When he pulled back, Jonah laughed. "Fucking finally!" He pressed against Vaughn, collarbone to knee, and Vaughn could feel the thinness of the sheets separating them, the hardness of Jonah's erection, the tightening of Jonah's arms around his neck.

Vaughn's cock twitched. He locked eyes with Jonah because there was no way Jonah hadn't felt it. Something passed between them in that gaze, something deep and yearning. Something dangerous.

Another kiss, then Jonah's arms unlatched and his hands smoothed down Vaughn's chest. "Upstairs."

Vaughn reached up and caught at Jonah's hands. "No."

Jonah's eyebrows flew up. "No?"

"Can't we just dance?"

"You came here in a toga just to dance with me?" Jonah was sarcastic, but Vaughn could have said those words with complete sincerity.

"No." He'd wanted to kiss him too, and he was still reeling from how good that had been.

"Then *what*?" Jonah's fingers pressed into his chest now.

"I just don't want to."

Jonah's eyes went glitteringly hard. "*Fine*," he snarled. He stepped back, pulling his hands away from Vaughn. "Three o'clock. Redhead."

Vaughn looked obediently. Yes, there was a red-haired man on his right.

"This is what *I* came here for." Jonah marched over to the redhead, twined his arms around him, and within seconds had his tongue down his throat.

Vaughn had never been hit in the gut, but he imagined it would feel something like watching Jonah do that. Was he surprised? No. Disappointed? Wrenchingly yes.

He needed more beer.

Someone clapped his shoulder. "Sorry, man." Vaughn glanced over to see one of the guys Jonah had introduced him to earlier. James? Jeremy? "He goes kind of nuts at these things sometimes, but he always calms down. You probably still got a chance. You sure you don't want to tap that?"

Vaughn narrowed his eyes at him. "He's a person, not a 'that.'" A nearby girl swivelled to look at him so quickly she risked whiplash.

Jeremy/James rolled his eyes. "You know what I mean. If you want a lesson in unnecessary pain, you can watch them go upstairs. We're going for beers."

That sounded like an excellent idea. Vaughn made to follow the guy to the kitchen, but found himself blocked by the girl. "Oh my God," she breathed. "Please tell me you're straight or bi. *Please.*"

"I'm so sorry. I can't."

She pouted. "Damn it. *Every* time. Any friends who are?"

"None here." He patted her shoulder. "I'll dance with you later, if you're around."

"That'll have to do." She did have a smile on her face when he moved past her though. At least dancing was enough for *someone* here.

James/Jeremy had joined the hockey buddies in moving through the kitchen. Vaughn darted after them, grabbed a beer, and caught up as they went into the living room. People already in there added to the group as they watched the game, complained about the size of the screen, then somehow found the game on Carson's cable and set it to replay from the start of the second period.

Infinitely better. And he didn't have to watch as Jonah dragged Red somewhere to fuck that snarl off his face.

Vaughn decided not to think about that.

By the end of the second period, there was a small crew of toga-clad men and women shouting at the TV from the sofa and spots on the floor. Vaughn fell into conversation with Bryce, one of Jonah's friends. By the end of the third period, the Bruins had won 6-3 and howls of dismay filled the room. The music blared louder in the other room to compensate.

Bryce slumped back. "Shit."

Vaughn scowled. "I know. What the hell was that?"

"Being a Leafs fan can be goddamn heartbreak."

"Amen."

They *chink*ed beer cans. Vaughn sipped, noticing how low the mood of the room was. Even the guys who'd been cuddling looked a little upset. Something was needed to distract everyone from the loss. A game of some kind? Something Greek would be fitting, but the only Greek drinking game he knew, Kottabos, would destroy the carpet.

There was a deck of cards under the TV. *Aha.* Once in hand, he turned to the room and held it up. "Circle of Death, anyone?"

Moments later, they were sitting on the floor, a large measuring cup in place as the King's Cup. Someone had brought in a beer crate, and Vaughn had spread the cards in a circle. A new can of beer was open and at the ready. Somehow, he thought the Greeks would have approved of this.

During the first game, he saw Jonah watching from the sofa. When they made eye contact, Jonah stared evenly at him, then frowned and turned away, leaving the room. A few cards later, Vaughn saw Jonah leading someone else through the room.

So, that's how things were going to go. *Fine.*

Two games and however many beers later, during which he didn't look beyond the circle of participants, Vaughn withdrew into the other room to dance. There the girl from earlier caught his attention, and before he knew it, he was doing the Macarena with most of the room. When the song changed back into a dance track, the girl was replaced with a guy who shimmied up to him with a cheeky grin. After a while and a few sensuous moves, Carson cut in and forced him into a slow dance just so he could look dreamily into Vaughn's eyes.

He must've looked a little suspicious, because Carson leaned forward and shouted over the music into Vaughn's ear, "I'm trying to make someone jealous."

Vaughn relaxed. "Playing dirty, huh?"

"Oh sweetie, *I'm* not the one playing dirty," Carson purred, rubbing his groin against Vaughn's. His face came closer and warning bells jangled loudly in Vaughn's head. Too tipsy to react in time, he couldn't stop the kiss that came next, or the tongue that wiggled its way into his mouth. *Ugh. Nowhere near drunk enough.*

Repulsed, he ended it as gently as he could. "Is it working?" he asked, hoping his disgust didn't come across.

Carson glanced to his side and preened. "Oh yeah."

A hand landed on Vaughn's shoulder. "Carson, can I borrow him?" Adrian yelled beside them.

Carson let him go with a pout and lingering hand brushes. As Vaughn turned away, he resisted the urge to wipe his mouth. *God.* He would never understand why people liked frenching. Just so sloppy. *Yech.*

His earlier kiss with Jonah hadn't even reached the tongue stage, but it had been blindingly amazing in contrast.

Adrian steered him into the kitchen, and Vaughn made for the tap. As Vaughn poured water for himself, Adrian leaned against the counter. His "toga" had shifted, and one part was now thrown over a shoulder. *Taken off and put back on*, Vaughn's brain informed him helpfully.

"Carson's told us you can come by anytime," Adrian said dryly.

"A repeat invitation." Vaughn took a healthy gulp. "Mother would be so proud."

Adrian snorted. "For someone who's barely moved beyond two rooms, you've made quite an impression."

More water. "After the hockey—"

"Stop. No. Don't fucking mention that shit to me. God, what a nightmare."

He nodded. "Right? A travesty."

"Listen, you have no clue. I was in a bar watching it on Wednesday, and the whole place went into meltdown. Grown men practically crying into their pitchers." Adrian shook his head. "You know you're in Canada when, am I right?"

"Utterly." Vaughn poured another glass and downed it in one.

"So have you and Jonah had sex or what?"

Vaughn gave quiet thanks that he'd already swallowed the water, because the choking that happened now would have sent it back into the cup. "*What?*"

"I saw you two. Don't know what went down, but he's pissed." Adrian adjusted his toga. "Not that it's any of my business, but I like it when my friends have a good time, rather than try to piss off other guys. You know that's what he's doing. My question for you is: what are *you* still doing here?"

That was a good question. Vaughn wasn't sure he had an answer. "Didn't feel right to leave."

"Seriously? He's disappeared with like three other guys tonight."

Three? Wow. "At once?"

"What? No. God, no." Adrian made a face. "The mechanics of that are just . . . No. One after another." He paused. "You're not upset."

He was, but it wasn't a big deal, because Vaughn totally *got it*. Like, Jonah wanted to sex him up and he'd said no, and because Jonah wanted sex, he'd moved on. He couldn't *blame* him for that. It made sense.

The anger on Jonah's face was something else, though.

Vaughn had a suspicion that if he kept drinking water, he'd start having more feelings about that. Like worry. And anger of his own.

"Beer is a wonderful thing," he answered.

Adrian snorted. "Right. How about another glass of water, bud?"

"Maybe."

"You gonna start something with him?"

Vaughn didn't know if he meant fighting or fucking. "No."

Adrian nodded, apparently satisfied. "Okay. I don't know where he picked you up, but take this from a friend? Whatever you're hanging around for, he's not going to appreciate it unless it involves cock."

"I know that." And he did. Even if there was a kind of sadness in the pit of his stomach now that he was thinking about it.

"Jeez, I didn't need to talk to you at all." Adrian patted his arm. "Good chat. You ready to take a load off?"

Vaughn hoped he meant sit down. "Oh yeah."

He downed the water and followed Adrian into the living room. Some people were playing a new card game in one corner, while a bunch of others discussed something heatedly on beanbags and the sofa with a joint. He and Adrian made for an empty spot on the sofa and got comfy.

"I'm *saying*"—one of the girls on the beanbags waved her hands limply in the air—"there's no one solution. It's complicated, not a black-and-white problem. It needs, like, work from multiple angles, you know?"

"What are we talking about?" Adrian hissed to a guy near him.

"Racism," he replied.

Vaughn rested his head against the back of the sofa. Tiredness washed over him, and he closed his eyes. It had to be after midnight. Long after midnight. He should call a taxi and get home. What *was* he hanging around for?

Someone prodded his knee. "Here, man." He looked down to see the joint being offered. He pulled on it, then passed it to Adrian, exhaling slowly. By the time it came back around, they'd moved on from racism to queer politics. He'd just accepted the joint again when someone's fingers stroked his hair.

Who the fuck? Vaughn looked up, ready to tell the guy off, and found himself staring straight into hazel eyes.

"Hey." Jonah's lips were swollen, and his hair was mussed. He'd lost his laurel crown, and there appeared to be stains on his toga. *Debauched* was the word that came to mind, and he wore it well.

"Hey." Resignation and anger were there, but they were very far away. Vaughn lifted the joint to his lips and took a drag, eyes on Jonah's.

"You're still here." Jonah sounded warily surprised.

He held for lengthy seconds, examining those green-brown depths. Exhaled, the smoke scratching his throat. "Yeah." Passed the joint over to Adrian.

"Why?"

To apologize. To change my mind. To explain. "Waiting for you. See if you're okay."

Jonah glanced at Adrian, then his mouth set. "I'm joining you."

He jumped over the sofa and lay across Vaughn's and Adrian's laps, head on the sofa arm next to Vaughn's elbow.

"Didn't take you for a stoner," Jonah said once he was settled.

Vaughn's hand went to a fold of sheet by Jonah's waist, rubbing the fabric against his fingertips. "I'm not."

"You inhale like one."

After all the beer he'd drunk, Vaughn had doubted the weed would do much for him, but there was a familiar softening in his mind and body. He smiled dreamily. "Practice."

Jonah wriggled and Adrian cursed. "Fuck's sake, keep still!" He slapped Jonah's ass for good measure, and Jonah aimed a knee threateningly at Adrian's groin.

Vaughn eyed Jonah's hair. Mussed and teased, it swirled in various directions over his head. Without meaning to, his free hand dipped into it.

The teasing expression on Jonah's face dimmed, and as Vaughn pushed through his hair in a gentle circular pattern, Jonah's eyes closed sleepily. "Feels good," he murmured.

"Does it?"

"Yeah."

"You as drunk as me?" Vaughn asked.

"No. One's my limit."

Trust him to be the sensible one. "You're not angry anymore."

"I'm all fucked out." Jonah's eyes opened slightly to narrow, tired slits. "You didn't give a shit. You still don't."

"I do, actually, but there's nothing I can do about it."

Jonah gazed at him, hurt flickering over his face. "I don't get it."

"I know." His hair was so soft. "Tomorrow . . ."

"You still want me over for games tomorrow?"

Did he? Vaughn's chest ached at both prospects: him being there and not being there. *True masochist.* "Yeah. I do."

Jonah nodded, then his eyes closed. Vaughn kept his fingers moving because it was nice. All he *could* do right now.

"I think you can argue for their inclusion, actually," one of the girls was debating. "The term 'queer' is nice in that it's broad enough to encompass everything that's basically not heteronormative."

"But that would mean 'gay' fits under 'queer' in a kind of hierarchy, and as a gay man, I would never describe myself as queer," one guy said.

"Oh, shut up. We're talking about asexuals, not gay guys." She scowled at him. "Just because you're gay doesn't mean you can define what queer is."

"Just because *you're* queer doesn't mean you can tell me where my identity fits in the entirety of the LGBTQ umbrella or that my opinion is invalid," he responded. "And if we're talking about asexuals, I don't think they should be included at all."

"Oh really?"

"Abstinence doesn't mean shit to anyone except right-wing loons in the US."

She grinned in triumph. "Asexuality isn't abstinence."

"Sure as fuck looks like it."

"Abstinence is *behaviour*, which isn't what asexuality is about," the girl continued. "It's about the direction and manifestation of your *sexuality*. Gay guys are attracted to men, right? And you have a libido, ergo, you want to sleep with men. But what if you got drunk and slept with a woman? Are you still gay?"

"Yes." He scrunched up his face. "No. I think it depends." He shook his head as if to clear it. "You got a point?"

This was . . . What was this? What were they talking about? He'd heard similar discussions plenty of times at university, but never about *this*. And hardly ever this eloquent at stupid o'clock over a joint.

"My point is that it's personal. Identity is personal. But people like labels." She sipped her beer. "As I was saying, asexuality is when you're not attracted to anybody, whatever that means for you. Your sexuality isn't directed at any particular group in society. Maybe you don't have much of a sexuality at all, low libido or lack of aesthetic connection to other people or something. Doesn't stop from you from having sex though. How is that *not* queer? Heteronormativity demands active sexual attraction between two binary sexes. It *requires* it."

Vaughn blinked. That was . . . That sounded . . . *Holy shit.*

"It's too late for this kind of bullshit." The guy stood and left the group. Vaughn mentally tallied that as a win for the girl.

And he felt like dawn had just broken in the room. Asexuality. Why hadn't he ever heard that term before? What she'd just described sounded like *him* and all his issues around sex and attraction and feeling things for people.

Sort of. He was still so aware of Jonah. The texture of his hair through Vaughn's fingers. His body, all heavy and warm on his lap. The steady rise and fall of his chest and the infinitesimally delicate movements of his eyelashes against his cheek as he dozed.

"I agree with you, actually," Adrian said, the edges of his words slurred with sleep. "By that definition, yes, asexuals belong under the queer umbrella."

"But the queer label isn't just 'anything that's not heterosexual,'" another girl said. "If there's no sexual attraction to anyone, no sexual component at all, that doesn't fit under queer *or* heterosexual. And let's not even get into the long history of active oppression queer people have suffered that asexual people haven't."

"How do you know they haven't? Why do you think queerness is defined by how long and how much you've been oppressed, anyway?"

The first girl shook her head. "Jesus. Whatever. Then where would *you* put them? Because they're still people who want relationships."

"I don't know."

They glared at each other.

Jonah shifted onto his side in Vaughn's lap, a sigh escaping, warm against Vaughn's arm. What was Vaughn going to do with him? Here, like this?

"Seeing as alternative sexual behaviour can be considered queer," Adrian said, "and celibacy is seen as alternative—"

"Then what about sexless marriages?" the second girl asked. "You think those heterosexual couples suddenly become queer, just because they're not having sex?"

"They're seen as strange by society, yeah," Adrian replied. "So why not?" That prompted a few angry retorts and a thrown cushion.

"Just how important is sexual behaviour in defining a label?" the first girl asked.

"Damn important," the second girl said.

"Oh yeah?"

"Yeah. I only have sex with women."

"But how often?"

She shifted uncomfortably. "Mostly in relationships."

"So you have spells where you don't have sex at all."

"Yeah, but that's normal. Everyone has those, regardless of orientation."

The first girl crushed her beer can. "Then if a lack of sex is as common to the human experience as having sex is, why would that alone exclude asexuals from the queer label?"

Good Lord. "Are you, by any chance, on a debating team?" Vaughn asked her.

Laughter rolled around the group. The first girl ducked her head. "I was president of an LGBTQIA club in university."

"When you run for prime minister, let me know, eh," Adrian said. "I'll vote for you."

So would Vaughn. Weed and beer had made his thoughts slippery, but no way was he going to forget this. The moment he got home, he'd be googling the hell out of asexuality. See if it was what it seemed to be. See if it was *him*.

Jonah shifted on Vaughn's lap. Vaughn teased a lock through his fingers, the movement as hypnotic for him as it seemed to have been for Jonah. He took the opportunity to look at Jonah's face without self-consciousness. Jonah looked younger at rest, more peaceful. None of his wicked, magnetic energy was at play now. Vaughn ran his eyes over the lines of Jonah's body, the way the muscles bunched and relaxed and rested, the way the fabric rolled and gathered around him. He looked like something out of a Rococo depiction of a Greek myth. Or, rather, a Greek youth in Bacchus's entourage. He'd fit perfectly into Natoire's *Bacchus and Ariadne.*

Vaughn's fingers itched to draw him. Almost to draw *on* him, to trace his figure by feel in order to better capture it later. Vaughn's other hand, the one not in Jonah's hair, still held a fold of toga. Without quite bidding it to, it moved to Jonah's hip and gripped his body.

It had been so long since he'd touched anyone like this.

Instantly, there was a warm palm against his chest, worming its way under the sheet to rest on his skin. Vaughn sucked in a sharp breath.

It appeared Jonah wasn't as asleep as he pretended to be.

"I have to get you drunk and sit in your lap to get your attention," Jonah muttered, his eyes dark slits as he looked at where his fingers curled through the hair on Vaughn's pec, catching on it. Vaughn exhaled shakily. It had also been a very long time since he'd *been* touched like that.

"Jonah . . ."

All Vaughn wanted was to keep touching him like this. Hold him closer. Kiss him again. But that was it. Nothing more. And judging by the way Jonah was looking at him, the way he was thumbing Vaughn's nipple, he was mentally a lot further than second base. Again.

But these were lazy, slow touches. Nothing urgent. Vaughn thought he could leave now and Jonah wouldn't snarl at him again. He could leave and look up the new word sliding in his brain like a barely gripped fish.

"It's late," Vaughn said. "I need to go."

Jonah's hand pressed firmer against his chest. "Don't."

"See you tomorrow. Today. Later."

"For fuck's sake, Vaughn. Stay."

Vaughn turned to Adrian. "What time is it?"

Adrian was watching them, eyebrows raised. "Time for all good boys and girls to go to bed," he said, before yawning. A chorus of yawns followed his.

"See? Get up," Vaughn said to Jonah.

"Make me." Jonah rooted further into his lap, scowling.

Vaughn slid his hands under Jonah's torso and lifted him up and onto Adrian. "Here. A present for you."

Adrian winked at Vaughn, then mock-scowled. "I don't like this present. Got a receipt?"

Jonah flipped him the finger as Vaughn stood up. He waved good-bye to the group and walked to the entryway to get dressed and call a taxi.

Jonah didn't follow him. Vaughn wasn't sure if he was relieved or upset by that. Either way, he needed time to research and reflect.

CHAPTER EIGHT

Jonah strode towards the shiny apartment building, squinting bleary-eyed at it. The sun was bright in the wintery blue sky, making the slush and snow around him sparkle. Big freaking difference from last night, which was down in Jonah's memories as *That* Toga Party now. The one where Vaughn Daisy Scarf Hargrave had finally shown some interest, and Jonah had fucked it up by throwing a goddamn fit because the dude didn't want to screw right away.

There was nothing wrong with that. He listened when people told him no. But Vaughn's no had been different somehow. After that scintillating kiss, Jonah had thought he'd finally had the guy locked down, that he'd get the tension, the *itch*, fucked out of him by a guy who knew his name and where he came from, that he'd won Vaughn over.

But. *No.*

And he'd turned around to the nearest hot piece of ass, desperate for the mindlessness of sex and, in some little twisted part of him, to prove to Vaughn how replaceable he was. That Jonah might not push a rejection, but he'd sure as fuck show him what he was missing.

Good job, Jonah. He'd fucked someone, someone had rimmed him, blowjobs had happened, all of it releasing him from the sad sack currently masquerading as his head. He'd floated with endorphins, his anger drained as though sex had turned valves on an emotional grate.

And he'd found Vaughn waiting like none of it had mattered.

What the hell was wrong with him? With both of them? Last night didn't fit into anything Jonah knew about guys. He'd never reacted like that to a rejection before. And he'd never had a guy waiting for him before, especially when sex was off the table and the guy wore an expression like he'd been kicked.

It sat weirdly in his stomach along with the über-rich atmosphere of this neighbourhood. God, he hated this part of town. Vaughn was lucky he was worth visiting.

And *so* pretty. That stupid realistic toga of his hadn't covered all the goods. Those toned legs with the right amount of hair, lickable shoulders and arms, and his *chest*. Holy gods of gay men, Vaughn had been blessed with perfect chest hair. Jonah should probably thank Carson for the party theme, but after the shit he'd pulled dancing with Vaughn, tonguing him like that—because Jonah had been watching—it wasn't going to happen.

Today wasn't going down like last time. No way was he just going to sit on that sofa and play video games for a few hours again. Jonah wasn't exactly sure what to expect though. This was totally out-of-bounds for him. He knew what he wanted to do—redoing that kiss was a vital first step—but Vaughn's response was an unknown entity. All he could imagine was Vaughn finally fucking him or the guy listing all the reasons why he wouldn't sleep with him, then telling him to leave.

Was this what strings felt like? All these stupid questions running like squirrels in his head? Yet he still moved towards Vaughn's shiny building as though pulled there. Saying *Fuck it* and looking for the next guy wasn't even an option, because he knew Vaughn and Vaughn knew him, and somehow that made all the difference. Jonah couldn't not go. He couldn't not see him.

As soon as he entered the building, the concierge guy greeted him *by name*. Jonah waved, then paused, wondering if they were going to go through the whole calling-Vaughn rigmarole again. When the concierge gestured towards the elevator with a smile, he realized they weren't. *Oh. Nice.*

Upstairs, he went to Vaughn's door and pressed the buzzer, praising the gods again when the door opened to reveal Vaughn in a black sweater and jeans, barefoot and with bedhead. He had deep bags under his eyes, and dark stubble lined his jaw and neck. *Goddamn.*

"Good afternoon," Vaughn said.

Game time. No point in delaying the inevitable. "Hi." Jonah walked in, making Vaughn back up. "We've got unfinished business." He zipped off his coat.

Vaughn winced. "About that—"

"C'mere." Jonah dumped the coat, put his arms around Vaughn's neck, and kissed him. He tasted of mint and that underlying flavour of human, of Vaughn. *So good.* He flicked his tongue along Vaughn's lips, but they stayed shut—then kissed back. He pressed forward, lining himself against Vaughn, feeling those long arms close around him. And *yes*, that was a hard cock in the right place. Electricity rolled through Jonah, and he latched on tight, fisting shirt and hair. *Come here. Give me more.*

Vaughn groaned before breaking the kiss. "Jonah."

Jonah pressed his mouth against Vaughn's stubble to feel the prickle, fingers drifting through curls and down his neck, tasting the skin before he hit sweater. *So sweet. So good.*

"Jonah, we need to talk."

Uh-uh, bad idea. Jonah ran clawed hands down Vaughn's back. "Talking is overrated."

"I mean it." Vaughn pulled away ever so slightly.

This was really *not* going to happen? Again? "About *what*?"

Vaughn's mouth twisted. "I said it was complicated."

Right. His interesting complicated sexual shit. Fucking bring it on. "Whatever it is, I can work with it." Jonah leaned in to kiss his neck.

"I told you I don't like casual sex." There was a hitch to his voice.

"So we'll do this twice," Jonah murmured into his skin. Slight salt. *Mmm.*

Vaughn ducked away from his mouth. "What I didn't want to say in the food court or at the party," he continued, "is that I don't like sex at all."

Jonah opened his mouth, ready to argue, but the words filtered through, and he coughed instead. "Come again?"

Vaughn's heartbeat pulsed next to Jonah's. Quick, hard. Vaughn swallowed. "I don't like having sex. What we're doing is great, but if sex is where you're heading with this, then I suggest we pause and reevaluate."

Was this for real? Vaughn still had his arms around Jonah, and Jonah could smell him, taste him, *feel* him.

Especially in one place. Jonah pressed against his erection. "The hell's this, then? A paintbrush? A ruler?"

Vaughn shook his head. "I'm not impotent. And getting hard isn't exactly difficult. Like you never got hard in the middle of math class?"

Was he saying kissing Jonah was like goddamn *math class*? Humiliation flooded him. Jonah let go and tried to jerk away, but Vaughn's arms kept him there.

"I'm sorry." Vaughn's hand stroked his back. "I phrased that badly. Sorry. I think I'd have to be dickless to not be hard around you. What I meant was that everything works, but a boner for me isn't an automatic yes to sex."

Context was everything, Jonah understood that, but this context had them literally breathing on each other. How could they be this close and Vaughn not want him? Jonah pulled away, and this time Vaughn let him.

"If you get hard when my dick's next to yours," Jonah snapped, "I'd say you're feeding me some bullshit by saying you don't like sex."

Vaughn's mouth tightened. "I know it's confusing. I've been . . ." He glanced over his shoulder, at a laptop on the breakfast bar. "Maybe the way to put it is that my body's okay with it, but my mind's not on board. I don't *want* it, psychologically."

Psychologically. Like, what, his brain wasn't attached to his dick? Jonah had had surprise boners before—everybody past puberty with a dick had—so Jonah knew sometimes it genuinely wasn't anything sexual. But the other way around, when you saw a guy and you just thought *Holy shit* and everything in your body just pointed at him and you wanted him naked and under you so badly there wasn't room for anything else in your head—that guaranteed a boner. Dicks weren't always attached to the brain, but brains were solidly attached to dicks. So if Vaughn was at least down for kissing, it followed suit that he'd be down for more.

In Jonah's experience, anyway.

"I don't get it," Jonah said.

Vaughn slumped. "It's the best I have."

Was this going to be a repeat of last night? Another brush-off? "Try again," Jonah said, his voice thick. *Damn it.* What was he getting upset for?

At least *I don't like sex* wasn't *I don't like you.* As far as excuses went, that wasn't bad. Even if this felt a little bit like *I don't like you.*

Get a grip, Sondern.

Vaughn bit his lip, gazing at Jonah. Those grey eyes were sad, almost pleading with him to understand. "You said sex for you was like chocolate," he said eventually.

"Yeah."

"You prefer dark, but you have milk because it's still chocolate."

"Yeah."

"I don't like chocolate." His eyes were locked on Jonah's. "I can see why people like it." He grimaced. "Well, sort of. I see that it's sweet and melts and is pleasurable. But I don't understand why that's such a great experience. It's just okay. I'd rather," his mouth twitched, "I'd rather have cake."

Jonah blinked. "That's still something sweet."

"Well, yes. I don't mind kissing and touching people and things like that."

"But that's basically what sex *is.*"

Vaughn rubbed his hands over his face. "Not to me. When genitals come into play, it just gets . . . Look, I've spent half the night researching this. There's a word for it: asexuality. People were talking about it at the party last night."

Jonah stared at him. Asexuality. That sounded freaking *clinical.* Was that supposed to make sense to him? "Are you for real? Are you actually serious?"

Vaughn slumped. "Yeah."

"What the *shit*, Vaughn?" Jonah bent down to pick up his coat. He needed to get out of here before he embarrassed himself any further. Before Vaughn said something he really didn't want to hear, like *By the way, I only kissed you to prove a point about how much I don't want you* or *You keep coming on to me and I don't like you anymore so we can't be friends.* "You think you could've told me that before I freaking threw myself at you?"

Vaughn made a surprised noise. "What? When? It's hard to talk about. I didn't think it was normal."

"It's not."

"There's an entire community of people who say it is." There was a hard edge to his voice. He turned and gestured at his laptop. "Hundreds of thousands of people who share my experience. There's this whole"—his hands waved in front of him—"side of human sexuality no one talks about. It's so *validating*. It's like realizing I'm gay again. Only even better because it's somewhat more accurate. I have a clear idea of what I am."

Well, fucking good for him. Jonah put his coat on. "*I* thought you were gay." God, he was never going to live this down.

Why did *this* guy have to be the one who didn't want him?

Vaughn stepped towards him. "You're going?"

"Uh, yeah? Like I can stay?"

Vaughn frowned. "You can." He reached out and took Jonah's hand. "Please don't go. I liked your entrance." A small smile tugged at his mouth. "I didn't expect it, but it was kind of wonderful. I like kissing you. And I do like men." Vaughn's thumb stroked Jonah's skin. "I've thought of myself as gay for years. Just . . . just not particularly good at it because I didn't feel attracted enough to want sex, or enjoyed sex when I did have it." He looked down. "I know it's not what you want. But I like having you here. I want you here."

Oh man. *Oh man.* That wasn't what he'd expected. Sex or no sex, that was usually the deal. Not this in-between thing, this . . . They were *holding hands.*

Jonah took a deep breath.

The information all started making connections in his head. Sort of. Asexuality: that sounded vaguely familiar. There might have been a talk about it during his LGBT society days at university—not that he ever attended the talks. All the intense identity discussion parts of the club meet-ups weren't the parts he'd been interested in. Last night's discussion felt like it might have been relevant, but he'd been too focused on the feel of Vaughn's hands on him.

"*I liked kissing you.*" How did that not translate into further action? He studied Vaughn—the stubble, the floppy hair, the slim body, the hair he knew was under the sweater. God, it was *criminal* that this guy wasn't doing the deed.

And Vaughn looked uncomfortable now. He let go of Jonah's hand. "If you want to go, I won't stop you."

"It's not that. I'm processing stuff."

Vaughn dragged one hand through his hair. "I know it's out of left field. If it helps, I wish I could be what you're used to, but I can't."

"Huh?"

Vaughn crossed his arms. "I can't be sexual. Let you do whatever you were planning to do to me. Reciprocate. Pin you down and top you, or bottom, or whatever it was you wanted." He'd gone red now. "I wish I could."

"But you can't." The idea was starting to make a little sense now. "Because you don't want to do that." And it sounded like it was a deeper level of *don't want to*. Deeper than simply not being in the mood for it.

I don't like chocolate.

The food analogy helped. He could understand that. Sort of.

"Pretty much," Vaughn said.

A connection snapped. Their conversation over lunch. *Ah.* "This is why you don't do relationships." Oh, this explained it. This explained why Vaughn read as Serious Boyfriend Material but was still single.

Vaughn nodded, but he didn't look happy. "Yes. Boyfriends like their sex."

Wait. It wasn't about *him*. It was nothing to do with Jonah, not really. This wasn't in reaction to Jonah; this was a constant thing. This would have happened to any guy who'd hit on Vaughn. *Thank fuck.* Somehow, realizing that eased an unnoticed ache in his throat.

"You would seriously rather be single and without sex than in a relationship where you had to have sex?" he asked.

Vaughn gave him an odd look. "Which would you rather be: celibate or married to a woman and expected to have sex with her? And to enjoy it?"

Jonah shuddered at the choice. Both options were terrible. "Yeah, okay. Fine." He frowned. "But you've *had* sex?"

Vaughn nodded. "Men and women. Neither did much for me."

He'd had sex, and he still didn't like it? Jonah couldn't understand that at all. "*Dude.*"

"Whatever you're thinking, I've thought it before."

"Have you had it more than once?"

Vaughn raised an eyebrow. "Yes."

"With multiple people?"

"Yes."

"More than one guy?"

"Not at once, but yes."

"Did you come?"

Vaughn looked embarrassed. "Sometimes."

Sometimes. *Sometimes.* Jesus. Well, even *sometimes* meant orgasms had happened. "You came! Wasn't that a good thing?"

"Orgasms are easy." He shrugged. "They're fun."

He said they were fun like Jonah would say *I work out.* "So, you jerk off?"

"Sometimes."

Again with the *sometimes.* "But you don't like sex? If you can come, then doesn't that mean you *enjoyed* it?" Jonah asked incredulously

"No." Vaughn shifted his weight. "I didn't. With another person, it's . . ." He seemed to struggle for words. "Messy. And awkward. It doesn't feel natural to me. It's a lot of effort. I can do it, but no, it's not enjoyable. It doesn't bring me closer to the person, it takes me further away from them. It's lonely." He stared at Jonah for a long moment, then cleared his throat and glanced away. "So I decided not to do it anymore." He leaned against the wall of the short hallway. "Can I take your coat, by the way?"

"And that works for you?" Jonah ignored the coat question. He was standing next to the door with his coat and boots still on, so *what.* He wasn't letting Vaughn steer the conversation away from this.

Vaughn nodded, his face clearing. "Yes. Much happier without it."

Wow. Jonah couldn't wrap his head around that. "I can't imagine going longer than a week without sex."

"I've noticed."

"I love sex. Love it. Every guy I've ever met loves it. This confuses the fuck out of me."

Vaughn nodded, hair falling across his face. "Believe me, I know. I'm fully aware of what men are supposed to want. Imagine my confusion when I realized I didn't share that."

Jonah glanced at the laptop. "And there are other guys like you?"

"Yeah. It's a wide spectrum, so it seems slightly different for everyone, but there are other guys like me. Other people." Vaughn finally smiled, small and relieved. "Sex isn't everything, and that's okay."

It wasn't like Jonah hadn't thought that before, but he wasn't sure he'd ever heard someone else say it with such sincerity and calm. Such *peace*.

Especially when Jonah didn't think he could deal with life without sex there to send him flying. What else was there to ease the bad parts?

"So what's the deal with me?" Jonah asked.

Vaughn went pink. "The deal?"

"You don't want to do me because you don't want to do *anyone*. Right?" He thought he got that right, but he suddenly needed to hear it from Vaughn.

"I would like to assure you"—Vaughn's eyes bored into his and his voice went deep—"that were I possessed of the standard amount of sexual attraction and desire that people supposedly have, I would fuck you whenever you wanted me to."

A shiver ran up Jonah's spine. Oh *God*. The image of what that would be like was mesmerizing.

"G-good." Okay. That was clear. His voice had gone hoarse for some reason. "So what happened last night?"

Vaughn made a weird face, like he couldn't believe Jonah was asking that. "I like you. You're gorgeous. You know that, right? You must know that. I could kiss you for hours." He uncrossed his arms. "And I want to draw you."

A laugh escaped Jonah. "*What?*"

"I do. Your proportions are textbook. Your face is incredibly expressive."

Jonah put a hand up to his face, instantly self-conscious. Draw him? *Him*? Seriously? But he wasn't anyone. And what the hell were proportions?

"Obviously I won't if you don't—" A ringtone played, interrupting them. Vaughn looked at the breakfast bar, where his phone was now lit up next to the laptop. "Excuse me." He turned to answer it.

Jonah leaned against the wall, needing something solid under him.

What a revelation. Jesus. He hadn't been this surprised by a potential hookup's personal shit since the last guy who'd downright rejected him—a Grindr dude who'd taken one look at him and spat out that he'd expected someone taller and way younger looking, then marched away in a huff.

Asexual. Huh.

He pulled out his phone and made a note to look it up later, see if it really was as normal as Vaughn claimed it was. Jonah had never heard of a guy who blatantly did *not* want to have sex, but hey—what he hadn't heard of filled libraries. It reminded him of those geeky guys who wanted a relationship, the ones who didn't sleep around or hit up the scene the way he and Adrian did. Vaughn was basically the extreme version of them.

Which was disappointing. He had to admit it: he'd been looking forward to seeing what Vaughn's sex face was like, to taking those expensive, fitted clothes off him and exploring the skin underneath, and really seeing what he was like without the fancy shit gathered around him.

That kiss was probably all he'd get. He closed his eyes. Minty. Sweet. Vaughn had kissed back, then broken it off. He understood, but Jonah still felt a small sting of thwarted desire. There was that tiny ache in his throat again at the idea of never seeing Vaughn naked, of never running his hands through that glorious chest hair, of never kissing him again. Sure. No big deal.

It *wasn't* a big deal. It was fine. So what if Vaughn wasn't in the cards? Jonah had an app and an entire city full of gay men who *were* willing to have sex with him. He'd lost nothing by trying this.

Only, he didn't want to leave.

He opened his eyes and saw Vaughn sighing into his phone. Still hot, still causing little aches and shivers in Jonah just from being there in front of him.

Jonah looked around the apartment instead. He took in the gleaming kitchen, the huge living room and sofa and TV, the game console, the magnificent view out the windows. The sheer shininess of the place got to him.

Maybe it was for the best. Jonah had never had this, had never seen the inside of a place like this except in realtor pictures and magazines. He didn't belong in here, with all this perfection. He, with his multiple sets of foster parents and a mother who'd disappeared and a father he'd never known and his loan debt and a dream to someday live in a place a tenth as nice as this, was an alien here. This kind of wealth was intoxicating. He probably shouldn't be around it, looking at what he couldn't have.

"Dad, you know what Mom can be like. There is absolutely no call for you to come over," Vaughn said into his phone.

Oh, he was talking to his father.

Jonah glanced back at the TV. That was the original reason for coming over: finishing *Halo*. Hopefully that offer was still good, because even if he wasn't getting laid, and this place felt totally beyond him, *and* Vaughn had just come out to him, Jonah wasn't ready to leave yet.

"I like you. I want to draw you."

Sounded like Vaughn would be okay to hang out. They could play games for a while. That would be cool. After this discussion, Jonah was totally ready to shoot aliens.

He wasn't, however, ready to think about that *"I like you"* or how deep it went.

He glanced at Vaughn, who was scowling and waving a hand around. *"No.* Don't listen to her about that, she doesn't know what she's talking about. I don't go to those places." He paused. "Okay, I go to *those*, but can we seriously not talk about this?"

He looked really tired, even if he did have a kind of strange energy today.

Oh, yeah, he'd been up late researching his new community of people who didn't have sex. Celibacy? Or abstinence. Or both, even. What was the difference again?

He should probably look that up too.

"No. I have a friend over," Vaughn said. He glanced at Jonah sheepishly, then his eyes widened. "That would imply the brunch was mandatory. Dad, it's *brunch*. She has one every other weekend. Let me reiterate, *I said I was busy*."

He was arguing with his dad about *brunch*. It was like all the rich people stereotypes rolled into one. Jonah bet there would be mimosas and fancy yogurt and pastries and salmon and shit. He wondered what Vaughn's parents were like. Maybe his brunching mom was the way rich women were in Jonah's head: alcohol-fuelled and pretty beyond her years and addicted to shopping and covered in jewellery. And his dad was probably overweight, with a suit permanently fused to his skin and more credit cards than sense.

Or maybe Vaughn's dad had his son's dark hair and grey eyes. And he was chewing him out for not meeting his mother for a family meal, even though it was *brunch* and not dinner like most normal families had. Jonah had seen that expression on Vaughn's face before. He'd seen it on the faces of kids whenever their real moms nagged at them about doing their homework or staying out late. Or whenever their moms had hugged them and kissed them, and they'd protested because it had been *embarrassing*.

A pain hit him in the stomach. Tears threatened. He swallowed, then made himself breathe, forced the tears back. What was this? Where was this coming from?

When Vaughn tutted and said, "Of course I love you and Mom, but does that mean I have to spend every weekend eating eggs with you?" the tears returned in full force. Shit. *Shit*. Jonah turned aside and dashed his sleeve across his eyes.

Get it together, Sondern. Figure this out. You can't stand in some guy's hallway and cry because he told his dad he loved him.

God, he was pathetic.

He was way over the parents thing. Like, listening to his friends talk on the phone to their parents was annoying. So intrusive. *He* didn't have anyone with bad timing calling him, interrupting his life with questions about food and partners and shit. He didn't have to worry about that.

Maybe, a small voice said, *it's a thing you want to worry about and be frustrated by. Maybe you want what everyone else seems to have.*

Yeah, and if he was asking for parents, he'd ask for a home and siblings and grandparents and birthday presents and a goddamned dog while he was at it.

Claire's been calling you and interrupting your life, that small voice piped up again.

That, right there—that had to be it. The news that his mother's lawyer wanted to speak to him. *That* was the problem.

Time to cut it loose. Find out what this lawyer wanted and shut her down.

He pulled out his phone and texted Claire. *Hi. Pls send the #. Thx.*

Then he put the cell away, the churning in his stomach transitioning into a weird light-headedness.

"Look, I'll visit next weekend," Vaughn said. "I have to go. I have a friend over." Pause. "Bye, Dad." Another pause. "*Bye, Dad.*" He hung up and exhaled. "Sorry about that. When the parental units get started, they don't let up."

Jonah made sure his eyes were dry and turned around. Vaughn looked at him and startled, dropping his phone. It bounced off the edge of the counter and onto the hardwood floor. Vaughn didn't seem to notice. "Are you all right?"

Jonah blinked at him. "Yeah. Is your *phone* all right?"

Vaughn frowned and picked it up. "Cracked. Again." He looked straight at Jonah. "Are you sure you're all right? You look like you're about to faint."

"I'm fine."

Vaughn came forward and pulled him to the breakfast bar, sitting him on a stool. "Here. Sit for a moment. I don't know if you want to leave or stay, but at least have a cup of water." He rounded the counter and went digging in the cupboards.

Jonah shrugged out of his coat, head still trippy. Water sounded good. A full glass appeared before him, and when he drank, the coolness of it grounded him. The light-headedness retreated a bit.

"You brushed off your parents?" he asked. Vaughn nodded. Jonah stared at his glass, seeing the refraction of light and image through the water, the imprint of his lips on the rim. His hand curved lightly around it. Suddenly he was gazing across twenty years at an ice cream cone melting a thick vanilla dribble over that same hand. He blinked.

His throat tightened. That had been years ago. That had been the last time he'd seen his mother, and he'd been too busy licking the ice cream to pay much attention to her walking away.

This was a glass of water, and he was twenty-four years old.

"You should spend time with your mom," he said, throat suddenly raspy.

Vaughn shrugged. "So my dad says. It wouldn't be so bad if she didn't use brunch as a means to get my brother and me socializing. Making connections." He sighed. "It *is* important to her. I said I'd go next week." He looked aside. "He told me to invite you."

Jonah reared back. "*No.*"

Vaughn chuckled. "I don't blame you. Brunch can be tedious. The food is usually excellent though."

"Why would I be invited?"

"You're a friend." Vaughn seemed uncomfortable. "I mean, I hope you're still a friend."

He'd told his father about Jonah? And that was it? That was all he needed to be invited out?

And Vaughn hoped they were friends? Okay. Good. They could still spend time together. His gut started feeling weird again. Good weird this time.

Suddenly Jonah really needed to shoot at aliens. That sounded nice and simple and unrelated to strange feelings. "We cool to keep gaming?"

Vaughn's eyes lit up. "Yes. Absolutely!"

"Then yeah, we're friends."

A sly smile made its way onto Vaughn's face. Combined with the stubble and the hair and the eyes— *Shit*, Jonah's cock was taking an interest again. Vaughn crossed his arms. "I see how it is. You want me for my Xbox."

Jonah raised an eyebrow. "Seeing as your body is off the table, yeah."

Vaughn laughed. Actually laughed. "I'll set up the game." He went over to the TV.

Jonah's phone dinged with an incoming message, and he pulled it out. Claire had texted the number to him. *I hope this contact is something good. I'm always here if you need me.*

Yup. He was officially over this noise. He drank his water, turned his phone to silent, and joined Vaughn on the couch.

Vaughn couldn't believe how well that had gone. Like, *so* well.

Especially given how spaced-out he had been. He'd had maybe three or four hours' sleep, because after coming home from the party, he'd gone straight onto Google. A few clicks had brought up AVEN, some LiveJournal and Tumblr blogs, and one or two newspaper articles, and the next thing he'd known, it had been close to dawn, and he'd been nowhere near done scrolling through forum posts and articles.

He'd taken a break to sleep, but apart from that, he'd done nothing but read all day. He couldn't get enough information or personal stories, because for once he saw himself in them. All the spaces between his experiences and other people's, the gaps where there should have been lust and desire were *explained* and given a name.

The sites described an orientation directed at nobody, a kind of sexuality that manifested itself as no sexual attraction and minimal sexual behaviour. Not wanting people. Not liking sex. Being indifferent to sex. Liking sex, but no urge to have it. Not having a libido. Having a libido but disliking it or it being low enough to not matter. All of that was covered under the asexual label.

The language that was casually tossed around on these sites— *sex-aversion, romantic orientation, squish, grey-A*—seemed to pick up all of his confused, scattered thoughts and make them coherent, and it was *magical.* There were other people like him out there, other people who'd found meaning in the relative absence of their desires.

The last time he'd felt this validated was when he'd realized he liked guys and came out as gay. That at least had always been obvious to him. But this had been subtler, a break between the gay cultural narrative and his life, and it finally had a name.

And now Jonah knew too.

He hadn't known what to expect from today. After last night, he hadn't been sure if Jonah would want to spend time with him anymore, and he definitely hadn't been sure how Jonah would take the news. Because now that he could shape and hold out his reality in his hand, he could explain to him what his limits were and why, and be able to answer his questions. And that had gone so well!

Okay, reasonably well. Jonah had gone from guarded and wary to confused to quietly understanding. If he was disappointed, he didn't show it. Right now he swore at the TV screen as an Elite pwned his character. But there had been a moment there when Vaughn could've sworn Jonah had been almost *upset*.

But Vaughn knew Jonah, knew his proclivities. Especially after last night, which Vaughn didn't think he'd ever forget. Jonah had sex with strangers on a weekly basis. Seemed to need it in exactly the way Vaughn didn't. Who was Vaughn in the grand scheme of his sexual life? A blip. Someone who'd said no. So why would Jonah be upset about *him*?

But he was still here. And while Vaughn wasn't sure how he felt about being so easily processed and put aside, he was grateful Jonah had stayed and had *wanted* to stay. Even this, sitting on his couch and playing *Halo* with him, was great. They could still spend time together.

Friends.

But that kiss. The way Jonah had focused on him. The feel of Jonah's hair under Vaughn's fingers. The firm heat of Jonah's hands on him. Vaughn wanted more of that touch.

There was a whole section on the AVEN site about tips for being in a relationship with someone more sexual, how to handle each other's needs in a way that was respectful of each person's sexuality. He'd read through post after post of people talking about their relationships, how they made them work and how they failed, drinking in the idea that maybe he could be with someone, even though he was the way he was. That maybe all the things he saw as lacking weren't ever that necessary or important in the first place, and that what he wanted, in all its vanilla simplicity, was enough.

Winter daylight streamed through the window, bringing out the gold streaks in Jonah's hair. Vaughn mentally traced his profile, trying to memorize the angles between his nose and forehead and jaw for later. An explosion from the screen returned him to the game.

Jonah had shot him.

"Hey!"

"Serves you right for not paying attention," Jonah said.

Vaughn forced himself to settle back. "I'll make sure to never look at your face again." He respawned and set out to recover the rocket launcher he'd dropped.

After a moment, Jonah asked, "Were you doing the drawing-me thing?"

Vaughn felt himself blush. "Yes."

"I don't get that. Why me?" Jonah's gaze didn't shift from the screen.

You're beautiful, and I want to capture that. Lord. Vaughn should attempt to explain without sounding like he was trying to seduce the man. "Like I said earlier: your proportions are textbook. You're very expressive. It would be fun to draw you."

Jonah shifted. "You saying I'm hot enough to draw but not to fuck?"

Oh, for God's sake. "Drawing is different. Creating art is a different urge."

"Is it? You sure you're not taking all that sex you're not having and putting the, I don't know, the energy into your paintings?"

There was a grin on his face. He was teasing him. *Teasing.* Vaughn began to search the map for Jonah's character. Someone needed revenge pwning.

"I assure you that's not the case," he said. "Look, you're just . . . Your face would be interesting to draw because you have wonderful expressions. That's all I mean."

"I thought artists only drew hot people."

Vaughn wanted to roll his eyes. "No. They do not. They draw two kinds of people: those who are visually compelling and those who pay them for a portrait."

"Oh yeah?" Jonah's lip curled, and he pulled the trigger on his controller with unnecessary force. "So even an orphan like me could be in a picture in a gallery?"

An orphan?

Right, he'd mentioned being in foster care. So his parents were dead? Oh no. He didn't seem to like talking about them, so Vaughn needed to tread carefully.

"People's histories tend to add to the significance of their depiction on canvas," he explained. "It's not just the rich and wealthy who are immortalized. Servants, prostitutes, office workers, refugees . . . Entire families. Orphans. To answer your question: yes. Anyone can be in a picture in a gallery—it depends on the picture and the artist."

Jonah nodded once, sharply. "As long as they're *visually compelling*."

"You don't think you are?"

"I think I'm hot. But I'm one hot guy in a sea of hot guys." He gazed at Vaughn from the side of his eye. "I don't think that's enough to make me worth drawing."

"I disagree." The game had reached a travel section. Vaughn put down his controller and retrieved his phone. He pulled up his internet browser and searched for *Benefits Supervisor Sleeping*, then showed the picture to Jonah.

Jonah's eyes widened. "What the hell?"

"It currently holds the world record for the highest price paid for a painting by a living artist." Even though Lucian Freud had recently died, the record still stood.

"She's . . ." He watched Jonah struggle to describe her gently. "Not hot."

"That's not really relevant. Art isn't about what's considered attractive or beautiful. It can be. But beauty and symmetry in a face doesn't always make an interesting portrait. The expression on a face, who that person is, and the qualities the artist puts into their depiction—all of that goes into an arresting portrait."

Jonah watched him steadily. Vaughn gazed back, feeling heat rising to his face. What was he thinking? Oh God, he'd been rambling again, hadn't he? "What is it?"

"You're so fucking intelligent, you know that?" Jonah almost spat out. "It's unreal." He looked at the painting again, glanced back at the mural, then turned to Vaughn. "You think you can draw a good picture of me?"

Vaughn put his phone down. "Maybe. I'd like to try."

Jonah shrugged. "I'll think about it."

That was promising. Vaughn didn't know why Jonah wouldn't think he'd make a good subject, but if he was willing to at least consider it, that was very positive. Vaughn might actually get to do it, to re-create his features on paper. The idea was giddying.

But he still had questions about that orphan thing. He decided to keep his voice light and casual, as though they were discussing the gameplay. "You're an orphan?"

"Effectively."

"Is that why you were in foster care?"

He could almost *feel* the tension start radiating from Jonah. "No. My mother left me outside a grocery store when I was five, and no one could find her. I have no idea who my dad is because he's not listed on my birth certificate. *That's* why I went into foster care."

Oh. Vaughn had lowered his controller, ready to reach out to him, but a glare from Jonah quickly turned him back to the game. "I'm sorry to hear that," he said lamely.

"Most people are."

"I'm glad it hasn't affected your ability to—"

"Focus on the game, pretty boy. My tragic past doesn't matter."

Vaughn wanted to argue that he kind of thought it did, but the bitterness in Jonah's voice stopped him. A vaguely snippy Jonah on his couch was better than no Jonah at all.

And that was that. They finished the game, stretched, ate whatever food Vaughn had in his kitchen, and discussed the other Halo games. Vaughn tried not to overtly study him, because he didn't want to make him more uncomfortable than he already had, but it was difficult. He wanted to grab some paper and pencils, and while sketching his expressions, ask more about foster care and how Jonah had ended up at a Bay Street insurance company. He wanted to know about his university days and whether he considered Carson and Adrian and the other guys Vaughn had met at the party acquaintances or close friends. He wanted to know *everything* about him.

But after that kiss from earlier, Jonah had retreated into some inner, brooding place. He was still sharp, full of edges and jokes, but there were glimpses of hidden vulnerable depths—like that orphan mention and his inability to understand why Vaughn would want to draw him—that made Vaughn worry slightly. Only glimpses. And only slightly.

Maybe he just wanted an excuse to hug the guy.

And by the time Jonah left, with a promise to return for another afternoon of gaming, Vaughn was hopeful they had some kind of shot at being friends. It was better than the nothing he'd assumed they would have before last night.

Vaughn turned and surveyed his apartment. It looked much the same as before. An extra glass out, an extra plate of half-eaten food, a few dried salt marks from Jonah's boots. All little clues that someone else had been here.

The salt marks on the floor were from where Jonah had stood and kissed him.

Vaughn walked around them, feeling silly. He cleared away the dishes, then moved through his living room and looked out the window. The sunset cast long shadows and pink light away from his building, and the city was a dappled pattern of cool pastels and snow; Morisot could have painted it.

He turned his back on the view. His apartment felt empty now. His evening stretched ahead of him, unoccupied and somewhat listless.

The snarling lion mural suddenly looked out of place in this room. He studied it, then imagined a blank wall. What would fit better now? Not a lion. Perhaps a landscape. Or something with an abstract element. Perhaps even something surreal. He could paint a melting toilet in the middle of a desert, or the sea with a lit lightbulb bobbing on it. Something different.

Or, and this thought did make him move into his studio, he could try to sketch Jonah from memory again and see how close he got to the real thing. Would that be strange? Inappropriate?

Pathetic?

Did it matter anymore? Telling Jonah about his newfound identity was something he'd had to do, to be clear and honest. But Vaughn knew without a doubt that whatever had burst between them last night, the energy that had caused Jonah to rush straight into his arms today, was stopped short by his admission. If there was any sort of antithesis to passion, asexuality had to be it. Drawing him now would be pure indulgence. Vain indulgence.

But he couldn't stop himself from trying, just as much as he couldn't stop himself from kissing the guy back. He began outlining a head on his paper. These pencil lines would be as close to Jonah as he'd ever be. He might get a friendly hug, in time, but another kiss wouldn't happen. Vaughn's head could be in the clouds sometimes, but he was absolutely, completely certain that Jonah would never try that with him again.

Maybe this could be close enough.

CHAPTER NINE

Vaughn left his apartment building and crunched his way slowly through the snow. The weekend still swirled in his head, memories flickering in and out without any connection or control. Beer and pot. Hockey games. Discovering his sexual apathy had a name and forums. The feel of Jonah's hair in his fingers. *Halo.* Finishing a piece, actually *finishing* it. Sketching out a new mural. Replacing his phone's cracked screen with a new one. Logging onto Tumblr and realizing his follower count had spiked by fifty people.

A strange weekend but a good one overall.

Sort of. His chest ached every time he remembered those kisses.

He tried to force thoughts of Jonah out of his head by the time he opened the gallery. After all, the December exhibition was in, the entrance foyer looked very festive with Christmas decorations, and he really was inordinately excited about this year's exhibition. He completely adored it, in all its interpretive, probably blasphemous glory. Every day since it had been put in place, he'd circulated the floor, taking in the various ways artists had interpreted Christian symbols. There were iterations of the cross (one piece was broken sticks of wood), the *Pietà*, the *Last Supper*, altars, and so on. Barinski's *Veil* draped dramatically from the ceiling in one room. Some of the pieces were quite gory: mutilated limbs hanging off plinths, and a painting of a crucified woman bleeding from between her legs, which made Vaughn uncomfortable on multiple levels. Despite the controversial nature of some of the pieces, so far the reception had been excellent. A few critics had been by, and he expected reviews to appear in the press this week.

He automatically went through the usual morning routine: turned off the security system, locked the door behind him, changed his shoes—sky-blue espadrilles today—and stowed his snow boots in the closet near the front desk, opened the office, set up the coffee machine, read through emails.

Right before opening time, he did his usual meander around the gallery to double-check everything was clean and in place. The upstairs photography exhibition remained dauntingly harrowing, as did the Christian symbolism one on the ground floor. Limbs, sticks, blood, and all. Someone had left a bag of chips in the middle of the floor, and he picked it up with an annoyed huff.

As he completed the loop of the gallery, wondering if it was too soon to text Jonah about another game night, he turned the corner to the final room of the Christian symbolism exhibition and stopped dead.

Instead of a canvas depicting a crucified, menstruating woman, there was a blank wall.

Vaughn blinked. Blinked again.

The wall was still blank.

Shit.

He turned and swiftly checked the closets, but nothing.

Shit shit shit shit.

At the front desk, he pulled out his phone and brought up his contacts. His first instinct was to go to Maurice, but he paused over Maurice's name. Detective Meyer was also in his phone; she'd given him her number last week in case he "thought of anything she needed to know or if any new developments occurred."

This totally classified as a "new development."

She picked up, sounding perky for a police officer on a Monday morning. "Hello?"

"This is Vaughn Hargrave from the Delphi Gallery." He gazed out the front door at the grey, wintery day. Snow was falling. "There's been another theft."

"I'll be right there. Don't move or touch anything."

He already *had* though. He put up the Closed sign, then sighed deeply. This was going to ruin them. Was it too early for a statement like that? Who cared anymore?

After bracing himself, he called Angeline and told her the bad news, then left a message for Maurice. Then he pulled open his laptop and started checking for art-related vacancies in Toronto. There weren't many, so he expanded his search. By the time he'd found something in Vancouver and was seriously considering just how difficult that kind of move might be, Detective Meyer had arrived.

After letting her in, he guided her straight to the blank wall.

"I see," she said shortly. "This was the woman on her period."

"You remember it?"

She frowned at him. "Yes. It's pretty memorable." She turned around. "Take me through everything you did this morning."

He talked her through it all, step-by-step, even the coffee machine. When he made her one with the freshly brewed beans, she made a face but kept him moving.

"Do you always do a walk around the gallery in the mornings?" she asked.

"Yeah." They were on the second floor. "It's a nice, quiet time before visitors and management arrive. I get a chance to review and remember what's in here, plus check for any garbage."

"Uh-huh." She made a note, but her face was dubious. She made a few calls, took pictures of the bare wall, then turned to Vaughn. "You called the owners already? Good."

Angeline and Maurice arrived after the forensics team, so they had to wait outside while the team combed over the front door and the security system. From inside the gallery, Vaughn watched Maurice's face get purple with anger and Angeline grow very still and quiet.

"They're not happy," Detective Meyer remarked.

"No. This is the second theft in three weeks."

The insurance. Jonah.

He grimaced. "Oh God. The insurance people aren't going to be happy. Our premiums are going to go through the roof."

Detective Meyer was watching him closely. "Isn't it true that most galleries don't have theft insurance?"

He glanced at her. Hadn't Angeline already gone over this with her? "Yes."

"But your gallery does."

"Yeah. We can afford it, and I think Maurice thought it would attract artists to exhibit with us."

"Maurice?"

He nodded. "Yeah. It was his idea. Angeline and I didn't agree, but Cressida did."

Detective Meyer frowned. "Cressida? The other owner? *She* thought it was a good idea?"

He remembered the meeting they'd had. Angeline and Cressida had argued for half an hour while he and Maurice had kept silent and out of their way. "Yeah. She was all for it."

"And she persuaded her partner?"

Vaughn winced. "We keep Cressida happy." He paused, the memory of a furious Cress looming large. After the first theft last year, she'd picked up an office chair and smashed it in the alley behind the gallery, then vowed to do that to whomever had stolen from her gallery if her *connections* didn't get to the asshole first. "An angry Cressida is a bad Cressida."

"Bad how?"

He shook his head. "Bad. Don't piss her off."

Finally, Maurice and Angeline were allowed into the gallery. Angeline swept in first, aiming straight for Detective Meyer and Vaughn, while Maurice marched towards the gallery rooms.

"I cannot believe you called the police before calling us," Angeline said.

"I advised him to," Detective Meyer said crisply. "Will you follow me?"

Maurice rounded the corner, then they heard a loud, "*Fuck!*" from within the gallery.

"Which one is it?" Angeline asked.

"*Crucible*," Vaughn said.

"Goddamn it."

Maurice stormed back around the corner and went right up to Vaughn. "I'm done with this," he spat. "Where is it?"

Vaughn squinted at him. "Where is what?"

"The *piece*, Hargrave! Where did you stash it? How did you do this?"

What the *actual* fuck? Vaughn stared at him in shock, unable to process what he was hearing.

Angeline was frowning. So was Detective Meyer.

"A-are you implying *I* d-did this?" Vaughn managed to stammer out.

Maurice turned yet another shade of purple. "I'm outright *saying* you did, shithead."

"I didn't."

"Maurice," Angeline said warningly.

"Bullshit!" Maurice was so close Vaughn could feel spittle on his face. He stood his ground though. "You trust-fund, faggoty trash, don't lie to me. Think you can swindle us normal people, the ones with bills to pay and a business to run? Fuck you. Why us, Hargrave? Why?"

Vaughn's head spun. "Maurice, what the hell are you talking about?"

Angeline flung a hand between them, then stepped into the gap as they backed away. "Maurice, calm the fuck down, right the fuck now."

He glared at her but moved away. *Thank God.*

Detective Meyer just stood there making notes. Wasn't she supposed to step in at times like this?

"This is no time to throw accusations around." Angeline's brown eyes gored into Maurice's. "Give us some evidence or shut up."

Maurice looked aside and muttered.

"Thought so." Angeline turned to Vaughn. "You. Upstairs. We'll talk later."

Anything that would get him away from Maurice. Vaughn turned and collected his laptop with slightly shaky hands. Where the hell had that come from? Was Maurice on something? Unbelievable. Did almost three years of working together mean *nothing*?

He went upstairs to the office, followed by Detective Meyer. He sank into a chair with relief, his knees wobbly. Meyer stole Maurice's chair and rolled it over to Vaughn so they could talk.

"I didn't steal the pieces," he said.

She nodded. "I believe you."

Did she? Vaughn wasn't sure if he believed *her*. Weren't detectives meant to be duplicitously understanding?

"That was quite a performance," she said. "Interesting that he raised the wealth angle. Your family *is* quite wealthy."

He sighed. "So what?"

"So why put up with Maurice if you're independently wealthy?"

"It's not my wealth, it's family wealth. If it goes, it goes." He gestured at the office. "I love art. I want to work with it. Having enough money to live on for the rest of my life without a job lets me do work I want." He leaned forward, resting his elbows on his knees. "I wouldn't be able to live on this salary if I didn't have money."

Her lips thinned. "You might be surprised. So you do this for the art?"

"Yeah."

"Put up with Maurice for the art?"

He shook his head. "Maurice has never been like that before." He'd dropped the odd jealous joke about Vaughn's wealth occasionally, but Vaughn was used to that. He'd had it all through school and university. What he wasn't used to was someone actually screaming in his face.

Meyer crossed her legs and rested her notepad on one knee. "Right. And the piece that was taken," she went on. "Who painted it?"

"A newcomer, Sam Peynin."

"Title?"

"*Crucible.*"

"What's it of?"

He frowned. "A naked, ethnically ambiguous woman crucified on a cross. As well as bleeding from her crucifixion wounds, she's bleeding from between her legs. There are scattered lily petals at the base of the cross on a brown, lifeless ground. The cross and woman are set against a black background. The style is evocative of the Baroque, deliberately so, but the grandiosity and religiosity is undercut by the modern subject matter and omission of certain core Baroque elements." He shrugged apologetically. "That's all I remember of it. I may have missed something."

She coughed. ". . . Sure. What's it made out of?"

"Oils on canvas, varnish."

"Colours used?"

"Warm, dark tones: black, red, brown."

"Dimensions?"

Why all these questions? "Thirty by forty inches."

"Sale value?"

He froze, staring at her. She gazed back patiently. *Jonah had asked that question. Twice.* Why was he thinking of Jonah right now? "Twenty thousand dollars."

"You sure?" she asked. "This is on the record."

"Yes." He stood and walked to the filing cabinet. He pulled out the estimations for the pieces in the December exhibit and showed them to her. "See? The sales estimate that we place on each piece. We do this so buyers know their value and we have a figure to give to the insurance company. Even if the pieces are only on display and aren't intended for sale, we have to list a price."

She glanced through the documents. "Mind if I copy these?"

"Go ahead."

She went to their photocopier and started scanning them. He watched her, his fingers worrying at a thread in his sweater. The price. Why was it always the *price* that people focused on? Didn't they realize someone's work of art, a labour of love and time, had been stolen? A piece of *culture*?

"Why focus on the sale value?" he asked.

Detective Meyer looked over at him. "It's always about money, Hargrave. Money or pride." She finished with the documents and handed the originals back to him. "Thank you." Her dark eyes rooted him to the spot. "I bet you could tell me the stats of every single piece on display down there, couldn't you?"

"Probably," he admitted.

"You're here first every morning and you leave last every evening. I've heard you organizing that party while your manager talks to the press and makes himself cappuccinos. You might come from money, Hargrave, but you know your work. I wouldn't worry about anything Mr. Palomer says."

He released a breath he hadn't realized he'd been holding. "Okay."

Angeline stepped into the office. She regarded them both, then fixed her gaze on Vaughn. "If you don't mind, Detective."

Oh good. Time to talk with the boss, and she didn't look happy.

The detective left and Vaughn looked at Angeline, heart thumping. He was about to be fired. He *had* to be. Detective Meyer seemed to be on his side, but no way would Angeline take this lying down.

She sat in the chair the detective had just vacated and sighed deeply. "What a goddamn mess."

That seemed . . . promisingly not fired. Vaughn sat opposite her, hope rising. "Yeah."

"I really wish Cress hadn't sided with Maurice about that stupid insurance policy." She made a face. "Can you imagine what they're going to say when we make another claim?"

Oh yes. He could just picture Jonah's face. Hilarious, for the two seconds before he started telling them they were full of it.

"This is going to be difficult to handle," he said.

She nodded. "Yes. And I'm going to need you here to keep the press and public at bay when they inevitably show up to nose around."

Relief made his bones melt. He sagged into his chair. "You're not firing me?"

Angeline frowned. "Is there a reason I should?"

"No!"

"Good. Because we have a gallery to run and a party to throw." She stood. "But first, I'm giving you the day off. Maurice was completely out of line there, and I think you two should stay away from each other today."

He stood hurriedly. "Angeline, it's okay. I can—"

"No. I mean it. Go home. I'll talk to Maurice." She pointed at his laptop. "Shut it down and hustle, Vaughn."

He shut down his laptop and gathered his things. Ten minutes later, he was back outside in the snow, heading home. It wasn't even ten thirty yet.

He squinted up at the clouds, snowflakes making him blink as they landed on his face. Unreal. Today was beyond belief. When was the last time he'd had a weekday off like this? He could go anywhere, do anything. There were several exhibitions he hadn't seen yet. He could go ice skating in front of City Hall. Christmas shopping. A movie. The possibilities were endless. Maybe this wasn't such a bad morning after all.

Jonah stared at his phone. The lawyer's number stared back at him. The digits were burning into his retinas, but he couldn't look away. Ever since he'd left Vaughn's place two days before, the knowledge of this number being on his phone had haunted him. He'd worked out, hung with his roommates, blown a guy near his gym, and now he was at work and he couldn't focus for knowing that this lawyer was in her office right now, could be waiting for his call *right now*. It was almost lunchtime, and he hadn't done anything except look at his cell.

Turned out wanting to cut the past loose once and for all was easier said than done.

Did he really have to call? Maybe he could just forget about it. After all, he had his life together, right? He didn't need this.

His desk phone rang, and he dropped his cell in relief to pick up the call. "Sondern speaking."

"Mr. Sondern," Detective Meyer said warmly down the line. "Good morning."

"Hi, Detective."

"Have you heard from Mr. Hargrave yet?"

From Vaughn? "No. Should I have?"

"Oh! I assumed he would have told you." There was a pause, then muffled voices as she spoke to someone else. "There was another theft at the Delphi Gallery."

Jonah's jaw dropped. "*Another one?*"

"Yes. We're looking into it. I assume the Duforts will send you a claim shortly. When they do, will you scan a copy and send it to me?"

"Sure."

"Great. Thanks for your time." She hung up.

Jonah put the receiver back in its cradle, then picked up his cell and dialled Vaughn.

He picked up right away. "Hey. What's up?"

Jonah facepalmed. "Detective Meyer just called me."

"Oh, really?"

"Are you playing dumb, or did you really not think to *call me* about the theft?"

A pause. "Ah, right. I didn't think to tell you. Angeline gave me the day off, and I was deciding what to do with it."

"You have the day off?"

"Maurice got angry and said some rather unnecessary things. Emotions ran high and Angeline thought it would be a good idea if we were separated for today. It's not a big deal."

Unnecessary things? *Unnecessary things*? "What? What did he say?"

"Nothing of any consequence. In fairness, we were all very upset, and no one had had any coffee yet."

Jonah started to see red, and it wasn't just the light through his closed eyelids. "Stop deflecting, and give me an answer."

"Really, it's not important. I promise. I'm fine. Anyway, yes, another painting was stolen, and I expect you'll be getting paperwork through soon." His voice turned cheeky. "And before you ask, the sale value of this one was $20K."

He exhaled and sat back, staring at the ceiling. "How are you in such a good mood over this?"

"Because I have the day off. I'll be in your area! Are you free for lunch?"

He glanced at the time on his computer. "Unlikely. I expect a claim from a very rich client of ours any minute now, and my manager and I will have to hustle out to investigate it."

"Shame. Another time, then."

"Yeah." He definitely sounded too cheery. Jonah set his jaw. "What did Maurice say to you?"

Vaughn sighed. "I am *not* upset over this, all right? So don't get angry. It's only words." He paused, then quickly said, "He called me a faggot and trust-fund piece of trash or something like that, then accused me of stealing the piece, but it's all fine now, promise."

Before he knew it, Jonah was standing, one hand tight on his phone and the other curled into a fist. "What the literal *fuck*."

"Jonah, it's okay."

"*It's not okay*. That is *never* okay. God, I hope his head explodes from all the shit he's carrying in it. Did you hit him?"

"Of course not. Violence isn't the answer."

"I'd have hit him."

"Then let's be grateful you weren't there, because if you had, you'd've lost your job."

"Vaughn, I'm going to kick his ass the next time I see him."

"You don't have to. Angeline will talk to him." Vaughn's footsteps could be heard crunching on the sidewalk. "Save all that energy for gaming."

Gaming. Yeah right. Like he wasn't duty bound to correct homophobic assholes who insulted his friends.

"I can hear you thinking." There was a smile in Vaughn's voice. "Let it go, Jonah. It's only words."

"It's fucking homophobic, and you shouldn't have to put up with it."

"You're right, but there are worse things in the world." His voice turned hard. "Promise me you'll be professional when you go there today. I mean it."

Jonah blew out in exasperation, then realized he was still standing, ready to fight. He quickly sat back down. God, he needed to get it together. Vaughn was right. "Shit like that pisses me off. But okay."

"Good. Thank you." His tone turned teasing. "I appreciate the sentiment. It's not often someone defends my honour."

Jonah felt his face heat up. Defend his— Was that what he was doing? He was just being realistic. The idea of *Vaughn*, of all people, committing a crime was ridiculous. "Please," he sputtered. "Like you'd steal artwork. The guy's loonier than a cartoon."

"Thanks, Jonah."

Pride rushed through him at that grateful, warm voice. He'd made Vaughn Hargrave feel better. Oh *yeah*. He shifted in his chair, aware he was grinning like an idiot.

An email popped into his inbox. It was from Garrett with the subject heading: *ANOTHER DELPHI CLAIM KILL ME NOW.* "I gotta go."

"I'll be around the Eaton Centre for most of the afternoon. Do text if you're free." He hung up.

Jonah opened the email, read through it, then went to Garrett's office. He found Garrett facedown on the desk, hands in his hair.

"It won't be that bad," he said.

"I hate these people." Garrett's voice was muffled by the desk. "I hate them. I never want to see that Palomer guy again. If I ever find the asshole stealing from them, I'll pound him into the sidewalk."

"You ready to go?"

Garrett heaved a great sigh, then peeled himself off the desk and reached for his coat. "Let's do this."

In the end, it really wasn't so bad. Angeline was there the entire time they spoke with Maurice, who was unusually quiet and polite. They got their documentation and a few pictures, then headed back to the office. In the taxi, Jonah immediately flipped through the paperwork to the sales estimate. Two hundred and twenty thousand dollars. *Jesus Christ.* Who was pulling this shit?

When he pointed it out, Garrett grunted. "You sure it's wrong?"

"Vaughn told me the value is twenty thousand."

"The assistant?"

"Yeah."

"You spoke with him already?"

Jonah felt himself grow hot. "Yeah."

"About this?"

Oh shit. Maybe he shouldn't have done that. Potential conflict of interest. Well, if that was going to be an issue, he should've considered it before playing video games with Vaughn, dragging him to a toga party, then kissing him. Boundaries between work and pleasure were long gone where Vaughn was concerned. Conflict of interest was probably well and truly established.

Man, kissing him had been worth it, though.

Garrett raised an eyebrow. "Are you blushing?"

"No. It's boiling in here." He cleared his throat. "He mentioned the theft and that we could expect a claim. That's all."

"And the sale value."

"Yeah. I asked for it. Because of the last claim."

Garrett regarded him for a moment, then nodded. "Okay. Good work."

Phew. Potential problem averted.

Jonah sat back against the taxi seat. It was past lunchtime, which just meant a shorter line for food in the usual places. Maybe he did have time to duck out to the Eaton Centre and see Vaughn.

Two days' distance from Saturday, and he was no closer to understanding what had happened between them. He understood being attracted to Vaughn, and he understood that Vaughn wasn't attracted to him, because he'd googled asexuality and it turned out to be an actual thing, so, okay. Not into sex; weird, but it wasn't the weirdest thing about human sexuality he'd ever heard of, he had to give it that much.

No, the thing he was stuck on was that he'd hit on Vaughn, been brushed off, *then stayed to play games anyway*. That was new. He still wanted to hang out with the guy even though sex wasn't going to happen. He didn't think it was just because he'd had a minor freak-out over his stupid mom issues, which he was now regretting. Thinking back over events, maybe it was Vaughn saying he'd totally do him if he were into sex, or giving him a glass of water, or letting him decompress by shooting aliens.

Or kissing back.

That seemed like an important detail. The asexuality website he'd looked at was certain asexual people could have relationships, even if sex wasn't part of them, so if Vaughn had kissed him back without an agenda of blowing him . . .

It might've been reflex, douche bag. You surprised him.

And anyway, why did he even care? He didn't even do relationships, so why was he thinking about this so much? He kissed guys all the time. No big.

Only, he didn't usually know their name. Or where they lived. Or that they could paint like a boss and preferred going barefoot and made bad coffee and looked like sin in a bedsheet.

His chest ached, and his thoughts were going in circles. What the hell was wrong with him? It was only *Vaughn*. He'd gotten off with like two guys since Saturday, but kissing Vaughn was what stood out from the weekend?

Time to get a grip.

Garrett cleared his throat. "I like your proactivity, and usually I'd encourage a good relationship with our clients, but you might want to be careful with this guy."

Jonah blinked at him. "Huh?"

"Try not to talk about work with him outside of email." Jonah opened his mouth to reply, but Garrett raised one hand. "Look, I get it. He's a nice guy and making friends is good. I'm not going to care about you two being friends outside of work. Just, you know, cool it on talking shop until this Delphi thing is cleared up."

Jonah shook his head. "I don't discuss work with him."

"I didn't think you did." Garrett smiled encouragingly. "I'm not trying to worry you. You're doing a great job." He glanced at the paperwork Jonah held. "I hate to say it, but I don't trust the gallery people. Any of them. We need to be careful in what we tell them. Make sure our asses are covered in case this ends badly. That's all."

Ugh. He had a good point. Were they being obviously close in some way? At least Garrett thought he and Vaughn were friends. That was probably better than the alternative. He had no idea what Garrett would say or do if he came out to him, not that he wanted to be out at work anytime soon.

"So," Garrett said brightly, "what are your plans for Christmas?"

That annual tradition of obnoxious, consumerist frenzy was a mere three weeks away. Oh, he had plans all right. "Eating and sleeping."

Garrett laughed. "That's the dream. You heading home?"

Home being the place he rented. With his roommates going to their various family homes, he'd be there with movies, food, and the bathroom to himself for once. "Pretty much. You too?"

"Spending it with my parents this year. Sister'll be over as well, with my nieces." He rattled off a bunch of complaints about the full house and his wife trying to buy presents for everyone and how big the dinner was going to be. It sounded like something out of a Lifetime holiday movie. "I'll need a vacation from the holiday," Garrett finished.

"I hear that."

"You're enthusiastic!" Garrett clapped his shoulder. "You know, you don't talk about your family much."

Jonah emphatically did *not* want to have this conversation with his boss. "Not much to say. They're all lunatics."

Luckily Garrett found that hilarious, and his mirth lasted the rest of the trip back to the office. There, Jonah bought lunch and ate it at his desk, refusing to even consider leaving until he'd gotten his work done.

Hours later, his phone lit up with a call from Zay. He glanced at the time—seven! When had that happened? He picked up.

"Where are you?" she asked.

"Work. Why?"

She sighed heavily into the receiver. "We're having dinner tonight."

Oh shit. He'd completely forgotten. He stood. "Fuck. I'm sorry. I forgot." He started saving and closing things down. "On my way now."

"You better be."

He paused. "Where are we meeting?"

She gave him the address. He shut his computer down and ran out of the building. Fifteen minutes later, he arrived at the restaurant. Zay waved at him and he sat down.

"For real, I'm so sorry," he panted.

She glanced him over. "Did you literally just run from Bay Street?"

"Maybe."

"I'm touched." She leaned forward as he collapsed into his chair. "Work is crazy?"

"It's fucking insane. It's like people don't expect ice to damage their shit. Someone keeps losing documents. And the Delphi Gallery had another painting stolen."

Her jaw dropped. "No way."

"And my manager chewed me out for talking to Vaughn about it outside of email."

Zay's expression turned wicked. "Oh yeah?"

He squinted at her suspiciously. "Why are you looking at me like that?"

"Adrian said you two didn't do much talking this weekend."

Adrian?

The toga party.

Jonah glared at her. "Adrian doesn't know a thing about it."

She grinned, holding up her hands. "Hey, hey, I'm only sharing the gossip." The grin didn't leave her face. "Sooo—"

"So nothing."

"—ooo, what happened?"

Too much to get into. He picked up the menu. "Actually nothing. Oh my God, is this *Italian* food?" Did she secretly hate him? He scanned the menu for something not carbohydrate- or cheese-based.

"Adrian said he was petting you like a cat."

He slapped the menu down. "He was not."

"Is it true he was about to kiss you but got a huge boner and left out of embarrassment?"

He *wished*. "Also no."

A server approached them to take their order. After that interruption, Jonah tried to turn the conversation to Zay and her weekend. The key word being *tried*.

"Is it true," she asked, completely ignoring him, "that you took a guy to a party where people were actively having sex, and he ignored everyone else except you, and you two had a moment? *Several* moments, even? But *didn't* have sex?"

He shifted in his chair. "Why can't we drop this?"

"Because this literally never happens to you. Also, I'm avoiding girls until I figure my shit out, so I'm living vicariously through you."

He studied her, with her smooth brown skin and wide smile and slightly grown-out hair. Large, sparkly earrings dangled from her ears, matching the stud in her nose, and her eyes were warm and teasing. She wore a white top out of some fancy material that made her look more professional than he did in his now-sweaty suit. A wave of affection swamped him. After a year or so of not talking, they'd picked right back up like it had been nothing; that was something special. He was lucky. "You deserve to live for yourself, you know."

Zay blinked in surprise. "Oh my gosh."

"I don't get it. Your grades were better than mine, Zay. You got…" He grasped for the words. "You're smart and beautiful and amazing with people. How could all that shit with Parry happen to you? How are you not earning crazy money in some scary company?"

Her mouth twisted bitterly. "Shit happens, Jonah. Grades and potential don't count for much when your head's in a dark place."

He knew shit happened. He knew that very, very well. "I thought you and Parry were *it*, you know? You were so happy. She seemed to love you."

Pain crossed her face. Their server dumped a basket of garlic bread in between them, and she reached for a piece. "We did love each other. But drugs got in the way for her and we both changed. I still love her, but it's not a relationship anymore. I had to leave or her addiction would have sucked me down." Guilt added to the pain in her expression. Instead of eating the bread, she tore it apart, piece by smaller piece. "I still feel bad about that, you know. Leaving her. Choosing myself."

"Don't," he said immediately. "You made the right decision. Relationships are a trap."

She sighed deeply, and he cringed. That had been a blunt thing to say.

"Relationships *can be* a trap," she said. "You have to choose wisely."

"I'm sorry. That came out wrong."

A smile broke through the pain. "Don't worry about it, sweetness. It's how I feel right now. I know I'll get through it." She put a piece of the bread in her mouth. "I think it's more accurate to say that relationships can be a trap, but there's always a way out."

Yeah. He could still feel the hard wood of the bench under his short legs and the sticky ice cream on his hand and see the glimpse of his mother's back as she walked away. Not that he'd been the one leaving in that situation, but he remembered the panic and pain of separation very well.

"Better to avoid getting in them in the first place." His voice had turned thick. And fuck, the basket of bread practically begged to be eaten. It smelled amazing. He wanted nothing more than to cram each golden, buttery, garlicky piece in his mouth and revel in their chewy warmth. Let the carbs drown out just how horrible the world could be.

"When they're right, though, they're the best thing ever."

"I'll take your word for it." He paused, aware that what he was about to say made him pathetic. "What does it feel like? When it's right?"

Her eyebrows rose. "I'm not exactly an expert." Her wicked smile returned. "But then again, compared to you I am."

He grumbled and looked around for the server. "Forget it."

"No way. When it's right, it's . . . wonderful. Like, everything is awesome with that person, and they make your life better simply by existing. Lots of good feelings. Safe. Happy. Supported." Her eyes went dreamy. "And sexy."

He wanted to scoff. "That's basically how I feel being single."

"Oh, Jonah." She picked up another piece of bread, wafting garlicky, salty yeast straight into his face. His mouth watered. "It's not just that. It's the closeness to another person, you know? And the fact that they know all the stupid, boring, crappy stuff about you and love you anyway." The bread in her hand waved about as she gestured. "You can share stuff because they have your back. They give a shit about you, and you give a shit about them. It's like this big, perpetual loop of caring and feeling."

Jesus Christ. "Do you sing 'Kumbaya' together as well?" he asked. "Hold hands and give thanks to the universe for bringing you love?"

One greasy finger pointed at him. "You mock, Sondern, but it's only because you don't get it, and you've never had it. Not from your foster families and not from the guys you fuck against Toronto's buildings. One day you'll know. Plus, you asked." She finished the bread. "Uhn. This is so good."

He almost flinched. That was a low blow. She was right, but it was low. And if the server didn't come with their food soon, he was going to inhale that basket, carbs be damned.

"Man, this got deep." She sipped her drink. "This was meant to be you telling me if the gallery assistant kisses as well as he dresses, not me telling you what my relationship wasn't."

"He does," he said unthinkingly. "And I wanted to know. I'm sorry it didn't work out with her. But it totally validates my opinion that relationships aren't worth the trouble."

"*People* are worth the trouble, Jonah. Relationships are always about people." She smiled. "So, hot art dude can kiss. Good to know."

He felt his face go hot. "That's all you're gonna know, because that's all that happened."

"Seriously?" She took another piece of bread.

"He doesn't do sex."

Her jaw dropped, along with the piece of bread. She cursed and retrieved it from her lap, brushing at crumbs and butter. "What do you mean?"

"I mean, he told me he doesn't like having sex."

Her eyebrow raised. "Like, at all?"

"At all."

"So what happened?"

"Like I said: *nothing.*"

"Oh wow." She tore apart the bread. "Is he super religious or something?"

He shook his head. "No. He called it asexuality."

"*Oh*. Okay. That makes sense." She began chewing.

What the— How was she so chill about that? "That makes sense? Are you kidding?"

She shook her head. "Nope. There were talks about asexuality during LGBT meet-ups at Ryerson." She tilted her head. "Let me guess: you were too busy rimming someone to go."

"I'd never heard of it before." He recounted how he'd stood there asking questions and trying to make sense of it. "I mean, he's a guy. You know? Sex is great. Quick, easy sex is *awesome*. This is what we *do*, and there's no reason for him to make it complicated like that."

Zay leaned over and flicked him in the forehead. "You can't speak for every man in Toronto. Every gay man, even."

He glared at her, rubbing grease off his forehead. "I speak for every gay man *I* know in Toronto."

"Really? I'm pretty sure every gay man *you* know works the scene the way you do."

Oh hey. Not *quite* the way he did. Some of the others didn't seem to score as much as he did. *Heh*.

Zay scowled at him. "Focus, sweetness. You just know this one little part of the gay scene. In fact, you know this one little part of the gay scene within an entire umbrella of LGBT scenes."

He scowled back. "You ever want me to wingman *you* sometime, just say the word. I can handle ladies' night."

"Oh, that is a *promise*." She grinned suddenly. "So he's not into sex, eh? Betcha weren't expecting that."

Fuck it. He reached for the bread basket, only for the server to appear beside the table and set down their food. With gratitude born of desperation, he turned his attention to his saltimbocca instead.

"No," he answered.

She picked up her fork. "By the way, you're wrong."

"About what?"

"About him making things complicated because he doesn't have sex."

Oh, this he had to hear. "Really? Enlighten me."

She finished a mouthful of food. "Sex is highly personal. Not everyone has a weekly quota like you. Lots of people are pretty okay with not having it unless they're in a relationship. And some people are okay with not having it at all." She'd ordered gnocchi with a Stilton and walnut sauce, and the smell of it was heady. "You can't be judgmental like that. Is he happy without it?"

He could still see the expression of relief on Vaughn's face. "Yeah."

"So what's the problem?"

Wasn't it obvious? "I can't sleep with him, that's the problem."

"Oh, boohoo." She rolled her eyes.

"And I want to," he continued.

Her fork paused en route to her mouth. "Considering what you just told me about him, I think you're going to have to let this one go."

"But . . ." He studied his veal, knife and fork paused over it. Strange feelings swirled in his head and chest—lingering anger from the thought of Vaughn being shouted at by Maurice and then going home to his big empty apartment, the knowledge that he hadn't had sex in years. *Vaughn.* He was a total dork, but he was cute and nice. He should have someone who wanted to hold him and look after him. "I think it's a shame."

"What's a shame? That you can't stick your dick in him?" Her tone was cold.

"No." Well, yes, but he wasn't thinking about that anymore. "He told me he doesn't do relationships because he doesn't have sex. I think he wants to date, but thinks no one will be interested in him if they can't do him."

Her expression softened. "Oh. That *is* a shame."

"Exactly." He started cutting the veal into smaller pieces. "There have to be more guys out there like him, right?"

Zay nodded. "Definitely. There are guys who don't care about having sex all the time. I think he'll be okay."

"But it'll be hard for him." Jonah couldn't really see it happening, but he hoped she was right. He had to hope. The idea of Vaughn being lonely was awful.

"It's hard to find someone compatible no matter who you are." How did she know this stuff? "His thing is sex. Other people have their own preferences or quirks that might be hard for some people to take." One eyebrow raised. "You're very concerned about him."

He shrugged and picked at his food. "He's a sweet guy." He glanced at her. "I worry about you too, you know."

"Awww!"

He felt himself blushing again. "Shut up."

"No freaking way."

She stood and rounded the table. He held up his hands to ward her off but too late—she hugged him. *Oh God, this is embarrassing.*

"You know, Adrian's worried about you too," he said into her shoulder.

"I'll hug him the next time I see him." Her arms tightened. "I'm so lucky."

Aw, shit. He hugged her back, but was relieved when she finally let go.

She returned to her seat, a big grin on her face. "Thanks, Jonah."

He stared at his plate, certain his face was redder than the sauce on his veal. "Can we please forget that just happened?"

"Nope." She dug into her gnocchi happily. "You gonna keep hanging out with him?"

"Yeah. He wants me to play *BioShock* next. Thinks I'd like it."

"Oh yeah? Sounds good." She had a smile on her face Jonah didn't entirely trust, like she knew something he didn't. But he didn't press, and the conversation thankfully moved on. They finished their food and left, cursing the cold as soon as they hit the snowy streets. Jonah parted ways with her at the TTC, and on his way home, replayed the evening over with a smile. If this was what friendship after university looked like, he definitely could use more of it.

CHAPTER TEN

In the end, Vaughn had gone ice-skating, then shopping. Disappointingly, Jonah hadn't called by the time he'd lingered over a mocha in a Starbucks, so he'd headed home, cleaned the lion mural off the wall, and checked Tumblr. On a whim, he'd typed *asexuality* into the search box, which, like most whims related to the Tumblr search engine, proved an excellent idea. Soon he'd followed about a dozen new blogs with names like *queenieofaces* and *gaybeard-the-great*, some of which even seemed to be based in Canada. Promising.

He was back at work today, and the usual routine found him sitting at the front desk answering emails when Maurice turned up. He barrelled through the door as though it had insulted him, his mouth turned down grimly, and his eyes focusing on a point over Vaughn's shoulder. Vaughn braced himself.

Maurice glared. "Is the coffee machine on?"

"Yes."

He walked past without another word. Vaughn exhaled in relief. *Thank God. Business as usual.*

He kept his head down and tapped away at his laptop. The caterers emailed last-minute questions, the musicians sent their arrival time, and there was a small rush of visitors at ten thirty. The artist of *Crucible*, Sam Peynin, sent a terse but understanding email about the theft, which he left for Angeline to handle. Detective Meyer came by and greeted him, then walked into the gallery, presumably to do her detecting work, whatever that could be.

When Angeline arrived, she smiled at him. "Did you have a good day off?"

"Yes."

"And did Maurice apologize to you?"

Does Maurice even know how to apologize? "Was he supposed to?"

She dropped the smile. "Yes. I don't know what his problem is with you, but he needs to get over it." She strode away, and Vaughn wondered if they really had to go through a farce where Maurice pretended to sincerely apologize to him, and he pretended to believe it, and then they both pretended they could still work together amicably. He'd rather eat paint.

The door opened, and the *Globe and Mail* arts journalist from the other week came in. Vaughn didn't have any notes or reminders saying he was expected, which rang a multitude of alarm bells and meant he watched him approach with great wariness.

"Hey," the journalist said easily. "How's it going? Jules Mitchell, from the *Mail.*"

Vaughn shook his hand. "Hello again."

Mitchell leaned on the desk casually. "So I heard there was another theft."

Yesterday. Literally yesterday. Angeline hadn't sent out a press release yet, so how on earth could this guy know? "Did you?"

"Yup. Heard it was a major piece too. Your latest exhibition's only been up for, what, a week?"

Vaughn hated journalists. "Something like that."

"Damned shame. I'm here to take a few pictures and get a statement from you guys on the theft." He dug into his messenger bag.

Vaughn eyed him. "Did Angeline tell you to come by?"

"No, Maurice said I could—" The journalist cut himself off abruptly, his face turning pink. "I, uh, I mean—"

Maurice had said what, exactly? Vaughn quickly typed an IM to Angeline: *Toronto Mail journalist here. You or Maurice expecting him?* "I can't just let you in to take photos."

The guy leaned over the desk. "You sure? I mean, I was going to come in anyway to do a review on the symbolism exhibition. I heard it's stunning."

Stunning wasn't the word Vaughn would use, but the critics always were a weird bunch. "Sorry."

Mitchell rested one elbow on the desk while playing idly with the Yayoi Kusama pumpkin paperweight Vaughn kept there. "Did the police ever get a lead on the thief for the Yoon piece?"

"I honestly don't know."

"Do you think it's the same guy? What have the police said about it?"

"We don't have any updates about that." Activity on the screen caught his eye: Angeline was typing a response to his IM.

"Seriously? That sucks," Jules continued. "The police never catch the guy in cases like this. What do our taxes pay for, am I right?"

Vaughn knew Detective Meyer was somewhere nearby, so said nothing.

Jules acted as though he hadn't noticed. "And I heard Jai Yoon's furious about it."

What was his point? "Wouldn't you be?"

"Oh yeah, for sure. Thanks for letting me poke around last time. That was nice."

"Sorry I can't do it again." Vaughn tried not to show how irritated he was by the guy lingering. *Remember: good relations with the media are important. Even if the media in question clearly gives more of a shit about the scoop than about the art or about good relations.*

Angeline wrote back: *I didn't invite him over. Maurice says he didn't either. Send him away.*

And how was he supposed to do that? Especially when the guy had their Kusama pumpkin in hand?

"My editor loved the piece. Loved it. I got like two hundred new followers on Twitter after it was published." Jules set the pumpkin paperweight down. "This thing is psychedelic."

Vaughn moved it away. The paperweight was an original and likely cost more than he would be happy to pay to replace it. Also, Jules clearly had no idea what he was handling. Art critic, his ass.

Jules leaned closer. "Okay, if you're not going to let me in to look at the latest blank space, level with me. What's going on with the Yoon piece? I know the police are still investigating it, but why is Yoon so pissed? Isn't theft pretty straightforward? Wouldn't she get an insurance payout? The owner told me the insurance would cover it."

"Our insurance does cover theft."

"So what's the problem?" Jules picked up a pen now. "Because, dude, you have to know that Yoon's been warning people off your gallery."

Berkley had done the same, and the gallery had survived. If it didn't get through the attention this time, well, it wouldn't be like they hadn't seen the end coming. Vaughn shrugged. "It's between us and Jai Yoon. Could you please leave now?"

Jules sagged, a deep sigh escaping him.

Behind him, a man entered the gallery. It took several moments for Vaughn to realize it was Devon wearing a suit and a rather harried expression, the one that tended to precede a request that would seriously inconvenience Vaughn.

"Hello, sir. Welcome to the gallery," he said quickly.

Devon drew up short, the panic on his face turning to confusion.

Vaughn turned to Jules. "If you don't mind, I have a visitor."

Jules eyed him, then reached into his pocket and pulled out a business card. "Here. If you change your mind, contact me. Anytime." He turned and left.

Devon stared after the reporter. "Who was that?"

"Some hack from the arts section of the *Mail*."

He grinned. "He was hitting on you."

In the name of everything holy and good, was everyone he knew cursed with a one-track mind? "He was digging for a story, Dev."

Devon waggled his eyebrows. "Two birds with one stone. I like his style."

"What," Vaughn asked with great patience, "are you doing here at eleven thirty in the morning?"

"Isn't it obvious? Avoiding work." Devon leaned on the desk, eyes on Vaughn's face, his body settling into almost the exact position just vacated by the reporter. "I need an invite to your gallery's shindig next week."

"Your parents are already invited."

Devon winced. "No. *Me*. And a plus-one."

"No." Vaughn tried to get a clear look at his pupils. Was he drunk? High? This party had been announced over a month ago, and he wanted an invite the *week before*?

"Vaughn, please."

"I confirmed numbers with the caterers already."

"We won't eat a damn thing."

Oh please. Vaughn wasn't talking about food and Devon knew it.

His skepticism must've showed on his face, because Devon scowled. "Oh come on, you know there are always teetotalers at these things. My date and I will barely make a dent in the drinks."

A date, eh? Vaughn leaned forward himself. "Who's the date?"

Devon abruptly looked down, avoiding his gaze. He reached for the Kusama pumpkin, and Vaughn swiftly put it in a drawer. Devon shifted his weight, at a loss for distraction. The hesitation alone told Vaughn this was something serious. "He's a rookie sales guy in the company." His voice was quiet. "He's really into art, and he's always wanted to visit this place."

"Let me guess: somehow he's already under the impression he's coming," Vaughn said dryly.

Devon's face fell. "And my parents actually want to attend this year, so I can't use their invites." He grabbed Vaughn's hands and clasped them together. "My friend—my brother—please don't make a liar out of me."

"But, darling, you're doing so well on your own."

"*Please.*" Devon turned on his desperation face. "He'll be crushed. I know I don't deserve it, but *he* does! If not for me, do it for him. He'll be ecstatic. I just want to see him happy."

As if. "You just want him happy enough to blow the boss's kid."

Devon pressed Vaughn's hands to his forehead. "Name your price, asshole."

Vaughn thought, then grinned when he thought of something. "Leafs tickets." Devon's parents usually had season tickets that could be traded up.

Devon looked at him, eyes narrowed. "*Oh.*"

"Home game. Front row. Two."

"You complete bastard."

Vaughn raised his eyebrows. "I'll let you pick the game."

Devon pretended to think about it. "Done." He let go of Vaughn's hands and shook one. "Now that that's settled, there's a club I want to visit this week. You free?"

Not really. He was on a roll with the abstract thing he was working on, and he had high hopes for his next mural. Vaughn opened his mouth to say so, but Devon beat him to it. "It wasn't really a question. I haven't seen you in two weeks, so you're coming out with me."

Vaughn huffed. "Why did you ask me, then?"

"Because I'm polite."

Detective Meyer walked past him. Vaughn waved, and she nodded back, then left. Devon watched her go with wide eyes. "Was that a police officer?"

"Yes."

"Vaughn, why was there a police officer in your gallery?"

Vaughn grinned. Devon knew this already; everyone in their social circle did. "To listen to nepotism in action."

Devon frowned at him, then snapped his fingers. "Right! The theft! Yes, of course." He stared after her as she crunched her way through the snow to the road. "Wasn't it like two weeks ago? She's still hanging around here? Don't you find that strange?"

"There was another theft."

Devon's jaw dropped. "No shit."

"I assure you, there's plenty of it as far as we're concerned."

"I think your gallery's problem is luck, my friend. And possibly your security system." Devon tapped the counter. "Print out an invite for me, would you?"

"Do you honestly think we send out *laser-printed* invitations? Good Lord, Devon, we're not barbarians." Vaughn shook his head. "No. You'll just have to forget yours in your other jacket." He typed Devon's name into the guest list, saved it. "But see, you're officially on the guest list."

"You're a god among men." Devon clapped his shoulder. "Now, this weekend—dancing! I'll text you the place. You're going to love it." Somehow Vaughn doubted it, but it was true he hadn't spent time with Devon in weeks.

Vaughn watched him swing around and saunter out, amused despite his annoyance at Devon's request to be squeezed into the event. The only reason Devon even tried things like this was because he kept succeeding. Not that Vaughn could judge him too much; he'd given in for a pair of Leafs tickets.

But he was now the owner of hockey tickets for a home game. And he knew exactly who he wanted to go with. Jonah hadn't struck him as much of a Leafs fan, but they were Toronto born and bred, and it was a home game; he'd want to go. He *would* want to go . . . right?

The idea felt like a date in his head, but it wouldn't necessarily *be* a date, because friends did stuff like go to hockey games together all the time. Yeah. No big deal.

Even though Vaughn was pretty sure he wanted it to be a date.

But it wouldn't be. Because Jonah wouldn't possibly want to date someone he couldn't fuck, and Vaughn understood that. So. Friends and hockey.

He checked his phone. Nothing from Jonah, which was fine because what was he expecting? They had no plans, nothing beyond another gaming session that weekend. It felt strange not to be looking at a recent message, though. Not to be talking to him. Jonah wasn't the type of person who'd text him funny messages during the day of his own volition. No, Jonah was the kind of person who'd respond to something, who'd call him to check something.

Before he could think too much about it, he fired off a text: *Busy Saturday, can we do games on Sunday?*

Then he put his phone down and returned to the gallery emails. He only checked his phone once every ten minutes. By the time lunch rolled around, he was sick of himself, and he put the cell in the drawer with the Kusama pumpkin before running out to buy food. When he returned, he checked it again and found a text.

From Katie, the daughter of his mother's friend. The film student with a chewing gum addiction. She wanted to know if she could film a project in his gallery.

Vaughn swallowed his disappointment. Okay, a film project? Could be interesting, especially if Katie was doing it. She already had a portfolio of films under her belt, and she hadn't graduated university yet. He'd be willing to hear more, but the decision wasn't his to make. He could pose it to Cressida and Angeline; right now wasn't the best time to suggest anything to Maurice.

Another text arrived, and it *was* Jonah this time. He almost dropped the phone in his eagerness to look at it: *yh sure.*

Vaughn blinked. That was . . . concise. He'd expected a little more than a simple agreement.

Then he realized he was looking at a two-word response by a man who most assuredly hadn't been waiting for any kind of communication from Vaughn and who almost definitely wasn't driving himself insane in the waiting. One of those words wasn't even spelled out in full. And Vaughn realized exactly how much of a fool he was.

The games. The kisses. The lunches. The jokes. The drawings. This ridiculous attempt at forcing some attention his way.

What on earth was he doing? He sat down heavily on the chair behind the desk, awareness creeping over him with cold fingers. *I really like him. A man who doesn't spell "yeah" out in full and doesn't understand art and has more sex in a week than I've had in the totality of my life and who won't like me back. Who* can't *like me back, not in the way he needs.* Vaughn got that, so what was he doing to himself here? Was he *trying* to make himself miserable? He knew better than this. He had years of knowing better than this.

Fuck.

Suddenly the prospect of clubbing with Devon seemed not only necessary, but too far away. He couldn't allow himself to pine after Jonah. Absolutely not. He needed to get out, to do something that didn't give him the time and space to think about the man. He sent a text to Devon asking if they could go in the next few days.

For the first time in a very long time, Vaughn found himself (a) trying to not think about a guy and (b) specifically going out to distract himself. Devon's recommendation had taken them to yet another new club deep in another industrialized corner of Toronto.

He had no idea where the hell these old warehouses kept popping up from. This one was all concrete blocks and sweeping metallic embellishments. Stencil decals spray-painted in opportune places added some hits of colour, but the UV lighting over the dance floor was what gave the place an extra edge. Pots of UV body paint were available behind the bar for five dollars. The lighting was very dim, the better to hide just how expensive the drinks were and to heighten the effect of the paint. Despite all that though, when Vaughn realized this was a UV paint party, he'd turned to Devon with a huge grin, hugged him, then leaped forward to buy paint. For once, Devon had been right—he *loved* this.

Once he'd daubed a design on Devon's face, he turned to a nearby mirror to paint himself. Devon's hands latched on to his shirt.

"Come on," Devon shouted over the music. He tugged at the shirt. "Go crazy."

He wanted Vaughn to take his shirt off? Vaughn regarded himself in the mirror: he was a tall, dimly lit figure with no real standout feature apart from his height. A man who'd checked his phone so often over the last two days for messages from Jonah that he'd royally pissed himself off. Even right then, gleeful over the opportunity to create UV art, he wished Jonah was there.

Ugh. Perhaps he could stop being undeniably pathetic and have some fucking fun.

He pulled his shirt off.

Devon clapped in approval, then took his shirt and tucked it into the waistband of Vaughn's pants. Vaughn stared down at his chest, ideas curling invisibly in front of him. Using the mirror to check, he carefully outlined his rib cage, spine, and the part of his pelvic bones just above the waistband of his pants, then did his shoulders, arms, and finally, traced a skull on his face. Devon watched him, the lines and petals on his own face rising and wrinkling comically as he processed the design.

"It's not Halloween!"

"But it's *fun*," Vaughn cried back.

Devon shook his head. "Creepy. Cool, man, but creepy. You're only gonna score emo-goth whores looking like that."

Vaughn admired himself in the mirror. "Emo-goth whores don't exist." And if they did, they wouldn't be here. He handed the UV paint back to the bartender, who pulled out her phone and took a picture. He bought drinks, sank them with Devon, then they bounced out onto the dance floor.

As he danced, he tried to get lost in the music and the atmosphere of the place. It was carnivalesque with the paint and light. Smears and splatters of purple, red, yellow, and green danced in the darkness as people gyrated around him. He and Devon danced together, then Devon found someone else to dance with, and Vaughn was on his own.

Unfortunately, he couldn't switch off his head. Everywhere he looked, he saw someone who seemed to resemble Jonah in some way. Why did he have to be blond and of average height?

Maybe all he needed was another drink.

When he saw another blond twining himself around a guy, it was decided: he *definitely* needed more drinks.

He turned and worked through the crowd to the bar. On his way, two men passed in front of him: a tall and lanky man who gripped the second, shorter one by the wrist, and led him quickly through the crowd to the darker corners near the washrooms. Vaughn's eyes caught on the shorter one because his profile resembled Jonah's—then he did a double take because it *was* Jonah.

Jonah reached forward and grabbed the guy's ass. They hustled like the building was on fire. Vaughn felt something in his chest deflate. Nope, no way he could compete with that. A hand clapped down on his shoulder, but he barely flinched.

"Man," Devon crowed next to him. "This place is insane! Look at the handprints this guy just left on me." He turned and Vaughn flickered a glance down. The seat of his pants were a grimy nebula of green UV paint.

"I hope it washes out," Vaughn said.

"Me too." Devon frowned. "You okay?"

He had to snap out of this. What were two kisses? Especially from someone like Jonah? "Yes. Drink?"

"You're reading my mind."

Devon steered them to the bar. They made friends in the line and treated them to shots. More shots followed. Vaughn bought them all yet another drink, and suddenly it turned into the best night of his life, even though the guy he'd spent several weeks developing a crush on was being topped in plain sight by a guy next to the washroom. He was treated to that visual when he and his new friends whooped past on their way to and from the toilet.

But it didn't matter because then they did more shots and danced a lot together and suddenly one of them was dancing *very* close indeed, and he wasn't bad looking (but not as cute as Jonah) and his hands felt so, so good on Vaughn's skin (but they weren't his and he wasn't him), and Vaughn could feel one hand sliding down and messing up his skeleton paint (goddamn it) and reaching for his dick (oh hey there), and *that* wasn't okay nope—

He grabbed the guy's hand and pulled it away from his crotch, then used it to twirl the guy around and grind against him from behind. There. Still dancing, but the guy wasn't trying to grope him anymore (awesome), and *ahh* what a relief, he was making a face and flouncing away (thank fuck), and Vaughn decided what he really needed now was to touch up his paint, because he was an *artist*, and what was an artist without his art, only instead of the bar he found himself next to the washroom for some reason. Jonah wasn't there anymore. Well of course not, why would he be, it had been like half an hour. He blearily checked his phone. Wow, more like . . . He used his fingers to count. Two. Two hours. *Two* hours?

"How you doing, buddy?" Devon roared in his face.

Vaughn reared back in surprise. Devon's paint was smeared all over him and Vaughn grinned. "You gah a lil som'n there," he slurred, patting Devon's face.

Devon laughed and pointed at Vaughn's crotch. He looked down and saw very obvious finger marks on his pants edging over his groin. Gross. He scrubbed at one with a knuckle, but it just smeared.

"You hanging out here for a reason?" Devon asked. "Or did you just finish?"

Vaughn shook his head. "I don't *do* that, you know."

Devon cocked his head to one side, eyes crinkling as he regarded Vaughn. "Yeah, I know."

Someone thumped against the wall behind them and started moaning. Devon glanced over automatically and his eyes shuttered in appreciation. Which was also gross. Vaughn opened his mouth to tell him off when those eyes widened and Devon turned to him. "Vaughn! Don't look, but I think it's the threesome guy!"

Don't turn around, don't turn around, bad idea, bad idea—

Oh. Jonah was only having his cock sucked. Well, that was better than watching some guy work his way into his ass. Vaughn's gaze travelled to Jonah's face and he found himself staring straight into Jonah's narrowed eyes. Those eyes said *Fuck off* and were followed by a middle finger.

Right. Rude to stare. But his face and skin was all flushed and sweaty, and he was kind of gorgeous like this as well. Not fair.

Devon's hand gripped Vaughn's shoulder. Vaughn couldn't seem to stop watching Jonah, who glared back, then scanned him up and down and recognized him. He could tell when it happened because Jonah's eyes widened, and his jaw fell open, and he sagged against the wall. *You?* he mouthed.

Vaughn waved, then was yanked back to face Devon. "What are you doing?" Devon asked.

Wasn't it obvious? "Sayin' hi."

"To *him*?" Devon glanced between the two of them, then put both hands on Vaughn's shoulders and stared him straight in the face. "No. I'm saying this to you as a friend: Vaughn, darling, you're tanked. You need to go home. Forget the slut and go home."

Home? Not yet! He shook his head, then stopped because everything went all spinny. "And youuu," he patted at Devon's face, "are way too sob'r. Diyuuu drink the same as me?"

"No! You actually drank all those shots? Shit, Hargy, no wonder you're all over the place."

Wait a minute wait a minute *wait one minute*. Had Dev just said the word *slut*? About Jonah? Vaughn frowned. "Slut?"

"That just filter through? Jesus Christ. *Yes*. Look at him." They both looked. Jonah's eyes were slits and his expression said he was close to coming. They turned back to each other. "You can do way better than that," Devon said.

That? *That*? He was a *person*. And okay, he wasn't Vaughn's person and would never be Vaughn's person, for what were very obvious reasons, but that was no excuse to judge him. Vaughn glared at him. "Slut," he began, "isnnot a nice word."

The skeleton guy was Vaughn. Holy shit. Talk about hiding in plain sight. Jonah had spotted him earlier dancing in the crowd, but had already hooked a guy and was halfway to coming on the dance floor. Then he'd been taken over to the corner and brutally fucked against the wall. Good... but he needed more. Plus he hadn't actually come and the asshole had literally shot off and then shot off.

It wasn't enough. Nothing about tonight had been enough. Jonah was trying so hard to get out of his head that he was considering a dungeon visit. Despite taking it up the ass before and the twink now eagerly swallowing his cock, it wasn't *enough*. Maybe some dom letting loose on his ass would help him forget the conversation with the lawyer.

Jesus. That conversation. When he'd finally called the lawyer, he'd been put through right away. Turned out she represented his mother's estate and needed to contact him because his mother had died and mentioned Jonah in her will. Jonah wasn't being left anything—all assets were left to her family, meaning her other children—except a letter.

Her family. Her other children. She'd left him behind and started another family and *kept them*.

He groaned. He didn't want to think about it. The guy on his dick groaned in response and began bobbing, which helped. He closed his eyes and tried to get lost in the sensations of mouth over latexed cock, the music and bass line thumping in his bones, the deep ache in his ass, and the grimy sweat sticking him to the wall.

But Vaughn and his rich friend were nearby and he thought he could hear them arguing like a married couple over the music.

The twink swallowed him in deep, and his attention flipped back to the blowjob. Jonah put one hand on the guy's head and moved his fingers encouragingly. *So close.*

Something made him open his eyes. Vaughn was pushing his friend away, but his friend was sneering at Jonah. There was also heat in the guy's face and an obvious lump at his crotch; he was turned on.

No shit. Jonah was hot and getting some out in the open. They probably weren't his only audience. That knowledge sank deep hooks into him—*yes*, he was being watched and lusted over. Again. He'd been seen having sex in the open and now his cock was being sucked in front of anyone who cared to look. Anyone could watch and see him for what he was: a slut who would take anything dished out to him, who needed to be fucked as much as possible, by anyone willing, because that was all he deserved. Oh *God*, the filth of it. Intoxicating. Overwhelming. He moaned, unable to bear it, and stared back at Vaughn's rich friend. *That's right. Look at me. Look at what you don't have.*

That did it. He ground his head against the wall and came in a rush of black stars and that sweet, beckoning, brief oblivion. The darkness and shame of being exposed and desired swirled through his veins, and he gasped at the headiness of it. His body felt like it was levitating.

At his feet, the guy choked in surprise, bringing him back to earth. Jonah slumped against the wall, one hand scrabbling to keep himself upright. The guy eyed the full condom, then smacked Jonah's leg lightly. "You could've warned me, dirtbag."

"Sorry," Jonah breathed. Oh, that had been good. Shiiit, he'd needed that.

The twink stood and pressed himself against Jonah expectantly. Jonah took care of the condom and tucked himself away, then reached into the guy's pants and gave him a handjob, sucking on his neck halfheartedly. Exhaustion hit him abruptly, and he wanted the guy to come soon so he could leave.

He glanced around, seeing a few guys unobtrusively watching them. Some of them looked hopeful, like they were going to ask for a go too. He felt a mild thrill but also mild disgust at the idea. Compared to the feeling he'd had in that office—no, he wasn't thinking about that. *Better*. This was better.

His gaze fell on Vaughn and his friend. The skull gleamed in the dim light, turning Vaughn's pretty-boy looks into a surreal mask. His eyes were just black pits from here. The crazily great skeleton design on his bare chest swayed and waved as he talked to his friend.

The twink came in Jonah's hand. They cleaned up unceremoniously and the twink left for the dance floor.

The music throbbed and lights danced and luminous paint flickered around him; everything was abruptly overwhelming. The guys lingering by the wall seemed like too much now, and Vaughn was distracted by his friend, so Jonah moved away, aiming for the bar for some water, because suddenly there was a bad taste in his mouth.

This was a good point to go home: he'd fucked, he'd come, the itch in his blood was banked, the pain in his head was obliterated, and every part of him was loose and languid. Granted, his ass hurt, and he hadn't really reciprocated well, so not his best night, but he'd gotten what he'd wanted—

"Thass not fair, Dev."

Somehow he hadn't stumbled past them very quickly. That was Vaughn's smooth voice all right. Listen to him, trying to drunkenly tell his asshole friend off. Heh. That slur in his voice was kind of funny. Jonah hadn't heard that before.

"We are leaving right now," Dev said, "because— Oh Jesus." He reached out and steadied Vaughn. "Listen to me. Listen. You listening? He," and the douche bag pointed right at Jonah, "is just a hick scene queen who bends over for anyone with a dick and a wallet, and I am *not* here to hear you defending him."

What the fuck? Wallet? Hick?

Scene queen?

Oh sweet Jesus, no. No way did this rich asshole come here and insult him like that. No fucking way. Not in a gay club and not when there was already another couple sucking off in the corner behind him. Just who did he think he was? Anger rose, thick and sharp, and he strode forward.

Vaughn's hands tapped at Dev's arms. "Yurrrr terrible. *Such* a hipcrite." He cast about and saw Jonah. The skull stretched into a hideous grin. "Heyyy, Jonah."

He wasn't the guy Jonah had a problem with. "You got something to say to me?" Jonah demanded of his friend.

Dev, whatever the hell that was short for, leered at him. "Yeah. How much?"

Jonah rushed forward, ready to punch that expression off his rich face, but was blocked by Vaughn, whose hands were on his shoulders and who was yelling something like *no* and *stop*. Jonah tried to move around him, but Vaughn had gone heavy, and he had to turn around in order to prop him up. Jonah studied Vaughn, the way he swayed and the vacant expression on his face. Then Vaughn dropped completely, and Jonah wrapped his arms around him to stop him from falling to the floor.

Oh hell, he was *gone*. Jonah tried to get a good look at his face, but his head had flopped onto Jonah's shoulder. He instead turned to the worried face of Vaughn's asshole friend.

"I'll get some water," Dev said. "Try to wake him up." He dashed away.

Jonah hauled Vaughn over to the closest wall and propped him up against it. The paint on his chest and face was all smudged now. Jonah pinned him upright and started gently shaking him. "Vaughn? *Vaughn*?"

His head jerked up suddenly, and Vaughn squinted at him. "Jonah? Izzat you?"

"Yeah. What did you have?"

Vaughn lurched forward and hugged him. "Isssho good to see you."

Relieved he wasn't completely passed out, Jonah patted his back awkwardly. "Good to see you too. Stand up for me."

"Don' wanna."

"You have to."

"I'm here," Dev said breathlessly behind them. He came into view, bottles of water in hand, and smirked at Jonah. "How you doing there?"

Jonah glared back. "He's heavy."

Vaughn reared up. "No, 'm not." He stumbled backwards. Jonah held on to him to stop him from cracking his head against the wall. "Nooo musssles," he added as Jonah propped him gently against the wall again.

"How are you thinking of food at a time like this?" Dev asked, twisting open one of the bottles.

"He meant muscles." Jonah flexed his biceps while keeping Vaughn pinned to the wall with his other arm.

Dev rolled his eyes and offered the bottle to Vaughn. "Hargy, get this in you."

Vaughn glared at him. "Be nice."

"I promise I'll be a gentleman if you drink this."

"Youuu sh'be a gennelman all the time."

Jonah didn't like seeing him slurring and out of it like this. He grabbed the bottle from Dev and pushed it into Vaughn's hand. "Drink it," he snapped.

"Oooh, *okay*," Vaughn snapped back, then raised the bottle and bumped it into his chin. Both Dev and Jonah cursed and helped him aim it.

"What did he drink?" Jonah asked as Vaughn took big, slow gulps.

"Half the bar, apparently," Dev replied.

"He needs to go home."

Dev shot him a glare. "What do you think I was trying to do? He got all hung up on *you*. How does he know you, anyway?"

"Friennns."

"Drink your water," Dev told him.

"We know each other from work," Jonah said.

Dev's eyes widened. "My God. You have a day job?"

Vaughn made a noise behind the bottle. Jonah flipped Dev the bird. "Yeah, and I didn't need my daddy to help me get it."

They glared at each other. Jonah hated him, his tight jeans, his styled hair and his stupid expensive shirt with a horse on it. The paint smeared across his face couldn't hide his smirking, judging expression. Ugh. It had been an artsy display of ivy and flowers of some kind, which was totally wasted on the jerk. *This* was the guy Vaughn had dated?

"Ow," Vaughn said.

Jonah realized he was pressing too hard against Vaughn's shoulder. He carefully eased off without letting go. "How's the water?"

Vaughn closed his eyes. "'S good."

"No, no, no. Stay awake, Hargy." Dev tapped Vaughn's face.

"Drink more," Jonah added, gripping his hand and raising the bottle for him.

"Don' wanna." Vaughn blinked at him. "Yurr here, Jonah."

Yes, he was. He was somehow still there, propping up a wasted friend/client and getting UV paint all over his clothes. Normally he would be halfway home by now. What had happened? What had he done to find himself in this situation?

"I'm going to have Bogard drive around." Dev pulled out his phone.

"Bogard?"

"My driver."

For fuck's sake. "Get a taxi like a normal person."

Dev's fingers tapped away over his screen. "But where's the fun in that?" he said in a singsong voice.

"Yurrr so pretty," Vaughn said.

Jonah glanced at him. He thought Vaughn had been speaking to him, but he was focused on the water bottle. Which was empty. Good.

"Besides, the car has a bucket in it," Dev continued, "and the last thing I want is to stand in this ridiculous weather watching him upchuck for half an hour."

"So nice of you to do him a solid," Jonah muttered.

"You say something?"

Jonah bared his teeth. "I'll help you get him out."

Dev nodded and put away his phone. "Let's get our coats."

Together they half handled, half dragged Vaughn to the cloakroom and into his coat, then outside. Jonah had shrugged his on as well and shivered once they hit the cold air. Snow was falling and the path from the club through a parking lot to the main road was already slippery. As they marched Vaughn over, his arms around their shoulders, Jonah had to admit he didn't like the idea of being out here either, and he'd only had his usual single beer. God knew what was currently swimming in Vaughn's body and how that would react with the cold if he were left alone. The idea made him tighten his hold on Vaughn.

A glossy black Beemer waited for them. Dev threw open the door and gestured. "Come on, Hargy, your bed awaits."

Vaughn squinted. "Thass not my house."

Jonah patted his side. "Get in."

"Buh isso pretty." Vaughn was staring at the sky in joy. Jonah followed his gaze to see dark clouds and spiralling snowflakes lit by orange streetlights.

"You know what's pretty? The heated seats in the car." Dev got in and held his arms out. "Give him to me."

Jonah's grip tightened around Vaughn's torso. His jaw set. *Give Vaughn? No.* Then Vaughn staggered to one side and he remembered that, dickish as the friend was, he was helping. "Down here," Jonah said to Vaughn.

Vaughn looked down at him and smiled. "Heyyy, you're here!"

"You're going home."

Vaughn frowned. "Wi' you? But tha' dun make sense."

"Hargy!" Vaughn followed Dev's bark, then took a step forward and dived headfirst into the car. Jonah heard Devon swear, then Vaughn's body was dragged farther inside. Jonah helped push his legs in. Dev manoeuvred Vaughn into sitting upright in the middle of the backseat, then stared at Jonah. "You getting in?"

Jonah blinked. "Me?"

"Yeah."

"Heeey, Jonah." Vaughn waved at him.

Aw hell. He had to make sure he was okay. And he couldn't refuse a ride. Jonah slid in and closed the door.

Dev leaned back. "Wonderful. Bogard, do you remember Vaughn Hargrave's address?"

Jonah watched as the driver turned to confirm he did. He started driving and a black screen rose up to hide him from them. Or, more likely, them from him. Either way, this car was seriously like something out of a movie. The inside was all leather and there was a *cabinet* right in front of him with bottles of booze and plastic glasses. The windows were tinted, and there were cupholders in the doors and in the sides of the interior. This car probably cost more than several years of his wages.

Vaughn was looking at him. Jonah looked back. "You okay?"

Vaughn blinked slowly, then opened his mouth and carefully said, "Hockey."

It took Jonah a minute to get it. "You mean the Tuesday game?" Jonah patted Vaughn's knee. "I know, it was a close one."

Dev leaned forward and pulled a bucket out of the cabinet, as well as a beer. Jonah's jaw dropped. "Are you for fucking real?"

"It's either this or coke." Dev twisted the cap off and took a healthy glug. Jonah didn't think he meant the soft drink.

Fuck this asshole. Jonah reached over Vaughn's shoulder and pulled his seatbelt around to clip him in place, then took the second bottle of water from Vaughn, opened it, and handed it back to him. "Drink this," he said.

Vaughn stared at it. "Buh I already dran' the water."

Dev took the water and replaced it with the bucket. "Hold this for me, Hargy."

"Okay."

Jonah glared at him. "He needs more water."

Dev held up one finger. "Au contraire. He needs to throw up all the shots he stupidly drank, *then* he'll drink more water."

What the...? "Has he done this before?" Jonah asked. "Is this like a *routine*?"

"Please. The last time he got this drunk was years ago." Dev sipped his beer. "It was memorable though."

"So what happened tonight?"

"I'm hardly his keeper." Dev patted Vaughn's shoulder. "You were just having a good time, weren't you?"

"Jooonah."

"He seems to have taken a shine to you." Dev sipped his beer. "I can't imagine why."

"You don't know shit about me," Jonah said.

"I know what your cock and ass look like. Oh, wait, so does half the club." Dev's face held no heat or lust whatsoever now, just judgment. "And I know this guy is picky to the point of lunacy, but he deserves better than some backroom slut to fool around with. So whatever you're doing to reel him in, I'd advise you stop it."

Jonah scoffed. "What are you, his mother? He can make his own friends."

"You are not his friend."

Cold tendrils wiggled deep in his gut. "I am. And I'm not *reeling him in*, whatever the hell that even means."

"Stop," Vaughn said. Jonah turned to him. He was looking sickly now, but he seemed more alert. "Youuu guyser bein' loud." He paused, then his mouth twisted. "Thin' I'm gonna be sick."

Dev patted the bucket. "Go right ahead, Hargy."

Vaughn nodded, then hunched over the bucket and barfed.

Jonah tried to ignore the splattering sounds. "He drank shots. *He* did. Why?"

Dev looked uncertain for the first time. "I don't know. He did seem a bit down earlier. We were supposed to visit this place on the weekend, but he suggested tonight."

Jonah watched Vaughn heave and dug into his coat for some tissues.

"Montgomery Devon Darvell, by the way," Dev said.

It took him a few seconds to realize Devon was introducing himself. "Jonah Sondern." He smirked. *Montgomery.* What a name. But Darvell sounded familiar.

"*His* last name is Hargrave, in case you hadn't got that far yet," Devon said.

Wasn't Darvell the name of a pharmaceutical company? Jonah could've sworn he'd read that name in the news. He rescanned the interior, then met Devon's smug gaze.

"Yes," he said. "That Darvell."

"That didn't sound rehearsed at all."

"I met him at university, though our parents have known each other forever," Devon continued.

"Let me guess, his daddy raises investment money for your daddy, and you've been promised to each other since birth."

"Hardly." Devon pointed with his beer bottle. "But let's ask about you. Who the hell are you? Who are your parents? Where did you go to university, assuming you did go? Where do you work? And how long have you been hanging around Hargy?"

He hated that nickname. "Ooh, gosh darn it, Monty, you got me. I'm just your regular moose in a suit looking for a quick buck." He grinned at the way Devon's face darkened. "No one gives a shit about that. All his money isn't stopping him from puking his guts out."

Devon's mouth twitched. "I'll give you that."

"'M sorry," Vaughn said from within the bucket.

Jonah rubbed his shoulder. "Just get it out."

By the time the car pulled up outside Vaughn's apartment building, Jonah was ready to fling the bucket out the window. Vaughn hugged it, one cheek against the rim. "Feel terble," he moaned.

"Just you wait until tomorrow." Devon clapped his shoulder. "Time to go outside again."

"Nooo. Isss warm."

Devon drained the rest of his beer and dumped it in a small trash can next to the cabinet, then opened the door and climbed out. Jonah unbuckled Vaughn, handed Devon the bucket, and together they managed to get him outside and the bucket cleaned with snow. Devon slammed the door shut and spoke to his driver while Jonah hustled

Vaughn inside, bucket in one hand. He heard the car drive away, and then Devon was on Vaughn's other side.

"Good morning, Mr. Hargrave, Mr. Darvell, Mr. Sondern," the concierge called to them as they staggered into the building.

"Hi, Pete," Devon replied.

"Hey, isss my house!" Vaughn crowed.

"Please tell me he's easy to put to bed," Jonah said as they called the elevator.

Devon snorted. "The last thing Hargy is is *easy*. Especially in bed."

Vaughn roused himself. "Hey."

"I love you, buddy, but it's true." Devon winked at Jonah. "Barely reacts. Sometimes I wondered if he was even gay."

Vaughn had slept with this asshole? Right, they'd been boyfriends. Still. What the shit. *How?* Jonah would've thrown up on principle if he had to fuck him. And what was with that last statement? Weren't they supposed to be friends? Un-fucking-believable. Jonah felt sick to his stomach. "How can you talk about him like that?"

"Hey, just giving you a heads-up so you don't waste your time."

Just like that, he was ready to punch the guy again. "He's right here. If you have so much money, buy some class."

Devon just laughed.

They hustled into the elevator and didn't say a word again until they got to Vaughn's door. Jonah found Vaughn's keys in his pocket and let them in. Devon leaned Vaughn against a wall while Jonah locked up behind them, then Jonah dug around for a towel while Devon tried to take off Vaughn's jacket, Vaughn fighting the entire time. Jonah noticed with a sinking stomach that it was almost 3 a.m., according to the timer on the oven.

"Iss warm." Vaughn held his jacket closed. They'd zipped it on over his bare chest because his shirt had disappeared somewhere.

"Darling, how big is your latest painting?" Devon asked.

Vaughn blinked, then stretched out his arms. "Thisss big." Devon tugged one sleeve off, then the other. "Iss gonna be blue."

Jonah approached with the towel. "Hold still." He started with the paint on Vaughn's shoulder. To his surprise, Vaughn went very still. Jonah gently wiped off the paint, taking care not to tug too much on Vaughn's chest hair, and noted with a scowl that someone had left finger marks on his pants over his groin. When he got to Vaughn's face, he gripped his chin and carefully rubbed the towel over him. Vaughn looked at him steadily, his expression turning uncertain as Jonah wiped.

"You're angry," he said.

Something in Jonah's chest twisted sharply. "I don't like seeing you like this."

"I'm sorry."

"It's fine." Most of the paint was gone by now, but Jonah wanted to stay close like this, to see those eyes focused intently on him. For someone so totally hosed, Vaughn was surprisingly lucid. He gently rubbed away small smudges of paint along Vaughn's cheek.

"I dun wanyew to be mad. I like you a lot."

"I like you too, buddy."

"Nooo, I mean I *really* like you. Like you sooo much." Vaughn frowned. "I wusn gonna tell you that."

That twisty thing turned further. *Oh.*

Jonah's hands stilled on Vaughn's jaw. He was so aware of Vaughn's bare skin, the slight stubble under his fingers, and the heat coming off his body. *All that skin.* Beautiful, even while drunk, and Jonah tried to focus on the bad stuff, like the fact Vaughn'd let someone else grope him and how gross his breath was and that it was 3 a.m. and that they all should've been in bed hours ago. Literally any other part of this night except what Vaughn had just said, because that couldn't be true. How could he *like* Jonah? It had to be the alcohol talking.

And now Vaughn looked embarrassed. The last thing they needed was a sad drunk on top of an apologetic one. Luckily, Jonah knew drunk logic. "I'll forget about it."

Vaughn's expression brightened. "You will?"

"Yeah."

"Yurrr amazin'. Tha's why I like you. Can I hug you?"

Jonah lowered the towel. "You're going to bed."

A puppy couldn't have looked more disappointed if Jonah had told it no more toys for today. "Okay."

Jonah tossed the towel down and put one of Vaughn's arms around his shoulders. Then he noticed Devon standing there, watching them in silence. "You enjoying the show, Monty, or you wanna help me?"

Devon gestured. "Play on, Sondern. He listens to you."

Jonah walked Vaughn into his bedroom and sat him on the bed. He dug through the pile of clothes at the foot of the bed and found a T-shirt and sweatpants that looked promising. "Arms up."

Vaughn obeyed, smiling as Jonah tugged the T-shirt over his head and down his body. "Thisiss fun."

"I'm so glad you're having a good time." He patted Vaughn's hip. "Pants off."

"Buh I tol' you abouh my aseshuality."

Jonah rolled his eyes. "I'm not sexing you. Pants off."

Vaughn crossed his arms. "No."

He dropped the sweatpants. There was no time for this, not at three o'clock in the morning. "Fine." He knelt and pulled off Vaughn's shoes, then rolled back the covers. "Bedtime."

Vaughn climbed clumsily under the covers and lay back. Devon appeared with a bottle of water and the bucket in hand. He placed them next to Vaughn, then bent over him. "See you in four hours, Hargy."

"Thansh, Dev."

Jonah went out ahead of Devon and retrieved the towel. He paused when he saw the empty wall in the living room, the one where the lion mural had been. Vaughn was starting a new one?

Behind him, Devon opened the linen closet and began pulling out sheets. "You wanna shower or you hitting the sack?"

There was a hamper next to the bathroom. Jonah dumped the towel in there. "I'm heading home."

"Why?" Devon held a spare duvet. "Man, I live around the corner and there's no way I'm heading back outside. Stay the night and sleep in."

"I have work tomorrow."

"So do I."

"I don't have clothes." All he had were his paint-smeared clubbing clothes.

Devon put one hand on his hip. "It's such a shame we don't live in the middle of a city full of clothing stores."

He had a point. God, Jonah was so tired. And no, he didn't particularly *want* to go back outside. "Fine." He grabbed the duvet. "I'm taking the couch."

"We both are."

Jonah held up a finger. "I'm not sleeping with you."

Devon scowled. "Don't worry, I'd like to remain STD-free."

"Fuck you." Jonah hauled himself and his duvet to the couch, stripped down to his boxers, and curled up with his head on a cushion. He listened to Devon use the bathroom, turn off lights, then bed down on the opposite section of the couch.

His thoughts turned straight to what Vaughn had said. He couldn't've meant it. Drunk people spouted all kinds of crap.

Only, Vaughn didn't strike him as being the kind of guy who'd say crap like *that* for no reason. Even when drunk. What if he *did* like him? Seriously like him? What if he wanted to be more than friends?

The idea was . . . Jonah could see it. He could see other nights where they partied and gamed and danced and ate together, he really could. Their time would be theirs, all theirs, separate from anyone else. All that Vaughn was, his art nerdiness and stupid clothes and blushes, would be Jonah's to enjoy and look after. Stereotypical scenes ran through his head: lying in bed, shopping, eating food, cuddling on Vaughn's massive couch. Nice scenes. Scenes that woke up an old, forgotten ache under his ribs.

Yeah. That wasn't so crazy. Having this sweet guy as a boyfriend would be . . . good. The kind of good that Jonah thought he could maybe handle. Like, if things kept going the way they were, that would be awesome.

But why him? What could Vaughn, who was on this whole other level from Jonah, possibly see in him? And what about sex? How would that work?

A pit grew in his stomach. Had Vaughn and Devon seen him ass up as well as the blowjob? The idea was mortifying now, outside of the club and hours later. No way could Vaughn have seen everything he'd done tonight, because if he had, he wouldn't have said that to him. No one in their right mind would say that to him if they knew he slept around as much as he did. Especially if they knew he fucked to chase that hard, numbing feeling with each orgasm, the delicious shame of being exposed and desired by anyone who cared to look. And definitely not if they knew he needed it, craved it, *loved* it.

Devon was right—he did bend over for anyone with a dick, and he wasn't right for someone like Vaughn. He wasn't right for anyone. He was sick and unwanted, and Vaughn would be better off with literally any other guy, even Devon.

Had his mother seen it? Had she somehow known about him, that there was something wrong with him? Was that why she'd left him so long ago?

Don't be stupid. You were five. She left because . . .

Well, he didn't know why. No one had been able to find her, not for him. He'd read his case file: *abandoned; mother unable to be found, father not known.* And now she was dead and he'd never find out.

The effect of that orgasm, the dark, uplifting freedom of it, was long gone. He needed it again, in this precise moment, to shove all these thoughts out of his head. But he was stuck in this sleek, silent apartment with snow falling outside and work six hours away. Him, his head, a guy who hated him, and the guy who apparently liked him passed out in the room next door.

He curled the duvet around himself more tightly and tried to fall asleep.

CHAPTER ELEVEN

His alarm woke him up, but once consciousness had been reached, Vaughn wished he were still asleep. His mouth tasted like decaying bile, his stomach rolled, and his head pounded. He was fairly certain he stank. Hangovers really did get worse with age; death had to be preferable to this.

Someone knocked on his door, then opened it. "Good morning!" Devon called.

"Nooo," Vaughn groaned.

"I'll get coffee going!" The door closed.

Vaughn forced himself to open his eyes and take stock. He wore a T-shirt. And his pants from last night, which stuck to him uncomfortably. *Ugh.* And there were smears of UV paint on his bedsheets. *Great.*

A dim memory of Jonah putting the shirt on him came to mind. Jonah had been here? Was he still here?

Vaughn sat up, swore at the way his head throbbed, then forced himself to stand. He downed the bottle of water next to his bed, then stripped off his pants and replaced them with sweats. When he opened his door, he saw two piles of laundry on his couch and one Devon in his kitchen.

"Is Jonah here?" he asked.

"Oh, he left ages ago." Devon pressed buttons on the coffee machine. "How are you feeling?"

"Like death threw me up."

"You won't remember, but I told you so."

Vaughn ran one hand through his hair, surveying the couch. "You two slept here?"

"Don't worry, I remain unmolested."

Vaughn tried to replay last night. He remembered the club and shots and dancing with people and seeing Jonah, but after that it got very fuzzy. There was a lingering sense of anger and surprise. He frowned. "Did I yell at you?"

Devon scowled at the machine. "I called Jonah some unworthy things and you got a bit angry, yes."

"What did you say?"

"Nothing of any consequence." Devon looked far better than Vaughn did. Knowing him, he'd already showered and needed only coffee and his shoes to leave.

"What did you *say*?"

Devon pouted. "Do I really have to repeat myself on such a beautiful day?"

It *was* a nice day. Early morning light streamed through the living room windows, and he blinked against the brightness. What time was it? Later than he normally woke up, but not by much. Before nine at least. Vaughn rubbed at his face. Ugh. He need to shower and wake up. "Hold that thought." He stumbled to the bathroom.

Ten minutes later he came back out, towel around his waist. Devon was pounding the machine with his fist. "I think I broke your coffee machine," he called as Vaughn lumbered into his bedroom. He dug out an outfit and returned to the kitchen, tucking his shirt into his chinos.

"Let me look." He pushed Devon out of the way. "And while I fix it, you sit down and tell me what you said about Jonah."

Devon retreated behind the breakfast bar. "Nothing more than what I'd said when we only knew him as the threesome guy."

"This is too early in the morning to be evasive."

"This is too early in the morning to be judgmental." Devon yawned.

The machine looked fine. He dug in the freezer for the bag of coffee grounds he kept there for guests, and suddenly a memory returned. He turned to glare at Devon. "I remember what you said. You called him a slut, among other things."

Devon shrugged. "I call 'em as I see 'em."

"You're terrible."

Devon cast him a level look. "Like you have ever given a shit before."

Vaughn turned to his coffee machine rather than respond to that. The machine wasn't used much—perhaps all of three times before now. He opened a lid uncertainly and poured the grounds in.

"I will never comprehend how you can be so envious of promiscuity and so disapproving of it at the same time." Vaughn slammed the lid shut, then pushed the On button. Nothing happened. "Why do you care about him anyway?"

"Because in the four years since we left university, I haven't seen you be interested in anyone." Devon leaned against the bar. "You've danced with a lot of guys, you've kissed exactly five, and you've had sex with zero."

Oh God. He *had* noticed. Vaughn's face burned. He hid it by checking the plug—which wasn't plugged in. Ah. He did that, then pushed the On button. Things lit up. Promising.

"And I *know* you're blushing there."

Vaughn glanced at him. "I *might* have had sex—"

Devon fixed him with a knowing smile. "Hargy, look. I'm not stupid. I'm not *blind*. I totally get it."

He . . . did? No, he couldn't. He'd come to his own conclusions. Vaughn mentally braced himself.

"You're aiming long-haul. You want a boyfriend."

Vaughn stared at him, wondering if Devon was still drunk.

Devon spread his hands. "I know you. You like the scene, but you don't want grinding and alley sex. You want domesticity." He fluttered his eyes at him. "The adoring boyfriend who cooks you food and plays games with you and goes to weddings with you."

His face burned again.

Someone else in this space with him. Someone who knew how to use his coffee machine. Someone who *would* use his coffee machine. Maybe, if Vaughn were being entirely honest, he sometimes thought that was a nice idea. That it would be good—wonderful, even, or ideal—to wake up with someone he liked and who liked him. Share the morning. Share dinner. Share a life. Ease the strain of family brunch.

Jonah would fit into the role surprisingly well.

The only hiccup was that that arrangement came with sex. It *always* came with sex. For Jonah, the sex would absolutely be a given. Vaughn had done some reading about what other mixed-orientation couples did together, and he had ideas about borderline sexual stuff he'd be comfortable doing with someone that might ease the sex side of things, but he didn't think Jonah would be satisfied with that. Hell, he *knew* Jonah wouldn't be satisfied with that. Last night was just the latest example of how not okay he'd be.

"Hey. I get it," Devon continued. "That's the dream eventually, right? And I'm glad you still come out with us, because we like having you. By the way, is that thing meant to be making that noise?"

It was still beeping. Vaughn turned around and started pulling at handles on the machine. Eventually a deep tank came out, which he filled with water.

Devon kept talking. "So you're holding out for the right guy. Can't say I agree that's the best way to approach it, but you do you, right? You're my brother from another mother. I'll support you all the way." Devon's toned changed. "But I'm telling you—this guy? Not the one."

Vaughn sighed and pushed a random button. The steam wand spat out dust and water before hissing steam. "Jesus!" He hit the button again to make it stop. "Is your only problem with him that he sleeps around?"

Devon scoffed. "He wears cheap shoes, cuts his own hair, buys condoms in bulk, and has a crappy attitude. Shitty clothes aside, he'll sleep around. Plus what does he do? Who's his family? Darling, you deserve better than that."

Vaughn reached into a cupboard for a mug. "Bitch really *is* your colour."

Better than that? This from the man who'd joked they could marry and who promised to cheat discreetly on him? Unbelievable.

Vaughn shook his head, pushed another few buttons, and finally brown liquid began streaming from the machine into the mug. "Your inner snob is showing."

"You know people would ask."

"You know how little I care. And I do like him," he admitted. "But you'll be relieved to hear it's not going to go anywhere. You're right, we're not suited." He glared at him. "But it's not for the reasons you're thinking."

Devon raised his eyebrows in clear disbelief. "So you say."

"Also, I'm not trying for a boyfriend."

Devon waved his hand. "Your delusions about the depths of your loneliness would be hilarious if they weren't so sad, my friend."

"I'm not lonely."

"Paintbrushes don't count as friends."

The machine stopped pouring coffee. Vaughn placed the mug in front of Devon, who gazed at it warily.

"I have friends," Vaughn said. "I have a job. I have family. I have interests. I'm not lonely, and I'm not looking for a relationship. And even if I was, like I said, he and I aren't suited, so it wouldn't work out anyway."

Devon sipped his coffee slowly. "I approve of your pragmatism. You should know that you told him you liked him and he couldn't leave quick enough this morning."

Vaughn's stomach bottomed out. He held on to the counter, needing something solid under him. "I did *what*?"

"He was wiping paint off you, and you were charmingly out of it enough to tell him you, quote, 'really like' him." Dev smirked. "Honestly, it was very sweet."

Oh no. Oh *no*. Vaughn's head sagged until it touched the kitchen counter. "He won't take it seriously, will he?" he asked against the granite.

"I have no idea."

"What else did I do last night?"

"Throw up on the way home."

Vaughn winced. So that *was* bile he'd tasted. "Give my apologies to Bogard."

"And pass out for a moment, which made both of us worry." Devon grimaced. "To give credit where credit is due, Jonah stepped up admirably when he realized how wasted you were."

He never got that drunk. *Never*. This one time, Jonah had to be there. Of course. Life wasn't cruel enough. What did he think of him? *Did* he think of him? Vaughn wanted a sinkhole to erupt in his kitchen floor and swallow him whole. Yes, death was preferable to waking up this morning.

"Much as I'd love to rehash this some more, I believe we're both gainfully employed and need to move on with our days." Devon stood, pushing his cup away.

"You can leave me here to rot."

"Oh, *come* on."

Devon herded him out of the building and in the direction of work. When Devon left, calling Bogard as he walked away, Vaughn began traipsing to the gallery and immediately pulled out his phone to call Jonah. It rang, then went to voice mail. Damn it.

He paused and sent a message. *Thank you for looking after me last night. I'm sorry if I said or did anything crass. I'm incredibly hungover and barely remember a thing. Devon said you had to leave early. Did he say anything to you?*

No doubt Devon had said something to him. Devon's idea of tact was about as subtle as a brick. Vaughn hoped it hadn't been too bad. Jonah could give as good as he got, but there was no need for unpleasantness to begin with. If Devon had been as judgmental as Vaughn knew he could be, then he had a lot to apologize for.

Now that he was outside, the full force of the day's beauty hit him. The sun shone in a clear blue sky, a fresh coat of snow made everything sparkle, Yorkville was decked out in Christmas decorations, and people wore smiles as they ambled the streets. How dare today be so pretty when he felt this vile. A memory of orange-tinted snow falling onto him, of a strong arm around his body, flashed back from last night.

There was no way he hadn't disgraced himself. The question was how badly. He hoped Jonah still wanted to talk to him, but judging by what Devon had said, that looked unlikely.

He stopped at a café to pick up tea and breakfast and ate it on the way to the gallery. Still no return call. Opened the gallery, did the rounds, checked emails, all the while with one hand on his phone, waiting.

Jonah didn't call until the evening, when there was one lingering visitor in the gallery and Angeline was digging in the closet near the front desk. Vaughn saw Jonah's name appear and swiped to answer so quickly he almost sent the phone flying off the desk.

"Hello," he said.

"Hey." Jonah sounded tired.

"How are you?"

"I've been better."

Oh no. Vaughn swivelled his chair away from the closet. "I'm so sorry about last night. I'm sorry I got drunk, I'm sorry for everything Devon said to you, I'm sorry you were dragged into looking after me—"

"Hold up, pretty boy. You're not a bad drunk. You need better friends, though."

He *knew* it. "Devon's an acquired taste. I promise he was much nicer when I first met him."

"Do you even remember half the shit he said?"

Vaughn leaned back. "I remember him calling you names. I'm certain he'd say them to your face."

"Forget the shit he said to me, he talked shit about *you*."

Oh. He was angry about that? "That's not really anything new. He likes to run his mouth. It's how we communicate."

"It's fucked up."

"I don't disagree, but I find he's easy to get along with provided you only take a pinch of what he says with any seriousness." *And watch what he does rather than what he says.* "He did get us home."

"I guess." Jonah didn't sound convinced.

Vaughn moved up to the windows that fronted the foyer. "He told me I said something to you."

Silence on the line. Vaughn's pulse hammered in his head and throat.

When Jonah didn't say anything, Vaughn made himself continue. "I know it's not . . . ideal. For you."

"For me?"

"That I like you."

"Dude, did you *see* me last night?"

"Briefly." Throughout the day, he'd remembered the odd thing: Jonah's face twisted in concentration against the wall, being pulled towards the washroom, being very close and angry. "I remember some things."

"I had sex with two guys in that club, Vaughn. I topped a guy the day before that, and gave a blowjob the day before *that*, and I'm not going to tell you how many handjobs I've had in the last two weeks. Do we see a pattern here?"

Vaughn swallowed. "I know you like to—"

"It's more than *like to*. I want it. I need it. Don't you get it?"

He did. Vividly. "My feelings would be less of an issue if you could sleep with me, yes."

"Oh my God, *no*." He could imagine Jonah pacing, cell to his ear, his other hand waving emphatically. "It doesn't matter how much you like me, or how much you'd let me do you, I'd still fuck other people. Because I'd want to and need to."

"I don't care about that." Because he'd thought about it, and he really didn't.

A stunned silence came down the line. "What the hell is wrong with you? How can you *not care* about your boyfriend fucking other people?"

Boyfriend. He'd used the word *boyfriend*. Vaughn's mouth went dry. "Who you have sex with is your business. I would never tell someone what to do sexually. Sex is fundamental, like wanting kids and having similar life values. People need what they need, and something like that isn't negotiable."

"Well good for you, but over here in the real world, people give a shit about that kind of stuff. They care who you fuck and how and when and where, and if it's not with your partner, then you'd better not have one."

Where was this coming from? "Who cares about other people? Jonah, is that what *you* think?"

"It's what I *know*."

"You *are* aware open relationships exist?" If he'd entertained the concept of *boyfriend*, then maybe he'd thought about that? Perhaps there was hope for them yet. "You could do whatever you wanted to with other guys. I wouldn't care. Whatever happens between us is between us."

"And just how well would that go down at brunch?" Jonah put on an accent. "'Oh yes, Mother, we had a *lovely* evening together. Jonah bottomed for a stranger in a bar on the way home from work, and I made cassoulet for dinner and let him use my shower while I painted an overpriced masterpiece; it was *tremendous*. By the way, let's ignore how Jonah's poor and doesn't have any family and likes sex with strangers instead of with me, and be grateful he knows how to use cutlery.' I don't think so."

Vaughn froze there, next to the glass, eyes fixed on the snowy street outside. The cold seemed to be leeching into his body through his fingers and stomach. He'd expected anger, but not mockery. "Is that what you think I sound like?" His voice wavered a little. "What you think my family would care about? That you were raised in foster care? *Cutlery?*"

"The *point* is I don't fit."

"I think you do. You could fit in anywhere you choose. But being a judgmental prick is a bad look no matter where you're from."

"I don't give a shit."

"Clearly."

"We done here? Because I have to find someone who pays taxes and rent and has a real job to blow me."

Unwilling to listen anymore, Vaughn hung up. He stared at his cell. It was ridiculous, but he half expected it to apologize to him for letting such a terrible conversation happen. An urge to smash it on the floor rose thick and harsh, and he took a few deep breaths, hand clenching around it. He'd just gotten it fixed. He'd just—

"You okay?" Angeline asked behind him. He startled, then felt a piece of plastic give under his clenched fingers. Half of the back of his phone flipped up and fell on the floor.

They stood over it in surprise. "Sorry," she said.

"Not your fault. It's gone through a lot lately." He picked it up and tried to press it back onto his phone. Jeez, his phone looked as though he *had* thrown it on the floor. He could picture it on a plinth, tape around it to mark viewing distance, and a placard: *Modern Anger.*

"Sounded like a fight."

He gazed at her. She stared back, brown eyes steady. *A fight.* She and Cressida argued occasionally, but never like that. Jonah had sounded bitter and almost hateful. Was Vaughn's family really that big a deal? Did Jonah really think they'd care about his background?

Devon.

Ah, yes, Devon's family would. No doubt he was responsible for some of what Jonah had just said. Vaughn needed to have words with him about privilege and people's feelings, especially if he was bringing a rookie employee as a date to this place next week.

What if he wasn't responsible for that, though? What if Jonah genuinely thought he and his family were ridiculous stereotypes?

Who cared? It didn't matter. Not anymore. Vaughn couldn't get rid of his family, and Jonah clearly didn't give a shit about him. Hadn't Vaughn expected this all along? He'd told himself not to hope, that there was no way anything real would happen between them.

It just went to show—what did he know, really? He hadn't been this close to something romantic in years. And the funny, awful thing was, they hadn't even been that close.

Vaughn sighed. "It was. But it's nothing. I'll get over it." Maybe.

"Other fish in the sea."

"I'm an awful fisherman, Angeline."

She bumped his shoulder. "I've seen the way some of the boys look at you. This one's obviously a dud. The Christmas party's next week, then you won't have to see me or Maurice for two weeks."

That thought *was* encouraging. Christmas. The gallery would be closed for two weeks while Angeline and Cressida visited family in Europe. He'd spend time with his parents, brother, and impending sister-in-law, eat good food, paint a lot, maybe even drive out of town for a day or two. Niagara Falls frozen in the winter was one of his favourite winter phenomena. Devon would be skiing somewhere with his family, so Vaughn wouldn't have to see him for a while.

All good things.

The prospect of a holiday distraction still didn't make him feel any better.

CHAPTER TWELVE

Jonah checked the time on his computer. Again. He had an appointment with the lawyer representing his mother's estate at one o'clock, and even though he'd been watching the clock, he was irrationally scared he wouldn't leave work on time to get to it.

Around him, the office buzzed with the sound of people talking and typing. Tinsel glistened on the edge of each cubicle, and the requisite Christmas baking took up a spot a few desks away from him. Not that he was interested anymore. His appetite had decreased over the last few days. It was a good thing; he'd been eating too much as it was. The office was in a minor uproar over the discovery of someone in the Processing Department who'd been found shredding claims documentation. Jonah's job had become easier since they'd been fired, but he couldn't find it in himself to be relieved about it.

No. He felt like shit because the previous week's argument with Vaughn still wasn't sitting well with him. He thought by now, after a weekend of clubbing and working out and the hookups he'd scored during those things, he'd be over it. But he wasn't. Every time he thought of how he'd raged at Vaughn, so angry at his refusal to see reality, his palms went clammy and his stomach clenched.

Now, mentally rerunning the argument for the several hundredth time, Jonah cringed. Mocking the way Vaughn talked? Whacking his feelings back in his face? Jonah wasn't great on the whole making-friends-and-keeping-them thing, but he knew you didn't do that. You didn't make fun of people and tell them something was wrong with them. And he'd said that to *Vaughn*.

The guy who'd thought something was wrong with himself for years because he didn't want sex. Dick move.

Vaughn had been a dick too, though. Okay, Jonah knew he couldn't control his feelings, but what was with him thinking they could be together and everything would be okay? Didn't he see what a fucking mess Jonah was? The sex was one thing, but didn't he realize Jonah could never be like him and his friends, with their ridiculous chauffeured cars and shiny apartments and family money and expensive clothes? Sure, one day Jonah was going to have his own money, but he'd never have that lazy ease with it Vaughn and his asshole friend Devon had.

Much as Jonah hated to admit it, Devon had been right about one thing: he didn't have family or connections, and that alone meant he was nothing to the people Vaughn knew.

Didn't Vaughn see all that? Didn't he understand how different they were?

A buzz from his cell announced a text from Adrian. *Dude. Not seen you in forever. Movie this weekend?*

In forever? It had been a week at most. *Jeez, Adrian.* He put his phone aside and glanced at the time. Another fifteen minutes had passed.

Last week had been something else. Apart from the events of That Night, waking up foggy-brained in Vaughn's apartment wasn't something he wanted to repeat. Devon had grumbled at him for setting a six thirty alarm, not that Jonah had cared. The guy could deal with the wake-up time of the proletariat. He'd pulled his clothes on, grimacing at how smelly they were, then checked in on Vaughn, who thankfully had been breathing softly in his bed, fast asleep. No more puke, water untouched, his face at peace. Okay. Then he'd left, thwacking the couch by Devon's head with his phone as he passed by.

The fogginess had hung around for the rest of the day, all through buying fresh clothes so he didn't go into work looking like he'd stopped by on a walk of shame, and while processing claims. He'd called the lawyer again and arranged an appointment for today. Before he knew it, the day had passed and he'd barely eaten or stopped. Calling Vaughn at the end of the day, when he'd been so tired and frustrated, had probably not been the best idea he'd ever had.

Honestly, if he never again heard Vaughn's voice crack the way it had during that call, it would be too soon. Vaughn had to hate his guts after that. *Had* to.

He ignored the way his chest hurt whenever he thought about it.

Time to stop dwelling on what had happened. There was nothing he could do about it now. That ship had been torpedoed, sunk, and torpedoed again. No, he just had the small matter of formally acknowledging his mother had ever existed to look forward to, then he could return to life as planned.

Finally it hit quarter to and he could step out. He rushed down the street to the lawyer's office—so convenient to work in Toronto's legal and financial district—and announced himself to the receptionist. Within a few minutes, he was led into an office with the lawyer, a middle-aged woman in a suit so sharp he wondered how she didn't hurt herself. And where she'd gotten it, because the fabric was amazing.

"Mr. Sondern," she greeted him warmly. "I'm so glad we finally reached you."

They shook hands and sat down. His stomach twisted and clawed at him, and he had to force himself to lean back and relax. "Nice to meet you."

"You too. As I said on the phone, I've been charged to settle your mother's estate." She pulled a file of documents towards her. "I understand you hadn't been in contact with her for quite a long time."

"Yeah." His voice was hoarse. "Since I was five."

She nodded like that was completely normal. "I've been given permission to tell you a few details about her life. Would you be interested in hearing them?"

He nodded, a lump in his throat.

"After she left you, she assumed a new name, married a business owner in Waterloo, and had three children with him. I understand she struggled most of her life with various addictions—alcohol, tobacco, cocaine, among other things—but managed to stay sober and clean for the last five years. She died a few months ago, of heart problems and complications related to early persistent drug use."

Drug use? Alcohol addiction? *Cocaine*? This didn't sound like the woman he barely remembered. But at age five, he wouldn't have noticed stuff like that. Was that why she'd left him? Drugs?

"Her children and husband weren't aware of you," the lawyer continued. "The will was a surprise to them." Boo-freaking-hoo. He had no sympathy for them. "Your mother left instructions to give you this letter." She pulled a yellowing envelope out of her file and placed it on the desk. "This is her only bequest to you. You have the right to take it or to refuse it. If you refuse it, I must have you fill out an official waiver."

Jonah stared at it. The envelope had *Jonah* scrawled on it in pen. "I'll take it," he said around the lump in his throat. She passed it to him, and he held the envelope between his thumb and index finger. It felt so light.

The lawyer hesitated. "I imagine this is difficult for you."

No shit. He set the letter down. "Did you know her?"

"No. I'm not her official lawyer. I was charged with finding you and executing this part of her will because I'm based in Toronto."

"Sounds expensive."

She smiled. "Not for you. My time is billed from her estate."

"Is there anything else I should know?"

She paused. "Her husband is curious about you. I've been instructed that if you wish to contact him or your half siblings, I can give you his name and phone number."

Half siblings. He had three half siblings and a stepfather. "What's he like? What's his name? How old are the kids? Can I ask that?"

She lost the smile. "You can ask, but I can't answer."

He was twenty-four. If she'd married someone else and had three kids, then they'd have to be pretty young. They'd lost a mother too. He felt a pang at the idea of that, of her leaving behind more kids. "I'd like his name, please."

She nodded, pulled out a business card, and passed it to him. He pushed it into his suit pocket without looking at it. "Is that everything?"

She spread her hands. "That's it. Sign some paperwork for me and we're done."

He did that, then left her office, the letter tucked beside the business card in his pocket, and his body hardly there, like he was mist or a mirage. He barely paid attention to the receptionist or to the jolt of the cold air outside the building.

A few steps down the street, he stopped, pulled out the envelope, and opened it. A single sheet of paper rested inside, a letter in cursive writing, the same ballpoint and neat curves as on the envelope.

Dear Jonah,

I'm not sure how to begin this letter. I don't know how old you'll be when you get it. You may not remember me much, but I think about you every day. I imagine you must hate me, or perhaps that's my own feelings talking to me. I think I would hate me.

I wanted to write this to tell you that I'm sorry. I know I did a terrible thing to you. Here's how it happened. I had you alone because your daddy didn't want to be a father, but I couldn't handle you. I was young and not good at making the right choices, and I wasn't looking after you right. You probably don't remember, but there were times I forgot to feed you or play with you because I was high or passed out. Sometimes I hated you and thought you hated me. I felt so bad and messed up, and I left you because I thought that was the best thing I could do, to let someone better look after you.

I feel differently now. I regret doing that and I'm sorry. You were a sweet kid and I didn't appreciate you. Nothing that I did was your fault.

I hope a nice family took you in. You were probably adopted right away because you were such a cute kid. I hope you got a mother who looked after you properly and fed you right and loved you. I hope you have a nice life, one with a good job and people who love you. I hope you don't do what I did and drink too much and chase bad experiences and push people away. It's not worth it. I sometimes imagine your life and I see things like you marrying a pretty girl or graduating university or flying around the world. But I think my favourite way to imagine you is sitting in a restaurant with your friends and having a good time.

As you can maybe tell, I'm not very brave. I wish I could say I wanted to find you and meet you, but I never did. I think I'm too scared of seeing you in real life. I messed up your life enough already and meeting you again would maybe have messed it up more.

I hope this letter answered some of your questions. I'm sorry again. Part of me hopes this letter doesn't matter to you at all because you've moved on. I think that's probably the best way I could picture you.

Your mother,

Anna

His hands shook. His cheeks stung. He wanted to simultaneously rip the letter apart and clutch it protectively to his chest. Three apologies, some fantasies and life advice, and that was *it*? Years of being shunted from place to place because the system didn't let kids form attachments to temporary carers; years of being looked over for adoption because he was too old, which wasn't a problem that ever, ever went away; years of bullying and rules and moving and hurt, all because *she couldn't handle raising him*?

She was right to be scared. If he'd gotten this when he was younger, if he'd met her again, he'd have screamed at her. This letter was cowardly. The last word in a conversation he'd never had a voice in. How was he supposed to use this? To deal with this?

It wasn't enough. It wasn't anywhere near enough.

He read it again. Had she taken any time over this? Was this the best way she could express herself? What kind of person had she been? Was this really how she felt?

"You okay there?"

He looked up. A smartly dressed elderly woman stood near him, her face concerned. He realized he stood in the middle of the sidewalk and that the stinging on his cheeks was from tears exposed to the cold air. He wiped at them hurriedly. "Yes. I'm okay."

"You sure?"

He nodded.

"You don't look too great."

"I'll get inside." He needed to get lunch, return to work. "I'll be okay."

"Okay. Look after yourself." She walked on, and he folded the letter away. In a daze, he went through the motions of choosing food and paying for it, then navigating through the busy TD Centre back to the Laigh and Sanders building. There was a surreal edge to everything, like he wasn't really there. Or like he was only pretending to be a functioning man, that inside he was nothing and would disappear as soon as someone noticed he wasn't real.

Approaching his office building with a salad in his cold, gloveless hand, he saw Maurice Palomer step through the front door, face like a thundercloud. Jonah froze. After Maurice came Vaughn, lean and elegant in a winter blazer with a red carnation sticking out of one pocket. His hair flopped around his face and he looked distracted.

That lump returned to Jonah's throat and his chest ached. *Yes. Him.* Jonah suddenly wanted nothing more than to drag Vaughn back to his apartment and curl up on the couch with him, because Vaughn would know how to deal with something like this.

But he couldn't. Not after last week.

Vaughn looked incredible. Suave and sophisticated. But Jonah knew that under the tailored silhouette was an art dork who liked gaming and didn't take care of his cell phone, and was incapable of making a good cup of coffee. He'd helped Jonah figure out a painting and defended his slutty ways to his friend and fed him food he wanted to eat. He was wickedly hot but blushed so easily. He'd wanted to draw Jonah. He'd looked at Jonah like he was somebody important and amazing, and how had Jonah not *seen* that until now? How had Jonah missed what a total gift this man was?

He'd thrown all that away.

Why? Because Vaughn didn't know just how fucked up Jonah was, so there was no way he really liked him? That had been his fault; Jonah hadn't shared anything with him. Nothing except how awful he was. God, Jonah really *was* fucked up.

"Jonah?" He startled. Vaughn had noticed him and was frowning. "Are you all right?"

"I wondered where you were," Maurice sneered.

Vaughn moved towards him. Jonah watched him approach, unable to think with all the feelings swarming in him.

"You look like you're about to faint." Vaughn peered closely at him. "Have you been *crying*? What's wrong?"

Typical. Jonah had said awful things to him, and Vaughn was still being concerned and nice. If their places were swapped, Jonah would have ignored him completely. Jonah opened his mouth to tell him he needed to grow a pair, but to his shock, a sob came out instead.

Vaughn's face turned stricken. "Jonah."

"Why are you so nice?" Jonah asked, each word shaky and thick.

"Can I get you something?" Vaughn reached out. "Let me help you inside."

Jonah shrugged off his arm, then changed his mind and grabbed his hand instead. "I was an asshole to you," he managed. "But you're talking to me anyway."

"You should see the expression on your face. You look sick. And I still— I can't not help you." He tugged gently. "Get out of the cold."

Vaughn's gloved hand was warm and dry in his. Jonah set down his salad and grabbed both of Vaughn's hands, focusing on them because he couldn't look at Vaughn's face. "My mother died." His cheeks started stinging again. "She left me a fucking letter."

Vaughn paused, then pulled his hands free of Jonah's. One moment later, Jonah was wrapped tight in a hug, cheek pressed against close-woven wool and chest against chest. He squeezed his eyes shut and let out a shaky breath. This. *This* was what he needed. The smell of the carnation, the scent of Vaughn's skin, the way Vaughn's jaw brushed Jonah's hair, and the comfort of his arms—alive, warm things. This was real, this was happening. Nothing like cold ink on dead paper. So much better than clubbing and Grindr.

Jonah gathered him in, wishing he could somehow distill this feeling into a jar so he could open it whenever he needed to remember what it felt like to be cared for.

He could hug him all day.

"I'm sorry." Vaughn's breath was warm in his ear. "I really am."

Oh God. Did he maybe still give a shit about him? Jonah didn't want to let him go. His words caught in his throat, and he shook his head and pulled Vaughn closer.

"Cuddle on your own time, Vaughn," Maurice yelled. "Taxi's here!"

Vaughn's arms eased from around him and Jonah clutched at them because he wasn't done yet, they'd barely had a few seconds, *he wasn't ready.*

"I have to go," Vaughn said. He looked worried. "Go inside and eat something. Call Zay."

"Don't," Jonah begged, though he wasn't totally sure what he was asking Vaughn to not do. Leave? Stop hugging him? Stop talking to him?

"I'll see you around." He pulled his arms free and walked towards Maurice.

"What the hell was that about?" Jonah heard Maurice demand from inside the cab.

"Absolutely none of your business." Vaughn shut the door.

Jonah watched the taxi drive away, colder now than he had been before. He sniffed and rubbed at his cheeks. *I'm losing it. Freaking certifiable.* A letter had brought him to tears and that hug was the official highlight of the past week. Vaughn gave excellent hugs. How long had it been since someone had hugged him like that? Just because he'd needed it?

He was an idiot. Not only because he was still standing in the freezing cold but because he'd let Vaughn slip away without telling him he was sorry for spouting his insecurity at him instead of listening to him. The guy liked him—or had liked him. Jonah still thought Vaughn was stupid for that, but he'd at least *tried*. If he were Vaughn, he'd have turned around quicker than you could say *abandonment issues* and run in the opposite direction.

Yelling on the phone wasn't sexy. Crying in the street wasn't sexy. Asking for hugs, seeing someone puke, and fucking so hard he hurt in order to distract himself from other hurt wasn't sexy. Feelings weren't sexy.

But Vaughn didn't care about being sexy. And if he still liked Jonah despite all that sheer unsexiness, then Jonah owed it to Vaughn and to himself to at least try to meet him halfway somehow. What was it he'd said? An open relationship? Well, maybe. He could at least hear the guy out, right? Jonah didn't want to leave things like this. He wanted Vaughn. He wanted a second chance. Whatever was growing between them—nameless, formless, momentous—it wasn't worth dropping like this.

He wiped his face again, took a deep breath, picked up his salad, and pulled out his phone. He tapped a text to Adrian saying yes to the movie and asking if he was free that evening. Then he texted Zay and asked if she was free too. Jonah didn't know much about friendships or saving relationships, but luckily he had people who did. He'd made a mistake with Vaughn by not telling him things; he needed to make sure he didn't do the same thing with them. That meant getting Zay's and Adrian's opinion on what had just happened, because Jonah didn't know if that was a good thing or not.

Then he wrote one final text before going indoors to eat his now-subzero salad.

Hi Claire thx for lawyers #. Do u want 2 catch up smtm soon?

CHAPTER THIRTEEN

Vaughn attached the checklist to his clipboard and put a pen behind his ear. Laptop docked. Phone in his back pocket. Suit jacket on a hanger in the closet downstairs, ready for his postsetup outfit. He tweaked his sweater and flexed his feet in his Sanuks. Yes, he was ready to set up the gallery for the party.

He left the office, ignoring Maurice's dark muttering as he passed his desk. Ever since the utter failure of a meeting with Garrett Barlow yesterday, Maurice had been in a terrible mood. Vaughn wasn't surprised; Barlow was still refusing a payout on the basis that the police report was forthcoming, and Maurice was losing patience.

He'd also made a few cutting remarks about Jonah in the taxi back to the gallery, something about how if they were that close, why hadn't Vaughn gotten them to pay on their claims? Vaughn felt it prudent to withhold just how close he and Jonah were, i.e. not at all. Not anymore, at least, if they'd ever been close.

But Jonah had looked so lost and upset, Vaughn couldn't help hugging him. Hearing his mother had died had just about broken his heart, not that Jonah would want to hear that. Even the hug had probably been overkill. Vaughn hoped his manager had given him the rest of the day off; Jonah had looked as though he needed it.

And Vaughn was *done* thinking about Jonah today.

Downstairs, he did a rotation to make sure there weren't any visitors still in the gallery, then blocked off the stairs to the upper level and wheeled the front desk and the chair to the side of the foyer. By the time that was done, the catering manager had arrived with her team, and he propped the door open so they could bring their equipment in.

While staring in dismay at the sludgy water the caterers were tramping in, he heard someone knock on the window next to the front door. He looked up to see Detective Meyer waving at him. *What on earth?*

She followed a trestle table inside and stamped snow off her boots. "Evening, Mr. Hargrave." Her cheeks were bright with the cold.

"Good evening."

"I see setup is in full swing." She eyed the flow of caterers.

"It is." He waited to let her explain why she was here, but she kept watching the catering team. "Can I help you with something?"

She shook her head. "Nope. I'll stash my coat in the normal place."

"Stash your coat . . . ?"

"I'll be rotating through the party."

"You will?" He gripped his clipboard and flicked through the papers to the guest list. "I didn't add you to . . . Did Maurice or Angeline ask you to join the party?"

"I'm not joining it, I'll be watching it. See if anyone takes special interest in one of the pieces." She took off her coat, revealing a glittery shift dress and metal matinee necklace. Vaughn caught a whiff of something floral. *Matching metals and Dior perfume.* She *was* joining the party.

She caught him eyeing her outfit and frowned at him. "Official police business."

"If you say so."

"You're not very dressed up." She gazed at his shoes. That was harsh—they were his nicest pair of Sanuks.

"I have a dress suit in there." He gestured at the nearby closet.

"I see." She scanned the foyer. One caterer was assembling a coatrack near the gallery coat hooks, two people pushed in a massive bin with bags of ice in it, and the rest carried boxes of food.

"You're a little early." *And eager.* "It doesn't start for another hour and a half."

"That's okay." She pulled a clutch out of her coat pocket, then walked towards the coatrack.

"Vaughn."

His head snapped to the side. Cressida stood there, obviously just arrived. A shimmer of pink peeking under the edge of her coat promised a statement dress. "Honey, the lights are all wrong."

The *lights*? He cast about. The fairy lights he and Angeline had strung up in quiet moments over the last few days were on and looked enchanting, if he did say so. "What's wrong with them?"

"They're meant to be zigzagging in the other direction." She pointed at the ceiling to illustrate.

"Cressida, it's too late to change them."

She pouted. "How did they go up so wrong?"

I am not paid enough for this. "Could you ask Angeline?"

Cressida twisted around and made a beeline for the office stairs.

The catering manager approached him with a worried look on her face. "Mr. Hargrave? There's a situation at the back door."

A situation? He followed her to the fire exit at the back of the gallery. It was in a cleared section, and the caterers were using the area to temporarily stack empty crates and boxes while they unloaded drinks into the ice bin. A burly caterer held a limp and slightly overweight figure by the arm.

Vaughn recognized the person and his annoyance ratcheted up a few notches. "Jules Mitchell."

The reporter smiled at him sheepishly.

"You know him?" the manager asked.

Unfortunately. Vaughn nodded. "Let him go."

"Tried to tell me he was with us." The burly caterer dropped Mitchell's arm. "Like we don't all know each other."

"I'll handle him." Vaughn gestured for Jules to follow him.

They walked into the gallery. Vaughn steered him right to the foyer and aimed him at the front door. "Go."

Jules spun. He wore black dress pants, a white shirt, and a black tie under his coat. One hand clutched a phone protectively. "Look, I can explain."

"You're not welcome here. Please leave."

"I just need *one* picture of the gallery interior for my story." He deliberated. "Maybe another one of the party."

Media hacks. All the same. He didn't have time for this. The quartet was due any moment now, and who knew when Angeline and co. would come down to check on him.

"You can have a picture of the gallery from the outside like everyone else."

Mitchell stayed resolutely put. "Look, I'm not even in the way here—"

"Coming through!" the burly caterer shouted as he barrelled towards them with a stack of empty boxes.

Vaughn yanked him aside, then shoved him at the door after the caterer. Jules spun around and growled at him. "Touch me again, and I'll have you arrested for assault."

"Keep standing there, and I'll have *you* arrested for trespassing," Vaughn spat back, straightening to his full six feet and one inch and glowering at him.

"*Wow.*"

They both glanced over. Jonah stood in the front door, sharp in his work clothes, his eyes wide. "Vaughn, I didn't know you could be so butch."

Vaughn stared at him in surprise. *What the hell is he doing here?* He hadn't invited him either.

"Who are you?" Jules demanded.

Jonah scowled. "Who the fuck are *you*?"

"What's going on?" Detective Meyer said behind Vaughn.

He glared at them. "These two were just leaving."

Jonah stepped forward. "Vaughn, I need to talk to you."

"I'm not leaving until I get my photo," Jules declared.

Vaughn turned to Detective Meyer. "They are *both* trespassing here."

She glanced them up and down. "Nice to see you again, Mr. Sondern." Then she pulled her badge out of her dress pocket. "Unfortunately, I have to ask you both to leave."

"Come on!" Jules protested.

Jonah's mouth set firmly. "Vaughn, seriously—"

Jules took off into the gallery. Vaughn swore and turned to go after him, but Jonah gripped his arm. Meyer ran after Jules, and Vaughn was pulled to the side of the foyer, next to the closet and out of the way of the caterers.

"We need to talk," Jonah said, his face intent.

"Not now." Vaughn craned his neck to look into the gallery, where sounds of a scuffle could be heard. "Oh God, I hope they don't pull down the Barinski."

"Yes, now. I mean, I didn't realize the party was tonight, but I'm here already, so this has to happen now."

The hell with that. "There's nothing to talk about."

"I disagree." Jonah grabbed both of his arms. "You like me, right? Still?"

Vaughn froze. Embarrassment bubbled up until he could barely stand still or look at him. Admitting that and then being shut down so adroitly was something he was more than ready to forget.

"We discussed this already. No need to rehash old news. I have a million things to do right now, and you need to leave." He waved the clipboard at him.

Jonah made a noise of frustration. "Don't *do* that. God, it drives me fucking crazy when you don't answer a simple question." He shook Vaughn's arms, making him drop the clipboard. "Vaughn. You hugged me yesterday. That's got to mean I didn't completely screw up with you."

Those hazel eyes of his. *So gorgeous.* Heat rose on Vaughn's cheeks. "You were upset. Anyone would have—" A bang from within the gallery made him jump. Fucking hell, what was going on in there? He took a step towards the commotion.

"Pay attention to me!" Jonah shook his arms again.

He turned back to him. "Jonah, now is *really not*—" He stopped short as Jonah opened the closet. "What are you doing?"

"Getting your full attention."

Vaughn was pushed into the closet, and he stumbled back as Jonah closed the door behind himself. They were plunged into darkness, and Vaughn scrabbled for the light. Once he hit it, the dim lightbulb showed the closet in all its constricted glory—shelves stacked with stationery and gift items on one side, a bucket and mop on the other, his suit in a hanger bag on a hook in the wall. It was a tiny space, and Jonah pressed against him, face resolute, ensuring he stood between Vaughn and the door. Absolutely no room to manoeuvre around him.

Shit. Despite the sheer craziness of the move and his very real need to get out, Vaughn had to admit, it had the desired effect: his focus was entirely on Jonah. He retreated, brushing past his suit and hitting the back wall. "Let me out."

"In a minute." Jonah pushed against him again, hands on his chest. "I have something to say. I'm sorry about last week." He shook his head. "I was totally out of line. I didn't mean any of it. I was tired and frustrated and angry."

"Got it. We're good." He tried to move forward.

Jonah stopped him with heavy hands. "You don't get it."

"There is a *reporter* loose in my gallery, I really can't emphasize how important—"

Jonah kissed him.

Warmth. Softness. A hard body against his. Hands cupped his face and neck, holding him there. Oh, Jonah had his full attention now. Vaughn grunted in surprise. But God, it felt good. So, *so* good. He was ready to continue doing this for the rest of his life, even if that meant never leaving this closet. Hope rolled through him, and he tentatively touched Jonah's waist. Jonah pressed up harder against him, and the wall behind Vaughn creaked.

Jonah broke the kiss but stared into his eyes. "I like you too. I like you so much it freaks me out. I thought there was no way in hell a guy like you could ever seriously want a guy like me."

What on earth was he talking about? Wasn't it the other way around? "Have you *seen* yourself?" he asked in disbelief.

"No one wanted me." Jonah's gaze was steady. "My dad didn't, my mom didn't, hundreds of foster parents and adoptive parents didn't. And that was years, you know? After a while I stopped caring and told myself it was fine and that I didn't want *them* either. And sex, all the hookups—I think one reason I do that is because the guys want me, and it feels really good. Like, I can do that, you know? I can be hot and fuck and be fucked and it's all great. So that was enough for a long time." His breath was shaky. "But it's also kind of shallow. You liked me for *me*, no sex required, and it freaked me out because I know how to do the sex part, but I haven't had the feelings part much. I haven't let myself have it."

Vaughn's heart ached. *Oh, Jonah.* He pulled Jonah tighter against him, ignoring how Jonah was hard and how the wall creaked and shuddered behind him. Jonah made a small, happy noise. "Jonah," Vaughn started. "I—"

"I'm not done yet. I need to tell you all of this so you understand, okay? I freaked out at you, because you're this, this . . ." His brow scrunched as he gathered the words. ". . . *guy*. You're hot, and you're talented, and you're minted. I'm a foster kid, and I have loans to pay off, and I sleep around, and I don't know the fancy cutlery, like fish forks and stuff, and I don't have a passion for anything the way you do for art."

"I truly don't give a shit about cutlery."

"I *know*. But it's like you're in this whole other world that I've only seen in movies and news articles, and I'm not part of it. I'm not what *you* know. I'm fucked up in ways I'm still figuring out. How can you want to be with someone like me?"

The ache in Vaughn's heart had spread to his throat. "I'm fucked up too. And I live in the same world you do, but with people who forget that cutlery isn't important."

Was . . . Wait, was the wall behind him *tilting*? That didn't seem right.

Jonah smiled sadly up at him. "See? You get it. Don't you know how great that is? You could've been like Devon. *Ugh*. But," his laser focus returned, "that's not the point. I found out my mom died and left me a letter, and it wrecked me. But it also kind of woke me up. She was messed up, and she left me behind, and she hurt about it all her life. I'm messed up, but I don't want to leave you behind, even though I still don't get what you see in me. I want to try. With you. Even though I'm not sure how or if I can. All I know is I don't want to spend my life wondering about you and hurting over you, only to write you some shitty-ass letter twenty years from now." His eyes were shiny. "But I thought I'd already fucked it up. Then you were there somehow, and you helped me, so then I thought maybe I hadn't. Maybe I could try again. So here I am."

Vaughn was speechless. Blindsided. There weren't words to express even a tenth of the emotions rolling through him. Where could he begin? How could he hope to match what Jonah had just said to him?

"You're—" The wall behind Vaughn shuddered, then gave way with a *crack*. He fell back amid clouds of dust, and his head hit something hard. One blank moment later, he blinked in surprise.

Jonah crouched over him, hands brushing dust off his face. "Vaughn! Are you okay?"

Vaughn tried to make sense of what had just happened. Instead of standing up, he was now lying on the ground. Half of his body was in the closet, the rest was in some kind of extra space behind a very thin wall. Or, rather, resting in a hole in that wall, which he now saw wasn't a wall, but instead a very thin board painted to look like concrete.

Hands gripped his face and tilted it to Jonah's. "Talk to me."

"I'm okay," Vaughn replied.

Jonah sighed, relief relaxing his frame. "Good. I was afraid you hit something."

"Are you all right?"

"Yeah. I landed on you." Jonah glanced around. "What even happened . . . there . . ." He trailed off as his eyes caught on something beyond Vaughn. Vaughn twisted to look behind himself.

He found himself staring at a naked woman hanging from a cross, blood flowing down her thighs. *Actually*, his brain babbled at him, *it's not the object, it's a representation of the object. Ceci n'est pas une pipe.*

"Oh my God," he realized. "It's *Crucible*."

He gingerly sat up. Jonah helped him rest against the real back wall and they stared at the painting. Behind it, in the corner, was a deconstructed *Entrance*, the threads hanging from the canvas and the plastic tubing leaning against it.

"They're *here*." Vaughn couldn't believe it. Had they been here the entire time?

Jonah pulled out his phone and took a picture, then turned his attention to the board. "Why is there a fake back to this closet? Who would do this?"

Good question. Vaughn noticed a small hole at the far end, where *Entrance* leaned, and small hinges. "There's a door over there." The part he'd smashed through was on the other side of the closet.

"Maybe next time you'll use that instead of almost breaking your head." Jonah took Vaughn's head in his hands, and Vaughn felt deft fingers lightly stroking over his scalp. "Anything hurt?"

"No." He gazed up at Jonah, whose jaw set and brow furrowed as he checked Vaughn over. A wave of longing swept over Vaughn, so fast and heavy it almost hurt. *Did that really just happen?* Was he dreaming that Jonah was here, looking after him?

Someone knocked on the door, then opened it. Bright gallery lights hit them, making them blink.

"Vaughn," Angeline said dryly, "what are you doing in there?"

Vaughn realized he was sitting on the ground, Jonah practically in his lap caressing his hair, and both of them were covered in dust and wood chips. "Uh . . ." He and Jonah stood up. "Hi, Angeline."

Angeline crossed her arms. "There is a mess out here, guests are arriving in an hour, and you're having a quickie in the closet with our claims investigator. You'd better have a fucking excellent reason for not being out here."

Vaughn stepped forward, hiding Jonah behind him. The last thing he wanted was Jonah implicated in work-related trouble. "Not a quickie. Angeline, you need to see this."

She raised an eyebrow. "Lesbian, remember? There is *nothing* in there I need to see right now. Or ever."

He pointed. "The stolen pieces are here."

She went very still. "*Excuse me?*"

He and Jonah exited the closet, giving her space to go in and see for herself. Out in the foyer, he saw Jules Mitchell facedown on the floor, being sat on by the burly caterer as the other caterers joked and took pictures. Meyer spoke on the phone, her hair falling out of its bun, but otherwise she still looked ready to drink and schmooze. She caught sight of him and Jonah and started toward them. Someone knocked on the front door, and Vaughn spun to see a quartet of uncertain-looking musicians standing there, apparently just arrived.

This was a disaster.

Then Maurice walked in, ready in black-tie apparel. He stopped short, surveying the scene. "What the hell is going on here?"

The catering manager started snapping orders at her team and they dispersed. Detective Meyer looked Vaughn and Jonah over and then glanced in the closet. Angeline emerged, a manic grin on her face.

Vaughn turned to Jonah. "You should go. Conflict of interest, right?"

Jonah frowned at him, like he hadn't expected Vaughn to say that. "No. I *was* here. It'll be okay. I'll square it with the boss."

"Vaughn," Maurice snapped, "why aren't . . ." He took in Vaughn's appearance, then saw the closet and went white.

Angeline grinned. "Maurice, guess what our intrepid assistant and his boyfriend discovered at the back of this closet?"

"What the *fuck*?" Maurice roared. Everyone took a step back as Maurice changed from pale to furious red. He turned on Vaughn. "You. You did this. You *ruined* it for me. Two more pieces and I would have been done with this goddamn place. You faggoty piece of shit, you just couldn't leave it alone." He swung at Vaughn.

Vaughn dodged back, bumping into Jonah, who stepped around him.

"Back off," Jonah growled.

Maurice jabbed a finger at him. "And you! Why the fuck didn't you just approve the goddamn claim?"

"Why don't you make me, shithead?"

Vaughn saw the swing coming, saw Jonah's hands clench. He yanked Jonah back, and Maurice's fist swung uselessly by. "Don't fight him," he hissed.

"I can totally take him!" Jonah said, outraged.

Detective Meyer grabbed Maurice's arms from behind in a double armlock. "Calm down, Mr. Palomer," she soothed as he began bucking.

He looked ready to explode, and Vaughn didn't want to be anywhere near him when he did. He grabbed Jonah's hand and pulled him away, across the foyer. They stopped beside the reporter and the caterer, who were on their feet now, filming everything on their phones, mouths open.

"What the actual *fuck*, Maurice?"

No one had noticed Cressida come in. Maurice stilled, which let Meyer tighten the armlock she had on him. Cressida advanced, pink dress swishing and curls bouncing. "*You're* the thief?"

"Babe," Angeline said.

"Five years of working here and *this* is how you repay me? You lousy, lying sack of *shit*." Cressida picked up a nearby empty crate and raised it above her head. Angeline rushed to intercept her.

Maurice struggled against the detective, shouting and swearing, then kicked her shin and bodily tossed her to the side. He saw the cell phones, saw the audience, saw Angeline failing to tug the crate away from Cressida, and swore. He pointed at Vaughn. "I will *end you* for this!" Then he was gone, out the door and past the flabbergasted musicians.

Vaughn's heart hammered in his chest. *Did that really just happen?*

"Holy shit." Jonah squeezed Vaughn's hand. "He really hates you."

"This is *wild*," Jules said.

Angeline helped Detective Meyer to her feet. Vaughn realized he was still clutching Jonah's hand and dropped it. He went over to his boss and the detective, reaching into his back pocket for his phone.

"Are you all right?" he asked Meyer. She waved him off easily. "Do we need to call your team again?" Then he looked at his phone, which fell apart in his palm. Oh. It'd been in his back pocket, and he'd fallen on it. *Damn it.*

"They're already on their way here for him," Meyer said, gesturing at Jules.

Angeline looked ready to punch someone herself. "Considering the circumstances, I'd rather they go after Maurice."

"I agree," Meyer said. She looked down at herself, snow dirt now on her dress, and glowered. "Oh my God. This is dry-clean only."

"Vaughn," Angeline said, bringing her phone to her ear. "I'm calling you a taxi."

"What? Why?"

"Because you're going home for the night." She glanced around the foyer. "We have a party to throw, and if you're here, Maurice may come back."

Vaughn's jaw dropped. "You're still throwing the party?" She couldn't be for real.

"Yes. Mr. Sondern," she called, "bring the musicians in."

Jonah jerked into action. Angeline arranged the taxi as the musicians walked past, heading for the corner where they were supposed to set up for the night. Cressida sat down on the crate she'd picked up, pouting.

Jonah sidled next to Vaughn, hand on his arm, and his presence sent a rush of warmth through him.

Angeline ended the call. "Vaughn, collect your stuff and wait for the taxi outside." She bent down and picked up his dropped clipboard. "I'll take things from here. You!" This was directed at Jules Mitchell, who snapped to attention. "I won't press charges for trespassing *and* I'll let you have the exclusive on this"—she waved at the closet—"if you stick around and check people off the guest list and help with cleanup later."

Jules grinned. "Hell yeah, lady."

"That's *Ms. Dufort* to you."

How was this . . . Vaughn had spent so much time on this party, he couldn't just leave. "Angeline, I need to be here. I need to—"

"You need to go somewhere safe," Angeline said.

"I agree," Detective Meyer added, dabbing at her dress. "Palomer threatened you in particular. I would lay low until we catch him."

Cressida nodded, then threw her arms around Vaughn. "You did so good! I'll cut his balls off if he comes anywhere near this gallery or you."

"And I'll frame them," Angeline said. "That bastard has epically screwed us." She stared at the closet. "A fucking *false wall*. How did that shit-lord do it?" She shook her head. "We'll figure it out later. Go home, Vaughn."

Unbelievable. Vaughn didn't want to go home. Not after this.

Jonah pulled on Vaughn's shoulder.

"One more thing." Angeline smiled tersely at him. "Congratulations. You just got promoted."

What a night.

Jonah glanced at Vaughn. Ever since the detective had sat him in the taxi, Vaughn had been silent. He had one arm draped over his bag like a pet, and his broken cell rested in the other hand—probably out of habit. The detective had asked for his home address, but when Vaughn had given it and said that Maurice knew where he lived, she'd become worried. "Go somewhere he doesn't know," she'd said.

So the taxi was taking them to Jonah's place instead.

And Vaughn hadn't said a word since.

Jonah couldn't believe Maurice had been behind it all.

Scratch that—he *did* believe Maurice was behind the theft. What was unbelievable was that he'd had the brains to pull it off. Stealing pieces and hiding them on-site. Claiming more insurance money than they were worth and, Jonah was willing to bet, pocketing the difference between the actual sale value and the claimed value for the earlier two thefts.

Jonah knew he'd smelled a rat.

The police report was going to be a fun read whenever they got it. Hopefully they'd catch the guy soon. In any case, he and Garrett were going to enjoy finally refusing the gallery's two claims for the pieces. He wondered how the report would describe the discovery of the pieces and the hiding spot. *J.S. humped V.H. literally through the wall.* What a claim to fame. Maybe he could emphasize the part where he'd realized the claim was suspicious.

The quiet was getting to him.

Vaughn still had bits of dust in his hair. "How's your head?" Jonah asked.

"Fine."

Silence fell between them again. The taxi made more noise than they did, for fuck's sake. *Work with me, pretty boy.* Jonah pulled the wreckage that used to be Vaughn's phone out of his hand and stuck it in Vaughn's bag, then took his hand. Vaughn looked down in surprise.

"You recovered some stolen artwork, got the night off *and* a promotion, and you're coming home with me," Jonah said. "I might be biased, but personally, I'd be something other than sad about it."

That got him a smile. "I'm not sad about it. I'm still processing that Maurice did it." He grimaced. "I honestly had no idea. I'm shocked."

"Are you kidding me? You're *surprised* it was him?"

"Yes!"

"How? Literally, how? He's an asshole!"

Vaughn's smile grew wider. *Ugh. So gorgeous.* Jonah's heartbeat quickened. "Asshole doesn't always equal art thief. We worked together for almost three years. He wasn't always the easiest person to get along with, but I would never have expected him to do something like this."

Jonah snorted. "'Not the easiest person to get along with.' How the hell do you do that? Stay so freaking positive? I'd have decked him within a week if he treated me the way he treated you."

Vaughn shrugged. "His perceptions of me are his problem."

And there. That was the kicker. "I wish I could do that." Jonah felt his face heat up. "Not give a shit about people's opinions. Life would be so much easier."

"I do care about people's opinions." Vaughn's thumb rubbed along Jonah's knuckles. "Certain people's opinions."

He *knew* he was bright red now. Hand holding wasn't something he was used to. It was awesome to touch Vaughn, but his hand was going all sweaty, and he had to actively resist pulling it out of Vaughn's and wiping it on his pants.

The silence that fell now was different. Jonah looked aside, out the window at the dark streets. Man, he lived far from downtown.

It hit him that he was taking Vaughn home. *Him*. He'd never taken anyone home before. And it was Vaughn, the guy he'd been so desperate to get that he'd *shoved him into a closet*. The same guy who lived in a fancy apartment in Yorkville and wore shoes that probably cost more than Jonah's rent. He was taking him to a house he shared with six other people—"house" meaning a sprawling, barely legal pile of wood. His room was the smallest one in the place, which meant cheaper rent for him in an already cheap area, and everything he had, from the bed to his clothes, he'd bought secondhand or on sale or found on a curb somewhere.

He was nuts to think he could pull this off. Him? Be in a relationship with this guy? He could barely hold hands with him. What was he on?

He frowned. Had he eaten today? He couldn't remember eating. He'd been so keyed up after the previous day, with the letter from his mom, and Zay and Adrian talking him through his apology, that all he'd thought about was catching Vaughn at the gallery, telling him everything about his mom and his feelings, and asking for a second chance.

Wait. They hadn't got around to finishing that part yet, when Vaughn would give him an answer. He'd been too busy falling through that cheap-ass chipboard.

Shit.

Jonah turned to talk to him, but the taxi came to a stop, which meant they were finally outside his place. Vaughn let go of his hand to pay the driver and they left the cab. As they walked to the front door, Jonah palmed his keys and tried not to notice the peeling, patchy paint and the stopgap job on the doorbell.

At the door, he paused. "My place isn't as nice as yours," he said abruptly.

"I don't care." Behind him, Vaughn sounded amused.

"I mean it. I don't think it's been improved since the eighties. I live with six other people, and there's only one bathroom, and there's no couch to crash on, and my room is tiny, and don't you have a brother? You should stay with him tonight. I'll call a cab and you can go do that."

A hand pressed against his back, slight stubble grazed his ear. "Jonah, I'm cold and want to see where you live." Vaughn's voice was soft in his ear. Jonah shivered, but not from the winter night. *Okay then.* He opened the door.

Inside, heat and the smell of garlic and cheese settled over them like a blanket. A couple of his housemates yelled hellos from the kitchen as Jonah and Vaughn took off their coats and boots.

One of them, Romy, came through the kitchen door in her pyjamas. "Hey, Jonah, you missed pizza."

He grimaced. "Good."

"You're missing out. One of these days we're going to see you eat a whole slice." She scanned Vaughn up and down, her face lighting up. "*Hi.*"

"I'm Vaughn."

"Hey, Vaughn, I'm Romy." She sent a wicked look at Jonah. "Jonah *never* brings guys around."

"Pleased to meet you." Did Vaughn actually like her or was he just being polite? Jonah had no idea. All he could see were her knock-off UGGs and the bare floorboards and the peeling wallpaper on the walls. Everything looked so shabby.

"We're just hanging out," Jonah said stiffly.

"Oh really?" She turned towards the kitchen. "Guys! Jonah brought a *friend* home to *hang out!*"

Wolf whistles erupted and she grinned. Jonah could've killed her. And them. Great. This was exactly the impression he wanted to make. Not only was his house a crap-hole, his roomies were animals.

Vaughn *laughed.* And not a disbelieving, *where-the-hell-am-I-and-how-do-I-leave* laugh, the kind where he was entertained. An infectious one. Romy joined in, and Jonah almost did too.

Instead, he grabbed Vaughn's hand. "Upstairs."

"*Oooh,*" Romy called as Jonah led Vaughn past her up the stairs.

"I take it this is an unusual thing for you," Vaughn said behind him.

"You take it right."

"Your roommates are fun." He sounded serious. "Do you think they have leftover pizza?"

Jonah opened his bedroom door. "It doesn't matter if they do, we're not eating it." He didn't work out six days a week for nothing. "Four hundred calories a slice, we might as well just glue it to our stomachs and save it a trip."

Vaughn laughed again, walking in. He put his bag down and surveyed the room. Jonah saw it with fresh eyes: a square box that barely fit a double bed and dresser, hand weights stacked in one corner on an otherwise empty floor. The floor was clear out of necessity rather than inclination, because there were only a few feet between the bed, the wall, and his minimal furniture. Compared to Vaughn's palace-for-one, this place with its cheap sheets and his postcards from friends and his line of Star Wars and Japanese animation movie posters on the walls had to be like a slum, right?

Vaughn broke into a smile though. "I adore Studio Ghibli movies."

"Who doesn't?" He shut the door, cutting off the sound of talking from downstairs.

"This place is homey." Vaughn squeezed past the end of the bed to look closer at his postcards.

Ohthankgod. If he could handle this, then maybe things would work out okay. Now all Jonah had to do was be cool. Guy in his room for the first time, no big.

Yeah, right. A guy. In his room. Not just any guy, *the* guy. Jonah had no idea what to do. He had to get them back to that place in the stationery closet, the one where he could lay it all out and be honest. Talking, face-to-face, maybe even squashed against each other again, because he'd really enjoyed that part of it. *How do I do that?*

"So." Vaughn turned to face him. "We've established you do like me after all."

Jonah wanted to sag with relief. Vaughn had this. "Yeah. I do."

"Even though I don't like sex?"

Jonah nodded.

"Even though I apparently speak like I'm lodged up my own ass?"

Jonah would never live that down. "You really don't. I'm sorry."

One corner of Vaughn's mouth tipped up. "I do know people who talk like that."

"No way." That *smile*. How was he so cute?

Vaughn squeezed back towards him. "Even though my job isn't 'real work'?"

Jonah winced but nodded again.

"Even though I don't stand up for myself when I perhaps should?" He looked a little bit sheepish there.

"Yeah." Though getting out of the way of a fist *was* a lot better than meeting it. Smarter. That, or being pulled out of the way by someone who was now listing all the shitty stuff Jonah had said about him. It was embarrassing, but Jonah wasn't about to ignore that he'd said those things. Vaughn needed to know they didn't matter to him. Not really.

"It's okay. I'm over that. And I want to try again." Vaughn looked uncertain now. "But are you sure about the no-sex thing? That's really okay?"

Jonah took him in, the lean lines of him. Just like that, even with the third degree he'd been getting, he was ready to pull Vaughn's clothes off and get down to business. But it was more because he wanted to be closer to him, not because he needed the flying, burning edge of sex. *Huh. Would he let me do that? Take his clothes off?*

He cleared his throat. "I think you mentioned open relationships."

Vaughn nodded. "I did." He stepped closer, taking Jonah's hands in his. "The kind of sex you have, you said you needed it."

Oh God. Are we doing this? Having this *discussion?* Vaughn's hands were warm and steady, though. Jonah gripped them tightly.

"I think that even if I enjoyed sex, I wouldn't be able to keep you happy sexually," Vaughn continued. "I mean, I . . ." He ducked his head. "I've been thinking about this, and about what I could do with you that is . . . not full-on sex, but still sexual. So you could feel you can be like that around me, but I won't feel that I'm being pushed to be something I'm not. Does that make sense?"

"I'm with you." His voice had gone croaky. "But you don't have to do anything. We can, like, do other stuff. Play video games or go clubbing and dance together or just, like, *sleep* together. Actually sleep."

"We will do all those things." Vaughn said it like it was promise. "And we'll kiss and get naked together. But I also think maybe we could work up to me giving you a handjob someday." His face was bright red as he said that. "That's as far as I could go. I think."

Oh yeah. He could picture that. Vaughn's artistic hand on his dick. *Vaughn's. Hot.*

"I know it's not enough for most people. But I was thinking that, you know, what we have is different than what you get from the guys you hook up with. It's practically unrelated. And I don't care that you have sex with strange guys, or how much you have, as long as you're happy." He coughed. "And safe. Please stay safe."

Like he didn't already? Jonah wanted to roll his eyes but just smiled instead. Vaughn's red face was too cute. And what he was saying was too awesome.

"So, um, yes," Vaughn continued. "We can mess around between us, and you can keep doing whoever else you want, however you want. I'm okay with that. In a way, I'm glad you prefer quick hookups. I really am. It makes it very easy for me to be with you without worrying I'm somehow depriving you. So if you can work with that, if *you're* truly okay with that, then I'm in."

Is he for real? That's the deal? He could do that. He could totally do that. Jonah's face was starting to hurt from his smile. Being with Vaughn would be the opposite of depriving him. Being with Vaughn *and* being free to have the sex he needed; that would be some kind of perfection. This wasn't a sacrifice. This was a gift.

What a strange thought, to realize how sex didn't have to affect what was between them, but it felt right. The care and understanding in what Vaughn'd just said blew Jonah away. This talented, amazing guy understood his deal with sex, and he not only didn't care, he supported it. What the hell? How did Jonah get this lucky? "I can't believe you think that's the easy part."

"It is though! Not that you *need* my permission, but you can keep doing the usual stuff you do. Go out to clubs, use Grindr, get what you need from those places." Vaughn glanced at him shyly. "Then come home and let me take care of the rest. Yes, I think that's very—"

Jonah couldn't take it any longer; he pulled Vaughn forward and kissed him again. Let go of Vaughn's hands so he could wrap his arms around Vaughn's neck and press himself close against him, chase the scent and taste of him. Vaughn staggered back, clutching him close, and tripped over the side of the bed, falling onto it with a surprised grunt. Jonah lay out over him, needing to feel as much of him as possible: the softness of his hair, the slight stubble on his face, the hard, warm body under his. Dizzying. Vaughn smelled *amazing*, a hint of cologne with sweat and dust.

Even better, he kissed back feverishly, his fingers scraping through Jonah's hair, along his back, and down his sides. One leg came up to wrap around Jonah's legs, keeping him there. This was better than he'd imagined, like he was being surrounded and sheltered. His dick was level with Vaughn's stomach, rubbing against him with every movement, and Jonah groaned, breaking the kiss.

He rested his head next to Vaughn's on the covers, panting as he gathered his thoughts. "Can we make a start on that thing about handjobs?"

Vaughn laughed. "I think so."

Fuck yes. Jonah pushed himself up so he straddled Vaughn and pulled off his shirt. Time to get skin to skin and finally touch him. "What are your hard limits?" He reached down and undid Vaughn's shirt buttons.

Vaughn's hand stroked up his side, fingers pressing firmly on his abs. "No tongue. Underwear stays on, for tonight anyway. Don't touch my dick, and don't worry about getting me off. Just touch me and let me kiss you."

Okay. He could do that. Even though said dick was hard, and Jonah could feel it against his thigh, he could avoid going below the belt.

Something occurred to him. "When you came out to me, you said you jerk off. Can I watch you?"

Vaughn went red. "I . . . um . . . oh. Would that be interesting to you?"

The idea was making Jonah's dick sing. "Yes, that would be hella fucking interesting. That would be *riveting* to me." He finished with the buttons and opened Vaughn's shirt to expose that gorgeous chest.

"Okay. Then, yes. Sometime. Not right now. I thought I might watch you touch yourself. Or rub off on me." His voice turned tentative. "If that's something you'd want to do."

Rub off on . . . Jonah's brain short-circuited. Yes, he wanted to do that. He wanted to feel Vaughn's skin against his, to run his hands through the hair on Vaughn's chest, and to grind his cock against Vaughn's until he came all over Vaughn's stomach. The thought of his come on Vaughn's skin sent a possessive rush through him.

Probably too far for Vaughn, though. *For now. Maybe.* It could be a new life goal, along with the handjob.

Fingers gently brushed his lips, then closed his jaw for him. "I see the suggestion's not unwelcome." Vaughn grinned.

Jonah shook his head. He tugged at the sleeve of Vaughn's shirt, so Vaughn sat up and helped him pull it off, then kissed him hard. Somehow pants were shucked off, and Jonah was free to move against him with nothing but their briefs between them. The hair on Vaughn's chest was wiry, perfect to rub his hands through and feel against his own skin, and Jonah gave praise to anyone listening for this anatomical bounty. Vaughn's hands roamed, leaving trails of fire over his chest and back. Jonah groaned when fingers found his nipples, and suddenly Vaughn's mouth was on his neck, little nips of teeth that sent Jonah into distraction.

It seemed like mere moments before he realized he was doing it, rubbing against him, thrusting his dick in the pressured space between their bodies. Vaughn sucked at his collarbone, one hand pushing in the small of Jonah's back, encouraging him. Jonah couldn't wait—and *oh.* He didn't have to. Nothing to prove here. He could come whenever he wanted and Vaughn wouldn't care. *Oh hell yeah.*

He pressed his head into Vaughn's shoulder, grounding himself, and reached down into his briefs to grab his cock. So hard. So *good.* He panted as he jacked, the feel of hair under his cheek and a thumb working his nipple and his hand on his dick sending surges of feeling through his entire body. A tongue licked his ear, and the shudder it produced set him off; he came with a deep groan and slumped across Vaughn, gasping, his mind one clear, blissful blank slate. Not quite the same rush, but just as good.

And safer. Lying in a bed was nice for this. Everything was soft around him. And under him was *his guy*, who didn't like sex but just let him do that and was still holding him, stroking his back. *It must be love.* Or something close to it. Jonah didn't really know. Vaughn wouldn't let just anyone do this with him, right? So it had to be. Jonah decided he could stick around to find out.

He put his arms around Vaughn and burrowed in against his chest, ignoring the slippery feel of his spunk between them. He'd somehow gotten it on Vaughn *and* in his briefs. Schoolboy stuff, which ordinarily he wouldn't do unless the other guy asked for it, but this time it was a mistake. And okay, it was probably a minor thing, but he needed to check. Nothing else mattered except being here with Vaughn and making sure he was okay.

"Sorry." He patted Vaughn's side near where he'd spilled.

"It's not the first time someone's come on me, you know."

And *that* was something he didn't want think about, someone else seeing Vaughn like this. But at least he wasn't grossed out by jizz. That was a relief. Jonah burrowed deeper against Vaughn's body.

"Was it okay?" Vaughn sounded uncertain.

Ha. What a question. "That was awesome." *Devon doesn't know what he's talking about.*

Lips brushed his hair. "Good."

Vaughn's dick was still hard. Was he totally sure about just leaving it? Jonah shifted so he rested at Vaughn's side and could see him eye-to-eye. "I feel weird not reciprocating," he admitted.

"It'll go down in a bit."

Vaughn's neck was a cloud of bites and stubble burn. *Oops. When did I do that?* Had he enjoyed it? Jonah looked him over. Apart from attacking his neck, he'd barely done anything for Vaughn. Shit. He had to do *something*. "I want you to feel good. How do I do that?"

Arms tightened around him, he got a shy smile, and Vaughn kissed him. "*This* is good. This is perfect. Just like this."

Naked hugs and kisses. Touching. Right. Jonah could manage that.

He cleaned Vaughn up, then set about doing what he'd wanted to do since seeing Vaughn in that damn toga at Carson's party: run his hands over every inch of Vaughn's chest and belly, feeling the hair and exploring him. Vaughn's hands trailed over his skin too, sending postcoital shivers through him. It was slow and intimate. They had time and space and nowhere else to be.

So different from what he normally had. But . . . good too. Sweeter. Better, in a lot of ways. And not beyond him. This was something he could do.

Talking was new too. Vaughn asked about his mom and the letter, and Jonah lay back and told him. Somehow it wasn't so hard to talk about his mother and foster care and his newfound siblings when he was wrapped up with Vaughn, safe and warm.

Then Vaughn told him, under duress, about the sex he'd had, the good stories and the bad ones. That led to Jonah sharing his more memorable hookups, which actually reminded Vaughn of visitors to the art gallery, and before they knew it, it was past midnight and they were drifting off where they lay. And all of it was surprisingly easy.

Vaughn fell asleep first. Looking at his profile, Jonah took in the floppy, mussed hair and lean face and long jaw. Swollen lips. The smell of him. Remembered what it had been like kissing him. Sitting next to him while they shot at aliens. Watching him eat. Seeing him stare down that reporter. And standing between Jonah and the scary Dufort woman. Standing between Jonah and *Maurice*.

A lump rose in his throat. Things could have gone way differently, but some miracle had happened and everything had worked out. Vaughn was here, in his crappy room. Willingly. With him. Maybe this wasn't exactly the happiest moment of his life, but right now none of the others seemed anywhere close to matching it.

EPILOGUE

Vaughn checked his appearance in the gallery washroom mirror. Hair was in place, shirt and scarf were clean, blazer was pressed, and the hickey Jonah had left on his neck last night was out of sight. *Good.* He'd had to check on that throughout the day, make sure Angeline, Cressida, and their new assistant, Amir, didn't see and comment. Or cackle.

He left the washroom and collected his things. On the way down the stairs, his phone announced a message: Jonah was running late. *God, really? Why tonight?*

It wasn't the end of the world, of course. Just that Jonah had finally agreed to let Vaughn meet his friends in his capacity as boyfriend. Two months, it had taken him. *Two.* In the same two months, Vaughn had introduced him to his family, more of his friends besides Devon, some of his mother's brunch friends, and his Tumblr followers (albeit as a sketch).

Vaughn had the impression that Zay and Adrian meant a great deal to Jonah, and while, yes, he'd met them already, he wanted to make a good impression on them. Be approved by them. Be considered worthy of their friend. Make it clear to Adrian in particular that Vaughn was taken now.

He took a moment to respond, saying he'd meet Jonah at the restaurant, then shoved his cell in his bag as he entered the gallery foyer. His cell no longer fit in his pocket, not with the heavy-duty, extra-protective phone case Jonah had gifted him for Christmas. Vaughn didn't really think the case was necessary, as he hadn't dropped his phone since falling through the false wall and destroying his last one, but he liked using something Jonah had bought him.

He changed his shoes into snow boots, said good-bye to Amir, then walked out into the slushy February evening.

The gallery was, frankly, a joy to work at without Maurice around. Vaughn couldn't say he missed him. Especially after Maurice had been found by the police the morning after the Christmas party, lurking outside of Vaughn's apartment building, drunk and with various sharp implements on him. The concierge had called the police and the rest was history. Jonah had been livid, insisting that Vaughn stay with him until Maurice was officially arrested and charged, which Vaughn hadn't minded *at all*.

Detective Meyer, it turned out, had been investigating Maurice's background since she'd taken on the Delphi Gallery thefts. He'd worked in art galleries in Vancouver, Edmonton, and various cities across the United States under multiple aliases, and at each one had stolen at least one work of art. Usually he just sold them on the black market, but Delphi had been a step up in his game: with the first two works he'd stolen, he'd claimed the sale value was higher than it actually was on the insurance paperwork, pocketed the difference, and sold the pieces on anyway. He'd bribed someone at the security company to cover up his after-hours site access, installed the false closet wall over the holiday break in his first year of working there, and had tried to blame Vaughn in an attempt to divert attention away from himself. All very crafty, Vaughn had to admit, but not particularly good as a long-term burglary plan.

Angeline and Cressida had slammed him with a raft of charges related to the pieces he'd stolen, as had the artists. And they'd dropped theft coverage from their insurance policy. Jules Mitchell was having a field day covering the story.

Vaughn was just happy to be handling more responsibility at the gallery. It was mostly what he'd been doing already, but now he was better paid for it and he had a say in accepting pieces for exhibit. He hoped he could work his way into being the official curator for the gallery before long.

His own art was generating pleasant amounts of attention online, especially his murals. His latest one, which he'd finished over

Christmas, was of the ocean from beneath the surface, deep blue edging into black at the borders. Two tiny figures could be seen at the top of the mural, plunging deep into the water, hands together. Shadowy figures of indeterminate species floated in the far oceanic distance. Jonah had watched him paint it with what Vaughn thought was an excess of awe and pride, but considering the steamy kisses that had taken place during its creation, on the tarp among the paint and brushes, he wasn't about to protest.

He'd finally drawn Jonah too. Multiple times. Even managed to convince him to sit nude for him, but only once (so far). Jonah claimed Vaughn looked more excited drawing him than he did when they were naked together, but Jonah didn't seem too upset about it. Thankfully. Vaughn was certain he was usually much *happier* naked with Jonah than drawing him, but it was sometimes a close thing.

Winter still reigned, as it tended to do at the end of February in Toronto. The wind off Lake Ontario could be freezing and rough. The days were a bit longer, but still short, and there were no signs of the snow disappearing yet. Walking through the blustery, icy evening, Vaughn longed for summer. He wanted to take Jonah outside of Toronto for weekends and show him other places in Ontario. He wanted long, lazy, sunny days and blue skies; slow, boozy picnics; warm weather; marching in Pride; and meandering around the waterfront. With Jonah.

Two and a half months ago, he couldn't have imagined this amount of change. In a lot of ways, his life was the same: he still avoided brunch with his mother when he could, he still had to deal with artists and troublesome visitors, and he still went clubbing and felt slightly distant from the sexual atmosphere in the crowds. He would never stop needing to dodge drunks on the subway, the way he did tonight on the way to the restaurant, and his tastes in clothing hadn't changed. Outwardly he still looked and acted the same.

But that disconnect he used to feel, the gap between him and other people, was gone. The realization that he wasn't strange or weird or dysfunctional or somehow lesser because he didn't want sex had made all the difference. It was incredible how much easier things became when he knew there was a community of people who shared his experience, and he had the language to articulate himself.

Extra amazing—if not miraculous, wonderful, unbelievable, and any other word Vaughn could care to use—was that Jonah understood him. Having him around, falling for him as Vaughn knew he was doing, made everything just that much *better*. He couldn't imagine Jonah *not* meeting him for lunch or being in his apartment or letting him visit his warm, welcoming house and roomies, or telling him off for failing to buy vegetables. How had he gone for so long thinking he couldn't have this closeness with another person? Why had he closed himself off like that?

Jonah had confessed a similar sentiment several times. Foster care weighed heavily on him, and the stories he'd shared made Vaughn want to go back in time and rip certain people's faces off, to pull small Jonah out of the system and look after him. Jonah still sometimes needed to burrow into Vaughn's body and rant, and he probably always would.

But Vaughn thought he was calmer now, like some of his restlessness was settling piece by little piece. He didn't startle as much at an unexpected caress or get that dark look on his face that meant running out for bruise-inducing sex. Vaughn never stopped him— and never would—but he had noticed that the number of hookups seemed to have slowed down, and that Jonah talked about them differently these days. Vaughn listened, laughed at the funny ones, and tried to give Jonah everything he couldn't get from a one-night stand. Wanting to give Jonah everything; it felt right.

He reached the restaurant and spotted Jonah hurrying down the street towards him, coat wrapped tightly around him against the cold. Up rose the butterflies in his stomach, still, although it had been two months. His boyfriend was gorgeous, even when he was frowning into the wind. Vaughn waited for him, watching for the moment when Jonah would see him and smile.

Jonah saw him and scowled.

Uh-oh. Bad day. Or bad hookup.

Jonah barrelled up to Vaughn and leaned against him, resting his head on Vaughn's shoulder.

Vaughn hugged him automatically. "You're on time."

"Dude freaking catfished me," Jonah muttered. "He was at least thirty years older than his picture, and those thirty years must've *sucked.*"

"I'm sorry, love."

"So annoying." Jonah exhaled heavily against Vaughn's coat, then straightened and kissed him. "I'll live."

"Will you need to try again tonight?"

"Nah. Just wanted some fun. Buy me a beer so I can survive this thing." His body leaned back into Vaughn's. Vaughn still couldn't get over how much Jonah liked hugging him—not that he was complaining. Jonah was overdue many hugs.

"They're *your* friends."

"Yeah, and this was *your* idea." He looked nervous.

Vaughn smiled. "I've already met them."

"Not the point. You've met my roommates." Jonah's face turned deadly serious. "Zay and Adrian are worse."

Somehow Vaughn thought the problem was less that they were going to be teased and more that Jonah wasn't used to being teased by people who liked him.

"I'll buy you as many beers as you want," he promised.

A smile broke through the nerves, a big happy one, and Vaughn kissed him, just because he could.

"Hey! You with the gorgeous asses!" They looked over. Zay leaned out the door of the restaurant, waving at them. "The alcohol and excellent company are *inside*, numb-nuts. Stop sucking each other's faces and get in here."

"And so it begins," Jonah intoned.

Vaughn laughed, took his hand, and pulled him inside.

Explore more of the *Toronto Connections* at:
riptidepublishing.com/titles/universe/toronto-connections

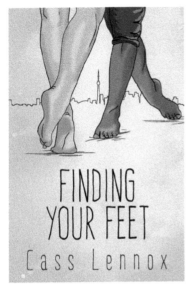

Dear Reader,

Thank you for reading Cass Lennox's *Blank Spaces*!

We know your time is precious and you have many, many entertainment options, so it means a lot that you've chosen to spend your time reading. We really hope you enjoyed it.

We'd be honored if you'd consider posting a review—good or bad—on sites like **Amazon, Barnes & Noble, Kobo, Goodreads, Twitter, Facebook, Tumblr,** and your blog or website. We'd also be honored if you told your friends and family about this book. Word of mouth is a book's lifeblood!

For more information on upcoming releases, author interviews, blog tours, contests, giveaways, and more, please sign up for our weekly, spam-free newsletter and visit us around the web:

Newsletter: tinyurl.com/RiptideSignup
Twitter: twitter.com/RiptideBooks
Facebook: facebook.com/RiptidePublishing
Goodreads: tinyurl.com/RiptideOnGoodreads
Tumblr: riptidepublishing.tumblr.com

Thank you so much for Reading the Rainbow!

RiptidePublishing.com

ACKNOWLEDGEMENTS

A massive thank-you to my enormously patient and understanding editor, Chris Muldoon. This book wouldn't be as coherent, polished, or North American without you.

Thanks to Riptide, for taking a chance on a newbie.

I must also thank my housemates, R.M., A.D.G., and W.M. who have to put up with my sleep-deprived babbling on a daily basis; my Canadian friends, who answered a lot of questions related to how they speak and go aboot their day; and A.B. and P.K., whose friendship and support I neither deserve nor can ever repay.

ALSO BY CASS LENNOX

Toronto Connections
Finding Your Feet (coming soon)
Growing Pains (coming soon)
The Wrong Woman (coming soon)

ABOUT THE AUTHOR

Cass Lennox is a permanent expat who has lived in more countries than she cares to admit to and suffers from a chronic case of wanderlust as a result. She started writing stories at the tender age of eleven, but would be the first to say that the early years are best left forgotten and unread. A great believer in happy endings, she arrived at queer romance via fantasy, science fiction, literary fiction, and manga, and she can't believe it took her that long. She likes diverse characters who have gooey happy ever afters, and brownies. She's currently sequestered in a valley in southeast England.

Blog: casslennox.wordpress.com
Facebook: facebook.com/Cass-Lennox-1704635609768647
Twitter: twitter.com/CassLennox

Enjoy more stories like *Blank Spaces* at RiptidePublishing.com!

All the Wrong Places
ISBN: 978-1-62649-420-6

Far From Home
ISBN: 978-1-62649-452-7

Earn Bonus Bucks!

Earn 1 Bonus Buck for each dollar you spend. Find out how at RiptidePublishing.com/news/bonus-bucks.

Win Free Ebooks for a Year!

Pre-order coming soon titles directly through our site and you'll receive one entry into a drawing for a chance to win free books for a year! Get the details at RiptidePublishing.com/contests.